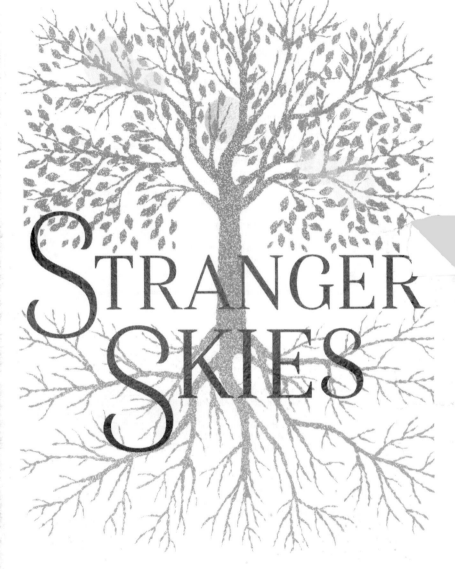

STRANGER SKIES

PASCALE LACELLE

SIMON & SCHUSTER

First published in Great Britain in 2024 by Simon & Schuster UK Ltd

First published in the USA in 2024 by Margaret K. McElderry Books,
an imprint of Simon & Schuster Children's Publishing Division,
1230 Avenue of the Americas, New York, New York 10020

1 3 5 7 9 10 8 6 4 2

Simon & Schuster UK Ltd
1st Floor, 222 Gray's Inn Road
London WC1X 8HB

Simon & Schuster: Celebrating 100 Years of Publishing in 2024

www.simonandschuster.co.uk
www.simonandschuster.com.au
www.simonandschuster.co.in

Simon & Schuster Australia, Sydney
Simon & Schuster India, New Delhi

A CIP catalogue record for this book
is available from the British Library.

HB ISBN 978-1-3985-2737-9
eBook ISBN 978-1-3985-2740-9
eAudio ISBN 978-1-3985-2738-6

Printed and Bound in the UK using 100% Renewable
Electricity at CPI Group (UK) Ltd

MIX
Paper | Supporting
responsible forestry
FSC
www.fsc.org
FSC® C171272

CONTENT WARNINGS: death, murder, grief, guilt, body horror, emesis, suicide ideation,
panic attack, bloodletting, self-harm, alcohol, amputation (off-page), war (mentioned),
violence, child abuse (brief mention), torture of a fantasy creature, exorcism

TO MY PARENTS, FOR ALWAYS
LETTING ME DREAM.

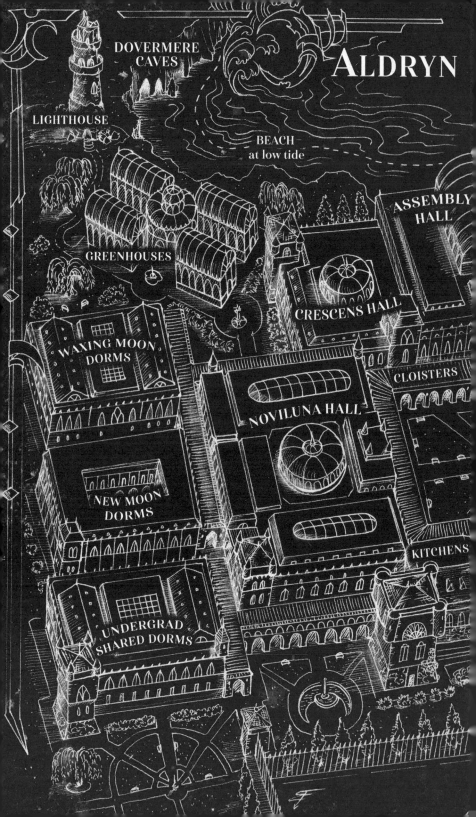

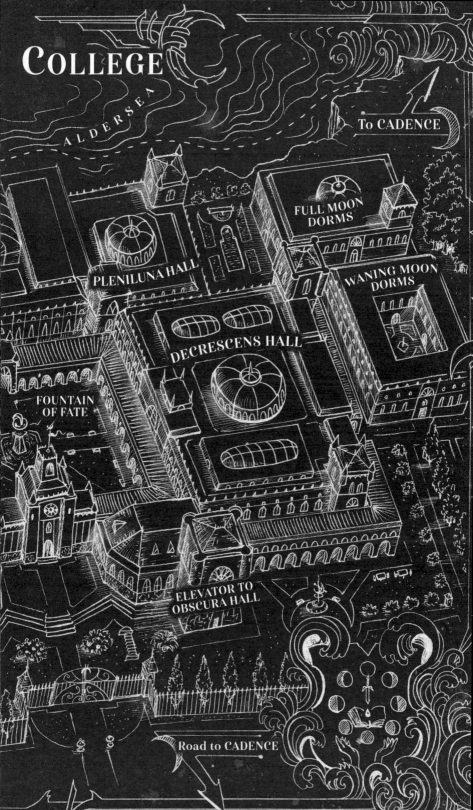

OUTERLANDS

TREVEL

A L D E R S E A

Dovermere
Cove

the
Caves

Cadence

Aldryn
College

ELEGY

Threnody

Harebell
Cove

TREVELSEA

THE CONSTELLATION ISLES

LUAGUA

OUTERLANDS

N

W

The Sacred Lunar Houses

& Their Tidal Alignments

HOUSE NEW MOON
Noviluna Hall

HEALERS (*Rising Tide*)
–ability to heal themselves and others

SEERS (*Ebbing Tide*)
–gift of prophecy and psychic visions

SHADOWGUIDES (*Rising Tide*)
–ability to see beyond the veil, commune with spirits

DARKBEARERS (*Ebbing Tide*)
–darkness manipulation

HOUSE WAXING MOON
Crescens Hall

SOWERS *(Rising Tide)*
–ability to grow and alter plants and other small organisms

GLAMOURS *(Ebbing Tide)*
–compulsion; charisma and influence over others

AMPLIFIERS *(Rising Tide)*
–ability to amplify the scope and range of other magics

WORDSMITHS *(Ebbing Tide)*
–ability to manifest things into being

HOUSE FULL MOON
Pleniluna Hall

—

SOULTENDERS *(Rising Tide)*
–emotion manipulation; empaths and aura-seers

WARDCRAFTERS *(Ebbing Tide)*
–ability to weave protection spells and ward magic

PURIFIERS *(Rising Tide)*
–ability to perform cleanses, balance energies

LIGHTKEEPERS *(Ebbing Tide)*
–light manipulation

HOUSE WANING MOON
Decrescens Hall

DREAMERS *(Rising Tide)*
–dream manipulation, dream walking; ability to induce sleep

UNRAVELERS *(Ebbing Tide)*
–ability to unveil secrets and decipher codes;
breaking through wards and spells

MEMORISTS *(Rising Tide)*
–ability to see and manipulate memories

REAPERS *(Ebbing Tide)*
–ability to reap life; death-touched

HOUSE ECLIPSE
Obscura Hall

Lunar eclipses produce variations
of other lunar magics

Solar eclipses produce rare new gifts
beyond other lunar magics

PART I:

THE
WITCH

I T WAS AN AUSPICIOUS DAY FOR A BURIAL, ASPEN thought.

Dense morning fog clung low to the ground where the coven gathered before the ancient yew tree. Their figures cut ghostly outlines against the pale dawn, the women clad in loose white muslin dresses, the men in billowing white shirts untucked from their breeches. They seemed like extensions of the fog itself, quiet spirits emerged from the soil, uncaring of the cold pine needles beneath their bare feet or the frigid breeze seeping through their unseasonable clothes.

The first kiss of winter had blown through the forest overnight. This would likely be their last burial before the earth froze over.

Aspen suppressed a shiver, conscious of her mother's eyes on her. This was no time to show weakness. She could already sense her mother's displeasure at her appearance: the unruliness of her dark hair, her red-rimmed eyes, the tiny crescent-shaped stains on her dress from when she'd hastily pulled it on, mindless of the dirt beneath her fingernails, which she hadn't bothered to clean after the digging she'd helped with last night.

A twilight grave for a dawn burial–such was always the way of the witch.

Somewhere above, a lark sang a deceitfully cheerful melody as the coven matriarchs guided Aspen's younger sister into the plot of earth where she would lie. Bryony's eyes met hers as she knelt in the grave, her own pristine white dress fanning around her prettily. Aspen's heart lurched. She saw herself in Bryony's strained expression, remembering how she had tried to keep a brave face for the coven during her own burial, even as fear pressed heavy on her chest. It was four years ago now, but Aspen would never forget the taste of earth in her mouth, the suffocating darkness as she was buried alive. The unbearable uncertainty that followed her into unconsciousness.

You'll be all right, Aspen mouthed. Her sister's chin wobbled in answer. No one seemed to notice but their mother, whose mouth tightened in a way that Aspen was quite familiar with. The High Matriarch did not approve of weakness in her daughters, and this small chink in Bryony's armor would displease her greatly.

What will the others say if my own daughter doesn't have faith in the Sculptress? the High Matriarch had asked Aspen on her own burial day. *The earth will receive you and sculpt you anew. This you must never doubt.*

Of course, to a thirteen-year-old girl about to be buried alive, such a thing was easier said than done. But this was the way of the witch. Once they came of age, they were buried at the foot of the sacred yew, where the Sculptress–the deity whose very essence ran below the earth and fed into the land–awakened in them their latent clairvoyance. Amid the gnarled roots of the yew tree, they were born anew, emerging from the earth as proper witches.

They were expected to be steadfast in their belief in the Sculptress and the fate that awaited them after their burial. *Faith conquers death*, the coven matriarchs taught them from a young age, forgetting, perhaps intentionally so, all the would-be witches who never rose from their graves. All those souls forever lost to the earth's embrace–or worse, snatched up by the demons who dwelled in the underworld far below.

This will not be Bryony's fate, Aspen told herself as her sister lay back in her grave, glossy black hair spilling around her like a pool of darkened blood. *She will rise again.*

The sun was beginning to crown over the treetops when the matriarchs began their chanting. Dawn drowned the world in hazy blues and pinks, a study in pastels that painted too gentle a backdrop for this grim affair. The matriarchs dug their hands in the earth and held fistfuls of dirt over the grave as their chants picked up tempo, the ancient words meant to protect Bryony's essence against demonic influence.

Bryony shot up, a broken plea bursting from her lips. "Please, I don't want to do this." Tears marred her face as she tried to stand, grasping for the hems of the matriarchs' dresses.

Her desperation broke Aspen's heart as well as her resolve. She tore from her place in the crowd and knelt at her sister's grave, ignoring the daggers her mother stared her way.

"Promise you'll be with me," Bryony managed through sobs as Aspen cradled her. "Promise you'll stay until it's done."

Aspen swallowed against the lump in her throat. She knew what Bryony meant, what she was asking her to do–just as she knew their mother was listening intently, and would no doubt give Aspen a verbal lashing later for this unruly interruption. "Promise," Aspen whispered, giving her sister a final squeeze before pulling away. "Be brave now." Louder, for her mother's benefit, she added: "The earth will receive you and sculpt you anew."

Bryony must have found courage in Aspen's promise, steeling herself as she lay back in the grave. The matriarchs picked up their chanting again, as though the ceremony had not been interrupted. Bryony closed her eyes as the first handfuls of dirt fell atop her. Tears glistened on her cheeks before more dirt covered her face. Her small body disappeared bit by bit, the witches' song growing louder and more frantic, the tense sound of it like a tree being uprooted from the earth. As the last of the dirt filled the grave, the song broke in one final, earsplitting note of triumph that sent the larks flying off in a frenzy.

And just like that, Bryony was gone.

In the sudden quiet, an unnatural wind wove through the yew's leaves. Its branches creaked and cracked and groaned, and deep below their feet came a rumble, the tree's roots moving to accept this offering of a witchling. For the next eight days, Bryony would stay buried beneath the sacred yew. Eight days to match the eight stages of a tree's life cycle: seed, germination, seedling, sapling, maturity, flowering, reproduction, decay–and from there, a witch reborn to start the cycle anew, if the Sculptress willed it.

Eight days for Aspen to worry herself sick over her sister's fate.

Aspen turned on her heel and ran from the clearing, narrowly escaping her mother's clutches. She would deal with the High Matriarch's displeasure later.

Her bare feet struck the earth, soles cutting themselves on pebbles and twigs as she ran through the woods she knew so well. The deeper she went, the denser and older and odder the woods became, full of magic from ancient witches whose decaying flesh and bones fed the trees and the Sculptress that had shaped them.

Few witches dared to venture so far, staying on the outskirts of the woods proper, where the coven lived. Ordinary towns-folk tended to avoid the woods altogether, whispering among themselves about the evil spirits that dwelled there and the witches who consorted with them.

But Aspen did not fear the woods. She belonged to them, as they lived in her.

The leaves here were a thousand shades of gold and rust, beautiful in their decay. Coming upon a familiar ravine, Aspen welcomed the spongy moss that bordered it, so soft and pil-lowy beneath her feet. Frost lined the edges of the water. Cold seeped through her, and though she longed for the hearth in her room and the warmth of her bed, she couldn't deny the grounding effect of walking barefoot through the woods. How it reminded her of her connection to the earth—that one sprouted from the other, and each fed on one another. A cycle eternal.

She could only hope the earth would be kind to her sister. That the Sculptress would deem Bryony worthy and awaken the witch in her.

Aspen followed the familiar melody of a nearby waterfall. It was unremarkable as far as cascades went, not very high or very powerful, but beautiful all the same. Strange, too, for a twisted tree trunk sprang from the ravine at the bottom of the waterfall. It was split down the middle to form an arch through which the cascading waters fell. Aspen had always found her-self drawn to it. This was her place of refuge, where she came to practice her scrying and tap into the stranger parts of her abilities. The parts her mother did not want her to use.

Witches could divine things from the earth, see hidden meaning in bones and leaves and the rings on the trunk of a tree. Some could map out root systems invisible to the naked eye, feel the needs of plants and animals, sense the coming of a storm or a drought and tend to their crops and gardens accordingly. Others had their inner eye turned to the future or the past, seeing repeating patterns and webs of possibilities in people's lives.

The magic that the Sculptress awoke in them manifested differently in every witch, but always it was tied to the earth and the connection their body had with it. Magic lived in their bones, sharpening their five senses and calling forth a sixth. In most it manifested in some form of art, guiding their hands to give shape to their visions. Sculpting, unsurprisingly, was most witches' preferred outlet; Aspen's mother had an entire gallery of wood carvings and ceramics and marble busts, each more detailed and strange and beautiful than the last. The work of witches long dead yet forever immortalized.

Aspen knelt by the ravine and ran her hands through the cold water, making the surface ripple as she scrubbed off the dirt beneath her fingernails. She stared at her reflection in the muddied water, trying to see Bryony in her own reddish-brown features. Four years separated them, but the sisters looked quite similar: the same deep-set, dark eyes flecked with golds and greens, framed by thick lashes and strong brows; the same shade of black hair, though Bryony's was lustrous and straight where Aspen's was curly on good days, frizzy on any other.

The rippling water became hypnotic as Aspen felt the tug of her scrying power.

Her magic was an anomaly, in that it was not connected *only* to the earth. She would often lose herself in a trance while watching the rhythmic dropping of rain in a puddle, or as she listened to the crackling of flames in a hearth or felt the wind dance around her. Her inner eye would awaken at these entrancing elements, often without her meaning to, and let her see through other people's eyes—animals, too.

It was a rare scrying gift, and harmless for the most part. But the vessels whose consciousness Aspen flitted into had no sense of her being there, which posed somewhat of a moral conundrum. She not only saw through their eyes but *felt* everything they did: the five senses their bodies experienced, and more intimate things too—old hurts and pleasures and memories imprinted on their muscles and bones and sinews.

Aspen took great care not to overstep boundaries, but her curiosity could not be helped. She loved experiencing the world as others did. It was her way of escaping the life she was bound to, the woods she was sworn to. A way to sate her ever-growing desire to see what lay beyond the coven.

Her mother, on the other hand, thought it immoral and had all but forbidden Aspen to scry in such ways. But Bryony had begged Aspen. *Promise you'll be with me.* An invitation for Aspen to see through her sister's eyes as her world went dark and quiet and scary. To have someone hold her hand— metaphorically speaking—as the air left her lungs.

Aspen remembered her own burial all too well, that suffo- cating, agonizing, endless moment where she waited for death to come and the Sculptress to break her bones, bending and cracking her body to shape her into a proper witch. She would have given anything to have someone hold her hand then.

If she could bring her sister this small comfort, then she would.

Aspen let her mind sink into the pull of her magic, her face inching closer to the still-rippling water–

"What do you think you're doing?"

Her mother had her arm in a vise grip, pulling a dazed Aspen up and away from the ravine. Her seething words cut through her like a lash. "First that outburst at your sister's grave, and now this?"

"I was just–"

"Don't start with your excuses. I know very well what you were about to do. How could you interfere with your sister's ascension this way?"

"I didn't, I swear."

"And if I hadn't stopped you? Your presence in Bryony's mind might have altered the Sculptress's work or called on the demons."

Guilt churned in Aspen's stomach. She hadn't thought of it– had been too emotional, swayed by her sister's pleas. Aspen hung her head. "I'm sorry, Mother." She should have known better.

"Foolish girl." Her mother let go of her with a sigh. "I expect better of you, Aspen. You are the Sculptress's *chosen*, and you must act accordingly."

Aspen stayed quiet despite wanting to grumble at those words. She didn't need the reminder.

To be chosen was to be blessed, according to her mother, but Aspen always thought *cursed* felt more appropriate a term. To bear the mark of the Sculptress meant becoming the next High Matriarch, tasked with the safekeeping of the woods and the protection of the coven. Never allowed to leave because of it.

At least such a burden would not fall on her sister. Only one witch per generation bore the Sculptress's favor, meaning Bryony could be free of the woods if she wanted.

But not Aspen. The woods had roots in her that she could never sever, tying her to these parts until the day she died and her body returned to the earth.

"What is that?"

Her mother was staring at the ravine, brow furrowed. Aspen followed her gaze and stilled. She hadn't noticed it before, how the leaves grazing the water's surface were black. Not the ordinary sort of decay that autumn brought about, but wrong. An unpleasant smell hung heavy in the air, thick and sickeningly sweet.

Rot.

Some of the trees along the ravine were *rotting*, blackened by some sort of sickness. How had Aspen not felt it? Her connection to the woods should have alerted her, but she'd been so focused on Bryony, she must have missed it.

Her mother moved closer to the blighted trees, and Aspen followed, eyes tracking the rot all the way to the murky water's edge farther down.

Where two bodies hid beneath moldering willow leaves near the waterfall.

Two girls, from the looks of them. Half-submerged in the

ravine, the rest of them draped lifelessly on the mossy bank.

Aspen's mother stopped dead in her tracks. When Aspen tried to step past her, the High Matriarch gripped her wrist. "Don't," she said with inexplicable terror in her voice, her eyes.

"We have to help them," Aspen urged, prying herself from her mother's grasp.

There was something pulling her toward the bodies, a tug she couldn't deny. The girls' manner of dress was strange. They wore trousers, for one thing, and the fabrics and patterns were like none that Aspen had ever seen before. Their hair was unbound. One had long blond tresses all matted together in the mud. The other's hair was barely shoulder-length, shorter than Aspen had ever seen on a girl around these parts, with pine needles and seed pods and twigs tangled up in her brown curls. The short-haired girl's head was perched lifelessly on her arm, and her hand was oddly clutched, the skin burned black. The other girl's hand lay a hairsbreadth away from it, as if she had been reaching for her companion.

On both their wrists was a faint silver scar in the shape of a spiral.

"Mother, quick, come see," Aspen breathed, heart pounding painfully against her chest.

Her mother was beside her in a moment, hand trembling at her neck, terror-filled eyes glued on that familiar symbol on the girls' wrists. The same symbol the Sculptress had carved on Aspen's ribs. The spiral scar tissue that marked her as keeper of the coven, High Matriarch to be.

"They're here," Aspen's mother said in a foreboding tone. "They have come, and so it begins."

Aspen didn't understand the dread in her mother's words. All she felt was an odd sort of excitement, her mind opening up to all the possibilities of what this could mean. Her curiosity getting the better of her again.

The eyes of the blond girl fluttered beneath their lids as she began to stir.

Not dead, then.

They have come, Aspen thought in echo of her mother, and though she did not know who *they* were or what her mother meant by it, her fingers tingled with a sense of purpose she had often felt before, though never quite so strong. There was a rightness in her bones, a momentous melody sweeping through her soul, as if everything were finally aligning into place.

Aspen's lips parted as the girl opened her eyes and looked directly at her.

And so it begins.

1

BAZ

B AZ BRYSDEN WAS MOST AWARE OF TIME WHEN HE WAS running out of it.

The night before a paper was due, for instance, when he realized the days he'd spent procrastinating instead of doing the work meant he now had to forego sleep in order to finish. Or when he was so engrossed in a book and a strong cup of coffee, he realized with only minutes to spare that he was going to be late for class.

Of course, Baz could make the minutes stretch so that he was never truly late for anything as trivial as papers and classes. What was it to him, the Timespinner, to make time run in his favor? He had only to pull on its threads so he could squeeze in a few extra sentences here, that extra bit of research that would earn him full marks there, the basic human tasks that would make him look at least somewhat presentable before leaving the Eclipse commons, like brushing his teeth and throwing on a clean shirt and making sure his hair wasn't sticking up every which way. He had done all these things just this morning, scrambling to hand in his final papers and stop by Professor Selandyn's office to drop off her solstice gift before leaving for the holidays.

And yet here he still was, hurrying across campus to catch his train.

Had anyone else possessed this power to manipulate time, they would not know such things as scrambling and racing against the clock and worrying about missed trains. But Basil Brysden was a peculiar specimen who preferred to use his power as a last resort—and strictly in the most innocuous ways—which only served to enhance his already anxious nature.

And the pock-faced Regulator that stopped him dead in his tracks made that anxiety spike.

"Mr. Brysden. Heading home for the holidays, I see?"

"Are you following me on campus now?" Baz gritted out in annoyance, adjusting the weight of his travel bag on his shoulder.

"My, my, so defensive." The smug satisfaction in the Regulator's beady eyes did not go unnoticed by Baz.

Captain Silas Drutten had been the bane of Baz's existence for the past two months. Ever since Baz helped break out his father and Kai from the Institute, Drutten had been on him relentlessly, trying to catch him in a lie and pin their escape on him. But Baz had gotten very good at lying—or maybe it was just that Drutten had very little evidence to go on. Either way, it was easy enough for Baz to stick to his story, no matter how many times he had to suffer through one of these pointless interrogations.

Today, it seemed, would be another one of those times.

"This meeting is purely accidental," Drutten said, adjusting the medals of valor pinned to his Regulator outfit. "I'm here for the donor banquet."

That explained the full regalia. While the students of Aldryn College were currently getting ready to leave for the weeklong

winter solstice break, faculty members were dressing in their best
suits and gowns to host their annual donor banquet. Everyone
of note with ties to the college would be in attendance tonight.
from high-ranking Regulators to the mayor of Cadence to families
whose names were likely carved on the very foundation of the college. It was said to be a grand affair, with a catered seven-course
meal and an open bar and people full of their own self-importance–Selandyn's words, not Baz's.

"Well, then," Baz said, glancing pointedly at his watch, "if you'll
excuse me, I have a train to catch."

"I take it that means you *are* heading to Threnody, then?"

"Obviously." There was no point denying it. "You of all people
know that's where my mother lives."

Drutten himself had made it a point to scour every corner of
Anise Brysden's house for signs of her fugitive husband. Of course,
he'd come up empty-handed–and yet he kept hounding her and
Baz both, making Baz's blood boil and his mother feel unsafe in
her own home. It sickened him to his core.

Drutten fixed him with a hard stare. "I'm sure I don't need to
remind you that harboring fugitives is a crime, even during the
holidays."

"I'm quite aware."

"But if you *were* to talk, give up the whereabouts of said fugitives,
I might find it in my heart to be lenient. My solstice gift to you."

Baz wanted to laugh at that. As if he would ever trust the Regulators to show any semblance of leniency toward him in this matter.

"We can keep doing this little dance of ours, Drutten, but my
answer hasn't changed from all the other times you interrogated
me." Baz held up three fingers, taking one down for each statement he made: "Yes, I was the last person to have seen my father at
the Institute. No, I did not help him or Kai escape, and no, I haven't
seen or spoken to either of them since. So unless you have solid

proof to dispute all of this–which I know you don't–I'll be going now. Enjoy your banquet."

Baz walked past Drutten without a second glance, surprised at his own brazenness. This blatant disregard for authority was still unfamiliar to him, despite everything he'd gone through these past few months. He felt a bit like a child about to be scolded by his mother for reaching for the cookie jar before supper, though the stakes were much higher.

But Drutten did not reprimand him. He only called after him with a falsely cheery "Give your parents my best."

Baz only dared to throw a look over his shoulder when he was about to round a bend farther down the corridor. Drutten's attention was no longer on him; the Regulator was shaking hands with Dean Fulton, who wore her usual tweed suit, evidently not yet ready for this evening's banquet. She had a friendly smile for Drutten, but it wavered when two more people joined them.

Baz's stomach dropped as he recognized Artem Orlov, dressed in an expensive fur-trimmed coat, red hair blazing like a torch. At his side was Virgil Dade, another member of the Selenic Order, who had been close to Artem's sister, Lizaveta, before she died. Virgil was also dressed to impress, which reminded Baz that a select few students were always invited to the donor banquet. It was the school's attempt to show off its best and brightest.

Virgil, it seemed, had all but replaced Keiran as Aldryn's golden boy–as well as Artem's lapdog.

Before either of them could spot Baz, he disappeared down the hall. Another look at his watch told him he would just barely make it to the station on time. Though trains to Threnody left every hour, he needed to be on *this one* specifically.

Magic thrummed at his fingertips, eager to be used. *Not yet,* Baz thought as he picked up the pace. He would reach for it only as a last resort.

Give your parents my best.

His blood boiled at Drutten's lingering threat, his hollow offer of leniency. Once, Baz might have been naive enough to believe Drutten had his best intentions at heart. But Drutten was like every other Regulator, upholding a legal system that made it a point to spit on justice when it came to the Eclipse-born. Something Baz had been forced to come to terms with after he and Jae had taken their case to a trusted attorney, who'd presented their accusations against Keiran Dunhall Thornby, Artem Orlov, the Selenic Order, and the Institute at large to the courts of Elegy.

The only hard evidence Baz and Jae had had was what little they'd managed to take from Artem Orlov's office the day they helped Kai and Theodore escape from the Institute: ledgers that detailed how both Artem and Keiran had used the former's status as a Regulator to harness silver blood from Eclipse-born who'd Collapsed—blood they then used to create synthetic magic wielded by the corrupt secret society known as the Selenic Order, of which they were both members.

But as incriminating as their evidence was, the Institute's corruption—and the Order's power—ran deeper than they could have imagined. All that proof was written off as inadmissible. The case got thrown out before it could even go to trial.

All that planning, all that hope that they would finally get justice for the Eclipse-born, and it had amounted to nothing. Artem walked away with his head held high and his job as a Regulator intact. Keiran's name remained unsullied, and his and Lizaveta Orlov's deaths were ruled as tragic drownings—the same way Emory's disappearance was declared a casualty of Dovermere. Three more souls lost to the Belly of the Beast, nothing more. As if one had not disappeared through a mythical door to other worlds after the other two had all but tried to kill her for her Tidecaller blood.

Baz nearly collided with a group of students gathered in the cloisters. They were exchanging last-minute gifts and farewell hugs before leaving for the holidays. A feeling of yearning smacked him like a tidal wave. Once, Baz would have given anything to be as alone as he felt now, with the Eclipse commons all to himself and no one to disturb his peace. A ghost meandering about, flittering unseen between the shelves of Aldryn's many libraries. But things had changed. The Eclipse commons were like a crypt without Kai, unsettlingly quiet. The Decrescens library felt like it was missing a vital piece of its soul whenever he looked up at the empty spot Emory would have sat in. Even Romie's greenhouse had lost all its appeal after a Sower professor cleaned it out and repurposed it for her first-year students.

For the first time, Baz was well and truly alone. And so very starved for connection.

He pushed past the students, mumbling apologies as he went. The skies above were a threatening gray, the air crisp with the coming of snow. Baz hoped the storm would hold off until he got to his destination. The weather had been unpredictable of late, something that experts blamed on a disturbance with the tides. Massive flooding of coastal towns, beached ships that affected commerce, a record number of drownings due to flash swells—and this was all over the world, too, not just Elegy. A phenomenon that had started soon after the door in Dovermere was opened.

An eerie coincidence, perhaps.

Baz reached the bustling station just as his train started to pull away. He cursed Drutten's name—if it hadn't been for his interruption, Baz would have made it on time. Now he had no choice but to give in to his magic.

Huffing a swear, he grudgingly reached for the threads of time. The world around him came to a halting stop. The sea of students stilled; the whistling of engines quieted. Baz wove through the platform trying not to think of how *easy* this was. He hopped on the train, brushing past the frozen porter who hadn't fully closed the door yet, and with a breath, Baz let go of the threads of time.

The world resumed its motions, oblivious to the fact it had ever stopped at all.

Baz plopped down in his seat and flexed his hands, trying to shake off the unsettling ease of what he'd done. He hadn't gotten used to his Collapsed magic yet, despite having lived most of his life with it.

The Collapsing was what awaited Eclipse-born who used too much power, an implosion of the self that there was supposedly no coming back from. But Baz had discovered that to Collapse did not mean inevitably succumbing to the dark curse that was said to await them. Instead, it was meant to broaden the scope of their power, making it feel almost limitless.

Though the knowledge of his condition opened many doors— too many he didn't want to consider, the idea of such power at his fingertips making him nervous—he didn't feel different in the slightest. Perhaps it was because he'd kept this limitless power in check all these years without even knowing, for fear of reaching a limit he had unwittingly already reached.

Then again, he wasn't exactly pushing himself to see how deep his Collapsed power went, either. Still the same scared boy, never reaching further than he thought he should. Cautious to a fault.

As the train pulled out of the station, Baz thought of Drutten's threat again and smiled to himself. At least his ruse was working. He'd known full well the Regulator would expect him to head to Threnody. Where else would he be going for the solstice holidays if not home?

But *home* had lost all meaning to him. His childhood house hadn't felt like one in years, and though the Eclipse commons had been a refuge to him in the past, they were too empty now to soothe him the way a true home should.

There was no going home for Baz. So he was going somewhere no one would expect him to be.

The train screeched loudly along the tracks, pulling Baz from the half sleep he'd slipped into. His face smooshed up against the fogging window, he was briefly disoriented at the sight of the busy station they were pulling into, despite having been here more times than he could count. He blinked the sleep from his eyes, urgency making his senses come alive as he recognized the blue, green, and white tiled sign on the brick wall that read *THRENODY CENTRAL*.

While people filed into the narrow corridor outside of Baz's otherwise empty compartment, he remained seated, eyes searching the platform wildly. Panic seized him when he didn't spot the person he was looking for. And then, just as the worst scenarios began to play out in his mind, the door to his compartment slid open, nearly giving him a heart attack.

"Mind if I join you?"

"Oh, I–" Any excuse Baz might have drawn up died on his lips, replaced by relieved laughter. "Thank the Tides it's you."

Jae Ahn smiled down at him, dark eyes full of mischief, and Baz had never been happier to see them. "The timing could not have been more perfect," Jae said as they shut the compartment door behind them and sat down across from Baz.

"Do you really think it'll work?"

Jae nodded toward the window. "See for yourself."

Standing on the platform with everyone else getting off the train was Baz–or rather, a perfect copy of him, dressed in the same clothes and hauling the same luggage that the real Baz had on him. Jae had truly outdone themself with this illusion; even the expression of this make-believe Baz was the same, a mix of worry and aloofness that had the real Baz feeling a tad self-conscious. Was that really what he looked like?

Jae had planned all of it, this grand illusion that would deceive anyone prying into Baz's whereabouts. If the Regulators had eyes on Baz on this very train, they would be duped into seeing him get off here, at Threnody Central, while the real him kept going south, cloaked in whatever illusion Jae now cast over their compartment. And if anyone looked in on the Brysden household over the holidays, they would find Anise and Baz holed up in their quiet home, neither of them wanting to venture outside or have company over, what with the shame of Theodore's escape from the Institute weighing heavy on them.

As the fake Baz disappeared in the crowd, Baz couldn't help but ask, "And you're sure the illusion will hold?"

"Of course it will." Jae kicked their feet up on the cushioned seat, looking pleased with themself. "I've been playing around with sustaining illusions long-term, and none of them have failed me yet. Now, if someone stops you in the streets and tries to have a *conversation* with you, we might be in trouble." They smirked. "Though you ignoring them wouldn't be too far off from the real thing, would it?"

"No, I guess it wouldn't," Baz had to admit. The sheer control Jae had over their Collapsed magic never ceased to amaze him.

Jae had been Collapsed for a long time now and had since been keeping tabs on both Baz and Kai, for whom this was all still new. Unlike most Eclipse-born who Collapsed, all three of them had managed to escape the Unhallowed Seal that strove to put their magic to sleep.

The train lurched forward, and as Threnody slowly disappeared behind them, Baz felt like he could breathe again.

"So how've you been, Basil?"

"Fine, all things considered. How's the training been going?"

At this, Jae lit up with pride. "Honestly? Better than I could have anticipated."

For the past few months, Jae had been living in Threnody under the guise of a research trip, but what they were really doing was training other Collapsed Eclipse-born in secret. Jae had managed to get in contact with others like them who had avoided getting branded with the Unhallowed Seal and offered to help them manage their limitless power. Most of these people were leading normal lives like Jae and Baz, hiding the fact that they had Collapsed from those around them with varying degrees of success. But others were on the run from the Regulators after having very public Collapsings, living in shadows, struggling to survive, praying they never got caught. Jae's training provided them with much-needed asylum.

The point, as Kai would put it, was to ensure everyone had their shit under control so they could eventually prove to the world at large that Eclipse-born who Collapsed were not a threat to society. That they could overcome this Shadow's curse that Collapsing was supposed to plunge them into.

"Makes you wonder if this whole curse business is bogus," Jae said, as if reading Baz's mind. "A cautionary tale, nothing more."

"How do you mean?"

"Have you ever felt this darkness we're warned of? Has your Collapsed magic changed who you are at your core, turned you into someone who craves power no matter the cost?" Jae shook their head, not letting Baz answer the clearly rhetorical question as they pressed on: "Our ability to control our Collapsed magic seems only to be tied to how powerful our magic already was to begin with. Take me for example. Illusions are a rather benign ability, one that I'd already mastered long before Collapsing. And your Timespinner ability—well, I wouldn't say it's mundane, far from it, but then again you were always careful with it, so it makes sense for you to have control over it now. But others whose magic is darker in nature, or whose grasp on their ability was already flighty to begin with . . . Well. It makes sense for them to have a harder time dealing with this heightened magic, don't you think?"

A certain Nightmare Weaver came to mind at this. Jae seemed to have the same thought. "He's getting better," they added in a gentle voice. "Like I said, it's an adjustment. And Kai's magic is . . . There's much we don't know about it yet. But we'll get there."

Baz looked down at his hands. The Nightmare Weaver he'd known had always been in control of his magic, but now that Kai was Collapsed, it was like the nightmares were controlling *him*. Nightmares spilled into his waking hours against his will, making it hard for him to distinguish what was real from what was not. Like the bees he'd once jokingly conjured out of Baz's dreaming, only no one was laughing now, especially not Kai.

Soon, twilight settled outside. Baz watched the jack pines and spruce trees rushing past, their branches drooping with snow. When the train stopped, Baz and Jae were the only ones to step off. Unsurprising, given the remoteness of their destination. The station wasn't even that, only a tiny, solitary outbuilding on the side of the tracks, with no one there to greet them.

Baz tightened his coat around him, pulling up the lapels around his neck to fend off the biting wind. He and Jae started painstakingly up the snow-covered road, and though Baz knew Jae had a cloaking illusion around them, he couldn't stop glancing over his shoulder to make sure they weren't being followed. Streetlamps were few and far between here, and Baz tensed at every sound, imagining Drutten's face hiding in the darkness between trees. His mind spun uncontrollably when they got off the road to borrow a narrow trail that wound its way through the wintry forest, hugging a jagged coastline.

The crashing of waves was unsettling in such a wild, forlorn place. Anyone could easily be made to disappear here.

"Almost there," Jae said up ahead.

By the time Baz glimpsed the lighthouse at the edge of the world, his cheeks were pink with cold and exertion, his breath forming clouds around him. The blue-painted door at the base of the lighthouse opened just as Baz reached for its handle. From inside came warm light and laughter and music and the mouthwatering scents of fresh bread and chowder.

And there stood Henry Ainsleif, reddish-blond hair a tangled mess that fell to his shoulders, a broad smile in the midst of his beard. "Come in, you two. You're just in time for supper."

Henry opened the door wider, and as Baz stepped in from the cold, his eyes fell on Theodore and Anise Brysden. His parents both paused in setting the small kitchen table. There was a happy yelp, a clang of silverware, and then Baz was being smothered in a big hug and a familiar scent.

"Hi, Mom," he breathed into Anise's hair, his heart soaring to see her so full of life.

"Oh, I'm so glad you made it," she said, squeezing him tight before holding him at arm's length, her big eyes—so much like Romie's—taking him in. "Was there any trouble? Are you well?"

"I'm fine, Mom." He smiled to see Theodore and Jae clasping each other affectionately on the shoulder. "All thanks to Jae."

Jae made a nonchalant motion before Anise smothered them with a kiss on the cheek, thanking them profusely. Baz's father took the opportunity to wrap his son in a hug that rivaled Anise's, and Baz closed his eyes, savoring the moment, still in disbelief that his father was here. A wanted man, but free of the hellhole that was the Institute, at least.

Baz looked into his father's smiling face and noticed all the ways it had changed since he last saw him, after the horrors of years spent at the Institute had all but hollowed him out. Life had returned to Theodore's eyes, and he no longer looked frail and broken, but healthy and whole. The Unhallowed Seal on his hand had been taken off, thanks to Baz's magic, because even though Theodore had never actually Collapsed, he'd still had his magic put to sleep by the Regulators. All because of Baz, whom Theodore had wanted to protect.

Baz, who'd been the one to Collapse that day in his father's printing press, the blast of his unbridled power killing three people in the process.

A familiar guilt reared its ugly head up inside him. And though there was no blame in Theodore's eyes, Baz felt an aching pressure to apologize, a desperate need to make things right between them. To make up for all those years Theodore had suffered in his place. He opened his mouth, willing the words to come. They wouldn't.

A voice like midnight, one he would recognize anywhere, came to his rescue.

"'Bout time you showed up."

Kai hovered on the last step of a steep, narrow staircase, dark eyes fixed on Baz. His mouth was turned up as if they were sharing a private joke, and the whole world seemed to disappear around them, taking all of Baz's worries with it.

"Hi," Baz breathed, feeling silly for not having a better reply. He was distantly aware of the others busying themselves in the kitchen, but his focus remained on Kai—on the casual way he flitted toward him, hair still damp from the shower he had clearly just taken. On the faint smell of pine that followed him, and the way his eyes sparked with unguarded joy, a slip of that sharp stoicism he usually wore like armor.

For a split second, Baz didn't know how to react. Were they supposed to shake hands? Hug? Kai saved him the mortification of having to decide: he gave Baz a playful nudge on the shoulder, like it was the most normal thing in the world, completely oblivious to the strange fluttering in Baz's stomach that this small touch elicited.

"Welcome home, Brysden."

And Baz realized he *was* home, in all the ways that mattered.

2

EMORY

EMORY NEVER BELIEVED IN FAIRY TALES UNTIL SHE found herself living in one.

Amberyl House could have been pulled out of a storybook. Every time Emory thought she'd seen the entirety of the witches' sprawling estate, she discovered some new curio to puzzle over. Sculpted marble busts and vases adorned with strange beasts and collections of gemstones the likes of which she had never seen before. Lifelike statues of armored knights and fair maidens that made her wonder at the hands that had carved them. Glass jars filled with peculiar-shaped mushrooms and even odder-looking bones, all of which Emory was forbidden to touch because of whatever mystical properties they held.

There was the sunlit room on the first floor where dried herbs and plants and flowers hung in carefully tied bunches from the rafters on the ceiling, left there to dry until they were ready to be crushed up with mortar and pestle and used for purposes unknown. There was the lilac-painted room on the second floor that felt colder than even the cellar, empty save for a massive clump of amethyst atop a marble altar, and the outside gardens full of fountains and parterres and shady nooks hidden among the hedges.

Even the massive library next to the herbarium was a marvel, containing titles in languages Emory didn't know, in alphabets she'd never seen. Other titles were written in her own tongue. Some of them she vaguely recognized, certain she'd read them before. She wasn't a big enough bookworm to tell if the author names were the same as those half-remembered stories. If Baz were here, he would know. She had perused a few of the books to keep herself busy, but whatever sense of déjà vu she'd had vanished as she read, the stories wholly unfamiliar to her.

It was difficult to grasp what was real and what was not. Was she trapped in a dream? Was this the Deep, masquerading as a lush land full of green things and the kind of rich, earthy smells that filled your lungs and made you feel alive, all to detract from the fact that you were actually dead?

You're alive, and this is the Wychwood, Emory reminded herself, for that was what the witches who had found her and Romie called it, and this was what she must believe. Even if the idea of being in one of the worlds Cornus Clover had written in his book made her want to laugh, or cry, or both all at once.

She felt trapped in this endless loop of questioning her very reality. And Amberyl House, despite its beauty and the generosity of their hosts, was very much starting to feel like a prison.

Romie joked about them being like maidens locked away in a tower by some evil witch, awaiting their prince. Except no prince was coming to save them, and the witches who'd taken them in weren't exactly evil–though they would not allow them to leave, either. Emory and Romie could wander the sprawling sunlit grounds of the estate but never go beyond its limits. Never into the woods that grew at the edge of the gardens, dark and old and mysterious.

They had tried it once, meaning to return to the spot where they'd been found half-drowned in a ravine. But whatever magic lived here barred their way, a thicket of impenetrable vines growing across the garden gate that would have taken them into the woods proper.

"There are things happening in the woods that cannot be interfered with," Mrs. Amberyl had told them when they'd brought it up. "Magic that could easily be disrupted by a stranger's presence. Until the ascension, I'm afraid you'll have to stay here at the house."

The ascension, Mrs. Amberyl had explained, was a ritual sacred to the witches, though she wouldn't divulge the specifics of what it entailed. "It is a very private affair," she'd said in that stern way of hers that left no room for debate. "But afterward, I assure you, you will be able to leave if you wish to."

"We just want to go home," Emory had said.

Except none of them knew how they might do so. Neither Emory nor Romie had any memory of how they got here. The last thing Emory remembered was pushing open the marble door in the sleepscape. One second, she was reaching for the knotted vines that formed the doorknob, and the next, she was lying in the mud, looking up at Mrs. Amberyl and her daughter Aspen.

In a daze, they'd searched their surroundings for any trace of a door. Remembering the water sloshing at her feet in the sleepscape, Emory had been convinced the waterfall might be their way back home. That perhaps the water flowing down the star-lined path of the sleepscape had spilled into this world, along with them. But whatever door they'd come through was gone, leaving them without a clue as to how they might return home.

They were stuck here, in the verdant world of the Wychwood,

in the company of witches who seemed entirely unfazed by their appearance or by the fact that they claimed to be from another world. It was as though they'd been expecting them. Just as the witch in Clover's story knew to expect the scholar.

And here Emory and Romie were. Not one scholar, but two. Far from the shores they'd known.

The Wychwood may not be the worst place to be stranded in, but they were still determined to find a way out—and make sense of how and why they were here in the first place.

"You're being too obvious," Romie whispered as they flitted through the grand, echoing halls.

"Me? You're the one whose book is *upside down.*"

With a swear, Romie righted the book in her hand. "Well, yours is in another language entirely."

"It has illustrations."

Romie rolled her eyes, but it was an affectionate sort of gesture. The normalcy of it made Emory smile.

They were trying to look inconspicuous as they poked around various rooms, pretending to read their books. Voices drifted toward them from the kitchens. Romie waggled her brows at Emory and strode off toward them, all but abandoning her cover.

"Wait—"

They peeked into the sunlit kitchens, where such divine food was made that a suspicious part of Emory wondered if the witches were trying to fatten them up for some grotesque reason, or poison them with some untraceable ingredient. She really had no reason to believe any of this, though—they'd been eating the witches' food for eight days now without any ill effect.

Witches were clanging about as they cooked up a storm, laughing and speaking excitedly in a dialect that was similar enough to their own that Emory could more or less understand. Their common tongue made her wonder at how their two worlds came to share it.

Emory and Romie listened for *something* that might help them make sense of their situation. Unfortunately for them, the only thing the witches seemed interested in was petty gossip.

Romie groaned, whispering, "Can't they just talk about the ascension? Surely that's what all this food is for."

At this rate, they would never find out what this oh-so-secret ascension entailed. Mrs. Amberyl had told them they could join the celebrations that would take place in the gardens *after* the ascension, but not the ascension itself.

Her meaning had been clear: Emory and Romie were strangers—outsiders to their witchy practices, foreigners from distant lands—and though they'd been invited into the witches' home, they would not be invited into their world proper.

Everyone in these parts was referred to as a witch, though Emory couldn't tell what exactly *defined* them as witches. They all had an inner eye, Mrs. Amberyl had explained, a sixth sense that manifested differently in every witch in varying degrees of power—much in the same way lunar magic flowed differently in the blood of Emory's people. But Emory had yet to see a witch using their inner eye. They led what appeared to be mundane lives, those who worked within these walls tending to the needs of Amberyl House and its residents, doing the cleaning and cooking and groundskeeping.

Whatever magic they did, they did in secret. Away from Emory's and Romie's prying eyes.

And tonight would be no different.

"What are you doing down here?"

Emory and Romie drew back from where they'd been peering into the kitchens. Behind them, Aspen Amberyl, the daughter of the witch who'd taken them in, stared at them with her arms crossed.

"We were just—"

"I need more tincture," Romie lied smoothly, holding up her still-healing hands.

In fact, it wasn't a lie at all—Romie *was* running low on the tincture the witches had prepared for her. Emory's own healing magic did little to nothing when it came to the horrid burns Romie had gotten in the sleepscape while clutching a white-hot burning star in her hands to fend off the umbrae. But whatever herbs the witches had crushed up together to make this tincture seemed to be helping, even if slowly.

Aspen studied them with narrowed eyes, her expression so like her mother's it was almost laughable. Where Mrs. Amberyl was the epitome of severity, Aspen was a poor model of it, a student trying to imitate a master when she was so clearly made for something else. A daughter used to following rules but yearning to break them. "Tinctures are made in the herbarium," Aspen said, "not the kitchens. What are you really here for?"

Emory's gaze slid to Romie.

"All right, you caught us," Romie admitted with a crooked smile. She jerked her chin toward the busy kitchens. "We were curious about the preparations for tonight. Trying to see if we can piece together what exactly a witch ascension entails, since none of you want to tell us."

Aspen pursed her lips. "That's because our ritual is—"

"Sacred, we know." Romie rolled her eyes. "But if we could *see* it . . ."

"It isn't allowed."

Romie gave Aspen a pointed look. "You're apparently not allowed to talk to us, either, yet here you are."

Something like amusement danced in Aspen's eyes, though her statuesque features remained unruffled. Emory and Romie had overheard Mrs. Amberyl telling Aspen to keep her distance when they'd first gotten here. In fact, they were pretty sure Mrs. Amberyl had given the same directive to every single witch in the vicinity, which would explain why everyone gave Emory and Romie such a wide berth.

Once, when a young witch came to Amberyl House complaining of a sickness, Emory had offered to help with her healing magic—because here, in this foreign world, she'd gone back to pretending she was only a Healer, which seemed safer than admitting she was a Tidecaller. But the witch had vehemently opposed her using any kind of magic on or around him, treating her as if she had the plague.

The witch community as a whole was clearly wary of Emory and Romie, even though they'd generously offered them shelter. But Aspen seemed drawn to the two girls all the same, always finding excuses to bump into them despite her mother's wishes, clearly as curious about them as they were about her.

"What do you wish to know?" Aspen asked, giving in to that curiosity.

"For starters, what is it?"

"I should think it's pretty self-explanatory. The ascension is when a witchling ascends into their power. Tonight, if the Sculptress wills it, our coven will gain a witch."

The Sculptress, they'd learned, was the goddess the witches owed their magic to—much like the Tides in their own world.

"And if this Sculptress of yours *doesn't* will it?"

Romie had taken the words right out of Emory's mouth. The pause that followed was unsettling, to say the least. Something flashed in Aspen's eyes that Emory thought looked familiar—grief, fear, chased away by a fierce denial of both, as if she didn't want to even *consider* what might happen if the witchling did not ascend.

Whatever it was must not be pleasant.

"Is the ascending witchling someone you know?" Emory asked.

Aspen blinked at her as if just realizing she was there. Probably not used to hearing Emory do the talking; that was typically reserved for Romie.

Such had been the way of things since they got here: Romie taking the lead, and Emory letting her. They'd gone back to the way things were before they'd been separated by a mythical door, and in some ways Emory didn't mind. It meant things were normal between them, even after all this time, even in this strange new place. Romie was *back*, and Emory wouldn't trade that for anything. Even if it meant shrinking back to her old self, the Emory who'd let Romie take charge because Romie knew best.

Besides, Emory didn't exactly trust herself to make the right decisions at the moment. Not after everything that had happened. Not after putting all her trust in Keiran, only for him to betray her—unmasking himself as someone willing to do anything to wake the Tides, including letting his friends die and Emory become a vessel for drowned gods.

Romie, she knew, would never have gotten played by Keiran.

Before Aspen could answer her question, a voice made them all jump. "You two. What are you doing here?"

Mrs. Amberyl was staring at Emory and Romie, looking displeased. She was an austere woman, from her manner of speaking down to her very appearance. Her words were as sharp and precise as her cheekbones, her quiet authority as depthless as her dark eyes. She commanded respect throughout her household, and though nothing about her felt particularly motherly—as far as Emory's understanding of such a word went—the care and generosity she'd shown Emory and Romie since their arrival couldn't be overstated.

"Speak," Mrs. Amberyl pressed.

"They got turned around looking for tincture for Romie," Aspen explained. "I told them they'd find it in the herbarium."

Mrs. Amberyl looked between them with an air of suspicion. "Quite so."

Emory noticed the way the woman's gaze caught on her hand—more specifically, her right wrist. This wasn't the first time Mrs. Amberyl peered at the spiral scar that marked Emory and Romie as being part of the Selenic Order, the secret society that Keiran had led. Both Mrs. Amberyl and Aspen shared a strange curiosity for it, though they'd never outright asked about it.

"Run along to the herbarium, then," Mrs. Amberyl told them. "Mr. Ametrine is there; he can fetch you the tincture."

As she and Romie retreated down the corridor, Emory could sense the two witches watching them quietly, no doubt waiting for them to be gone before Mrs. Amberyl tore into her daughter for fraternizing with the strangers.

A spark of inspiration struck her. With the Lightkeeper magic she'd been practicing in secret, Emory could refract light and render herself invisible–or as invisible as she could with how little time she'd had to perfect the skill. She'd gotten the idea from Keiran, a trick of the light that would allow her to fade against the backdrop of the corridor, hidden enough that she could tiptoe back around the corner and eavesdrop on the Amberyls.

Emory gripped Romie's arm, pointed behind them, then tapped her ear, mouthing, *Stay here.* She almost expected Romie to argue, but Romie only gave a terse nod as she caught her meaning. Her eyes, though, were rife with worry–and something else Emory didn't want to consider.

Using their magic in this world proved more taxing than it normally would, but not so much that they couldn't do it. It was as if being in this strange place with a different moon altered the rules that governed their lunar magic. Romie could access her Dreamer abilities only through bloodletting, even under her ruling waning moon, and doing so always brought on a great fatigue.

Emory, on the other hand, could still access her Tidecaller abilities without bloodletting or having to rely on the current moon phase. And the kind of post-magic fatigue she experienced was not *quite* the same. In fact, she wouldn't describe it as fatigue at all but as a haunting. One she was fully prepared for now as she succumbed to her magic's pull.

Doing so was easy–*too easy*. In her mind, she heard Baz warning her about the dangers of Eclipse magic.

"Control is crucial because our magic isn't like the other lunar houses'," he'd said to her what felt like forever ago. "It's not exactly something you call on. *It* calls to *you*, and you have to learn how to resist that pull while at the same time succumbing to it just enough that the pressure doesn't become too much."

That had never been a problem for Emory back at Aldryn. But here, the pull of her magic was *unbearable*. It was like her Tidecaller ability was always close to the surface, desperate to come out. It had been this way since the immense feat of power she'd displayed in the sleepscape, where she *should* have Collapsed but hadn't. Like her power was eager for her to use more and more of it and finally tip the scales toward Collapsing. It was a pressure building painfully in her veins, the same way it had the summer after losing Romie, when the only thing that would lessen the pain was bloodletting.

Using her magic in small doses relieved that pressure more than bloodletting ever could, but it came with its own setbacks.

Don't think about it, she told herself as she called on the Lightkeeper magic. It must have worked, because Romie blinked, looking right through her. A shadow moved at the edge of Emory's vision, but she paid it no mind as she moved closer to the Amberyls.

". . . told you to keep your distance."

"I know, Mother."

"Once your sister ascends, you'll need to keep a close eye on her. I won't have her mixed up in this."

"They're not half-bad," Aspen replied meekly. "Maybe we shouldn't be so quick to assume the worst. Surely there's an explanation for why they have–"

"Don't be foolish. You know the stories. And with the rot that has started to spread . . ." Mrs. Amberyl smoothed her stiff dress. "We cannot take chances now, especially with your sister not yet ascended. Never again will a witch fall prey to a demon's cunning."

Her words slithered unpleasantly along Emory's senses–or perhaps the shiver that went through her was due to the ghost sidling up close to her, summoned by this echo of his own power. Emory jerked back, barely keeping a hold on her magic as she stared at the pallid face of the boy who haunted her.

This was the worst part of using magic here–the ghosts it conjured.

They manifested whenever Emory used even a modicum of magic: specters at the edge of her vision, death lingering in the shadows around her, beckoning to her. It was as if calling on one tidal alignment opened the gates wide for the darker ones to seep through against her will. Shadowguide and Reaper magic alike, leeching on her guilt and her fear and her desperation. Making her afraid of her own power, the way she had been when she'd first discovered her Tidecaller abilities.

Her ghosts never spoke to her, but it was like she could read their minds all the same. And Keiran's ghost was taunting her now, taking some grim, twisted pleasure in the fact that she was using *his* tricks, *his* magic. The thought made Emory feel dirty– even as some small part of her couldn't help but feel proud at how quickly she'd learned to use this magic.

Before she could lose her cool and reveal herself to the Amberyls, she rushed back to Romie's side, eager to leave the ghost behind.

Only once they were in the privacy of the small parlor that connected their conjoined rooms did Emory relay what she'd heard. She found it hard to focus as Romie rattled on with theories of what it all meant. She'd hoped the light filtering in from the large window might chase her lingering ghost away, but he was still there, smirking at her as if he knew the kind of hold he had on her, even in death.

He's not real, Emory told herself, pressing her eyes shut. He couldn't be. He was a figment of her imagination, called to the surface by the tangled web of emotions his death had weaved inside her:

Self-loathing at having let him play her like he had and not seeing the truth of him before she'd given him her heart.

Guilt at having let the umbrae kill him before her very eyes.

Relief that he was gone, that he'd gotten what he deserved.

Affection, still, despite it all, and this desperate need to understand why he'd done what he'd done, if only to justify her own part in it.

Emory wanted nothing more than to burn Keiran Dunhall Thornby out of her system. But his ghost would not let her, and maybe she deserved such a haunting.

After she'd hurt so many people she cared about, a small, ugly part of her took satisfaction in it—the pain of that pressure building in her veins when she resisted the pull of her magic, the ghosts it conjured when she gave into it. A twisted form of self-punishment.

"Did you use too much?"

Romie's face was scrunched up in worry, mistaking Emory's frayed state for the same post-magic fatigue she experienced. Something Emory was more than fine letting her believe.

She gave her a wan smile. "I'll be all right."

Romie leaned back against the window. There was that look in her eyes again that had Emory feeling inexplicably guilty. Ever since Romie had found out about Emory's Tidecaller magic, she'd been acting tense any time Emory used it or brought it up. Emory would have expected her friend to be excited over such rare magic. Instead, she had the distinct impression that Romie was *afraid* of it.

Or jealous.

Maybe both.

Whatever it was had Emory scared that the old rift between them might open again, and she would not let it, not so soon after getting her friend back. So she hid the full scope of her power, let herself appear weaker than she was, let Romie take charge of things while she followed along like the old version of herself would have. It felt odd to take a step back after having found such strength in herself in the wake of Romie's disappearance, but if this was what was needed to keep the peace–to find a sense of normalcy in this strange place–then so be it.

"This wasn't part of Clover's story," Romie said after a while. "Those who traveled through worlds . . . their magic was never affected like ours is."

"That was a children's story. I guess the reality is bleaker."

Emory tried to shut out the small voice inside her that was begging her to use more magic. Keiran's ghost began to fade into the shadows, denied its only tether to this plane. When he disappeared at last, the pressure in Emory's veins returned like clockwork. Her blood singing for more more more more *more*.

"You know, every time I see Aspen, I'm more convinced she's the witch from the story."

Emory didn't know how to feel about Romie's continued obsession with *Song of the Drowned Gods*. Yes, they were in a world that seemed plucked from the book's very pages, but while Romie was convinced their purpose was to play out

Clover's story to the end—and hopefully change its outcome—Emory had her doubts.

"There's just something about her," Romie continued, eyes unfocused and bright as stars. "I keep finding myself in her dreams, even when I'm not trying to. It's like there's this tug between us. A tether that keeps bringing me to her. And it's the strangest thing, but whenever Aspen is near, I swear I hear an echo of that damn song, like a phantom impression of it ringing in my ears."

"Could mean anything," Emory said lightly.

"Or it could mean Aspen hears the song too. The call to other worlds. Maybe she'd be willing to help us get to the sea of ash, if only she could get out from under her mother's claws for a second."

Emory said nothing at that. Ever since Romie had found the lost epilogue in the sleepscape, which centered on two characters who were clearly a Dreamer and a Nightmare Weaver, her belief in the story had doubled. She saw herself in the girl of dreams, more certain than ever that she had a grand part to play in this story. That her being here was fate.

But if that was the case, if Romie really was the girl of dreams and Emory the scholar on the shores and Aspen the witch in the woods, and they were all connected by this song woven between worlds, why then did Emory not feel the same tug between them, the same urgency to chase after this destiny and see the story through?

All she had were her ghosts and her guilt and her desire to go home. To see her father again. See Baz again. Laugh with him and Romie like they once did as children.

She'd done what she set out to do: she'd found Romie, alive and well. There was no need to keep going. No benefit to them seeking out the Tides in the Deep, to waking them as Keiran had wanted. Especially not if it meant Emory would become their *vessel*.

"Look," Romie said, twisting around to peer out the window. "I think it's starting."

Emory joined her to see a dozen witches slipping into the woods, the setting sun elongating the shadows they cast in an eerie way. Two figures stood out in stark recognition: Mrs. Amberyl and Aspen.

Romie turned to Emory with a mischievous smile. "If no one's here, what's stopping us from going after them?"

The answer to that was *nothing*–except, of course, for the thicket of vines that barricaded the garden gate. But without the watchful presence of Mrs. Amberyl, it was easy enough to get through, with a little help from Emory's Sower magic. The vines parted for them, and as they slipped into the woods proper, Emory tried to ignore the unsettling shadows that followed them.

The woods were thick with damp, smelling faintly of rot. They found the coven gathered before an ancient yew tree. At its foot was a grave being dug up as the witches chanted a low, humming tune. All of them wore flowing, diaphanous gowns and billowing shirts with ample sleeves, garments that were unseasonable and much folksier than their usual stiff skirts and suits and high-necked blouses. They were barefoot and wore bones around their necks and atop their heads like crowns–everything from massive antlers to tiny bones so fine they must have come from something no larger than a mouse.

The forest seemed to have quieted around them, so that the only sound was the strange hissing and murmuring of the witches' song. The sun disappeared, shadowing the clearing in the cold hues of twilight, and the chanting came to a sudden stop.

A weighted, anticipatory sort of silence settled over the witches. A shiver ran up Emory's spine, making the hairs on her arms rise.

And then a hand emerged from the earth, seeking purchase on the edge of the grave.

The corpse of a girl rose from it. She wore a once-white dress that clung in tatters over her small frame. Beneath the dirt streaked across her face, the warm tone of her skin held no trace of death. She was not a corpse at all but a girl very much alive.

"The earth has received you and sculpted you anew," Mrs. Amberyl intoned. "Arise, Bryony Amberyl, for now you are a witch."

Bryony was helped out of the grave by Aspen. It was then that Emory noticed the strange marking on Bryony's exposed rib cage, the skin visible through a tear in her dress. It looked as if the earth itself had torn her open and stitched her back up again, leaving a slightly raised pink scar on her skin.

A *spiral* scar.

Exactly like the one both Emory and Romie bore on their wrists.

"The Sculptress's mark," an old witch gasped, pointing at the scar.

"Another Amberyl daughter blessed with the Sculptress's favor!" someone else exclaimed, drawing a spiral over his forehead.

Bryony smiled up at her sister, her face mirroring the coven's apparent elation. And then her eyes went black, as if her pupils had been blown out.

She took a sharp intake of breath, opened her mouth, and let out a guttural sound.

For a terrible moment, Emory saw herself on Dovermere Cove, seeing Travers's would-be corpse spewing up water before he withered away, and Lia as she screamed and clawed at her throat, mouth burnt to a crisp by some invisible magic. It felt like déjà vu, like she was reliving those nightmares that haunted her sleep.

But the sea was not here. Dovermere could not touch them. And Bryony did not appear to be disintegrating into dust or clawing at her throat. In fact, she let out a strangled laugh that had Aspen jerking back from her and then began to speak in a strange tongue, her voice too deep to belong to a teenage girl.

Romie gripped Emory's wrist tight. A twig snapped, and Bryony whipped her head in their direction. There was no way she could see them hiding behind these bushes, yet it felt to Emory like those impossible black eyes were boring into her own. An odd sense of recognition settled in her bones—a kinship to the bloodthirsty wickedness that blazed in the dark depths of those eyes.

But then Bryony blinked, and whatever twisted spell she'd been under stopped. Her eyes were normal again, the whites flashing plainly in the moonlight. With a whimper, she fell limply into her sister's waiting arms.

An unsettling quiet fell over the witches until one of them hissed, "Hellwraith."

The word slithered from tongue to tongue, somber and chilling. Aspen's grip on her sister turned protective at the fear and violence radiating from the witches.

"You know what must be done, Hazel," said a sour-faced matriarch who stared down her prim nose at Mrs. Amberyl. "She will have to be exorcised."

Mrs. Amberyl stepped in front of her daughters. "Don't be foolish, Hyacinth. You all saw Bryony's mark. The Sculptress has blessed her."

"Then how do you explain this demonic possession?"

The High Matriarch swept a hand over the woods. "We've all noticed the changes in the air of late. The trees are rotting. Streams are running black. Leaves are festering and roots are moldering and branches droop as if they are too weak to hold up their thinning canopies. Putrefying animal carcasses are found in droves. The woods that are sacred to us, the very source of the magic we wield, are dying. There is a sickness running beneath the earth, spreading through roots like poison through veins. And all of it started when *they* arrived. Those who falsely bear our Sculptress's mark."

Romie's nails dug into Emory. There could be no question as to whom Mrs. Amberyl meant.

"We have seen this before," the High Matriarch continued. "The netherdemons finding their way out from their realm beneath the earth. And just like before, evil *will* be purged." Steel laced her every word. "I will see to it myself on the black moon."

Above, a pale waning crescent shone. Emory and Romie stared wide-eyed at each other, their hearts beating in tandem as cold, bone-deep fear set in.

This was no fairy tale.

It was a waking nightmare—and one with no escape.

3

BAZ

THE LIGHTHOUSE IN HAREBELL COVE HAD NOT BEEN Baz's first choice for a secret hideout, but it turned out to be the perfect spot, somewhere the Regulators wouldn't immediately think to look for their two most wanted fugitives. Though if they did, Jae had concocted an illusion that would conceal Theodore and Kai, so long as no one looked too close.

For a time, right after their escape from the Institute, Theodore and Kai had hidden under everyone's noses in Cadence, under the protection of the Veiled Atlas. Alya Kazan and her niece Vera Ingers had taken them in, hiding them away in the small apartment above the taproom they managed. It had been the perfect location, a place where all of them could gather to share information and start building their case against the Institute and the Selenic Order.

But after the case got thrown out, the Institute's search for Theodore and Kai seemed to intensify. The Regulators sowed the seeds of fear in Cadence and its surroundings, plastering the escapees' faces everywhere, painting them as dangerous, unstable convicts. The safest course of action for Theodore and Kai was to leave before someone discovered them.

The list of alternative hiding places had been a short one with no good options. Alya suggested they sail toward the Constellation Isles, even as far as the Outerlands. Kai thought it best if they stayed under the Regulators' noses at Aldryn College, in the Eclipse commons that only Eclipse-born could access. Theodore wanted nothing more than to see his wife again, though they all knew the Regulators had eyes on their house in Threnody—which also made Jae's offer of housing them with the other Collapsed Eclipse-born they were training unwise.

It was Baz who'd suggested Henry Ainsleif's lighthouse.

Baz had gone to visit Emory's father shortly after the events at Dovermere, when he knew rumors of Emory's supposed drowning would have reached him. Baz couldn't bear the idea of keeping the truth of Emory's fate from her father. He didn't think it fair for Henry to believe she was dead when she was decidedly not—especially not after telling his own parents the truth about Romie and seeing all their grief replaced with careful optimism.

"Telling them the truth will only give them false hope," Kai had warned Baz at the time. "What if Emory and Romie *are* dead?"

"They're not," Baz had countered, refusing to believe anything else.

And if they never came back . . . Baz didn't want to think of *that,* either. But he certainly didn't agree about the truth giving his parents false hope. If someone had done the same for him when he'd thought Romie had drowned—if they'd told him there was still a chance for her to make it out of Dovermere alive—it would have saved him an ocean of hurt and grief and doubt. It would have given him the hope he'd so desperately needed then.

So he gave that to Henry. He told him everything, making it as clear as he could that Emory was not dead but simply *gone*.

To Henry's credit, he'd taken the news about doors to other worlds and the fact that Emory was a Tidecaller rather well. It seemed Emory had previously written to him about having odd magic and suspecting her mother might have lied about her birth, and so all the pieces came together to form a coherent picture in Henry's mind.

It had felt good to talk to Emory's dad. To voice all these things to someone from outside of their little group. Baz had found himself saying more than he'd intended, venturing into the Eclipse situation of it all, their failed quest for justice against the Selenic Order and the Institute at large. He had certainly not anticipated it enticing Henry to their side.

"If my daughter is Eclipse-born, I don't want that to ever happen to her. I want to help. However I can."

And so Baz had taken Henry up on his offer, sending Kai and Theodore to hide away in Henry's secluded lighthouse in the tiny hamlet that was Harebell Cove. Emory's ties to the Selenic Order raised some concerns over this decision, because while the rest of the world might know Emory Ainsleif as a Healer, the Selenic Order knew she was a Tidecaller—and that might put a target on Henry's back.

But the Regulators had no reason to believe Henry Ainsleif might be involved in the harboring of two Collapsed Eclipse-born fugitives. To them, he was but a humble lighthouse keeper with little to no magic, a reclusive man who didn't overly concern himself with the outside world, the grieving father of a girl who, despite having ties to Baz, was believed to be dead. Another victim of Dovermere's dark whims.

It was a risk nonetheless. *Especially* the part where they'd let Anise Brysden in on the truth. Theodore had insisted on it, and

Baz couldn't deny the good it had done both his parents. He'd never seen his mother this happy. It was like she had shed all those years of loss like a second skin, making herself shiny and new again. But Baz feared it was the sort of precarious happiness that would make her spiral into despair again if it was ripped away from her—which was a very real possibility, if they were ever to be found out. Or if Romie never came back.

But as all of them drank mulled cider and exchanged gifts, their bellies full of savory chowder and fresh brown bread, music scratching away on the gramophone and laughter ringing in their ears, Baz couldn't help but think it was worth it. All his worries had slipped away, as if here in the lighthouse at the edge of the world, nothing bad could reach him. Not Artem or Drutten. Not the stress of figuring out the extent of his Collapsed magic or the burden of seeking justice for his fellow Eclipse-born.

Here was the connection he'd been craving. The sense of belonging he'd been robbed of at Aldryn College.

There seemed to be an unspoken agreement among them all to keep things light and festive tonight. Tomorrow, they would talk business—and business they did have. But tonight existed in a perfect bubble, and none of them wanted to undo this precarious magic.

As the evening started to wind down, with Theodore and Jae reminiscing about the good old days of the printing press, and Henry and Anise busying themselves with the dishes, Kai wordlessly slipped away from the table while Baz wasn't looking. Baz felt crestfallen, thinking Kai had gone up to bed without so much as a good night. But then he spotted him near the back door, slipping on his coat. Kai caught his eye and motioned for him to join before disappearing into the night. Without hesitation, Baz grabbed his own coat and went after him.

Snow fell in fat, unhurried flurries against the windless night.

Baz followed the foot tracks on the snow-and-pine-needle-covered ground until he found Kai sitting on a tree stump, head tilted up to the sky. The moonlight washed his features in muted silver, leeching all trace of warmth from his skin.

"So, how are all our friends back at school?" Kai asked in a mock singsong voice.

Baz snorted. "You never had any friends at school."

"Look who's talking."

"I have Professor Selandyn. We take tea together every day."

"Tides, what have you become without me?" Kai uncorked his trusty flask and offered it to Baz with a wink. "Here. Bit stronger than tea, though."

Maybe it was because of how blessedly normal their exchange felt, or the unexpected warmth that Kai's wink sent through him, but it had Baz reaching for the flask and taking a small sip. The taste of gin filled his mouth, as unpleasant as he had expected it to be. He coughed as it burned down his throat, the sound of Kai's laugh flooding his senses.

How he'd missed it, that laugh.

"So," Baz said haltingly. He cast a furtive glance at Kai. The flurries caught in his dark hair looked like stars in a night sky. "How've you been, really, with . . . everything?"

Kai snickered. "Amazing." He took back his flask and leaned casually against the tree stump. "I really think I've found my calling, you know? Shucking oysters and cleaning out lobster cages with two old men whose idea of fun is playing the same damn card game every night, discussing the same damn boring topics every day, and following this same damn routine of theirs like they're drowning and it's their only lifeline. It's great." His eyes slid to Baz. "No offense to your dad."

Baz shrugged the comment off. "Sounds better than feeling like a lonely ghost with no one to talk to." At least he had his sister's cat to keep him company . . . most of the time. "I swear even Dusk is growing sick of me."

Kai arched a brow. "Thought you liked the solitude."

"Things change, I guess."

It was funny. Baz *had* always enjoyed solitude, but perhaps it was only because he'd grown so used to missing the people in his life he cared most about. His father being sent to the Institute, his mother checking out, his sister disappearing, Kai Collapsing . . . They had all shaped this lonely existence of his.

But for the briefest of moments, these people-shaped holes in his life had been filled by Emory, and for a time he was reminded how much he craved connection. To exist in a space with people who knew him, share the burdens and joys of life with them, even in the smallest of ways. Like tonight.

"I can't stay here, Brysden," Kai said suddenly. His voice had gone serious, and he looked at Baz with a guarded sort of hope. "I need to go back to Aldryn."

"You know you can't." Baz looked away so as not to see that hope dwindle. "We can't risk someone discovering you."

"I'll stay hidden in Obscura Hall," Kai pressed. "I'll go out to the caves under the cover of darkness—"

"Kai . . ."

"You really want to know how things have been going for me? Ask your dad about all the horrible shit he's had to see me conjure up from his nightmares. Henry too. It's getting out of control. I'm pulling things out of nightmares without wanting to—fears I have no intention of bringing to life, things that should stay buried forever. Even when I'm not actively trying to absorb a nightmare's darkness, it clings to me anyway and follows me back into waking. And the things I bring out are taking longer and longer to disintegrate."

Like the epilogue, Baz thought. They'd been puzzling it over, why the epilogue Kai had found in the sleepscape hadn't turned to dust like all other things he pulled out of nightmares. It was still perfectly intact, perhaps following a different set of rules since it was a physical thing that had been put *in* the sleepscape to begin with. But if other horrors were now staying intact in the waking world . . .

"It's only a matter of time before I bring a fucking *umbra* into the lighthouse," Kai said. His jaw tightened. "Or something worse."

Baz shivered, but it wasn't from the cold. "I thought you said there were less umbrae, after what happened."

"For a few days, maybe. But more came. And it's not just that. There's this . . . *wrongness* in the sleepscape that's making the umbrae act bolder than ever. It's like they're clamoring for souls. For mine in particular." Kai fidgeted with the cap on his flask. "And I keep getting these glimpses," he added, avoiding Baz's eye. "Of Emory."

"What?"

"I can't tell if it's real or not. And it's never anything concrete. Just an impression of her, all tangled up in the darkness of the sleepscape. Like she's drowning in it. Like we both are."

Baz's mind raced. He thought of the sleepers who'd woken up shortly after Emory had gone through the door. News of it had spread quickly, how most of the Cadence Institute's sleeping Dreamers—eternal sleepers whose consciousness had been devoured by the umbrae in the sleepscape, leaving behind comatose bodies in the real world—had *awoken*. There was not a doubt in Baz's mind that it was somehow Emory's doing. The timing was too odd to be a coincidence.

Whatever she'd done in the sleepscape—whatever power she'd unleashed that had blasted a horde of umbrae out the door along with a dying Keiran Dunhall Thornby—must have woken up the eternal sleepers. Restored their minds.

According to the papers, some of these Dreamers had been

asleep for *decades*, tended to at the Institute with little to no hope of ever waking up. And now they were awake and alive and absolutely *fine*. None of them remembered anything from their time in the sleepscape, or if they did, they weren't talking.

That kind of power . . . If Emory had indeed wielded such magic as to wake the umbrae, undo what had been done to the sleepers whose souls had been lost to these nightmares, *surely* she must have Collapsed. And though Collapsing wouldn't destroy Emory–Baz, Kai, and Jae were proof enough–Baz couldn't help but fear for her. A Tidecaller was already limitless enough as it was, but a *Collapsed* Tidecaller?

And now Kai, who was struggling with his own Collapsed magic, was having dreams of her *drowning in darkness*.

"I'm sure she's fine," Kai said quietly, though there was an edge to his voice that Baz didn't understand. "Anyway, she probably only shows up in my head because of you."

"Me?"

"You dream of her constantly. And while I'm happy to be rid of that damn printing press scene of yours, I can't say Dovermere is much better."

Baz was glad for the darkness hiding the flush that crept up his neck. He'd hoped Kai wouldn't have noticed the shift in his nightmares, the way the printing press scene now bled into the caves to show him one of the many horrors he'd witnessed inside Dovermere: the umbrae feasting on Baz's fears, dragging Emory to her death, bending to Kai's will. Emory going through the door. Keiran dying in his arms. The portal whispering in his mind.

Sometimes, when the nightmare involved Emory–which was more often than he cared to admit–it shifted out of the caves to show Baz other moments with her, all twisted up with the horror of his subconscious. The pain of losing her. Her betrayal of his trust. The moment she'd pulled away from him when they'd kissed that one time, the rejection starker and crueler in the darkness of his mind.

Now he knew Kai had been present for at least a few of those nightmares and had seen how much it ate away at him, this childish pining for someone who was *gone*, who might never come back. Of course, Kai had never said anything about it to him. It was like Emory was this unspeakable thing between them, the one subject they never broached.

Until now.

Baz cleared his throat, kicking at the snow. "Sorry," he said, though he wasn't entirely sure what he was apologizing for.

"Not your fault I keep getting pulled into your nightmares." Kai took a swig from his flask and stared angrily out at the darkness. "If Collapsed magic is supposed to be limitless, you'd think I'd have better control over it. Not whatever the fuck this is."

Baz's gaze drifted to the unmarred Eclipse tattoo on Kai's hand. "I know how you feel about this, but . . . my offer still stands if you need it."

Not long after their escape from the Institute, Baz suggested using his time magic to bring back the Unhallowed Seal on Kai's hand–temporarily, of course, just to give Kai a bit of a reprieve from the uncontrollable nightmares. It had been a thoughtless question, asked in a moment of despair after seeing Kai struggle against invisible demons in his sleep. Kai had told him to fuck off. Baz had apologized. And they'd never spoken of it again.

Kai looked like he might throttle him now that he'd dared bring it up again. "You sound just like your dad. He's been playing around with his Nullifier magic to try to help me suppress my own magic. Keep the nightmares at bay."

"That's great." Baz beamed. Why hadn't he thought of this before?

"But it's not a solution, is it?" Kai bit back darkly. "It means your dad doesn't sleep so long as he's helping me get some nightmare-less rest. It means I have to stay here."

"If that's what you need to make this work . . ."

"What I *need* is to be closer to Dovermere and to try opening the portal again. What was the point of that damn epilogue if I can't go through the door?"

Kai had gone back to the caves shortly after Emory went through the Hourglass, trying to get it to open again at his touch. If Clover's epilogue had any truth to it, both Kai and Romie were like Emory in that they, too, had the power to traverse worlds. But the door would not open at Kai's touch, no matter what he tried.

Baz would never dare admit to it, but the truth was that he would give *anything* to hear the song of Dovermere, the same one that had called to Romie and Emory and Kai. He'd come to terms with not seeing himself reflected in *Song of the Drowned Gods* the way they were. He had no role to play in this story; he wasn't the boy of nightmares or the girl of dreams or the scholar on the shores who went through worlds. He was the reader, doomed to watch his favorite heroes from the sidelines as he'd always done. He could try to put the pieces together, but he would never have the power to push the story forward.

And Baz was okay with that. He had to be.

The magic of the night seemed to have died around them, and Baz didn't know how to reignite it. The wind picked up suddenly, and he tightened his coat against it. "Want to go inside and play a boring game of cards?"

"Fine." If Kai minded the abrupt change in subject, he was good at pretending otherwise as he slid off the tree trunk with a mischievous smile. "But we're making it into a drinking game."

Baz couldn't help his own smile or the inexplicable warmth that went through him as they walked quietly back to the lighthouse, their shoulders occasionally brushing. But even this tiny sliver of normalcy couldn't mend the magic for long. Before they reached the door, it burst open to reveal a frantic-looking Henry hurriedly slipping on his coat, an everlight lantern swinging from his hand.

"What's wrong?" Baz asked.

"The tide's swallowing everything up!"

As if on cue, Baz realized the night was no longer quiet: ear-splitting roars came up from the shoreline, and he thought he heard some sort of siren blaring in the distance. He and Kai hurried after Henry down to the water's edge, where the sea had already swallowed up half the shore. Large, powerful swells crashed along the smooth rocks, reaching as far as the tree line. The faint light of the lantern cast a sorry picture: lobster cages and fishing gear were being battered by waves and then pulled back into the sea, and Henry's fishing barge was now beached, caught in the boughs of trees.

Henry was already knee-deep in what must be freezing water, grabbing hold of whatever he could and tossing it farther up the shore. Kai didn't hesitate to join him. He threw Baz a dire look as he hauled things out of the water. "The time, Brysden!"

Right. Time—the one thing Baz had power over.

He grasped the threads of it, bending the tide to his will. The next wave paused before it could reach them, frozen in time, and the three of them worked around it to heave things out of the water. It still amazed Baz how easy it was to reach for his magic. Once, this big a feat would have appeared *too* big, the kind of magic he would have feared might bring about his Collapsing.

But this was only a drop in the ocean of what he could do.

When they'd secured everything, Baz let go of the magic, and the tide resumed its unnatural battering against the shore. Panting, the three of them watched the sea in silence, not daring to voice the eerie reality of what they were seeing.

Baz looked at his watch for confirmation. It was midnight—the point at which the tide should be at its lowest. If there was one thing they could always count on, it was the rise and fall of the tide, the science behind it. There truly had to be something wrong with the world for it to be so out of sorts.

And Baz couldn't help but think it had something to do with Dovermere, and the door they had opened within its depths.

4

EMORY

"WHAT THE FUCK," ROMIE WHISPERED. *"WHAT THE FUCK?"*

"So I wasn't imagining things?" Emory asked, closing the door to their parlor behind her. "The spiral–"

"It makes no sense. How can it be the same?"

The resemblance to their own spiral mark was too striking, too *impossible*, to be mere coincidence. In their world, the Sacred Spiral was attributed to the Tides, but here, it sounded like it was the mark of the witches' own deity, the Sculptress.

"And don't even get me started on the ascension," Romie said with a hysterical laugh. She started pacing, tracking mud on the floor. "How long do you think that poor girl was buried for? I can't believe they *bury their children alive* for them to ascend into their power. And then to suggest exorcism!" Another gruff laugh. "And Mrs. Amberyl had the audacity to call *me* barbaric when I explained bloodletting to her."

Emory remembered that conversation well. Mrs. Amberyl had

sneered at Romie's description of the bloodletting practice those of their world relied on to use magic outside of their ruling moon phase. "How incredibly barbaric."

A laughable statement now that they'd seen how a witch's magic came about.

Emory kept seeing Bryony's blackened eyes, hearing that strange voice come out of her. "Demonic possession," she said in a horrified murmur. "That can't be possible, right?"

"Sure looked like it." Romie plopped down on the divan. "But that voice—I've heard it before."

"What?"

"I didn't want to freak you out, but . . . there's something really weird happening with the sleepscape."

The blood rushed from Emory's face. "Weird how?"

"You know I can sense umbrae hovering at the edges of dreams, right? That's usually my cue to leave, to come back to the waking world before they devour the dream I'm in. But ever since we've been here, I've felt something *darker* than the umbrae hovering at the edges of the star-lined path." Romie worried her lip. "That's where I heard that voice. From that dark presence, whispering in that strange tongue. I can't shake this idea that whatever it is, it's trying to escape the sleepscape."

"You think what possessed Bryony was an umbra?"

"Demon, umbra . . . Is there really a difference?"

Emory thought back to the umbrae that had attacked them in the sleepscape right before they came here. The way she'd *healed* all of them—how such power should have made her Collapse but had left her totally and utterly fine.

What had Kai said to her once? That umbrae were attracted to new magic. Like the kind of magic she'd used. Perhaps it had gotten the attention of something worse, too.

She frowned. "But how could an umbra *possess* a witch like that?"

"What Mrs. Amberyl said, about their rotting woods . . . What if it really is our fault? We opened the door between this realm and the sleepscape. Maybe a crack was left open for all kinds of horrors to slip through."

A nervous laugh bubbled out of Emory. She felt on the verge of tears, and there was an unpleasant acidity in her mouth that tasted very much like fear. "Let's not admit to our possible guilt out loud when they're talking about *purging the evil* from their world. They want to get rid of us, Ro."

"Well, it's not like we're planning to stay here, anyway. We'll just have to leave before the new moon." Romie eyed her with that wariness again. "What I'm saying is, whatever you did in the sleepscape must have caught the umbrae's attention, and now that we're here . . . maybe they're coming after us."

Emory ignored the blame in those words. "All the more reason we have to find a way home."

"No, you don't get it. I think the forces within the sleepscape are after us because they want to *stop* us."

"Stop us from what?"

"From reaching the sea of ash, of course."

There it was. Emory's shoulders slumped. "Ro, be serious."

"I *am* being serious. Look around you, Em. We're quite literally in a world from *Song of the Drowned Gods*, called here by a song we both heard. If this is real, then why shouldn't the rest of the story be?" She pointed to Emory, then to herself, saying, "You're the scholar who found a portal to other worlds. I'm the girl of dreams who was slumbering among the stars. And now we've found a witch with the same spiral mark that we have. Two witches, apparently! Bryony and Aspen are the missing pieces we need. They're the reason we're here."

"What if you're wrong?"

Something shifted in Romie, that fervor in her eyes banking, bringing her back down to earth. She swallowed hard before say-ing, "Look, I know I messed up back at Aldryn. Obsessing over the epilogue the way I did . . . I lost sight of what was important to me and nearly lost everything in the process. I don't want to do that again. But I *swear*, Em, I'm right about this. All I'm asking is that you trust me."

"Of course I trust you."

"Then let's do this together. The way it always should have been."

Hearing those words resonated with Emory. For a long time, she'd resented Romie for her secrecy and obsession, for throwing away their friendship along with everything else that had been important to her—like Romie's budding romance with Nisha and her relationship with Baz.

But now a part of Emory understood. Because while Romie had lost herself searching for the epilogue, Emory had lost herself searching for Romie.

She, too, had alienated and used the only real friends she'd had left in search of power and acceptance, which she'd sought from people who, in hindsight, might not have been the best influence on her. Keiran sure hadn't been. Neither had Lizaveta, despite her veiled warnings. Virgil and Nisha had been the only Selenic Order members Emory had connected with, but it still felt to her like she'd been too consumed by Keiran to give them a proper chance.

"Can we make each other a promise?" Romie asked.

At the solemnity in her voice, Emory sat next to her on the divan. "Of course. Anything."

"We're in this mess because of the secrets I kept."

"Ro . . ."

"No, let me finish. I hate that I lost you even before I went to Dovermere. And when I thought I might be dead, I hated that I would never be able to make amends. But we're here now. Together. And I don't want any secrets between us anymore."

Guilt stabbed through Emory. "I don't either."

"So no secrets, then?"

Everything Emory was keeping from Romie rose to the surface. The pull of her magic and the ghosts it conjured. Tides, even the truth about Keiran. Romie knew of his betrayal, how the entire Selenic Order had fallen for his lies, but she didn't know about Emory's relationship with him. Emory had kept that detail out, too embarrassed to admit she'd let her feelings for Keiran cloud her judgment.

She didn't *want* to lie to Romie. But it wasn't like Romie was being entirely truthful with her, either. Whatever she felt about Emory's magic hung between them like an impenetrable wall. But Emory wasn't ready to tear it down just yet and find out what lay behind it.

"No secrets," she said with a smile she hoped reached her eyes.

"Good." Romie rested her cheek on Emory's shoulder and sighed happily. "You know, as much as I love being here with you, I feel bad for my brother. The dork would have a field day with this."

Emory snorted on a laugh. "He'd probably pass out from excitement." The thought of Baz made her heart sink. Quietly, she added, "I do miss him, though."

Romie leaned back and waggled her brows at her. "Like, miss him, or *miss him* miss him?"

This, at least, was one truth Emory hadn't hidden from Romie. How close she'd become to Baz in Romie's absence. How confused she was about what she felt for him.

"I'm not sure," Emory said with a sad smile. And she genuinely *was* unsure. She missed him more deeply every time she felt homesick, because she realized that Baz had become her anchor. The one person she knew she could depend on.

She missed his friendship, his companionship, his solid presence. But she wasn't sure she missed him *like that*.

There was that kiss on the beach, and their goodbye in the cave, playing still in the back of her mind. But those weren't the first things that came to mind when she thought of Baz. And that made her feel awful all over again, remembering how she'd used his feelings for her to get something out of him.

Maybe if they made it back home, she would give him a chance. A proper chance this time, to see if these feelings he'd always had for her could be reciprocated.

Or maybe it was best to let it go.

Emory let out a long exhale, glancing at the window. From the looks of it, the witches had returned from the forest: the gardens around Amberyl House were all alight, and music drifted toward them.

"We'll have a hard time convincing Aspen and Bryony of anything, with how deep Mrs. Amberyl has her claws in them," Emory said.

Romie raised a brow. "With that rebellious streak in Aspen? Please. The girl is begging to be let free from her mother's rigid rules." That bright fervor reignited in Romie's eyes. "Let's go do some sleuthing, shall we?"

If the ascension festivities were meant to be *festive*, the reality sorely fell short of expectations.

The gardens surrounding Amberyl House had been transformed for the night, full of ribbons that fluttered in the breeze and glass jars alight with the glow of fireflies trapped within. It should have been enchanting, but the scene was underscored with an eerie quality. The music was erratic and haunting, and the movements of those dancing were twisted, as if they were trying to conjure the Sculptress herself or summon more witches from their graves.

The clattering of bones from the witches' necklaces made a shiver run up Emory's spine. Everyone who looked her way felt like someone out to get her. But no one said a word to her and Romie. They pretended the two of them didn't exist, as if they weren't complicit in Mrs. Amberyl's plan to purge them on the black moon–whatever that might entail.

At least for tonight, they were safe. Though judging by the thinness of the waning moon, they would have no more than two days before that changed.

Romie actually looked *thrilled* by it all, which should have come as no surprise given her nature, but still felt unwarranted under the circumstances. She picked up two intricately carved goblets that contained a deep purple drink from a table laden with fruits and meats, sipping on hers as she handed the other to Emory.

"What are you doing?" Emory asked in a horrified whisper, trying to stop Romie from drinking. "We don't know what's in these."

"Oh, relax, will you?"

"*Relax?* They want us gone, Ro."

"And we're not going to get answers from them if they know we know that." Romie swayed to the music, smiling at the witches around her. "So start acting like you're having fun."

Emory sniffed at her drink–it smelled *divine*, like mulled wine– but resisted the urge to try it. She did attempt to loosen up as Romie grabbed her hand and pulled her through the crowd, but all she wanted to do was run off into the woods away from these people and never look back. Romie had other plans. She coaxed Emory onto the dance floor, laughing as she twirled her around. Something loosened in Emory's chest at the sound of Romie's laugh, at the sight of her dancing. She was suddenly reminded of a younger Romie, running barefoot in the sand with her arms spread out as she pretended to be one of the gulls. So free and full of life.

Life–Romie was *alive*, something Emory had yet to fully wrap her mind around. For so long she'd thought Romie was dead, then lost to the magic of Dovermere. But she was alive, and here with her. And for a tiny moment as they laughed and danced, it felt like nothing had ever changed, like they were still the same two girls they were before Aldryn College, before the Selenic Order, before Dovermere and the epilogue and the doors.

They weren't. She knew that. They were different girls in a different world, playacting at who they'd once been, at least on her part. But Emory clung to the feeling nonetheless.

Romie suddenly pulled Emory through the crowd to where the High Matriarch and her two daughters stood beneath a flowery arch on a dais that overlooked the festivities.

Mrs. Amberyl was all polite smiles, but Emory could tell it was a mask. There was worry hidden in those sharp eyes, a protective grip to the hand resting on her younger daughter's shoulder. And with good reason, given the anxious looks and whispers the witches kept throwing Bryony. A mother shielded her small children as they passed by the dais, as if afraid Bryony might grow fangs and eat them.

Emory had to give Bryony credit. The young witch's smile never slipped, even as her eyes gleamed with unshed tears. Aspen, on the other hand, didn't bother with feigned niceties; she looked fiercely territorial standing on the other side of her sister, fingers laced through hers as if ready to whisk her away at the first sign of trouble.

"Mrs. Amberyl, thank you so much for inviting us," Romie said with a winning smile. "What a fabulous event!"

As if they hadn't just overheard the witches talking about the evil they'd brought upon their land.

Romie did a double take of Bryony. "Sorry, I don't think we've had the pleasure yet."

Emory bit on the inside of her cheek to keep from smiling; Romie was a natural at this.

"This is Bryony," Mrs. Amberyl said in a tight voice, her fingers digging deeper into her daughter's shoulder. "My youngest."

"Hello," Bryony said in a sweet voice so unlike the guttural one that had overtaken her in the woods. She had apparently bathed and changed since being dug up from her grave, a vision in a rich cream-and-emerald dress. Her dark hair had been styled up and adorned with pale green jewels.

Bryony leaned into Aspen. "Are those the ones you were telling me about? From the other world?"

Aspen's gaze cut to her mother, whose lips were pressed tight in displeasure. "Yes," Aspen answered. "But–"

"How does it work, your magic?" Bryony asked Emory and Romie with a tilt of her head, full of innocent curiosity.

"Well, it's influenced by the moon and tides, you see," Romie started, gaining Bryony's rapt attention.

With a quick, pointed look at Emory, Romie launched herself into a lengthy explanation of the particulars of lunar magic. Emory immediately understood what she was asking of her.

It wasn't only Lightkeeper magic she'd been practicing these past few days but Memorist magic too. Romie had begrudgingly let Emory try it out on her, though Emory could tell it had made her uncomfortable. She couldn't blame her: the concept of Memorist magic had always felt intrusive to her too.

It was one thing to use Memorist magic on a willing mind; it was quite another to use it on unsuspecting ones. Back home, it was considered taboo to use such magic without consent. But Emory wasn't home, and she was desperate for answers.

Feigning interest in the conversation, she called on her Memorist magic. Instantly, the pressure in her veins lessened, making her want to sigh with relief–even as the wrongness of what she was doing made bile rise to her throat.

Predictably, getting past the fortress in Mrs. Amberyl's mind proved no easier than before. Emory had found that all witches' minds were warded in some way—their own magic, perhaps, acting as a natural barrier to hers. Mrs. Amberyl's was the most heavily guarded she'd come across, a fortress of thorny vines that coiled tighter together at Emory's probing.

Such a fortress had to be hiding secrets.

But they weren't secrets Emory would ever be privy to, it seemed. No matter what she tried, she couldn't get past the barrier. She knew Memorist magic was strongest when touching the person or staring directly into their eyes, but she couldn't do either while remaining inconspicuous.

And now the more magic she called on, the more the shadows around her grew, her faithful ghosts taking shape. She could feel Keiran at her side, ever taunting. There were others, too. Lizaveta. Travers. Lia. Jordyn. All of them clamoring for her attention as she struggled to weasel her way into Mrs. Amberyl's memories.

Emory turned her sights to Aspen, hoping to have better luck. Nothing—save perhaps a deep sense of love for her sister, and a bright passion at the thought of someone Emory couldn't make out.

She gritted her teeth as she felt one of the ghosts tugging on her arm. But she couldn't let go of the magic just yet. She slithered into Bryony's mind, bracing for memories of being buried alive, or of her being possessed by that *thing* back in the woods. Before she could glean anything, Bryony's eyes cut to her in a way that had Emory jerking back, both physically and mentally.

Her grip on the Memorist magic slipped. Pulse beating rapidly, she wondered if Bryony had sensed her presence in her mind. She wasn't the only one watching Emory with a puzzled expression— the other Amberyls had noticed her stumble, heard her gasp.

"Sorry," Emory said, setting her cup down on a table. "Must have had too much to drink."

"Is it wise to let your *guests* partake in our celebrations?"

This came from Hyacinth, the sour-faced witch from earlier. She hovered near the dais with two boys caught somewhere between their teen years and early adulthood. Her sons, no doubt, given the striking resemblance and the same contemptuous curl of their mouths.

"I see no reason why not," Mrs. Amberyl retorted curtly.

Hyacinth's gaze slid to Bryony, full of distrust. "And your poor daughter, after such an ordeal . . ."

"Bryony is perfectly fine, I assure you."

"That remains to be seen." Hyacinth scowled at the Amberyls. "I think we'll take our leave now. But don't go thinking the coven won't keep a close eye on you until the black moon."

As they left, one of the boys muttered something that had Bryony blanching and Aspen drawing her closer. Goose bumps rose on Emory's arms as what he said registered.

Hellwraith.

Her ghosts stirred at the word. Without thinking, Emory pushed into the boy's mind to find out what exactly a hellwraith was. A cold hand was suddenly at her throat. Her magic slipped as Emory jerked back from Keiran's ghost, knocking into Romie.

"Easy," her friend said, holding her steady.

"I think perhaps you should both retire for the evening," Mrs. Amberyl suggested.

The hard look in her eye broached no room for argument. As Emory and Romie made their way back to the house, the music grated on Emory's senses. Everywhere she looked, she expected to find a ghost: in the shadows between the hedges, in the revelers dancing like specters themselves, in the faces limned by flickering firefly light.

"What happened back there?" Romie asked when they got to their parlor.

"I'm not sure." Emory sat on the divan, trying to catch her breath.

"Did you get anything from Mrs. Amberyl's mind, at least?"

Emory shook her head. "I don't think I've mastered Memorist magic enough to be able to do some proper digging." She wasn't sure she ever wanted to; bile still burned her throat, and all she could think of was Penelope West, who'd had her memories wiped–something Emory couldn't help but feel responsible for.

The disappointment in Romie's eyes made it clear she believed such power was wasted on someone like Emory. That if it were Romie who had Tidecaller magic, she would have mastered Memorist and Lightkeeper and every other alignment long ago. In fact, she would be *excelling* at them. And here Emory was, barely able to glimpse a flimsy memory from these witches' minds.

She caught sight of Lizaveta's ghost in the mirror, as if the girl were drawn to Emory's smallness.

Mediocre.

Emory shut her eyes tight, willing her to go away.

"Em, are you all right?"

Emory opened her eyes to see Romie frowning at her. The worry in her voice had her plastering on a smile. "Yeah. That magic just took a toll on me, I guess."

The promise they'd made earlier left a bitter taste in her mouth. *No secrets.* But this wasn't entirely a lie.

Surely that made it okay.

5

ROMIE

ROMIE WAS DREAMING AGAIN.

The sleepscape was strange and foreign to her here, as if being in another world strained her connection to it. It was still the same dark expanse, but there was a distinctive quality to the stars that made them *feel* different. Romie could tell the dreams they bore belonged to the witches, for they left in her the impression of earth beneath her feet, the scent of rain and moss in her nose. Their dreams were tinged green, as if they carried the woods in their souls even in sleep.

She'd never noticed how dreams in her own world were imbued with sea salt and brine, the faint scent of iron and copper, as if the sweetness of blood—of magic—made up the very fabric of people's subconscious. Only now that she was here did she miss it.

One thing remained steadfastly the same: the song woven between the stars. It anchored her. She could trust that she remained on the right path so long as she still heard the call of her destiny, this song tethered to her soul.

Romie knew Emory wanted nothing more than to return home, and though Romie herself yearned to see her brother again and her parents and Dusk and Nisha–Nisha, whom she thought about constantly, knowing the Wychwood had been her favorite part of Clover's story–she couldn't turn from this path now. Not after everything she'd lost to get here, the relationships she'd let burn to ashes in her wake.

She wasn't one to dwell on past mistakes. What was done was done. To turn back now would mean Travers, Lia, Jordyn, and all the other Selenic Order initiates would have died in vain. To turn back now would mean she had broken things off with Nisha for nothing, when together they could have been *everything*.

The only way was forward.

Romie walked through the sleepscape with purpose, her feet guiding her to that one star that always shone brighter than the rest. She was called to it the same way that song called to her. Even when she tried to avoid it, she felt that she couldn't, nor did she particularly want to.

Aspen's dreams were always lovely, rich with the life of the forest she was intricately tied to.

But tonight Romie paused before slipping into her dreaming. There was a second star shining just as bright beside Aspen's, tugging on Romie's soul in a similar manner.

Without hesitation, Romie reached for this second star, knowing who it might belong to.

It occurred to her only once she had stepped into Bryony's dream that what she'd find here might not be so peaceful after what happened at the ascension. Romie braced for the worst, thinking whatever had possessed Bryony might be lingering here in her sleep. But what she found was laughter and merriment, the rich taste of chocolate sneaked out of the kitchens by younger versions of Bryony and Aspen.

No demonic possession here.

But there was a different sort of darkness pressing against the edges of her dream. The umbrae looking for something to devour.

These creatures of nightmare feasted on dreams, turning them into something bleaker than nightmare, like black holes of despair. If a Dreamer like Romie found themselves in a dream that the umbrae chose to feast on, they needed to pull themselves out of it before the monsters could devour them, too. If not, their consciousness would remain trapped in the sleepscape forever, severed from the body they left in the waking world. They would become an umbra themselves, hungering for dreams.

Like Jordyn, Romie thought with a pang. A part of her wished she had Emory's ability to heal the umbrae the way she'd done in the sleepscape, to set these trapped souls free.

Romie was used to the umbrae's presence by now, though she *had* noticed that they were quicker to appear here in this world. She could never stay for very long in a single dream without them pressing in, as if they were tracking her through the sleepscape, eager to devour her soul.

And then there was that other thing, looming in the darkness just as the umbrae did. Though it didn't feel like a typical umbra. It was darker, stranger, *older* than anything Romie had ever encountered here. Whispering in that strange tongue, an unsettling melody that seemed so at odds with the lilting song that tugged on Romie's soul, like dissonant harmonies.

Romie wasted no time leaving Bryony's dream behind, hoping that dark presence would not follow her. Back on the star-lined path, she looked for the other bright star, longing to find herself in Aspen's dreaming again.

But the other star was no longer there. Aspen must have woken up. Crestfallen, Romie began to walk around aimlessly–and stopped dead in her tracks as she spotted someone else in the sleepscape.

Aspen was here. Not in dream form, but *here*, standing on the starlit path as though she were another Dreamer wandering around.

Back home, it wasn't uncommon for Dreamers to cross paths in the sleepscape. They weren't exactly corporeal here, but they appeared to each other exactly as they did in waking, clothes and all—something many Dreamers had learned the hard way, after falling asleep barely clothed or wearing nothing at all, only to slip into dreaming where other Dreamers saw them stark naked.

Aspen *was* clothed, wearing a flowing white nightgown, her dark hair unbound. The frizzy curls around her face were damp with sweat, and she had the look of someone who had just woken up.

So how was she *here*?

"Aspen?" Romie's voice was soft; she didn't want to scare Aspen off. But even as she got nearer and repeated herself, Aspen did not look at her. In fact, her eyes were glossed over, covered in a diaphanous white film.

Romie stared dumbfounded around them, then back at Aspen. She was certain the witch wasn't dreaming; she'd visited her dreams enough times now to know what those looked like, and this was about the furthest thing from it. And Aspen was certainly no Dreamer.

The only explanation Romie could think of was that Aspen was *scrying*, though that still didn't explain how she was here.

Aspen suddenly gasped, her face tilting upward, neck muscles pulled taut. Her hands were clutched in front of her chest, over her heart. She looked like she was in pain.

Romie tried to shake Aspen out of her trance, but when she touched her arm, the witch's skin warm, the muscles beneath strong, she realized Aspen's face and body were no longer her own. She had shifted into a young man, beautiful and chiseled like a battle god, who in turn transformed into a beast twice his size, growing teeth and claws as its molten eyes found Romie. A low rumbling sounded in its throat. Flames swirled between its open maws–

Romie wrenched away with a start and stumbled out of the sleepscape.

She sat up in bed drenched in sweat, heart pounding in her chest. For a moment she was tempted to run to Aspen's room, make sure she was all right. Wondering if Aspen had been possessed by the same demon that had overtaken Bryony–the same dark presence Romie herself had felt looming at the edges of the sleepscape.

But as she sat there in the dark, willing her breaths to slow, all Romie saw was the color of the beast's eyes.

Not black, but amber. Eyes that burned like molten suns.

It couldn't be the same thing that had possessed Bryony, because the emotions Romie had felt coming from Aspen as she transformed into it had been . . .

Not fear, but something like affection.

A bright, burning kinship that Romie herself felt thrumming in her own veins, even now. As if this odd pull she felt toward Aspen were mirrored in this fiery beast.

BAZ

THE MAGIC OF THAT FIRST SOLSTICE NIGHT ENDED WITH the tide's ravaging of the shore. They'd managed to save most of Henry's things thanks to Baz pausing time, but as the tide pulled back out again the next morning, their party set out in search of missing lobster cages and fishing nets that had washed up farther down the coastline.

In the daylight, with the calmed seas and wintry sun trying to pierce through the heavy mist, Baz couldn't help but see his surroundings through new eyes. These smooth gray rocks lapped by frothy waves, the white-dusted pine trees standing like proud sentinels overlooking the sea, the harebell flowers persisting through the snow—they were images of the place Emory had called home. Baz imagined her keeping an eye on the horizon as a young girl, waiting for her mother to return. But the woman she knew as Luce Meraude would never come back to Harebell Cove. In fact, she might no longer even be in this world.

The infamous lost epilogue that Kai had pulled from the

sleepscape had passed from hand to hand these past few months as they'd tried to make sense of it. Baz, Kai, Jae, Selandyn, Alya– it was clear to them all that the person who'd left the epilogue in the sleepscape had to be Luce Meraude, otherwise known as Adriana Kazan. They'd found proof of Luce's true identity in the journals Keiran had left lying around the Institute, and her being a Dreamer suggested she was capable of hiding the epilogue in the sleeping realm.

"You're telling me I have a *cousin*?" Vera Ingers, the daughter of a third Kazan sister, had mused. "I never had cousins. What's Emory like? I mean, I know I met her at the equinox festival, but I didn't *know* then."

Baz had told Vera everything he could think of about Emory. All the best qualities. All the things he missed about her. Vera had given him a funny look. "Oh, you have it bad," she'd teased him.

He often wondered if Emory knew the truth about her mother. Surely Keiran must have told her. Or perhaps Romie, who'd been the one to chase after the epilogue in the first place, had pieced it together.

This landscape was far from the sandy beach and singing tall grasses where he and his sister and Emory had chased after seagulls, but it left him with a pang of longing all the same. He suddenly wished he'd brought the sketchbook his mother had gifted him for the solstice, but it waited for him back at the light-house, blank and begging to be filled.

"You used to love to draw," Anise had told him earlier this morning with a teary-eyed sort of fondness. "Remember all those drawings you'd give me? Characters from your books. The willow tree behind our house. I kept them all, you know. And now you can make new ones."

Baz longed to pick up a pencil and ingrain this landscape in his memory. But for now he picked up a fishing net instead, all tangled up at the base of a rock. Farther down the beach, Kai carried the remains of a battered lobster cage beneath an arm, dark hair unbound and damp from the sea mist. Kai suddenly stopped in his tracks, dropped the wooden pieces at his feet—and disappeared out of thin air, as if the mist had gobbled him up.

Baz's stomach dropped. "Kai?" He picked up the pace, heart in his throat as he tried not to slip on the slick rocks. "Kai!"

"In here."

Relief surged through him at the sound of Kai's voice. Baz came upon an opening in an outcropping of rocks. A cave mouth, slender and dark. He could just barely make out Kai's outline inside it. Baz took a careful step in despite the warning bells screaming in his mind. But this cave was nothing like Dovermere, only a small grotto carved in the rock, and not even fully enclosed; there was an opening above their heads that let a muted streak of light in, right in the middle of the circular space.

Kai ran a hand over the smooth walls slick with lichen. "Henry told me there were a few caves like this dotted along this side of the island. I found some of them, though most are collapsed due to erosion." He splayed his fingers out beneath the curtain of sunlight, tufts of mist swirling around his fingers. "Never seen this one before."

Baz hung back, a sinister feeling rooting him in place. "Come on, let's get out of here."

Kai side-eyed him. "What are you scared of? This isn't Dovermere."

"I know that."

And yet he couldn't help but think it felt *exactly* like Dovermere—couldn't explain the tug he felt on his magic. Or maybe that was only the fear. Perhaps all dark pockets of the world shared the same sense of mystery, the same strange allure, the same inexplicable eeriness that would forever set him on edge after what they'd lived through in Dovermere.

"We should head back," Baz pressed, adjusting the weight of the tangled net on his shoulder. "There's nothing here."

Kai finally relented, his own morbid curiosity apparently satisfied. Or maybe just to appease Baz's fear.

They bumped into Jae as they made their way back to the lighthouse. There was a twinkle in their eye as they clapped them both on the back.

"There you two are. Come on, it's time we get to work on your training." Jae winked at Baz. "We need to get you ready for the Quadricentennial."

Baz groaned, wishing he'd stayed back at the cave. This, he wasn't looking forward to.

"Remind me again what this Quadricentennial entails?" Baz's mother asked as they all sat around the kitchen table later that evening, a frown of consternation on her face.

The Quadricentennial was to be the biggest event of the century, marking Aldryn College's four hundredth anniversary. Every centennial, Aldryn hosted a month-long celebration to which students from other magical colleges around the world were invited. In the past, deadly, cutthroat games had been held, pitting student against student as they sought glory and knowledge. But these games hadn't been held since the school's Bicentennial; no one knew exactly what happened that year, but it was catastrophic enough that the college not only discontinued the tradition but also canceled their Tricentennial celebrations altogether.

This year, there was a buzz of excitement surrounding the Quadri, because the college had decided to bring the games back, though in a way that focused more on academia than anything else. The college would be hosting panels and workshops led by the world's leading magical experts as well as academic challenges that students could enroll in to showcase their magic.

There would be theoretical challenges where students would solve complicated equations revolving around tidal bulges and moon position degrees, and practical challenges where they would form teams with students of other houses and alignments to solve complex puzzles using only the magic at their disposal. With scouts from the area and abroad watching like hawks, it would be a chance for students all over to prove their worth, to make connections that might land them highly sought-after jobs and internships and scholarships to the most prestigious postgraduate programs.

And Baz had been roped into participating.

While Eclipse-born were allowed to compete in the challenges, not many of them had signed up. Understandable, given the stigma surrounding their abilities and the very real fear of Collapsing. Baz had always known his final year at Aldryn would be the school's Quadricentennial, though he never anticipated entering the games should they ever be reinstated. But all that had changed now.

Now his participation in the Quadri was a crucial part of their grand plan to bring justice to Eclipse-born. Because despite their case getting thrown out of court and the odds being stacked against them, what with the corruption of the Institute and the power that the Selenic Order wielded over the Regulators, they had no other option but to keep fighting.

It was Jae who'd had the idea for the Quadri.

"If Baz wows everyone with his magic—and I've no doubt he will—it might sway the public opinion in our favor. Academic scouts use the Quadri to assess talent, but most of them won't expect to find it in an Eclipse-born, especially not one with such a rare gift as our Timespinner. They'll marvel at his precision and control, and when we finally reveal that Baz has been Collapsed for years now—without giving away the, ah, unfortunate details of his Collapsing, of course—people will recall that precision and control and realize Baz was never a danger to them. They'll see that Collapsings aren't inherently bad."

"Or they'll twist it around and condemn Basil for putting all these people in danger," Anise countered.

Jae merely shrugged. "It's a risk we have to take."

"And why does Basil have to be the one to take that risk? Why can't it be someone else?" Anise stopped herself with her eyes on Kai, as if just remembering that Baz was the only Eclipse-born left at Aldryn. Her gaze softened. "Someone from another college, perhaps."

Theodore patted his wife's hand. "Basil can handle himself. Isn't that right, son?"

Baz nodded shyly, feeling the weight of everyone's attention on him.

"He'll show all the assholes at that school how it's done," Kai said with a sardonic smile, and Baz was grateful to him for breaking the tension.

"And we really do need to put all chances on our side," Jae said, "especially as more and more Collapsed Eclipse-born seek to join our little revolution." They cleared their throat, a somber look in their eyes. "Word of what I'm doing in Threnody is getting around faster than I can take people in, which is wonderful, but also comes at a risk."

Jae had always been a secretive type, full of mysterious connections from all around the world, and Baz now understood why. They communicated with other Eclipse-born through secret channels, by telegraph and letters and other ways Baz wasn't privy to. Jae had sent out the call to find other Collapsed Eclipse-born in need of help, and magically the news had spread without raising any alarm with the Regulators.

Theodore was squinting his eyes at his former business partner. "What are you not telling us, Jae?"

Jae sighed. "Do you remember Freyia Lündt, a woman who Collapsed in Trevel a few years back?"

Theodore's eyes bulged. "The *Reanimator*?"

"Yes, the Reanimator." Jae thrummed their fingers on the table. "She asked to meet me in Threnody."

A deathly quiet settled over the lighthouse. Baz remembered reading about the Reanimator in the papers a few months after his father had been taken away to the Institute. She had magic as rare as his own Timespinner abilities, but far more sinister. She could bring things back to life, so to speak–though from what Baz understood, the corpses she brought back from the dead weren't exactly *alive*. They were empty vessels that only imitated life. Her Collapsing had been brought on after she'd killed a dozen people for the sole purpose of testing the boundaries of her magic on them.

Freyia Lündt had escaped the Regulators' clutches, narrowly avoiding the Unhallowed Seal, only to spark more terror wherever she went. Death followed in her wake–as did the *undead*. There were rumors of gruesome murders and corpses brought back all wrong, their bones bent at odd angles and their magic acting up, as if being brought back from the dead rotted their powers from the inside out.

When people told each other horror stories of Eclipse-born who'd succumbed to the dark curse of their Collapsing, it was the Reanimator who haunted their thoughts.

And Jae wanted to *meet* with her?

"You can't be serious," Kai said with a gruff, nervous laugh. And if *Kai* of all people thought this idea was absurd, then it surely must be.

"All those people she killed . . ." Anise whispered, eyes wide with horror.

"*Supposedly* killed," Jae specified. "Freyia deserves the benefit of the doubt just as any of us do."

Baz shifted uncomfortably at that. *He* had killed people too. His Collapsing had brought down his father's printing press, killing three victims in the blast. He knew it wasn't the same thing as the kind of murders Freyia was said to have committed, but it still weighed on his conscience. In his mind he saw Keiran dying a slow, agonizing death on the cave floor. The blame in his eyes as Baz told him the truth, that he was the one who had killed Keiran's parents. It was an image that haunted him often, and Baz told himself it was punishment enough for his crimes. That, and the knowledge that he was to blame for ripping his own family apart—sending his dad to the Institute, his mother into depression, and his sister on a reckless pursuit of mythical doors.

"Maybe it would be best to let the Regulators have her," Anise pressed. "Instead of putting your own life on the line."

"No one deserves to suffer at the hands of the Regulators, my darling," Theodore countered, his face blanching at the memory of the Institute. "No one."

Though Baz sympathized with his father's sentiment, the idea of reanimation magic sat uneasily in his stomach. Death, he thought, should not be tampered with. It was final. Just as he didn't dare use his magic to turn back time and save those who had died because of him, the Reanimator shouldn't be allowed to use her gift to bring corpses back from the dead. At least not without owning up to the consequences.

"If I can help her control her magic," Jae said, "we'll all be better for it."

Baz hoped Jae's definition of *control* meant learning not to use magic at all. But that was Jae's problem now, not his. He had the

Quadri to focus on, and only a few days left to enjoy the solstice holiday with the people who mattered most to him before he'd have to play his part.

Before he had to say goodbye again.

They spent the rest of the week training with Jae, who had Baz and Kai pushing the limits of their Collapsed abilities until the holiday didn't feel like one at all. But in the bits between training and discussing strategy for the Quadri and playing those boring card games every night that were really not boring at all–even Kai seemed to enjoy himself–Baz found solace in his sketchbook.

It was odd how much he'd missed drawing; odder still how his mother had seemed to anticipate this longing inside him when he himself hadn't seen it. Picking up a pencil felt like the most natural of things, and though Baz fumbled his way through pages of ter- rible sketches, he slowly found his stride again.

He'd never considered himself an artist with any real sort of tal- ent, but he could admit he wasn't a bad one either.

Despite the peace that drawing brought him, it did nothing to erase his anxiety as they inched toward the end of the week and the start of the Quadri. But there was something else bothering him that he couldn't quite put his finger on until the last day of the holiday.

Baz found his father sitting on a stretch of coastline behind the lighthouse, staring out at the sea. His heart ached at how peaceful Theodore looked. Eyes closed, a small smile playing on his lips, face tilted up to the sea breeze. He looked content. Free of worries.

And as guilt surged inside him, Baz understood that this was what had been slowly eating away at him this week. Not his anx- iety over the Quadri, but this unending guilt. Despite the bliss of being with his parents again–of seeing them happy–a shadow loomed over them. Nothing was right. This peace was fleeting.

A mere illusion. Their family was broken in more ways than one, with a crucial part of it missing behind a mythical door, and Baz was to blame for all of it.

Baz had robbed his father of all those years where he could have been free instead of rotting away at the Institute for a crime he hadn't committed.

Baz was the reason his mother spent years as a ghost of herself, withering away under the burden of grief as she desperately tried to keep it together for her children.

Baz was to blame for Romie distancing herself from their family, from everything Eclipse-related, because she didn't want to live with the shame of what their father had supposedly done. What *Baz* had done. He was the reason her fate now remained unknown. And if she died or never came back, what was left of their broken family might never recover, and he would be to blame for that, too.

His father must have sensed his presence. He turned toward him, but Baz headed back inside before he could see him.

With too much nervous energy to do much else, Baz started packing. He didn't realize he was crying until a voice jolted him out of his spiraling thoughts.

"You okay?"

Baz quickly wiped at his cheeks. Kai stood in the doorframe, his expression unreadable.

"Yeah." Baz cleared his throat, busying himself with his folded clothes. "Just getting ready for the inevitable return to Aldryn."

"You're anxious about the Quadri."

"Of course I am." If only it were just that.

"Don't be."

Baz snorted. "Easy for you to say."

Kai came to hover at Baz's side. He reached for the sketchbook laid open on the bed, but Baz snatched it back, tucking it away safely into his bag. Kai's piercing gaze caught his. "I could come with you. You know, for moral support."

Baz sighed. "This again? You know you can't."

Kai rolled his eyes as he plopped down on the bed. "I thought you'd changed, Brysden. Where's the rule-breaker who got me out of the Institute? I liked him. He was fun."

The comment was like a knife wedging itself in an open wound. "That was never me."

Was that what Kai thought of him? That he was interesting only when he acted the part of the rebellious hero, when he wasn't being his careful, disciplined self?

Fighting back tears, Baz pulled on a sweater lodged beneath Kai. "Do you mind? This boring rule-follower needs to pack."

For a moment, Kai didn't budge. He searched Baz's gaze, the slightest frown creasing his brow. Baz thought he would press him, but at last he got up and snapped a sarcastic, "Sorry to keep you," before heading out the door.

Baz's soured mood could not be remedied. Henry and Anise pre-pared a feast for their last night together, but despite the laughter and chatter and comforting food, all Baz could think was how he didn't deserve any of this. He could feel Kai trying to catch his eye, had no doubt that the Nightmare Weaver saw right through his forced smile. Baz couldn't bring himself to look at him for fear of breaking.

"Come get some air with me, Basil," Theodore said after they'd finished eating and everyone was busy clearing the table.

Baz donned his coat and followed his father outside, if only to escape Kai's insistent glances.

They stood in silence at the water's edge for a time before Theodore said, "I'm proud of you, son. Everything you've done, everything you're doing . . . I know we're asking a lot of you."

Baz swallowed past the lump in his throat. "I don't know if I can do it."

"Of course you can."

"You taught me that magic was like breathing. That the key was using it in short, measured breaths. And all my life, that's what I did. But now that I'm Collapsed, suddenly I'm told I can use it in big, heaving bursts, and I'm–I'm scared, Dad. I don't know what I'm capable of. What if I take it too far?" He stared off into the distance, surprised at this outpouring of honesty. But he couldn't stop. "I have all this power at my fingertips, and I don't know how to use it. I don't know that I . . . that I deserve it. Not after what I did."

Theodore clasped Baz on the shoulder, forcing him to look into his eyes. "Listen to me. What happened is not on you."

"How can you say that when I have blood on my hands? When I stole years off your life?"

"Oh, Basil." His father's eyes were bright with tears. "Don't ever think that. I *chose* my path, and I don't regret it for a second. This strength you have, it's precisely why I did what I did all those years ago. So you could thrive, and fight to free yourself and others in the process."

Baz wasn't able to fight back the tears that fell on his cheeks. It was everything he didn't know he needed to hear. His father drew him in for a hug, and Baz broke down against him, letting all the years of resentment and fear and this newer guilt pour out of him.

"I love you, Dad," he whispered. Resolve replaced what had been crumbling inside him. He wanted nothing more now than to make things right–to succeed and be worthy of his father's sacrifice and belief in him. For the first time, he believed himself capable.

They watched the rhythmic waves lap to and from the shores for a time, until cold seeped through their bones and the warmth of the lighthouse called them back inside. Kai wasn't there, and

Baz was suddenly desperate to seek him out. Apologize for snap-ping at him earlier.

He found Kai upstairs, but not in his own room. The Nightmare Weaver stood by Baz's bed, his back to him, hands hovering over his bag.

"What are you doing in here?" Baz asked quietly.

Kai turned at his voice. His mouth was tight. "Thought I should apologize for being a jerk earlier."

"Funny, I was looking for you to do the same thing."

Kai's expression didn't change. He looked slightly on edge. It was then that Baz noticed his sketchbook had been pulled out of his bag and now lay open on top of his folded clothes.

Baz's stomach dropped. "You went through my things?" He grabbed the sketchbook. The page it was open to was full of quick sketches of Emory, scenes he'd pulled from his memory. Her laughing. Her standing before the Hourglass. The moment before they'd kissed—her tearstained face, his hand cupping her cheek, her lips parted.

"These are good," Kai said, dodging the question. "I didn't know you were such an artist."

"I can't believe you went through my things." Baz shoved the sketchbook into his bag, a flush creeping up his cheeks. He was acutely aware of Kai watching him. Of the fact that Kai had been looking at his most intimate recollections of Emory. He didn't know why he felt a surge of guilt when it was Kai who'd been caught red-handed.

"What was she to you?" Kai asked, his voice barely above a whisper.

Everything, Baz wanted to say, just as a more doubtful part of him thought, *Nothing at all.*

An elusive sunset, a ship in the night, a comet he was less certain he'd seen with each day that came and went without her in it. That was Emory to him. She was a door he'd once thought shut creaked open again, for the briefest moment in time. A fissure through which he'd glimpsed all the golden-hued might-haves and could-bes, before they slipped from his hands like water as the door sealed shut again.

She felt more and more like a dream as concrete memories escaped him in a flight of fancy, leaving him to wonder what was real and what was but a romanticized version of reality. Was Baz misremembering things? All the hours they'd shared in the library, heads bent over textbooks. The day he'd drawn blood from her, the sound of her laugh as she asked him to distract her. The night they'd found Lia on the beach. All the times they'd saved each other, the broken ache he'd feel whenever he watched her slip into dreaming.

That kiss . . .

The more he thought of it, the less certain he was that it had meant anything at all to her, even though it had meant *everything* to him at the time. But she'd gone through that door, and Baz knew that even if–*when*–she returned, things would never be the same between them. He wasn't sure he'd want them to be. Between the sting of finding out she used him and the desperate fear of watching her slip through worlds, he hadn't quite resolved his feelings for her.

Missing her was an ache that hadn't yet dulled, that might never leave. And yet, in his starkest moments of loneliness, it was not Emory he thought of, or even his sister. It was the boy staring at him now with such disarming vulnerability, the one whose absence had always weighed on his heart, even when Emory was still here.

What was she to you?

Baz didn't know how to articulate any of this, especially not to Kai. So he said nothing at all.

Silence stretched on. When Kai finally left, muttering something about going to bed, it felt like another door closing before its time.

7

EMORY

B RYONY'S UNNATURAL EYES HAUNTED EMORY EVEN IN sleep.

Here in the darkness of her mind, her ghosts were inescapable. They hovered around her in a circle, trapping her. They were in a cave she could never forget, standing on the platform where the Hourglass stood. Except there was no Hourglass here—*she* stood in its place, for she was like a door herself.

The ghosts drew nearer, tightening the circle. They felt more prominent, more corporeal here in sleep, as if not ghosts at all but *real*, as if the sleepscape had torn down the barrier between the living and the dead, and here they all stood together in echo of the night that sealed their fates.

There was Travers, water trickling down the side of his mouth, weeds and barnacles clinging to his body, his face sallow and his body deteriorating before her eyes. "This is all your fault," he said in a watery voice.

There was Lia, blackened, tongueless mouth opened on a silent scream. *Your fault*, her frightened eyes echoed.

"Why couldn't you help us?" This from Jordyn, barely human, with the depthless eyes of an umbra and claw-tipped hands reaching for Emory.

"I tried to warn you it would come to this." Lizaveta, arms crossed and expression as haughty as it had been in life, blood pooling from the hole at the base of her neck.

And Keiran. Worst of all, Keiran.

But Emory's attention went to the two people beside him. The circle, it seemed, was not complete with only the dead; the living had joined in, just as eager to blame her for what she'd made them suffer.

The first was Penelope West, eyes red rimmed and haunted. "You let them manipulate me," she said. "You let them take away my memories. I can't believe I ever called you a friend. You weren't worth the effort."

The second was Baz, who looked at her the same way he had after realizing she'd betrayed him. "Everything you touch crumbles to dust."

Tears sprang to her eyes. "Please, I'm sorry . . ."

Keiran stepped into her space, and she was too stunned by how real he looked, too broken by all their accusations, to back away. His hand closed around her neck. She felt the biting cold of him against her skin, a touch of death that seeped into her soul.

Keiran's ghost did not speak, but the hungry, hateful look in his eyes left no room for interpretation.

He blamed her for leaving him to the umbrae. Loathed her for letting him die. And as his icy grip squeezed tighter around her, she knew this was a promise as much as a threat.

She had killed him, and he would haunt her forever because of it.

He had a hold on her even in death.

Emory did not fight him off, even as every part of her screamed at her to move, to shove him back, to close her eyes and wake up. Keiran's chokehold tightened, and the voices of everyone else she had hurt rose in the depths of Dovermere, echoing off the walls, slithering along her skin, sinking their teeth into her tortured heart.

And they were right. It was her fault. If it weren't for her, none of this would have happened.

Maybe the world would be better off without her.

Keiran lifted his other hand to brush her face, his eyes going tender now, like he agreed with the ugly, intrusive thought worming its way into her mind. Like he was offering her the death that would silence it forever.

Maybe it was what she deserved.

"You know they're not real, right?"

A voice like midnight, cutting through the gloom.

Kai detached himself from the dark. Their gazes locked.

The hand around her neck relinquished its hold. Her ghosts, both dead and alive, disappeared, drifting away like dust on an imaginary breeze.

It was just her and Kai now, alone in the Belly of the Beast. They blinked at each other in the quiet.

"Are *you* real?" Emory asked.

Kai frowned. Before he could answer, the darkness shifted between them. Out of it emerged the stuff of actual nightmares, all sightless eyes and clawed hands and skeletal figures. The umbrae.

They shifted and swirled, immaterial and restless, as something else formed among them, something darker and stronger and older than the umbrae. Fear settled in Emory's bones, even as something kept her rooted in place, staring wide-eyed at the giant umbra that was taking shape, a terrifying sort of recognition singing inside her.

Kai swore, snapping her out of it. His eyes locked with hers again. "Wake up. *NOW.*"

And so she woke.

Emory lit the candle beside her bed, desperate to chase away the shadows. She wasn't sure how long she sat there trying to get her heart to slow as she puzzled over the nightmare. Kai must have been real. But how could that be when they were worlds apart?

And that dark presence . . .

It was still night out, but she couldn't sleep anymore. Grabbing the candleholder, she ventured out into the hallway. The house was quiet, the ascension celebrations over from what she could tell. Her feet led her unbidden to the lilac-painted room on the second floor, where Bryony stood in a robe and nightgown before the marble altar. Tendrils of smoke wafted from an incense burner hanging at the back of the room, making the air smell woodsy.

Emory watched quietly from the doorway as Bryony held a fisted hand over the altar. She opened it, letting pieces of bone fall atop the bowl-like clump of amethyst that sat on the altar.

"I can feel you there, you know," Bryony said without turning.

Emory stepped into the room, which was as unnaturally cold as ever. She tightened her own robe around her. "Sorry. I didn't want to interrupt. Were you scrying?" She had yet to see a witch scry.

"Trying to." Bryony grimaced as she looked at the bones atop the amethyst. "I don't think I've found my scrying method yet. Bones are decidedly not it."

"How do you find what scrying method works?"

"Trial and error, mostly. My sister tried everything before she realized what works for her is getting lost in the rhythms of the elements. My mother, on the other hand, knew from the very first breath she took after ascending that her sixth sense unlocks with sculpting." Bryony sighed. "I wish I knew mine. But then . . . I'm also scared to find out."

"How come?"

"At my ascension, I was . . . Something happened that wasn't normal." Her eyes flitted to Emory. "But you saw it, didn't you? You were hiding in the woods, looking in on my ascension."

An excuse was already on Emory's lips, but Bryony merely smiled, saying, "It's all right, I won't say anything."

"We were just curious, really."

"I understand. I'm like that too. My mother always says *curiosity kills the cat*, but she forgets that cats have nine lives."

Emory laughed at that, an image of Dusk, Romie's stray tabby, coming to mind. "Well, thank you for keeping it a secret." She studied the younger girl. "Is that why you're afraid to scry? You think what happened at the ascension will happen again?"

Bryony nodded. "Some of the witches believe what happened means I'm a–a hellwraith. That a demon took hold of my essence while I was buried, and now it's fighting back against the Sculptress's claim on me."

A shiver ran up Emory's spine. So this is what a hellwraith was. "Is that . . . possible?"

Bryony lost herself in the pile of bones atop the amethyst, a crease forming between her brows. "I felt it when I was underground. This demon in my mind, desperate for a way out of the netherworld. The Sculptress won, but I'm afraid if I tap into my scrying ability, it'll find me in the astral plane and seize my essence for good."

She gave Emory a furtive glance. "I'm not supposed to say any of this to you."

"Why not?"

"My mother thinks you coming here, in this world you don't belong, is what attracted this demon in the first place." Her eyes fell to Emory's wrist. "That spiral—it's a sign of our Sculptress."

"Where I'm from, this mark relates to *our* divinity," Emory said. "The Tides. They're at the origin of our lunar magic, much like your Sculptress is at the origin of yours."

Bryony seemed to mull that over for a while. "There's a story that's told to us when we're young. About twin sisters who ruled the coven together, long ago. They rose to power during a great blight that started after demons broke through the seams of the underworld and corrupted the woods, the magic that flows through it. Many a witch tried to cast them back without success. Until, on a black moon, when the veil between this plane and the underworld is thinnest, the twins were able to cast the demons back to their realm. The woods healed, and the witches lived on happily.

"The story never made it clear how the demons escaped the underworld in the first place. Some think it was a cunning demon king leading his army to conquer the world of witches. Others, that a witch fell prey to a trickster demon and parted the veil for him." Bryony eyed Emory's wrist again. "My mother believes you might be trickster demons here to hurt us."

"I promise you we're not. We just want to go home."

From Bryony's expression, she wasn't sure if she believed her.

Emory thought of her nightmare, of all those people she'd hurt in some way or other. She vowed to herself that neither Bryony or anyone else would become one of them.

8

KAI

KAI WAS IN THAT DAMN PRINTING PRESS AGAIN.

It was the printing press one minute, with Baz held in his father's arms, and the next, it was Dovermere, with Baz holding Emory in his. The scenes bled into one another, making it hard for Kai to follow. Baz's father taken away by the Regulators. Emory disappearing through a door. Baz alone in the rubble of blasted machinery, then in a crumbling cave filling with water.

Through it all: Baz's fear, which Kai tasted as his own.

Kai called out to him. And when Baz twisted around at the sound of his name, it was not Baz at all but an umbra, featureless and empty eyed.

This wasn't Baz's nightmare. It was Kai's.

Kai backed away from the umbra but realized it was not *real* as it faded away suddenly, and the whole scene shifted before his eyes.

A room he recognized from his time at Trevelyan Prep. A chess board. Farran Caine smiling at him with that brilliant smile of his, blue eyes crinkled in laughter.

"You're such a sore loser," Farran teased as he captured the king on Kai's side of the board with nothing but a humble pawn.

Farran's smile dropped, eyes locking with someone across the room—Keiran Dunhall Thornby, his teen face etched in grief. Farran's chair grated loudly against the floor as he rushed toward his friend, not even throwing a glance back at Kai.

"Don't leave me," Kai heard himself say, his voice soft like his younger self had been.

It was a dream that was a memory that was a nightmare. The beginning of the end of an era, ushering in Kai's understanding that Eclipse-born were on their own, that loyalty among the other lunar houses would always come before loyalty to theirs.

Kai picked up a knight from the board, the only piece of his left standing, and vowed to build matching armor around his heart.

The scene shifted again. Kai found himself pulled back to Dovermere, watching Baz watch Emory leave through the door. Except . . . no. Emory *was* the door, and she was begging the students closing in around her to leave her alone.

Again Kai found himself puzzling over whose nightmare this was. He certainly didn't care enough about Emory for this to be one of his own fears. Baz was there, but this didn't taste like his nightmares.

He focused on Emory, something inside him tugging him to her like she was an anchor in a dark, stormy sea. He focused on the very real tears in her eyes. The plea that slipped past her lips as Keiran Dunhall Thornby's hand wrapped around her throat, begging to be released from the torment of these students' accusations.

"You know they're not real, right?" Kai said.

Emory's eyes cut to his. The scene dissolved around them until only the two of them remained.

"Are *you* real?" Emory asked.

Kai frowned, noting the dress Emory wore that looked centuries old. Something, perhaps, from another world.

Was this real?

This was not, as he'd told Baz, the first time he'd seen Emory in his sleep. But it was the first time they'd spoken to each other, the first time it'd *felt* like the real her.

Before he could figure it out, darkness exploded between them, a great big wave of it looking to drown them both. Only it didn't–it merely swirled around itself like a spiral, growing darker as it did. Fear cut through Kai as umbrae materialized in its shadowy folds. He swore, looking at Emory. If this was really her, she couldn't get overtaken by the umbrae. Baz would never forgive him for it.

"Wake up," he said. *"NOW."*

Her eyes widened–and then she was gone.

And not a moment too soon. From the center of the darkness emerged a towering umbra with a crown of obsidian atop its head. Nightmares rippled around him like a billowing cloak of shadows. It spoke in a tongue Kai did not understand. It felt old, guttural and melodious all at once. And though he could not distinguish the words, he knew their meaning, deep in his soul.

Open the door.

The umbra launched itself at him. Kai fell backward, holding his hands above him to fend off the umbra–only for it to dissipate at his touch, like dust blowing on a breeze. As if it'd never been there at all.

In his hand was a crown of obsidian.

And then the nightmare was crumbling around him. Kai was in the printing press again, in the caves again, with Farran again, machinery and rock falling on him, chess pieces clattering around him, the sea rising up to swallow him, even as darkness pressed in from all around, the sleepscape seeping in, looking to dig its claws into Kai's subconscious.

Kai screamed himself awake.

At least, he thought he was awake. It was hard to tell in the dark, in this room that was not his. A light switched on, and then Baz's face was hovering over him, big brown eyes open wide. He wasn't wearing his glasses. He spoke words Kai didn't understand. Fear surged in him, wild and uncontrollable.

This wasn't Baz.

Kai lunged out of bed and wrapped a hand around the umbra's neck, shoving him against the wall. "I'm not afraid of you," he hissed in its face.

"K-Kai," the creature sputtered, claws seeking purchase on Kai's wrist. "Stop. *It's me.*"

Not claws, Kai realized. *Fingers.*

Not an umbra, he registered, but *Baz.*

Kai let him go at once, stumbling back. Something slipped from his other hand and clanged at his feet, but Kai paid it no mind. He stared horrified at Baz, who rubbed at his neck, where the beginnings of a bruise had already appeared.

"I'm sorry," Kai panted. He slumped on the bed and grabbed his head between his hands. "I'm so sorry."

The narrow bed shifted with Baz's weight as he sat next to Kai. Their shoulders brushed ever so gently, the only tether Kai had to reality.

"It's all right," Baz said. "It's over now."

On the bedroom floor before them was a crown of obsidian. Kai did not understand. He could take others' fears out of their night-mares, pluck them from their heads and conjure them in real life, but he'd never brought an object out of his own dreaming.

The crown remained for a time before it disintegrated, as all dreams eventually did. And then it was just a memory.

9

BAZ

THE SOLSTICE HOLIDAY CAME TO AN END TOO QUICKLY. Before he knew it, Baz was on a train back to Cadence, watching Harebell Cove and all sense of joy recede. And though Jae was with him–making their way back to Threnody and the Eclipseborn who awaited them there–Baz couldn't help but feel a pang of loneliness already setting in.

He hadn't been able to find Kai after saying goodbye to his family. There wasn't a doubt in Baz's mind that Kai was avoiding him after what happened–the Nightmare Weaver screaming in his sleep, his magic spinning out of control, his hand around Baz's neck, the forlorn look in his eyes.

Baz had no choice but to leave without saying goodbye.

"Here," Jae said now, pulling Baz from his thoughts. "My belated solstice present to you."

Baz reverently picked up the old leather-bound journal that Jae set beside him. "You're giving me Clover's journal?"

"*Lending* you Clover's journal. Alya's been pestering me to get it back, and I don't trust a courier to handle this. Figured you'd like to peruse it before giving it back to her for me."

Baz ran a finger along the spine. A fraying black leather rope was bound around the journal to keep all the random scraps of paper tucked safely within its yellowing pages. From what Jae had told Baz about it, Cornus Clover's personal journal was an eclectic collection of writings, ranging from notes on magic to early passages of what would become *Song of the Drowned Gods.* Jae had fought tirelessly to get his hands on the journal. It'd taken a fair amount of bribing to get Alya Kazan, a supposed descendant of Clover's, to lend it to Jae for them to study.

And now here it was, in Baz's hands. There was a peculiar sort of magic in that, he thought.

"I put the epilogue in there too," Jae pointed out. "Though you can take that out before giving Alya back the journal."

"Did you find anything of note in here?" Baz asked as he carefully untied the leather rope and opened the journal.

Jae grumbled. "It's just as I remember it," they said, having perused the journal once before, back when they'd been dating Alya. "It's full of nonsensical things I can't help but think are code for something else. Verses that make no sense. Lists of random names or words that sound made-up. Passages written in alphabets I've never seen before—which reminds me, have Beatrix look over some of those passages, will you? If anyone can make sense of the languages, it's her."

Baz nodded. Professor Selandyn was an Omnilinguist, able to understand and speak any language fluently. Perhaps her ability would extend to these possibly made-up languages Clover had penned.

"That man remains as much of a mystery as ever," Jae sighed, "even to those of us who've dedicated our lives to researching his work. Why do you think he's held so much fascination over us for so long? Not much is known of his life to begin with, and this journal's no help at all. Although he does mention a sister in there–Delia–but I'd heard those rumors before."

A sister! Baz thought as he perused the journal. He stopped on a quickly sketched illustration of an armored knight facing off against a dragon. The warrior from the story.

"We know he was enrolled at Aldryn," Jae continued, "that he was an excellent Healer, that he had a sister–but other than that, it's as if they're both ghosts. Came out of nowhere and disappeared without a trace. Even the name Clover and all the wealth that's tied to it seemingly appeared overnight, making it impossible to trace its lineage. It's as if he and his sister stepped out of another world entirely and disappeared back to it without a trace."

Which might very well be the case, Baz thought, and he knew Jae was thinking the same. They had proof that a door to other worlds existed. Who was to say Clover hadn't indeed lived through the events of *Song of the Drowned Gods*? That he wasn't the scholar on the shores himself?

When the train pulled into Threnody Central, Baz and Jae hugged a quick goodbye before Jae motioned to the window with a wink. "Someone ought to give that poor boy a hand."

On the platform, the illusioned Baz had apparently taken a bit of a tumble, and his luggage had come open, spilling out all its contents. An indignant laugh bubbled out of the real Baz. "Now I'm just offended."

Jae grinned. "Wanted to make sure eyewitnesses saw you here today."

It made sense; they did want everyone to believe Baz had spent the holidays in Threnody, so if the Regulators were watching, they would give them a show. Jae thrummed their fingers on the compartment door, looking back at Baz with a fond sort of sadness. "Take care, Basil."

"You too, Jae. And please—be careful with the Reanimator."

He still thought Jae was being far too trusting of this particular Eclipse-born they were meeting up with in Threnody, but he had to believe Jae could handle themself.

Baz watched Jae disappear on the platform with an inkling of dread, wondering when they'd see each other again. If they'd see each other again at all.

No. He was worrying for nothing.

The illusioned Baz had finally picked himself up off the floor and was hurrying onto the train when the real Baz noticed someone watching *him* outside his compartment.

All the blood rushed from his head. The man wore a stiff tweed suit under a large woolly coat. The tapered brim of his hat sat low on his forehead, shading his eyes. And though he turned away as soon as Baz looked up, making his way to another compartment, there was no doubt in Baz's mind that his attention had been fixed on him.

Had the Regulators found him, then? If so, he could only hope Jae's illusion had worked.

The rest of the journey to Cadence was spent in a state of agonizing anxiety, even as Baz tried to tell himself that everything was fine. Surely if the Regulators had seen through Jae's ruse, this man would make a move while the train was still moving, cornering Baz when there was nowhere for him to go. A unit of Regulators would be waiting for them at the Cadence station, and Baz would be taken in for questioning, much to Drutten's satisfaction. Theodore and Kai would be brought back to the Institute, and everything would be ruined.

But when the train pulled into Cadence and Baz stepped out of his compartment, the man he spotted a ways down wasn't looking at him. When Baz grabbed his luggage and made for the door, the man did not run to follow. And when Baz stepped onto the busy platform, no Regulator was there waiting for him.

The place was crawling with students coming back from their holidays. There was an odd energy on the platform, a grim excitement that Baz didn't quite understand but attributed to the start of the new term. Glancing over his shoulder, he noticed that same man following him. His steps were unhurried, his manner casual; probably just heading toward the exit like everyone else. Still, Baz picked up the pace, heart in his throat as he sought to put some distance between them—and tripped over someone's luggage, flying to the floor with it as a result.

"Oomf."

"Hey, watch it, asshole."

"I'm so sorry. I—" Baz extricated his limbs from the fallen suitcase and glanced up at its owner. The rest of his apology died on his lips. "Oh."

An eager sort of cruelty lifted the corner of Artem Orlov's mouth. "Well, well. Isn't this a pretty sight."

Baz tried to get up, but Artem pushed him back with a booted foot to the chest, making Virgil Dade snicker behind him, ever the faithful lapdog. Hostility flashed in Artem's glacial eyes. "Have a nice holiday with your family of fugitives, Brysden?"

Baz's stomach dropped. Surely he was only taunting him. He couldn't know the truth. . . .

"Some of us don't have families to spend the holidays with anymore, thanks to you Eclipse-born," Artem continued. "But you'll get what's coming." He pressed harder on Baz's chest, leaning in to say, "Won't be long now till your father and that friend of yours are back at the Institute where they belong." He pressed harder still, eliciting a grunt from Baz. "Better watch your back, Brysden."

"Artie," Virgil warned in a clipped tone, jerking his chin to where two uniformed Regulators were approaching with a grim air of importance.

Artem immediately took his foot off Baz and helped him up. With a gentlemanly smile, he brushed the dust off Baz's coat. "Be careful out there." He spoke loudly for the approaching Regulators' benefit. "Wouldn't want anyone getting hurt over tripped luggage, now, would we?"

An image of the illusioned Baz tripping on the Threnody platform came to mind. Had Artem seen through the ruse? Baz couldn't breathe as the Regulators appeared, certain they would take him away. But the Regulators paid him no mind as one of them pulled Artem aside to whisper something in his ear. Artem's face lit with a sort of perverse excitement that set Baz on edge. But whatever it was, it seemed to have nothing to do with Baz. Taking advantage of the distraction, he grabbed his luggage and slipped through the exit door unnoticed.

Only when he was outside did he drop his guard. Letting out a breath he'd been holding in only made things worse as the pain in his chest sharpened. He doubled over in the shadows, pressing a hand to his chest. Artem hadn't been gentle, and he feared he might have a bruised rib. The first solution his mind supplied was asking Emory to heal him before he remembered Emory wasn't here.

But someone else was.

Out of the corner of his eye, Baz saw that same strange man watching him. And he was coming straight toward him.

With a grunt, Baz moved toward the line of cabs. Someone grabbed him roughly by the arm, but it wasn't the man stalking him.

"You and I aren't done, Timespinner," Virgil Dade said in a menacing tone. He was alone, Artem and the Regulators nowhere in sight. The Reaper dragged Baz toward a car with tinted windows that hinted at money, pulling the back door open for him and gesturing inside. "Time we had a little chat."

Baz gulped–and got in, settling on the smooth leather upholstery. Virgil slammed the door after him and got in on the other side. As the driver pulled away from the train station, Baz threw a nervous glance out the back window. The strange man was still standing there, watching their car driving away.

Virgil punched him on the shoulder, abandoning the hostile mask as a lazy smile split his face. "How've you been, Brysden?"

Baz rubbed at his shoulder. "I've been better." He winced as he breathed in painfully. "I think your *friend* bruised my ribs."

"Yeah, sorry about that." Virgil's face scrunched up with genuine consternation. "Can't you do your freaky time shit to reverse the damage?"

Why had the thought not crossed Baz's mind? "Yeah, maybe later." He didn't want to experiment with his magic here, in a moving car, in front of Virgil and this driver he didn't know. "Don't you think it's a bit risky, being seen getting in a car together?"

"What, you don't think I played my part well? And you! The fear in your eyes! Face as white as a sheet!" Virgil laughed. "Tides, it's like you thought I was actually going to hurt you."

"I thought a Regulator was following me," Baz muttered defensively. "He was on my train. Might have seen through . . ." He cut himself off, giving a furtive look to the driver.

"Relax, we can talk plainly in here," Virgil said. "Hector's my private driver. Won't say a word."

Baz still lowered his voice. "Whoever was following me might have seen through Jae's plan."

"I wouldn't worry about it. Artem doesn't seem to suspect, at least."

Baz forced a tight smile at the reassurance in Virgil's voice. He trusted Virgil implicitly–had to, considering Virgil was their eyes and ears within the Selenic Order.

It was one of the first things Baz had thought of after what had transpired at Dovermere, to get those of the Selenic Order who'd been in the caves on their side. Virgil hadn't wanted to hear anything at first, too broken up over Keiran's and Lizaveta's deaths to care, too torn over what to believe. It was Nisha Zenara who'd come around first. She'd wanted to trust Baz, and perhaps it was easier for her to do so than the others because of how close she'd been to Romie. When Baz told her the whole truth—about Artem, Keiran, and the silver blood they took from Eclipse-born—the revulsion on her face could not have been feigned.

"I swear we didn't know about the blood," Nisha had said to him, and Baz believed her. "Artem and Keiran were the ones to develop this new type of synth. If I had known they were made with stolen Eclipse blood . . ."

She'd vowed then and there to do everything in her power to help them take the Order and the Institute down. Virgil had soon followed suit after Nisha showed him what proof they had. Since then the two of them had been playing double agents within the Selenic Order. With Keiran gone, Nisha had been appointed as the new leader of the Order's current cohort, and Virgil had stepped up as Artem's confidant, his right-hand man, bonding with him over the deaths of Keiran and Lizaveta. Using that bond to gain Artem's trust.

The rest of the Order's current cohort of students was kept in the dark as to what Nisha and Virgil were doing with Baz; the fewer people who knew the truth, they agreed, the better.

"Listen," Virgil said now with uncharacteristic somberness. "Something *did* happen back there, though."

Dread filled him at those words. "What?"

"The Regulators got wind of a high-profile fugitive setting foot in Threnody. Apparently they've just captured an Eclipse-born—a Reanimator called Freyia Lündt."

Relief flooded through Baz. For a second, he'd thought Virgil would tell him something happened to Theodore and Kai–that the Regulators found them at the lighthouse, despite how careful they'd been. But his relief was short-lived as Jae flashed in his mind. Jae–who'd been on their way to meet up with Freyia today.

If Jae had been caught with Freyia, if their involvement with the Eclipse-born came to light . . .

"Shit," Baz muttered in defeat.

"Shit indeed." Virgil ran a hand over his short-clipped hair. "You saw how Artem was when he got the news back there. He was almost . . . *gleeful* about it. He didn't tell me what he's planning, but I know the Order's up to something, and I think the Reanimator is the piece of the puzzle they've been waiting for."

"What would they need a Reanimator for?"

"I don't know. From what I overheard, it didn't sound like they were planning on branding her with the seal. At least not yet. Which I'm thinking means they're planning on studying her or something."

Baz swore as it all came together in his mind. "They're going to use her against us."

The Regulators would indeed study her. They'd push to see how her magic had been influenced after she'd Collapsed, and they'd use their findings to fit their own agenda. To show the world that it was the Shadow's curse that made her kill all those people and do such unspeakable things to their corpses. They'd say, *Look, this is why the Unhallowed Seal is so important. If she'd been branded, she'd never have committed such crimes.*

"No Eclipse-born will be safe," Baz muttered, feeling all hope dwindle in his chest. Everything they'd been working for, all the planning on how to show the world that the Shadow's curse was a falsehood, that those who Collapsed could live with their abilities intact, as Baz and Jae and Kai were proof of–all of it would be for nothing if the Regulators decided to weaponize the Reanimator against them. There would be no convincing anyone then. Fear of Eclipse-born would burn brighter than ever, spreading like wildfire through the town, the island, the world at large.

"What about Artem?" Baz asked, holding out a bit of hope as he remembered Virgil had spent the solstice at Artem's holiday home. "Did you find anything that could help us?"

"Other than Artie's weakness for whiskey? No. I swear, the guy can't hold his liquor. Thought he'd surely slip up at some point, but all he did was reminisce about Liza and Keiran and the good old days, getting so drunk he made *me* feel sorry for him. Then he'd spend hours locked away in a room he didn't want me going in." Virgil cleared his throat. "Pretty sure I heard him crying in there."

Baz's shoulders slumped in defeat.

"I'm sorry, Brysden." The car came to a stop halfway up the hill that led to Aldryn. "You should get out here so we're not seen together."

"Right. Okay."

"I'll let you know if I can dig up some more."

Baz got out of the car, hand on his chest at the pain his movements elicited. Before he could close the door, Virgil added, "And for Tides' sake, get that fixed before the Quadri. No one wants to see you hurt."

"Someone does," Baz muttered as he started walking up the hill.

The empty corridor that led to Obscura Hall was a welcome reprieve from the bustling campus—that is, until Baz spotted the man from the train hiding in the shadows. He detached himself from the wall he'd been leaning against. Baz held his luggage up, wielding it like a weapon, and *screamed.*

"Tides, calm down, it's only me." The man threw his hands up in the air in a show of surrender. He still had that hat tucked low, hiding his face, but that voice . . .

That Tides-damned, impossible voice.

"*Kai?*"

The Nightmare Weaver laughed as he took off the hat. He tugged his hair out of the bun he'd tied it up in, running a hand through the long dark strands. "Guess I nailed the disguise, huh?"

He looked absolutely ridiculous in that tweed suit and tie and that too-large coat, his fine golden chains hidden away somewhere beneath the stuffy collar. Even without the hat, Baz might have had a hard time recognizing him. Except maybe for that smug grin he wore.

"What in the Tides' name are you–ow." Baz winced as the pain in his chest knocked the breath out of him.

Kai was at his side in a flash. "You okay?"

"Fine," Baz grunted, though he was anything *but.* He should have turned back time to heal himself before walking up the hill, but instead he'd let the pain fuel his fire, his determination to make Artem and every single Regulator pay.

Kai swore. "It's that piece of shit Artem, isn't it?"

Baz couldn't believe he was *here.* He didn't know what to say, so he shoved past him to call the elevator, and didn't deign to speak to or look at Kai even as the metal gates opened and they stepped inside and the gates closed again, drowning them in silence. The elevator jerked into motion. Baz could feel Kai's gaze on him, but he didn't want to give him the satisfaction of speaking first.

"Come on, Brysden," Kai said at last, voice low and soft against the metallic grating around them. "I told you I had to get away from that lighthouse. I know being here's a risk, but after what happened the other night . . . I couldn't stay there anymore. I have to figure this out."

The elevator came to a stop. The doors opened onto the illusioned fields of Obscura Hall, the tall grass heavy with snow, the skies above a muted gray. Baz couldn't get out fast enough.

"*Baz.*"

Kai gripped a fistful of his coat to stop him. Baz whirled on him. "Did you ever consider it's not just your life you're putting at risk here? If they find you, that might as well mean the end for my dad, too. And what about the consequences for me and Jae and everyone else who's been helping? I guess you don't care about the risk to us, either."

Hurt flashed in Kai's eyes. Before he could say anything, a familiar voice sounded behind Baz.

"All valid questions."

Professor Selandyn stared at the two of them with her hands on her hips, looking sterner and more displeased than Baz had ever seen her. He was glad not to be on the receiving end of that displeasure.

Kai averted his gaze, kicking at the ground. "Look, I won't stay long, just—"

"Kai Salonga," the aging Eclipse professor interrupted, "you do realize this campus is about to be crawling with students from all over the world? Including *Eclipse-born* students who'll be staying with us for the duration of the Quadricentennial. *Here.* In Obscura Hall. Which is now home to a fugitive." She huffed, then looked at Baz. "And you, Basil. Of all people, you let him come here?"

"I didn't—"

"It was all me," Kai interjected. "He didn't know I was coming. No one did."

Professor Selandyn clucked her tongue. "Have you no sense, boy? Especially given what happened today."

Kai frowned. "What happened?"

"You heard about the Reanimator they captured?" Baz asked Selandyn.

"*What?*" Kai exclaimed.

Professor Selandyn nodded grimly. "That's what I was coming

down here to tell you. I just spoke to Jae–they're all right. They got to the location where they were supposed to meet the Reanimator, but she never showed."

Baz filled them both in on what Virgil had told him. Kai swore, running a hand through his hair. He had the decency to at least look sorry about coming here at the worst-opportune time.

Professor Selandyn looked older than ever as she said, "Things are about to get bad for us, I'm afraid." She fixed Kai with a hard stare. "So whatever it is you came here for, you'd best have it done quickly and leave before anyone finds you."

10

KAI

THE HOURGLASS WAS EXACTLY AS KAI REMEMBERED IT. As he and Baz entered the Belly of the Beast, the silence between them yawned open wider than the cavern itself. Kai could feel Baz's anger and hurt simmering beneath the surface. He wished Baz would just *let it out* already, because anything would be better than this silent treatment.

Kai knew he'd brought it on himself. First by coming to Aldryn behind Baz's back, then by trying to slip out of the Eclipse commons when he'd thought Baz was asleep–only to find him sitting in his favorite armchair in the dark, staring daggers at him.

"Tides, Brysden," Kai had exclaimed. "What are you doing?"

"Waiting for you." Baz had crossed his arms. "As if you thought I was going to let you go down there alone."

Kai hadn't even tried to convince him to stay behind. He might have used Baz's injury to do so, but Baz had finally relented and used his time magic to reverse the damage Artem had inflicted on him.

If Kai ever got his hands on Artem, he would *kill* him for what he'd done.

In silence, they'd gone down the hidden stairs carved into the cliffside that led to the cove, and here they now were, not a word spoken since.

"Well, go on, then," Baz quipped, breaking the quiet at last as he gestured to the Hourglass. "Work your magic."

Kai bristled at the annoyance in his voice. "Look, I was just trying not to risk anyone else, all right?" he said, echoing Baz's earlier accusation.

"Thanks for the consideration," Baz muttered. His gaze flitted from Kai to the Hourglass. "What was the plan if you managed to open the door? You would have just gone through it without even saying goodbye?"

"Come on, Brysden." The truth was, Kai hadn't thought that far ahead. He eyed the Hourglass as if it were a formidable foe that kept thwarting him—and it was. "We both know it won't actually open for me."

Suddenly it seemed pointless to have come here at all. After he'd found the epilogue in the sleepscape, after he'd read *The Sleepers Among the Stars* a million times trying to make sense of it, Kai had thought he and Romie must be the boy of nightmares and the girl of dreams that the text alluded to. That being the forgotten parts of the puzzle meant they must have the ability to open the doors between worlds just as Emory did. That he, too, must be a key.

But as he again went through the motions of opening the door—the slice of a knife across his palm, an offering of blood against the striated rock—it became painfully evident that the Hourglass still would not open for him.

Kai swore and punched the Hourglass. He swore louder as pain lanced through his hand.

"Yeah, like that's going to work," Baz breathed.

"Shut up, Brysden." Kai shook his hand, staring daggers at the Hourglass. "This is pointless. Why won't it open for me if I'm supposed to be a fucking key?"

"Maybe you're only half a key."

It was the same thing Baz had said to him the first time Kai had tried opening the door, and of course he must be right. Clover's epilogue painted the girl of dreams and the boy of nightmares as going to the sea of ash *together*, so it made sense that the Hourglass wouldn't open for Kai alone. It likely never would without the other half of the equation. The dreams to his nightmares.

"Then maybe it's time we find a Dreamer to test your theory out," Kai spat.

"And what Dreamer is going to want to help a runaway Nightmare Weaver?"

Kai slid Baz an irritated look. Oh, he was enjoying this–sulking in the corner waiting to prove Kai wrong, seeing this ridiculous, risky plan fall apart. Every line of Baz's body spelled out *told you so*. And he was right. No Dreamer would ever risk their life to help the likes of him. The only one he could think of was gone. He was on his own.

But there was one other thing they hadn't tried.

Kai looked at Baz, recalling the way he'd so easily pulled at the threads of time surrounding the door, when the Hourglass had nearly been torn down by falling debris. Baz had reversed time so that the crack running down its middle would be fixed. And if he'd been able to do *that*, who was to say he couldn't also turn back time on the door's lock, wind it back so that it unlocked as it had for Emory?

"You could do it," Kai said quietly, fearing the words might be too big. "You're strong enough to do it."

Though neither of them had ever broached the subject, he knew Baz had thought of it. He seemed to consider it now, inching ever closer to the door, as if he too felt its odd, gravitational pull. But Baz pulled back, shaking his head.

"I can't."

"Can't, or don't want to?"

"What's that supposed to mean?"

"It means you care more about protecting this damn door than helping me out. You don't *want* me to open it. Not if it might prevent Emory and Romie from coming back."

From the way Baz averted his gaze, it was clear Kai was right.

It was like Baz had taken it upon himself to become the guardian of the door. A safeguard against those who might try to breach it, a sentinel awaiting Emory and Romie's homecoming–if they were even still alive. Baz didn't want to try reversing time on the door for fear of slipping up, affecting the door's power in a way that might mean Emory and Romie could never return.

"You won't even consider trying, will you?"

Baz readjusted his glasses, palmed the back of his neck. He was nervous. "How is going through the Hourglass going to help you with your magic anyway? It might just make everything worse– both for you and them."

Kai's gaze slid to Baz's neck. He could practically see the imprints his fingers had left there. Shame roiled in his stomach. What happened at the lighthouse was *exactly* why he needed to figure things out–why he'd come back to Aldryn at all. "I can't keep hurting those around me."

"And I can't risk *losing* you," Baz cried out. "Not again."

The admission echoed in the silence. Something charged passed between them. It was the kind of rare moment where Kai dared to hope. Where he imagined Baz finally reaching for the bruised, broken heart laid out in offering before him.

But Baz looked away, fighting a flush creeping up his neck. As if the moment were too much for him. "We should get out of here.

Get some sleep. Jae will be here first thing in the morning to come fetch you. They'll make sure no one sees you heading back to the lighthouse."

"You really want me to go?"

"I want you to be safe. And with the Quadri starting tomorrow, this place won't be safe at all."

Kai didn't want to argue. He felt empty, hollow at the thought of leaving again. Of being at that lighthouse again, cut off from the world he knew and those he loved.

He'd managed to get a message across to his parents a few weeks back, letting them know he was safe. But they couldn't risk further contact; he didn't want to lead the Regulators to them. And anyway, it wasn't his parents he missed. That wasn't to say he didn't love them—he did—but he was used to spending time away from them. Their business meant they hadn't been a concrete part of his life for some time now, and he'd grown used to it.

Baz, on the other hand, had become a constant. A point of reference he could turn to, always. But as Baz walked away—from Kai, from the Hourglass—Kai felt for the first time like things might never be the same between them. Like maybe he'd messed it all up, and nothing could fix this.

He'd never been so scared to lose something in his life.

Kai did not wish to dream that night.

He knew what his own nightmares would show him. What Baz's would too. And so he sought something different. The sort of nightmare that would hold no true fear for him, that could not hurt him, because it was not *his* or anyone else's that he cared about.

He delayed sleep for as long as he could, sitting alone in the illusioned fields of Obscura Hall, with a night sky full of stars above him. He didn't dare fall asleep in the commons, where Baz would be susceptible to whatever horror he might conjure. Where Kai's hands might find themselves around his neck again, unable to tell where nightmare ended and reality began.

Sleep came inevitably. Kai drifted through darkness and stars, doing everything in his power to avoid the pull of Baz's nightmares, the pull of Dovermere, the pull of his own fears.

He felt a different sort of pull then. The hollow void of a familiar type of nightmare. There was nothing to it but oppressive silence and bleak despair. An infinite, empty sort of darkness.

Kai knew instantly that he'd slipped into the slumber of an Eclipse-born who'd been branded with the Unhallowed Seal. It was just as terrifying as he remembered, especially now that he knew exactly how it felt to have one's magic snuffed out by the brand. His own hollow dreaming when he'd been at the Institute had been unbearable.

Fury surged inside him, and he wanted nothing more than to tear the Unhallowed Seal off of this Eclipse-born's hand, to rid them of this unspeakable burden and restore their magic to them. Magic was *life*, and to take it away in such a cruel way was as good as a death sentence.

But there was nothing he could do here. No way for him to help.

Kai should have welcomed the nothingness, found solace in the fact that nothing here could follow him back into waking. Instead, all he felt was more despair than he'd ever known.

He bit down on an angry sob.

All this power coursing through him, and the only thing it was good for was sowing more fear.

Kai left the nightmare with an acrid taste in his mouth. Despair and bitterness must have called to each other here in the sleep-scape, for he immediately found himself in a nightmare that was brimming with both.

A woman in her midthirties, dark hair braided in a crown atop her head, sat hugging her knees amid a pile of bodies.

She was singing something Kai had heard before, a Trevelyan lullaby that mothers sang to their children despite the grim stories it told: young men lured out to sea in storms that drowned them, women who disappeared in thick coastline fogs, ships devoured by mythical sea creatures that spat out their bones on the other side of the world. Indeed, this woman held a small child in her arms that Kai hadn't seen at first, all bundled up in a blanket. The woman rocked him gently. Tears ran down her cheeks. Her singing was beautiful despite the breaking of her voice, the gruesome scene at her feet.

The woman set down the child atop the mound of corpses. The young boy looked peaceful in his sleep; the lullaby had worked its magic. The glint of a knife caught the light as the woman lifted it above the child. Kai took an involuntary step forward just as she brought it down upon the boy. Kai flinched and tripped over a corpse whose face was oddly familiar: a girl with red hair, her mouth set in a smirk even in death.

"I warned him it would not work." The woman was staring at Kai through tears, her hands slick with the child's blood. "The dead are meant to stay dead."

The corpses around them sat up in one great movement. In sync, their lifeless eyes turned to Kai. He stumbled backward, suspecting who this was, what he was seeing. He needed to wake up. But something darker caught his eye.

Watching the scene was a towering umbra wearing an obsidian crown. It spoke in that same tongue as before, uttering the same words that Kai understood instinctively.

Open the door.

Suddenly the corpses moved at an unnatural speed, scrambling toward Kai. He screamed as he willed himself to leave this nightmare behind and *wake the fuck up*—

When he opened his eyes, Kai found he was no longer beneath

the illusioned sky of Obscura Hall. He stood on the beach, waves lapping gently at his shins. In the pale moonlight, Dovermere's mouth seemed to laugh at him in the near distance. That unnatural tongue resonated in his mind. *Open the door.*

But Kai turned his back on it, only to find that another sort of door had been opened, and out of it had crawled an army of revived corpses.

ROMIE

A T FIRST LIGHT, ROMIE HEADED TO THE HERBARIUM.
It was a lovely place that reminded her of her old green-house. Whatever rot was affecting the woods had not yet reached the plants and herbs and flowers that grew in here, all fresh and verdant and healthy. Romie knelt to study a particularly interesting variety when a voice made her whip around.

"Careful. That one's poisonous to the touch."

Mr. Ametrine, an old, bent man with knobby hands, stood behind her, leaning on a sculpted wooden cane. Romie pulled away from the plant, which she *wasn't* going to touch; she knew better than that, thank you very much. "I thought it might be foxglove," she mused, "but I take it it's not?"

"Monkshood," Mr. Ametrine said. "Also known as wolfsbane. Very toxic."

Romie hummed. "It's always the toxic ones that are the prettiest."

The corner of his mouth lifted at that. "You have an interest in botany?"

"Oh yes. Very much." She thought of Nisha, their shared love of plants. Their secret trysts in the greenhouse. Tides, she missed her.

Romie lifted her still-healing hands with a self-deprecating smile. "I was actually wondering if you had more of that salve for me?"

Mr. Ametrine wobbled off to prepare it, leaving Romie to puzzle once more over why her hands had burned at all when she'd grabbed hold of those stars in the sleepscape. She understood that this space between worlds was not quite the same as the sleepscape she knew, in that it was a *tangible* place in which her physical body had been present, whereas when she visited it in dreams, it was only her subconscious. Grabbing hold of a star in sleep let her access whatever dream it contained; but doing so in the space between worlds, apparently, only hurt her.

Odd, then, why Emory had been able to do so without getting burned. A perk of being a Tidecaller, Romie supposed.

Tidethief.

The word came to mind against her will. She was still trying to make sense of it all, how the friend she'd known all her life had been a Healer when she'd last seen her but had since become a mythical Tidecaller, with all these powers at her fingertips.

Envy was not a color Romie enjoyed wearing. She'd never seen the point of it. If someone had something she desired, she used them as inspiration to fix what was lacking in her life instead of begrudging them for it. But she couldn't exactly manifest Tidecaller magic of her own, could she? And it was a particular sort of sting to realize that what she'd dreamed of her whole life–to know every facet of the lunar cycle as her own–was indeed possible, just not for her.

She wasn't even sure if Emory *wanted* this kind of magic. There was a haunted look to her every time she used it, something she kept hidden. A part of this new version of herself that she wasn't allowing Romie to see. And that, too, was a particularly nasty sting, to know that her best friend didn't trust her as much as she once did.

At least the feeling was mutual.

Romie flexed her healing hands at the obtrusive thought, pushing down this hint of distrust she had for Emory's magic. She convinced herself it was nothing. They'd gotten good at pretending things between them were fine. That nothing had changed. It was easier than to face all the ways they *had* changed.

A tingling went up Romie's spine as an odd sensation overtook her. Instinct had her glancing at the Selenic Mark, certain someone was calling her through it. But the spiral remained dull, as it had since they'd gotten here.

Salt water was needed to activate the mark, something Romie and Emory had no access to in these woods. A shame, since being able to talk to each other in secret while they were here might have proved helpful—as well as getting in touch with people back home, like Nisha. They'd tried to activate the mark by mixing all the salt they could find in a bowl of water, to no avail.

Mr. Ametrine appeared with Romie's salve. She thanked him profusely, pocketing the tin, and proceeded to ask him questions about various plants. At first he looked like he might ignore her to heed whatever warning Mrs. Amberyl must have given about her and Emory, but he surprised her by indulging her curiosity.

"I heard about the rot that's affecting the woods," Romie said after a while, hoping this new kinship between them would loosen his lips. "How does something like that happen?"

Mr. Ametrine gave her a long, thoughtful look before answering. "Typically, root rot sets in when an invasive fungus or insect is present."

Romie tried not to bristle at the implication—that she and Emory were the invasive species in this scenario.

"But the Wychwood is not a typical wood," Mr. Ametrine continued, "and this is no typical root rot. You see, everything flows from the Wychwood. It is the heart of the world, where all magic and life originate. If it fails, the rest of the world is doomed to follow."

"That's why your coven is its protector," Romie said as lines from *Song of the Drowned Gods* came to mind.

At the center of this world lies the Wychwood, a forest older and wilder than any other. It is the source of all growth and greenery. Veins run from it, pump magic and other nutrients into the land, and at its helm is the singular witch tasked with protecting it. She is the rib cage that wraps around the heart of the world, her very skin and bones made to keep the Wychwood safe. To ensure each cog in the wheel of life works as intended.

"And can the woods be healed?"

Mr. Ametrine looked conflicted at her question, something like pity in the way he regarded her. "Sometimes healing requires sacrifice."

The words sank like weights in Romie's stomach. Mr. Ametrine's gaze flickered to a spot behind her. He inclined his head and left.

"Thought I'd find you here," Emory said, eyes trailing after Mr. Ametrine. "What was that about?"

Romie tried to shake off the unease the aging witch's words had left her with. "Oh, you know, just trying to find a way out of this mess."

Sacrifice. Was that what Mrs. Amberyl meant to do with them?

Seeing the nervous way Emory fidgeted with her sleeves, Romie asked, "You all right?"

Emory worried her lip. "You know how you said you heard that weird voice in the sleepscape?"

From the look in her eye, Romie knew where this was going. "You heard it too?"

Emory nodded, face pale. "There's something else. I think I saw Kai."

"Kai?" Romie echoed, grabbing Emory's arm in surprise. "How?"

"This isn't the first time I've seen him in my dreams. Back home, when you were gone, I kept dreaming of Dovermere, and sometimes he was right there with me." Her brow creased. "Which makes no sense because he was at the Institute at the time and shouldn't have been able to use his magic at all. And now we're worlds apart, and still he shows up. The same way I managed to see you in my dream when you were on the other side of the Hourglass."

Romie's thoughts raced. She had tried finding Kai in the sleepscape herself while she was here–Baz and Nisha and her parents too–but it was impossible. Like they were on another plane of existence entirely. She remembered trying the same when she was stuck between worlds. The only person she'd ever been able to reach was Emory.

"Maybe you being a Tidecaller means you're not constrained by doors," Romie mused. "Like you're a bridge between worlds, and that's why we can reach you in the sleepscape from wherever we are."

It would make sense. A key, a bridge, a door–they were all ways to get from one place to another, and that was what Emory could do.

"I want to go back to the waterfall where they found us," Emory said. "Surely we must have missed something last time."

Romie agreed. Now that the ascension was over, they didn't have to stay trapped inside here anymore–if what Mrs. Amberyl had promised them still held true.

"And then I think we should leave," Emory added. "Whether we find our door or not, we should get out of this place while we can."

Romie chuckled. "And go where?"

"The neighboring towns we heard of. The ones without witches. We could ask them for protection."

"We don't even know where those towns *are*. Besides, the witches are supposed to be our allies. In the book—"

"Oh, screw the book, Ro. This is nothing like it."

The harshness of her words caught them both off guard.

Emory sighed, brushing the hair from her face. "Look, we were clearly never meant to come here. I think you're right, that in going through the sleepscape, coming here, it messed with the balance between worlds. Maybe it is what's making the woods rot, what woke that thing in the sleepscape, what attracted the demon that possessed Bryony. The only way to fix all of it might be to just go home."

"And what if it fixes nothing? What if we leave and the woods keep rotting, and the witches lose their magic, and things just get worse and worse for them?"

Emory's face was set in grim determination. "If the alternative is them sacrificing us to heal their woods? Then I say we save ourselves while we can."

Romie stared at her friend in disbelief. "You have all this incredible power running through your veins, all this potential as someone who can open literal doors between worlds . . . and you want us to run back home like cowards?"

"That's not fair."

Romie gave a harsh laugh. "It's the truth, though, isn't it? We have the chance to do some good here, because yes, I believe we're here for a reason, that there's some semblance of truth to Clover's story and that we were chosen to see it through. We heard the call of *gods*, Em. If we abandon this idea now and just go home, it would mean everything we went through, everyone we lost, was for nothing. Would you be able to live with that? 'Cause I couldn't."

Emory averted her gaze, seeming to fight back tears. Romie felt bad, but she didn't take any of it back, her conviction unshakable. She'd always been the type of person who got bored chasing after dreams and goals, abandoning them whenever things got tough. This was the first time she wanted to see something to the very end despite all the complications, all the things she'd lost to get here. She couldn't give up now.

At last Emory gave a heaving sigh, and Romie knew she'd won her over. "Fine," she said, "but if they burn us at the stake for this, I'll never forgive you."

Romie threw her arm over Emory's shoulder, unable to hide her smile as she dragged her out of the herbarium. "Come on. Let's start by finding this damn door. No point arguing over something that might not even be there."

They were steps away from the garden gate when a voice echoed behind them.

"Where are you going?"

Aspen stood there with her arms crossed.

"We're not prisoners here, are we?" Romie asked with a raised brow. "Not now that the ascension's done, anyway."

"It's not safe to go into the woods on your own."

"So come with us."

A pause. "Where?"

"The waterfall where you found us. We want to make sure we didn't miss anything last time."

Aspen threw a look behind her as if debating whether it was worth displeasing her mother. Finally she crossed the garden gate ahead of them. They followed.

The woods seemed normal to Romie as they walked through them. But the deeper they went, the more obvious it became that something was wrong. An eerie stillness. A stench in the air. A state of decay that was unnatural for autumn.

Even the waterfall was all wrong, seeming completely dried

up. There was, of course, no door there. Just like last time they checked. The rot was worse here, the ravine nearly black with sludge. Aspen's face blanched at the sight. Then Romie noticed what she was staring at: a dead deer, its hide decomposing, flies swarming over its shedding antlers.

Romie covered her mouth. "Tides, that's *horrifying*." Her gaze drifted to Emory, who wasn't looking at the carcass, but rather at the decaying leaves beneath her feet, her fingers splayed out in front of her as if she were running them through water. Romie swore she saw a ripple of silver beneath her skin. A trick of the light, there and gone in a flash. Unease gathered in her stomach. "Em, you okay?"

Emory looked at her with an odd expression. "Don't you feel that?"

"Feel what?"

"It's like there's an electric current running under my feet, and the air feels . . . charged. Alive with power." Again she ran a hand through the air in front of her, mesmerized by whatever invisible force she was sensing. Her breathing picked up, chest heaving as if she were running. She pulled her hand back and looked at Romie with something like fear. "Don't you feel it?"

"I can't say I do."

"It's the ley line," Aspen said matter-of-factly, frowning slightly at Emory. "It runs right through here."

"Ley line?" echoed Romie and Emory.

"Paths of energy that run beneath the earth. Invisible to the naked eye, but we witches can feel them. Especially here in the Wychwood, where they're most concentrated. There's a certain vibration to them that we don't feel before ascending. But once we do . . . we can feel how everything is connected."

It was Romie's turn to frown at Emory, wondering how in the Tides' name *she* could feel these lines of energy. Another perk of being a Tidecaller, Romie supposed.

"Is there a way to use the ley line's power?" Emory asked Aspen with an eagerness Romie did not like. "Maybe this is how we find our door."

Aspen hesitated. "Standing on a ley line *can* heighten one's magical abilities, but its power cannot be used in the way you're thinking. It isn't something you can harness or control. It is simply . . . felt."

Romie noticed the way Emory's shoulders sagged at that. A thought crossed her mind. "If this is where magic is strongest, it might explain why this is where we appeared. Which means the door has to be here. We can't possibly have appeared out of thin air."

"This door of yours," Aspen said with curiosity, "you believe it will bring you to other worlds, yes? Like in that story of yours. *Song of the Drowned Gods*."

They gaped at her.

"How did you know that?" Emory asked.

Aspen bit her lip, realizing she'd said too much. "I . . . I heard you discussing it." At their insistent looks, she added, "When I was scrying." She let out a relenting sigh. "My scrying power is different from other witches'. I can see through people's eyes, feel what they feel, hear what they say."

Romie raised a brow. "So you spied on us."

"I only did it once or twice, I swear. Can you blame me for wanting to know more?"

The violation would have infuriated Romie had she and Emory not been *also* poking around the Amberyls without their knowing—in dreams, in memories. She caught Emory's eye and knew she was thinking the same thing.

"What exactly did you hear us talking about?" Romie asked.

"Only that book. And how you believe yourselves to be like its characters. I couldn't quite piece together the story, though. Will you tell it to me?"

And so Romie did. By the end of it, Aspen was frowning, and Romie couldn't tell what she was thinking.

"So you're seeking these doors to go to this sea of ash," Aspen said at last.

"Yes."

"And you believe I might be this witch of the woods who must go along with you to find these other . . . heroes?"

"Possibly, yes. Have you ever heard it, the call of other worlds? This song that pulls on your soul?"

The Sculptress, perhaps, calling her forward. Just like the Tides calling Romie to the sea of ash.

Aspen's eyes brightened, and it was all the answer Romie needed. But that spark was there and gone in a flash, replaced with that stoicism again. "My mother would never let me leave. My place is here, in the Wychwood."

Disappointment followed Romie like a shadow as they made their way back to Amberyl House. She was too consumed in her thoughts to notice the rot seemed to have expanded to the foot of the garden gate until Emory pointed it out.

Aspen quickly ushered them onto the grounds, evidently perturbed at the sight of the spreading decay. Her gaze caught on a shaded alcove of the garden, where Bryony sat in a bed of flowers. The hem of her cream dress was blackened with dirt, but she still managed to look flawless, with pale green ribbons in her hair and a smile on her lips.

Unaware she had an audience, Bryony blew on dandelion puffs and seemed mesmerized by the cloud of spores that danced around her. She closed her eyes and shoved a handful of dark berries in her mouth, the juices staining her lips red.

Romie's heart stuttered as she noticed what looked like nightshade growing all around Bryony. But Aspen stopped her before a warning could form on her tongue.

"We never pull a witch from her scrying," Aspen said in a low, clipped tone.

"But those berries are poisonous! Nightshade is deadly–"

"Those bushes are *black* nightshade, not the deadly variety. See? The berries form in clusters."

Romie relaxed, knowing very well that deadly belladonna produced *single* berries. Still, as Bryony convulsed before their eyes, it was hard not to intervene. The young witch's eyes flew open, as cloudy white as the dandelion fluff that suddenly froze around her, remaining suspended in the air.

Bryony was scrying.

A small smile touched Aspen's lips. "She's done it."

"Why the berries?" Romie asked.

"They're her tether. When scrying, a witch's essence needs to be firmly tethered to the physical world through at least one of the five senses. Taste, it appears, in Bryony's case. We do this to remind our bodies that we are *here*, while our essence, our sixth sense, wanders the astral plane."

"What happens if you pull a witch from scrying?" Emory asked.

"You would sever their essence from its tether, leaving room for–"

Aspen stopped midsentence as a girly giggle suddenly bubbled from her throat, sounding so unlike Aspen that Romie recoiled. The look on Aspen's face was equally as confusing: gone was that stoicism, replaced with a doe-eyed wonder as she glanced dazedly around the garden. She sighted Bryony's scrying form amid the cloud of dandelion puffs and tilted her head to the side, uttering a single sound.

"Oh."

Aspen blinked, seemingly coming back to herself–just as the dandelion puffs around Bryony fell in one great motion to the earth at her feet. Bryony's eyes found her sister's, void of their previous milky appearance that showed she was scrying.

A smile split Bryony's face, the red berry juices still staining her lips. "Aspen, I found it! My scrying power—it's just like yours!"

Aspen stormed over to her sister, looking very much like their mother as she gripped Bryony's arms. "You have to keep this secret. This is not *natural*, Bryony. And after what happened at your ascension . . ."

Bryony seemed caught off guard by the sternness in her sister's voice, the fear in her words. "But it's just like what you can do."

"No, it's not. I can't *take possession of others*."

Romie met Emory's gaze as it all clicked into place. What they'd just witnessed . . .

Bryony had *taken over* Aspen's body.

A rustling sound had the four of them spinning around to see the two boy witches who'd called Bryony a hellwraith at last night's festivities. They were staring at her now like she'd grown horns and fangs. One of them pointed a trembling finger at her. "You really are a hellwraith!"

"We're telling our mother," the other spat.

"Please," Aspen said, pulling Bryony close. "This is all a misunderstanding—"

"Being Amberyls doesn't make you exempt from rules. A hellwraith must be purged."

Emory suddenly stepped toward them. "You're going to keep quiet about this. Whatever you think you saw here, you didn't. Got it?"

Before Romie knew what was happening, the boys nodded, their eyes oddly glazed as they turned on their heels and left.

And then it hit her.

Emory had Glamoured them.

12

EMORY

THE REACTIONS TO HER USE OF GLAMOUR MAGIC WERE almost as bad as the ghosts it conjured.

Emory had no time to explain herself before Aspen dragged her sister back to the house with a lingering look of suspicion at Emory—who she believed to be nothing more than a Healer, not someone capable of magically compelling others. Even Bryony, who'd warmed up to Emory last night, seemed fearful of her now, or perhaps she was just afraid for herself.

Romie watched her with that ever-present wariness that was beginning to fray on Emory's nerves. "You shouldn't have done that in front of them," Romie admonished. "Now what are they going to think of us?"

With her ghosts pressing in, Emory didn't have it in her to fight. She knew it was a risk to use her Tidecaller magic in such an obvious way, but she wouldn't take back what she'd done to those boys. Not as she thought of what *purging a hellwraith* might entail.

She couldn't fathom that Bryony might be evil. If the kind of magic *she* had used made her akin to a demon, what did that make Emory?

They'd only just gotten back to their rooms when a knock came at the door. Aspen pushed inside the parlor without so much as an invitation, a roll of parchment tucked beneath her arm.

"Is Bryony all right?" Emory asked.

"I told her to lock herself in her room. There's no knowing what those boys will do after what they saw." Aspen studied her. "What you did back there . . . You're not just a Healer, are you?"

"No."

Romie threw her hands up in exasperation, muttering something about how they'd be burned at the stake for this.

But the distrust in Aspen's eyes faded as Emory explained how the Glamour worked. "Will this enchantment last?"

Doubt lanced through Emory. She had as much practice with Glamour magic as she did with Memorist. What if her mastery of it was just as mediocre?

As if sensing she wouldn't get a clear answer, Aspen unrolled the parchment she'd brought, laying it out on the divan. "I found this the other day in my mother's study."

It was a map, beautifully detailed in sepia ink. Emory recognized Amberyl House at the edge of the Wychwood. There were other smaller houses all along the woods and, farther south, villages that did not border the woods at all, which must be where normal townsfolk lived. The Wychwood itself stretched northward, on and on, engulfing the full top half of the map. Curving lines of silver ink ran haphazardly through the entire parchment. One such line was thicker than the rest, and hugged the side of Amberyl House, leading deeper north into the woods.

"What are these?" Emory asked, tracing the silver lines with a delicate finger.

"The ley lines," Aspen said. She pointed to the tip of the thick silver line close to Amberyl House. "This is where we found you. But as we know, whatever door you came through clearly isn't here. So it got me wondering . . . what if we can't find it, because that was the door *in*? And to leave, you must find the door *out*."

Aspen traced the line where it curved upward, going deeper into the woods before curving down again, as if circling back to the initial point. Then it looped inward again, and Emory understood that it was forming a *spiral*.

But the line Aspen was tracing cut off, leaving the spiral incomplete. Her finger stopped where the line did, broken by a black smudge Emory hadn't noticed before. In fact, a whole section of the map had been smudged off, blotted out by what looked like a giant ink spill. As if someone had wanted to erase an entire section of the world.

"I believe you'd find this door at the center of the woods," Aspen said. "At the very innermost tip of the spiral ley line."

A door in, a door out.

A descent through worlds, spiraling deeper down until they reached the sea of ash.

"If I stand on a point of power on the ley line," Aspen continued, "it will amplify my scrying, and I can search for the door's location. I can help you find a way out of here before . . ."

"Before your mother comes after us on the black moon?" Romie supplied in a mock conversational tone. "When is that, by the way?"

"Tomorrow." Aspen didn't look the least bit surprised that they knew about that. There seemed to be a battle of wills raging on inside her. "You have to understand . . . things are happening here that have our coven scared and looking for someone to blame. My mother believes this all started with your arrival. Others are more inclined to point fingers at my sister, after what happened. I worry things will escalate and lead to Bryony getting hurt."

"You think with us gone, everything here will have a chance to go back to normal," Emory said.

A nod from Aspen.

"So why won't you come with us?" Romie pressed. "You and Bryony both."

"And go with you on this quest through worlds?" Aspen gave a wistful smile. "The Sculptress chose us to be the next High Matriarchs, not to abandon the Wychwood."

Emory could hear Mrs. Amberyl's influence in her words, but Aspen's eyes betrayed a longing for something she couldn't have.

"That's not how the story is meant to go," Romie said with a tinge of exasperation. "There's no point going through the door if the witch won't come with us."

Romie was clearly disappointed, but Emory wondered again if they were only grasping at straws, seeing meaning where there was none. In their world, the entire Selenic Order bore spiral marks, yet as far as she knew, it didn't mean they were *chosen*. So what was it that tied them to the fates of Clover's characters? It was Emory's Tidecaller blood that allowed her to open doors. It was Romie's Dreamer magic that let her travel unscathed between worlds. And it was presumably Kai's Nightmare Weaver power that made him hear the song that called to all three of them, and he didn't even have a spiral mark to speak of. Maybe Aspen's mark was purely coincidental.

"Please tell me I'm not imagining things, at least," Romie said. "That you do hear the call of other worlds."

Aspen seemed to chew on her next words. "When you first arrived, I did feel this instant sense of *kinship* toward you. I didn't know why then, but now . . . I think it's because you're not the first souls from other worlds that I've encountered."

Romie's eyes widened. "What? How–*Who?*"

"Like I said, my scrying is different from other witches'. Oftentimes, the eyes I see through . . . they see things that are too strange and inexplicable to be of this world. There is one mind in particular I keep coming back to." A small smile played on her lips. "Tol, his name is. His world is so unlike this one. And his magic . . . I can only describe it as shifting into a beast of sorts, and I can say with the utmost confidence that there is no such magic in these parts."

"Tides," Romie exclaimed, "that's what I saw! Last night, you were in the place where I normally see dreams. Except you weren't dreaming–you weren't asleep at all. You were *scrying*, weren't you? Wherever your third eye travels to when you scry– the astral plane, right?–it must be the same as the place where dreams are."

The sleepscape. The astral plane. A realm beyond realms, full of unseen possibilities.

"Your face transformed," Romie continued. "You were you one second and a boy the next–a boy who then turned into a beast. You think he's from another world?"

"Yes," Aspen breathed wistfully.

It dawned on Emory that Aspen might actually *want* to go with them through the door. To find this boy she shared an inexplicable connection with.

But it seemed the woods had roots in her that would not let her go.

"I can't go with you," Aspen reiterated. "But my offer stands. Do you want my help or not?"

Emory and Romie exchanged a wordless conversation. They wanted out: here was their out. Whether the door led forward to the next world or back to their own remained to be seen.

The sun had almost set when the three of them headed into the garden with provisions for the road. The inside of Amberyl House had been eerily quiet. The outside was quieter still. Not a single witch in sight.

Aspen blanched as they reached the garden gate. It was open, and lying before it was an unconscious Mrs. Amberyl.

"Mother!"

Emory readied her healing magic, but the High Matriarch's eyes were already blinking open as Aspen knelt beside her. In a daze, she sat up, hand coming away bloodied from a wound on the back of her head.

"What happened?" Aspen asked, voice pitched high in worry.

"They took her," Mrs. Amberyl muttered faintly, clutching something to her chest. She repeated herself, stronger now, as Aspen helped her to her feet. "They took Bryony."

As if on cue, a cry pierced the night, deep in the woods.

Mrs. Amberyl tore toward the sound without a moment's hesitation. Emory saw what she'd been clutching as it fell from her hand.

A pale green ribbon, flecked with blood.

They raced through the woods in a panic. It had gotten dark enough that it was hard to see anything, but both Mrs. Amberyl and Aspen seemed to know exactly where they were going.

They found Bryony at the site of the ascension, surrounded by at least half the coven. She'd been gagged and bound against the yew tree. A circle of white powder had been drawn around her, complete with small animal bones and skulls and candles that flickered in the breeze.

They were clearly going to try to exorcise the demon out of her.

"You fools," Mrs. Amberyl breathed.

Bryony cried around her gag as she spotted her sister and mother. The two boys from earlier held Mrs. Amberyl back, and a few other witches stepped in to keep Aspen, Emory, and Romie away from the circle. The sour-faced Hyacinth stared down Mrs. Amberyl. "You know it must be done, Hazel."

"You gave me until the black moon to handle the matter my way." Mrs. Amberyl flung a hand out to Emory and Romie. "They are the ones who need to be purged from–"

"Be quiet, Hazel. The problem is your hellwraith of a daughter. We all saw her at the ascension, and what my boys witnessed today . . ."

Emory blanched. So her Glamour hadn't lasted after all.

"I understand this need to protect your daughter, I do," Hyacinth continued, "but as High Matriarch, your duty is to the coven first." The witch squared her shoulders. "Since you won't do what needs to be done, we will."

As one, the coven began to chant. The flames around the circle intensified. Bryony screamed, her head tilting up to the skies. Mrs. Amberyl and Aspen fought against the witches who held them back as Bryony's screaming grew to a crescendo—and suddenly stopped.

When Bryony looked at them, her eyes were entirely black, just like they'd been during her ascension.

With an unnatural jerk of her neck, she twisted out of her gag. When she spoke, it was in that deep voice that was not hers.

"Where is it? I can feel it on you—where is it?"

She was looking at them all without seeing them, talking aloud but not to them. She squirmed against the ropes keeping her in place, slipping between languages. Without effort, she managed to free herself, then ripped the side of her dress open and began clawing at the spot where the spiral scar marred her skin—as if to tear open her own flesh.

Aspen lunged for her sister, begging her to stop.

Bryony set her black eyes on Aspen, sniffing intently. "You have it too," she said in that strange voice.

And then Bryony's hands were around her sister's neck, strangling her.

Emory opened her senses wide, calling on a mixture of magics— Healer, Glamour, Wardcrafter, Purifier, Unraveler—to try to exorcise whatever demonic entity had its claws in Bryony's essence. Using so much power opened the floodgates for the darker alignments Emory shied away from. Her ghosts pressed in as they tended to, but it was more than that now, the earth around her festering, turning black and oozing, as if she were killing it herself.

Still, whatever she was doing seemed to be working: Bryony screamed in pain, letting go of Aspen and recoiling back on herself. Emory couldn't tell if it was Bryony's screams or the demon's, couldn't tell if she was hurting Bryony more than the hellwraith possessing her.

But Emory couldn't stop. In truth, she wasn't sure she *wanted* to stop.

It was as if finally allowing herself to plunge into her magic after days of only dipping her toe in it had opened up a chasm inside her. She remembered how power tasted, how good it made her feel. That unbearable pressure in her veins was gone. The ghosts around her faded from view until all there was was her and her magic and this *thing* inside Bryony whose attention was wholly on her now.

Recognition flashed white-hot in those unnatural eyes, like they were suddenly ablaze with luminous flames. "Tidecaller," Bryony said in that deep voice that didn't belong to her, a certain hunger in it. Like whatever possessed her *wanted* Emory's power, like it craved this silver surge that was threatening to consume her.

Because that was silver dancing along her veins, heralding her inevitable Collapsing.

And yet . . . Emory didn't feel like she was burning out at all.

She caught the fear in Romie's eyes as she watched her glowing silver. And though she could hear her friend begging her to stop, to let go of the magic, Emory could not. She had the sudden thought of reaching for Romie's Dreamer magic and using it to will Bryony to *wake*, to pull herself from the astral plane that was also the sleepscape.

Her veins rippled silver with the effort, but still there was no sudden blast of silver, no feeling that she was teetering on an edge about to drop into the vast unknown of her Collapsing.

She *should* have Collapsed, just as she should have back in the sleepscape. She was right there, exhibiting all the signs, diving too deep into her power, and yet she still wasn't erupting the way Eclipse-born should.

Emory leaned into it, fearless and free. She could sense the ley line crackling beneath her, energy that was begging to be used. It vibrated through her, making her blood sing, and she couldn't help but revel at the power that flowed from her and through her, this incredible, heady *rush* it brought, as the black slowly receded from Bryony's eyes.

Emory smiled at the demon. He was no match for her with all this power at her fingertips.

Mediocre no more. Now she was limitless.

13

ROMIE

"EM, STOP."

The words were too faint to be heard over the din of power emanating from Emory and the screams of the witches and the eerie, pained cries from the demon possessing Bryony. But Romie couldn't manage anything louder, not as dizziness overtook her, making her fall to her knees. She felt nauseous, lightheaded, felt as if all the blood were draining out of her though she had no wound. She barely managed to lift a hand to her face, noting how ashen her skin was, before it fell limply at her side again, her muscles weak as unconsciousness pressed at the edges of her vision.

"Em," she tried again.

Silver lines danced on her friend's skin, but there was no blast. No Collapsing. Just Emory's smile, a gash of white against the night, as she grew more powerful and Romie grew fainter, fainter, fainter . . .

And then, all at once, it was over.

Emory was wrenched back by Mrs. Amberyl. The silver in her

veins faded, her magic falling silent. Romie was still on the edge of fainting, but this sensation of having all the blood drained from her veins ended, leaving her with a heavy head and a sudden thirst and a bleak, unfathomable realization.

Because now that Emory had been pulled off the ley line, now that her connection to this amplified magic was severed, Romie understood what happened. Why she'd started feeling the way she had when Emory first stepped on the ley line and called on this magic that had her veins rippling silver.

Emory had drawn power from Romie. Leeched the magic in her very blood.

Tidethief.

Emory met her gaze as if she'd heard the slur in her mind.

And then Aspen screamed as Bryony fell to the ground, eyes their normal color again, but fixed unseeing above her.

BAZ

MORNING CAME AND BROUGHT JAE ALONG WITH IT. It was barely dawn, but soon the campus would be flooded with students from all over arriving for the Quadri, and Obscura Hall would no longer be the refuge Baz knew it as. He soaked up his last moments of quietude in the commons, a strong cup of coffee in hand and Dusk, his sister's cat, nestled at his feet.

"Where's Kai?" Jae asked as they sat next to Professor Selandyn on the sofa opposite Baz.

"Still asleep, I think." Baz didn't want to think about the fight they'd had over the Hourglass. "Any word from Vera?"

For the past few weeks, Vera had been working undercover as a clerk at the Institute, where she kept an eye on the goings-on of the Regulators and their treatment of the Eclipse-born.

"I'm afraid it doesn't look good." Jae's face was grimmer than the grave. "Word is the Reanimator is being moved from the Institute today to be brought to an undisclosed location. Vera thinks that means the Regulators are planning to do tests on her. In an . . . *unofficial* capacity."

"And we're just going to let that happen?"

"Short of another jailbreak, there's nothing much we can do, I'm afraid."

Baz glanced up toward their rooms. Kai would be *livid* to find this out–and all for the jailbreak, no doubt.

"Now about *this*." Professor Selandyn held up Clover's journal, which Baz had lent her the day before to study. She tapped a ringed finger against it. "I stayed up all night reading it. Clover wrote something that piqued my interest, since it aligns with my own research into the Tides and the Shadow–and coincides with what's happening out there."

She gave a jerk of her chin to the window overlooking the sea, and Baz knew she meant the unpredictability of the tides, something she'd been poring over since news of it first broke.

Just then Kai burst through the secret door that led to the cove, still dressed in yesterday's clothes. "Sorry, I know, I'm late," he said, out of breath. His bleak appearance and the dark circles under his bloodshot eyes betrayed a sleepless night.

"Kai Salonga," Selandyn said sternly, "where in the Deep were you off to?"

Kai gulped. "I, uh, seem to have sleepwalked."

"Did anyone see you?" Jae asked.

"I don't think so." Kai tried to meet Baz's gaze, something pleading and desperate in his eyes. "I need to talk to you."

Baz glanced at his watch, a confused tangle of anger and worry knotting his stomach. He wasn't sure he believed the sleepwalking bit. What had Kai been doing out there? Reckless as usual. "You and Jae should go before the Quadri's opening ceremony starts."

"Brysden . . ."

"He's right, we have to go," Jae said, grabbing their coat from the sofa's arm. They squeezed Professor Selandyn's shoulder. "Beatrix, always a pleasure."

Baz locked eyes with Kai. He did not want to say goodbye—and Kai, he knew, was not the sentimental type. He wished Kai would make some quip or other, but there was this weird tension between them now that had him fearing neither of them would say anything at all. The thought had Baz reaching for Kai. He pulled him in and held him tight. There was a moment of hesitation or surprise on Kai's part, but before Baz could think twice about it and pull away, Kai's arms closed around him.

"Be safe, asshole," Baz murmured.

He felt the small chuckle that went through Kai. "Right back at you."

The campus was a flurry of activity at an hour when it would normally be still.

As Baz made his way to the assembly hall, he spotted groups of students he'd never seen before, some of them sporting uniforms from distant colleges. Despite everything, he was excited about the Quadri. This was truly a once-in-a-lifetime experience, and he would get to live it.

Though the opening ceremony didn't involve students showcasing their magic, it was imperative that Baz be there to start playing the part of dutiful Eclipse student who would smile like everyone else as they welcomed student delegations from around the world and—perhaps most importantly—the scouts that would be on the lookout for talent and intellect.

Near the Fountain of Fate, he came across a group of students speaking in what he thought sounded like Luaguan. They seemed agitated—but not with the excitement he would expect. One of the girls looked like she'd seen a ghost. Another was comforting a boy who was in near hysterics. Baz wished he knew what they were saying; Kai would know.

As he found a seat in the assembly hall, it was clear that the Luaguan students weren't the only ones perturbed. Baz picked up on threads of conversation he *could* understand, and though the words made little sense–ghosts, abominations, *undead*–they still had his nerves fraying.

What in the Deep was going on?

The doors closed with a loud clang that set Baz even more on edge. He'd never been claustrophobic, but something about this didn't feel right–especially as he spotted two Regulators standing before the doors. Barring the way out.

Other people had noticed and were murmuring uneasily among themselves. At the podium where Dean Fulton should have been giving her welcome speech now stood another Regulator. One that Baz knew all too well.

"Due to some safety concerns, the Quadricentennial opening ceremony has been canceled," said Drutten. "You are all required to remain here for your security as we conduct a sweep of the school grounds."

That got everyone talking over one another, confused questions and displeased shouts rising all around them in a cacophony of languages. Drutten lifted a hand to call for silence again. "Some of you might have heard of or witnessed firsthand the strange . . . *apparitions* sighted in Cadence early this morning."

Apparitions? What in the Tides' name was he on about . . .

Drutten cleared his throat. "We believe this to be the work of a highly dangerous and unstable Eclipse-born known as Freyia Lündt, a Reanimator who escaped from the Institute sometime last night."

Baz's stomach dropped as Drutten continued: "The fugitive is believed to be in the vicinity of Cadence, if those reanimated corpses roaming the streets are any indication. Now, rest assured, that matter has been taken care of, but Freyia Lündt poses an imminent threat so long as she remains out of the Institute's custody. She evaded the Unhallowed Seal after Collapsing nearly a decade ago, and the horrors she has committed since are unspeakable. We believe she escaped to join a movement of fellow Shadow-cursed—that is, Collapsed Eclipse-born like her whose magic hasn't been sealed—who have been gathering around Elegy and plan to use their dark, twisted magic to sow terror among us."

Horrified murmurs rose in the crowd. Baz couldn't believe what he was hearing. Freyia must have given away *everything* that Jae had been doing in Threnody. She'd betrayed her own people to the very Regulators she'd been running away from for a decade.

It was only a matter of time now before Jae was caught—and their entire plan would come fluttering down like a flimsy tower of cards.

Drutten gripped the podium in his beefy hands and swept a solemn look over the gathered students, drawing their attention as he waited for silence. "I share this information with you not to sow fear but because it is a matter of public safety and concern." He took an intentional pause, letting the tension build. "It's no secret that the tides have been acting up of late, affecting not only our ecosystems but our magic as well. This, combined with the uprising of these dangerous Shadow-cursed, indicates that there is some larger force at work." Drutten stood a bit taller, clasping his hands behind his back. "We believe the root of the problem lies in the appearance of a Tidecaller in our midst."

Baz's pulse beat so loudly it drowned out the gasps of surprise around him.

Drutten held up a hand again, somehow able to quiet the bewildered crowd. "A student of Aldryn College known as Emory Ainsleif lost her life to an apparent drowning a few months ago. She was a Healer of House New Moon, but recent information has led us to understand this was a *lie*. Dean Fulton has kindly provided us with evidence of a selenograph test that indicates Ms. Ainsleif's blood contained Eclipse magic. Multiple witnesses have come forth to confirm this and testify to the kind of dangerous magic Ms. Ainsleif dealt in. And though Ms. Ainsleif is presumed to be dead, we believe the Reanimator and her accomplices are looking to resurrect her. Because Emory Ainsleif is a Tidecaller. The Shadow reborn."

The world tilted beneath Baz's feet. This couldn't be happening. Who within the Selenic Order had spilled the truth of Emory's magic? It had to be Artem, though he wasn't here among the Regulators, from what Baz could tell. Likely out hunting down the Reanimator and these supposed accomplices of hers. Baz thought of Jae and Kai. If the Regulators believed the Reanimator had help from Eclipse-born allies, those two—as well as Baz's father—would be at the top of their list. He could only hope they were far from here by now, on a train back to Harebell Cove.

But then . . . if the Regulators were aware of the nature of Emory's magic, it wouldn't be long before they headed to the lighthouse to question her father.

Where they would find Jae and Kai and Baz's own father hiding from the law.

He had to get out of here, had to warn them.

It was only then that he noticed the furtive glances a few students were throwing him. Whispers of *Timespinner* and *Eclipse-born* reached his ears. Panic shot through him, especially as Drutten continued with his speech.

"Rest assured, all the necessary measures will be taken against these Eclipse-born. The college campus is being combed through to ensure your safety. Once we have finished this initial sweep, you will all be asked to return to your respective dorms. We will be making the rounds to ask questions. If *anyone* has information regarding Ms. Ainsleif and these Eclipse-born rebels, it is in your best interest to tell us."

Then, almost gleefully, he added: "All Eclipse-born students and staff, whether from Aldryn or another school delegation that has arrived here today, will be subjected to a Memorist's interrogation, so as to verify that they are not hiding any pertinent information regarding the Tidecaller."

This was *illegal*. It was like they'd gone back in time to when Eclipse-born were so feared that they were subjected to these kinds of humiliations on a daily basis.

Drutten's eyes found Baz's in the crowd, and the bastard *smirked*. He knew he'd won. A Memorist would crawl into Baz's mind and find all the secrets Drutten had been trying to draw out of him these past few months.

It was over.

"We'll start with that one," Drutten said, pointing to Baz. "A close friend of Ms. Ainsleif's, were you not, Mr. Brysden? Seize him."

Two Regulators were on him before Baz could think to move. Damper cuffs gleamed in the light as they held them up to his wrists, looking to prevent him from using his magic.

The floor suddenly exploded, blasting back the Regulators and sending Baz to his knees.

15

KAI

THEY WERE HALFWAY TO THE TRAIN STATION WHEN the streets of Cadence descended into chaos as people fled from the pale white *things* roaming around, yelling about ghosts. Except Kai knew they were no ghosts.

Jae stared in horror at the two corpselike, vacant-eyed creatures ambling down the street. "What in the name of the Tides . . ."

The sound of an engine cut off the rest of their sentence as a motorcycle blew past them, then came to a screeching halt. Vera jumped off and bounded toward them, face as white as the two monstrosities she kept eyeing.

"So, uh, bad news," she said. "The Reanimator escaped from the Institute."

"What?" Jae exclaimed.

"All I know is Artem Orlov was the one in charge of transferring her sometime before dawn. I saw him come in–with Virgil, which I thought was odd. She must have escaped while they were transferring her." Vera motioned to the reanimated corpses. "Clearly, she's been busy."

"That's not her doing," Kai said grimly. "At least, not *really.*"

Jae blanched. "Kai, what did you do?"

Kai bit back on the shame Jae's expression called up inside him—and anger at himself for not having brought it up earlier in the commons, but what was he supposed to have said? *Hey, sorry to throw yet another wrench in our plans, but I brought back reanimated corpses from Freyia's nightmare and, though I did manage to get rid of most of them, some got away from me and are now terrorizing the streets of Cadence?*

He'd thought at the very least the nightmares would have disintegrated into dust by now; it had been long enough. As he stepped closer to one of them, he did see it was slowly starting to fade. *Sleep,* he thought as he touched the thing of nightmare. It vanished before his eyes.

He turned to the other one and froze, recognizing the red hair, the scornful expression.

Bleak realization hit him. Because if Lizaveta Orlov's corpse had been in the Reanimator's nightmare—clearly more memory than dream alone—then maybe Artem really was at the center of all this.

"We need to find Brysden. *Now.*"

16

BAZ

B AZ TRIED TO CATCH HIS BEARINGS AS PIECES OF floorboards and other debris flew in every direction.

Roots had impossibly torn through the floor and were now darting toward the assembly hall's heavy door to blast it open. Students scrambled out of the hall in terrified confusion, screams filling the dusty air. Baz pushed unsteadily to his feet. One of the Regulators who'd been after him mirrored the motion. The Regulator lunged for him, but before he could reach him, vines encircled the man's ankles and jerked him backward.

Baz looked around wide-eyed and bewildered, searching for who or what was doing this.

Nisha nearly barreled into him, yelling at him unintelligibly over the commotion.

"Did you do this?" Baz asked with stupefied awe.

"Yes, now *run!*"

Baz didn't need to be told twice. Together they followed the frenetic students spilling out into the courtyard. A dozen Regulators were running toward the assembly hall, no doubt alerted by its uprooting. Baz whirled around to see Drutten making a beeline for him, eyes full of hatred. He knew he was done for.

But Nisha tugged on his arm, and before Drutten or the Regulators could close in on them, they managed to slip away into the crowd. It occurred to Baz that he did not know where they were running *to*, if there was even a safe place to hide at all, until Nisha veered toward Obscura Hall.

A place only Eclipse-born could access. The *only* safe place for him on campus.

"Where do you think you're going, Eclipse scum?"

They were stopped beneath the cloisters by a group of three students who looked at Baz the same way Drutten had. Inflamed by fear of a Tidecaller and what that meant.

"Over here!" one of the boys shouted, calling on a nearby Regulator. "We found—"

The ivy growing thickly around the cloisters wrapped around the boy's mouth, cutting his words off. Before the other two could react, Nisha was pulling Baz toward Obscura Hall. They nearly collided with another student as they reached the dark door that would lead to safety. Hands shot out to grab Baz. He struggled to break free of the student's hold, and just as Baz finally had the good sense to reach for the threads of time, desperate to make it to safety, a familiar voice cut through his fear.

"Brysden—it's me."

Baz stopped struggling. Kai was *here*, holding him steady, dark eyes boring into his with all the fear and anger and disbelief that Baz himself felt.

"What in the Deep are you doing here?" Baz breathed.

"No time for this—let's go!" another familiar voice snapped.

Professor Selandyn held the door to Obscura Hall open and was ushering them inside. Vera Ingers was there, too, helping a limping boy Baz didn't know.

Baz set aside his questions as they all hurried into the elevator. Just as the gate began to close, a Regulator burst through the door at the other end of the corridor. Baz sped up time around them so that the gate closed before the Regulator had even taken a step toward them. And then the elevator was shooting downward, accelerated by Baz's magic.

Once they were past the wards, the Regulator wouldn't be able to reach them. No one could come into Obscura Hall unless they were Eclipse-born—or unless they were *accompanied* by one.

Baz caught Kai's eye. Both of them were breathing quickly. The unfamiliar boy that Vera had dragged in here was being fussed over by Professor Selandyn, who was trying to stop the bleeding from a gash above the boy's eye.

"Who is he?" Baz asked brusquely.

"*He* has a name," the boy replied, wincing in pain. He brought a tattooed hand up to his wound, making Baz relax slightly at the sight of his Eclipse sigil.

"Rusli's a Luaguan student," Kai explained. "I bumped into him on my way back here. He got jumped by Regulators who tried to put damper cuffs on him."

Rusli gave them a slanted smile. "I fought back." He motioned to his cut. "They didn't like that."

Kai chuckled darkly. "Welcome to Aldryn, I guess."

Baz couldn't help but notice the spark of kinship between Kai and Rusli. He shoved down the hint of jealousy that flared inside him—now was *not* the time to dwell on what the Deep that even meant—and thought instead of all the Eclipse students like Rusli who had traveled here only to find themselves caught up in this horrible situation.

The elevator gate opened onto the illusioned field. Only when they were all in the safety of the Eclipse commons did Baz feel like he could breathe again. "Where's Jae?" he asked, looking between Kai and Vera. "And how did you get here anyway?"

"Jae's fine," Kai said. "We split up at the train station. They went to warn the Eclipse-born in Threnody–and get a message across to your dad at the lighthouse, of course."

Baz pulled at his hair. "This is bad. Freyia talked. The Regulators know about Jae, and it's only a matter of time before they make it out to the lighthouse." He eyed Vera. "How did this happen–how did she even escape?"

"We think it's Artem," Vera said. "He came into the Institute right before the Reanimator went missing." She threw a glance at Nisha. "Your friend Virgil was with him. I'm assuming this has something to do with the Selenic Order?"

Nisha looked puzzled. "If it does, it's news to me. Artem must have roped Virgil in at the last minute, otherwise Virgil would have told us."

An inkling of doubt rose in Baz. He wanted to trust Virgil–*did* trust Virgil–but what if he was wrong?

"A Reanimator," Rusli said, face pale. "So it's true, then, what they're saying about corpses running around town?"

"That wasn't the Reanimator," Kai said, avoiding everyone's eye. "It was me."

"What?"

"I accidentally slipped into Freyia's nightmares last night and woke up on Dovermere Cove with an army of reanimated corpses at my back. I tried to make them disappear. Got most of them, but some got away from me."

Rusli whistled a dark note. "Those are some gnarly nightmares to have."

"Why didn't you say anything before?" Baz asked angrily.

"I tried telling you this morning."

This morning. When Baz had all but shoved Kai out the door. He clamped down on a surge of guilt. "There's no getting out of this mess, is there?"

Professor Selandyn let out a breath. "Obscura Hall will remain safe for as long as the wards stand. But you two"–she motioned between Baz and Kai–"need to leave. If they find out you're Collapsed, there's no knowing what they'll do to you now."

Baz's gaze flickered uncertainly to the Luaguan student. Rusli had similar features to Kai, though his dark hair was cropped close to his head, and he was on the shorter side. He didn't bat an eye at Selandyn's admission.

"He's good, Brysden," Kai said tightly. "We can trust him."

Baz was unconvinced. "Look, no offense, but–"

Rusli rolled his eyes. "You think you're the only Eclipse-born I've met who've Collapsed? If this Jae you spoke of is who I think it is, then rest assured they're a mutual friend of ours."

Baz lifted a brow. "You know Jae Ahn?"

A nod. "I met them last year when they came to Luagua asking after a friend of mine who was in hiding after she Collapsed. Jae called her to Threnody a few months ago to help her deal with her newfound powers. If it weren't for them . . ." Rusli caught himself and cleared his throat. "The point is, I don't make it my business to rat out Collapsed Eclipse-born to Regulators. As far as I'm concerned, we're all on the same side here." He pointed to his wound to prove his point. "We Eclipse-born have to protect our own."

A sense of pride swelled inside Baz. This–this was what they were fighting for. Solidarity among their peers. The Eclipse-born coming together as one, unburdened by fear.

Limitless, and all the better for it.

But it was folly. All the ways in which things could go wrong swam in his mind, and Baz shook away the fancies that had started taking shape there, grounding himself in reality. "They're going to have *Memorists* look into all of our minds. If you know we're Collapsed, then they'll know. We're done for. There's nowhere to run."

"There is one place," Professor Selandyn said. "Somewhere no one will be able to follow."

"The door," Kai murmured.

Professor Selandyn nodded. "What Drutten said about Emory . . . If the world believes her to be the Shadow reborn, if they think she is the reason why the tides are acting strange and why we Eclipse-born are rising up, as if Emory has some kind of dark influence over us . . . then we need to bring Emory *home*. To show them all that she is not what they say she is."

"So it's true, then?" Rusli asked in wonder. "This Tidecaller . . . she's real?"

"As real as a door to other worlds is real," Vera said in a sing-song voice, earning a look of confusion from Rusli. She ignored him, asking, "So when do we leave?"

Baz looked between all of them. They stared back at him expectantly. He laughed a little hysterically. "We can't open the door, not without—"

"Oh, for Tides' sake, Brysden." Kai threw up his hands in exasperation. "We all know you're capable of doing it. And before you say anything about risk, *fuck the risk*. We're way past the need to tread carefully."

Baz turned to Professor Selandyn, hoping she would talk some sense into all of them. Instead, she said, "Things will only get worse here. All our fates might rest in Emory's hands now. In proving that this sickness spreading across the world is not due to her being a Tidecaller but something else. A greater evil that perhaps she alone can stop."

Selandyn took out Clover's journal from her pocket.

"Clover believed the disappearance of the Tides and the Shadow is what triggered the doors to close and fade from memory. As a result, this cutting off of worlds created a universal imbalance of sorts. Like organs being severed from one another and not being able to function properly because of it." She flipped open to a page full of barely legible script. "Here he predicts that a sickness would spread, affecting our magic as it worsens over time. The erratic motions of the tide, the slow decline of eclipses and, consequently, of Eclipse-born."

Professor Selandyn turned to a passage that wasn't written in any language Baz knew. She ran a bony finger along the strange script, her expression unsettled. When she spoke the line aloud, the words she formed were guttural and melodious all at once. They made the hair on Baz's arms stand to attention, slithering up his spine.

"I don't know what language this is," Selandyn said, "but it's old and powerful."

"What does it mean?"

"A Tidecaller must rise. Open the door. Seek the gods. Restore that which lies at the center of all things."

Selandyn handed the journal to Baz. She gave him a weighted look, her meaning clear.

She wanted them to fix what was broken, the way Clover had intended.

"Go now," Selandyn said, motioning to the door that would take them down to Dovermere Cove.

"Professor . . . what about you? You can't stay down here forever."

"Not forever, no. But there are other Eclipse students on campus, foreigners who came here for a month of academic celebration and instead walked into forced interrogations and brutality. They will need solidarity now more than ever. I won't leave them behind."

"But the wards . . . The Regulators are bound to make it past them eventually." Even if they had to force one of those Eclipse-born to bring them down here.

"I'll stay with her," Nisha declared. "I can find the other Eclipse-born. Bring them here. Then we'll slip away through the secret door and try to find someplace safe to hide."

"The Veiled Atlas," Vera said. "Aunt Alya will take you in."

Nisha nodded. "Then it's settled."

"My dear, after what you did back there, the Regulators will be after your blood more than mine," Professor Selandyn countered. "You *all* need to disappear."

"Come with us, then," Baz said.

Selandyn laughed at that. She patted his cheek gently. "Oh, Basil. I fear these bones of mine are too old for such an adventure. I'll be of better use here. Like I said, I'm not leaving Eclipse students behind."

"Then I'll stay," Rusli said. "I have some tricks up my sleeve that can help me pass unnoticed while I round up the rest of the Eclipse students." His features changed before their very eyes, and suddenly he was not a Luaguan boy at all but a uniform-clad Regulator wearing Drutten's face. He winked at them, breaking the illusion, and touched his angry-looking wound. "Besides, I still have a bone to pick with the Regulator who did this to me."

Baz couldn't deny the plan was sound, but he couldn't make himself move, didn't think he had the strength to.

For so long he'd been on the sidelines, watching those around him do the work. But here was his chance to step into the story at last, to carve himself a role in it, however small. Here was his chance to stand up and fight for Eclipse-born, even though it felt like he was running *away* from the fight entirely.

He could open the door, at the very least. The rest he could leave to the real heroes of the story. And together they would fix what was broken. They would bring Emory back to this wretched world and make it into one where she could live without hiding the truth of what she was–where *all of them* could.

He would be reunited with his sister again and mend their fractured family.

Professor Selandyn squeezed his hand, giving him the strength he needed. A wobbly smile stretched across her lips. "Go, Basil."

Take heart.

Baz pocketed Clover's journal and met Kai's gaze. "I guess this is where our story begins."

17

EMORY

EMORY WAS STILL VIBRATING WITH THE FORCE OF HER power—with the adrenaline that thrummed in her veins, no longer silver but red. She barely registered Bryony's limp form as Mrs. Amberyl whirled on her.

"You did this," the High Matriarch seethed. "You killed my daughter."

Emory recoiled. All the residual power inside her subsided, leaving her hollow. "I . . ." She looked at Bryony, held in her sister's arms. Oh Tides. *Had* she killed her? "I was trying to save her . . ."

"She's still alive," Aspen said, eyes wet with unshed tears. "Bryony's still breathing."

Still breathing, though her eyes remained vacant.

Emory's own breathing became shallow. Everyone started talking around her. Not a single word registered as shadows pressed in, the ghosts drawn by her magic. A heavy feeling rested on her chest, and she imagined as soon as she looked at the darkness, acknowledged it was there, she would shatter beneath its weight.

She was barely holding herself together as they were ushered back to the house, Bryony's unconscious body carried there by the strongest of the men. They took the young witch to her room. Healers were summoned. Sage was called for, in what Emory imagined was a way to prevent the demon from returning. Mrs. Amberyl had Emory and Romie sent back to their rooms, her normally stoic, sharp voice laced with a desperate note now. Like she, too, was struggling to keep herself together.

"What was that back there?" Romie asked as soon as they were alone. Her face was drawn and pale. "You looked like you were about to Collapse and wipe away the Wychwood altogether."

Shame roiled in Emory's stomach. She wondered if she *would* have eventually Collapsed if Mrs. Amberyl hadn't pulled her off the ley line when she did. But it hadn't felt like it. The power coursing through her had only made her want *more*.

"The ley line," Emory heard herself croak. "It's like it expanded my limits so that I couldn't Collapse."

"That's not the only thing it did."

"What do you mean?"

Romie watched her with a guardedness that broke Emory's heart. Like she expected Emory to Collapse here and now, hurting her like her father's own Collapsing had hurt others.

"I only wanted to help," Emory said in a small voice when Romie remained quiet.

But if she hadn't tried pulling Bryony out of that trance, the young witch might not have fallen into the comalike state she found herself in now.

Your fault. Your fault. Your fault.

"We should get some rest," Romie said, not daring to look at Emory as she headed to her room. "Who knows what the witches will do with us now."

The brusque dismissal might have stung more if Emory didn't suddenly crave the solitude. Alone in the parlor, she hugged herself to keep from falling apart as her ghosts clamored for her attention. All she could do was fight back tears.

Just like in her nightmare, her ghosts formed a tight circle around her. Accusations slipped from their lips in a cacophony of sound that called to mind the demon's guttural tongue.

Emory shut her eyes. "It's not real, it's not real, it's not real," she mumbled to herself, as though she could banish them by the sheer force of her desperation.

An icy breath caressed the side of her neck, sending shivers down her spine. She whirled on Keiran's ghost, stumbling backward at how close he'd been.

"Why won't you leave me alone?" she asked in a broken whisper, tears falling in earnest now.

Every part of her screamed at her to move, to shove him back, to close her eyes and pray to the Tides that these ghosts would disappear, that she would wake and find that all of this had been some horrible nightmare.

But she didn't think she deserved to be let off that easily, especially not after tonight. This was her fault—Bryony, and everything that came before it. All her fault, always her fault.

Just like in her nightmare, she thought that maybe the world would be better off without her.

But something else inside her revolted at the thought. These ghosts manifested when she used magic because she was ashamed of what she had done, what her power meant. The destruction it had left in her wake.

Everything you touch crumbles to dust.

Except—hadn't her magic also done *good*? She wasn't to blame for everything. And she was tired of making herself small as a form of self-punishment. She didn't deserve this. She'd done enough atonement for her mistakes, and her dampening herself, making herself mediocre again, helped no one, least of all her.

The ghosts around her seemed to sense the shift in her mind. The look in Keiran's eyes turned violent. The others around him too. And suddenly it was as if they were pouncing on her, drawing all the darkness around them and looking to suffocate Emory with it. Feeding off her guilt, shame, every negative emotion she'd been feeling.

She wouldn't let them.

"*Leave me alone!*" she screamed, throwing a vase at Keiran's translucent face. It went through him and shattered on the floor, eliciting a cruel smile from his ghost. Emory let out a defeated whimper and crumbled to the floor amid the broken ceramic. Drawing her legs close to her chest, she buried her face in the crook of her arms and waited for the darkness to pass as sobs racked her body.

When she looked up some time later, the ghosts were gone. Romie's door was still tightly shut, as if she had not heard the scream or the breaking vase or the sobs.

As if she had chosen not to.

Aspen knocked on their door at first light. "The matriarchs have come to a decision about what to do with you."

Emory's stomach dropped. The witches had wanted her and Romie gone after Bryony got possessed the first time; surely they would be out for their necks even more now that Bryony was in the state she was.

They followed Aspen to find Mrs. Amberyl at Bryony's bedside. The High Matriarch had bags under her eyes, her mouth lined with profound worry. Bryony's small hand was tucked in her mother's grasp. With her eyes closed, her chest slowly rising and falling, she appeared to be sleeping.

"Will she be all right?" Romie asked.

Aspen's face was grave. "We don't know. Her consciousness is stuck in the astral plane now. There's no knowing if she'll find her way back to her body."

It struck Emory how eerily alike this was to the eternal sleepers from her own world–Dreamers whose consciousness got lost in the sleepscape, leaving behind their bodies in a comalike state.

Mrs. Amberyl stared at Emory with an indecipherable expression. "What do you think happened in those woods?"

Emory blinked at the question. She wanted to defend her actions, to explain that she was only trying to save Bryony from the demon inside her. Instead, she said, "I think you're right to believe your forest is rotting because of us. Whatever it is we might have woken in the space between worlds, whatever it is that possessed Bryony . . . it's the same. And it's looking for *me*."

Tidecaller, it had said in recognition when it saw her silver veins. The hunger in that word, how the demon seemed to *crave* her power, excited by the prospect of her within its reach.

"Did Bryony tell you the story of the twins and the demons?" Mrs. Amberyl asked.

Emory blanched. "Yes. And that you believe we're trickster demons."

"That story is a lie designed to hide a darker truth," Mrs. Amberyl said. "The real story is this: long ago, twin witches *did* bear the Sculptress's mark, an anomaly in our long-standing traditions in which a singular witch holds that honor. Asphodel and Oleander, they were called. One day, a stranger appeared to them, bearing a spiral mark like yours. The stranger's coming opened the door wide for demons to escape the netherworld and poison our woods, the same way they are rotting now. The stranger convinced the more impressionable sister, Asphodel, that they were meant to travel through worlds together and petition the gods at the center of all things to heal our broken worlds.

"The other sister, Oleander, stayed behind, acting as a bridge between the Wychwood and her twin, who traveled from it, possessing the ability to scry into her sister's mind. Asphodel was always meant to come back, but she never did, not even once the rot receded and the demons were cast back to the netherworld. Oleander could no longer feel her twin's essence, could no longer commune with her through scrying. She tried to go after her, but found she could not go through the door. Asphodel was forever lost, and Oleander could only curse the stranger who had taken her to her death. A trickster demon indeed.

"Oleander swore she would never let our kind be tempted out of the Wychwood. She concealed the truth in her journals, hid away all evidence of doors to other worlds, even from the other matriarchs. The only one she shared this with was her successor. And so this secret was passed down from High Matriarch to High Matriarch."

Mrs. Amberyl turned pleading eyes to Aspen. "I would have shared this truth with you eventually. But then we found two strange girls half-drowned beneath a waterfall, and the woods began to decay, and your sister ascended bearing the Sculptress's mark and showing signs of demonic possession. I knew then that the past was repeating itself, and I swore I would not let my daughters know such fates.

"The others believed the problem lay in Bryony's possession. But I knew it originated with you." Mrs. Amberyl sneered at Emory and Romie. "That your coming here meant you would try to convince my daughters to follow you to the center of the universe, just as the stranger who came before you did."

Just like the scholar on the shores from Clover's story, who'd gone through worlds and convinced a witch and a warrior and a guardian to follow him to the sea of ash, where all their fates were sealed.

Stranger, scholar–that was who Emory was. And perhaps the thing that awoke in the sleepscape, that was trying to seep out of it by possessing Bryony, was the great beast in the sea of ash, looking for retribution.

"I have done so much to keep my daughters from harm, yet fate found them anyway," Mrs. Amberyl said. "One's mind is lost to the astral plane; the other might be the only one who can save our dying woods, even the universe at large. I've seen it in my scrying how this blight is spreading across worlds, and it terrifies me." Her eyes slid to Emory. "I have felt you prodding at the edges of my mind. This is what I didn't want you to see. But I'll share it with you now, if you wish."

Emory was hesitant to reach for her magic so soon after what happened. She caught Romie's eye, hoping for some encouragement, but was met only with distrust.

Wary of her own power, of the ghosts that would follow, Emory reached for the Memorist magic, convincing herself it was safe to do when not standing on a ley line. She sighed as the pressure in her veins disappeared. Thankfully, Mrs. Amberyl's mind was laid bare to her, and as soon as she brushed against it, images flashed between them:

An angry sea flooding a familiar coastline. A rotting forest. A barren earth growing cold and dark beneath a too-dim sun. A sky full of impossible storms. A world reduced to ash, where a small glimmer of hope still burned, like a torch against the coming dark.

Emory let go of the magic just as Mrs. Amberyl's wards went back up around her mind, casting her out. Her heart beat rapidly. Darkness pressed in, though not in the form of ghosts this time–just their accusatory voices whispering in her ears, an eerie tidal wave of sound that sought to pull her under. Emory faltered back, clasped her hands over her ears.

Not real not real not real.

"Em." Romie's familiar voice breaking through the din. She looked at Emory with consternation. "What did you see?"

Emory didn't know which was worse: Mrs. Amberyl's bleak vision or the ghostly voices in her ears. She had the sudden thought that maybe it was all related. That the darkness called forth by her magic might be connected to whatever blight was sweeping through the worlds. With a shuddering breath, she said, "The answer to fixing all of it lies at the center of all things. With us going to the sea of ash."

Just as Romie had always believed.

"You kept this from me," Aspen said to her mother, voice trembling with barely contained anger. "I have been hearing the call of these other worlds ever since I ascended, and you made me feel like what I was seeing was *blasphemous.* When all along, you were hiding this truth from me." Aspen wiped away angry tears. "Do you have so little faith in me?"

"Aspen–"

"You would have gotten rid of Emory and Romie and let our world rot away to nothing instead of trusting that I might be able to fix it."

"This has nothing to do with trust. I was only trying to protect you."

Aspen scoffed. "And look where that got us. If you'd told me the truth the minute Emory and Romie arrived, the three of us could have left the Wychwood before this sickness got to Bryony. I could have saved her."

The brokenness in Aspen's voice seemed to change something

in Mrs. Amberyl's demeanor, finally cracking that hard exterior.

"I'm so sorry," she whispered. "I thought I was doing what was best."

"You were wrong."

Emory's heart ached with empathy for Mrs. Amberyl. The High Matriarch had only wanted to save her daughters, even if it meant risking her own people, her whole world. She would have rather seen the Wychwood reduced to nothing than sacrifice either of her daughters. Two lives over an entire world—over *multiple* worlds, if her vision was any indication.

It felt selfishly cruel, in a way, but Emory saw it for what it was: a mother protecting her children however she saw fit. A part of her wished *she* would have known such fierce protection instead of a mother who'd cared so little about her that she hadn't wanted her at all.

Aspen looked between Emory and Romie, chin lifted in determination. "I'll go with you to find this door and all the ones after."

"Aspen–"

"No, Mother. You don't get a say in this. You've made a mess of things; now it's up to me to fix it." Aspen sat beside her sister, tenderly brushing a lock of hair behind her ear. "Maybe in restoring the woods, we can restore Bryony's essence to her body."

Romie looked at Emory expectantly. "Well? We need you, Em. You're a key piece in this. The scholar on the shores. We can't go through these worlds without you."

Everything in Emory wanted to say no, to just find the door and book it back home and leave her terrifying ghosts behind and the witches to deal with their own problems. But Mrs. Amberyl's vision haunted her. That all-too-familiar coastline ravaged by floods, as though the tides were all out of sorts, their link to the moon severed and skewed and wrong. If this sickness was spreading across worlds, then perhaps they wouldn't even have a home to go back to.

Unless they helped save it.

And perhaps, in the process, the ghosts that plagued her would finally leave her alone.

18

KAI

THE TIDE WAS LOW WHEN THEY REACHED THE COVE, making it easy for them to slip into Dovermere. A blessing, given the unpredictability of the tide. One good thing about this fucked-up day, at least.

The pull of Dovermere was undeniable, beckoning Kai forward with a hungry sort of eagerness. In his mind, he heard Selandyn's voice mingled with that of the umbra in his nightmares, speaking in that ancient tongue.

Open the door.

Despite the warning bells sounding in his ears and the feeling that something waited for him in the gloom of the caves, Kai's strides were steady, his sense of purpose unmarred.

There was no going back now anyway.

Behind him, Baz was still debating with Nisha and Vera on whether the two of them should be here at all.

"If you're going through the door to other worlds, I'm coming too," Nisha said. "I'm arguably just as big of a fan of *Song of the Drowned Gods* as you are."

"This isn't some fun little adventure we're all merrily going on," Baz cautioned. "We don't know what's waiting for us on the other side of the Hourglass–much less if we can actually *survive* it."

"We'll survive it," Vera said with unfounded confidence.

"You don't know that. We're not Tidecallers, and if Emory's blood is the only thing that allows her to go through worlds unscathed and not end up like Travers and Lia . . ."

Baz trailed off, but his meaning was clear. A withered corpse. A tongue missing from a charred mouth. That was what had awaited those who weren't Tidecallers, who couldn't travel between worlds. Travers and Lia had been spat back out onto these shores, only for their twisted magic to kill them from the inside.

"Wouldn't Kai's presence protect us the same way Emory's might have?" Nisha asked. "If he's mentioned in the epilogue as being one of these key pieces who can travel through worlds . . ."

"So is Romie," Kai snapped, "and that did nothing to save your friends." He didn't want to be held responsible should things go wrong.

"What about this?"

They all stared at Vera as she produced a familiar compass, the same one Baz had found near Keiran's body right here in the caves. Vera had nearly snatched it out of Baz's hand when he'd first shown it to her. *This was Adriana's,* she'd said, full of wonder. *The engraving on the back–VA. That's for Veiled Atlas. It was passed down in the Kazan family, and Adriana was the lucky sister to get it.*

"What about it?" Kai asked, failing to see how such a bauble might be pertinent. "It doesn't even work."

"I know, but my family's always had this superstition about it, using it as a talisman against misfortune. My grandmother gave it to Adriana to protect her on her travels. And if Adriana left it with Emory before going off in search of the epilogue . . . I can't help thinking it's got to be important." Vera slipped the chain around her neck. "Maybe it'll keep us safe."

"Gambling our lives based on all these guesses doesn't sound safe to me," Baz muttered.

"Look, we could stand here theorizing all day," Nisha said, "but we won't know unless we try. And the fact of the matter is, we really don't have a choice at this point. So, Tides willing, we'll be safe . . ."

"Or we'll all die horrible deaths," Vera finished for her in a chipper, unaffected tone. "Personally, I'd rather take my chances than go back to the Regulators. And if something goes wrong, Baz can always turn back the clock, right?"

Baz grumbled something under his breath, clearly displeased with their odds and this responsibility Vera was thrusting upon him. Still, the four of them kept forging deeper into the caves. Nisha was right; they had no other choice.

They reached the Belly of the Beast. The Hourglass beckoned to Kai darkly, as it always did. He looked at Baz, who was sizing up the curious rock formation as if it were a formidable foe he had to destroy. Baz caught his eye, throat bobbing as he swallowed back the fear that Kai could feel rippling off him.

"You can do this," Kai said in a low voice only Baz could hear, trying to convey all the faith he had in him. If only he had the power to make Baz see himself the way Kai did—the strength in him, the power he exuded so effortlessly, without even knowing.

Baz glanced at the Hourglass again, and something shifted in him. He squared his shoulders, blew out a breath. Shed his fears as though this were a nightmare and Kai had absorbed them for him.

But this was real. And as Baz pulled on the threads of time around the Hourglass, visible to his eyes only, Kai couldn't help but marvel at him. This infuriating boy who barely believed in himself, despite having the power of *time* running unimpeded through his veins, amplified with his Collapsing, and completely under his control.

He was magnificent.

As though it were the easiest thing for Baz to do, the door wound back to a time it had been unlocked. The Hourglass split open to other worlds. Velvety darkness full of stars yawned open before them, beckoning them all forward.

Baz gaped at the door, murmuring a bewildered, "I did it." He looked at Kai. "I really did it."

"Never doubted you for a second, Brysden."

They held each other's gaze, the world narrowing to just the two of them. But then the sliver of a song reached Kai's ears. He turned to the door, itching for that darkness, all too eager to answer its undeniable pull.

Kai was the first to step past the threshold. The others followed behind him, and then they were standing on a path laden with stars, a shallow stream of water rushing past their feet, spilling into the darkness on either side of the path in trickles and cascades that sparkled in the starlight.

"This way," Kai said, already moving along the path in the same direction the water flowed.

"How do you know?" Baz asked, catching up with him.

"There's music coming from over there." The same damn song he heard in his sleep, here now in waking form. Kai gave a sidelong glance to Baz. "You don't hear it, do you?"

Baz shook his head, something like disappointment swimming in his eyes. Before Kai could say anything, Vera exclaimed, "Look!"

The compass had come to life, glowing golden in the dark. Its whirring hands came to a stop to point them in the same direction the song came from.

A sudden prickling sensation crept along the back of Kai's neck. The taste of fear flooded his mouth, so poignant he thought he might choke on it.

Something was coming.

"Brysden–"

The rest of his warning died on his lips. Kai's head snapped backward as shadows rushed him and bound him, filling his open mouth until he was choking on them. Something grabbed his neck, claws cold against his skin. A giant umbra towered over him. A cloak of billowing shadows trailed behind it, and atop its head sat a crown of obsidian. It had no mouth to speak with, but its voice–old and guttural and melodious all at once, a voice he had heard before–spoke in Kai's mind.

Fear Eater. Nightmare Weaver. Have you come to free me at last?

Kai struggled against its grip, feeling himself drift toward unconsciousness as the creature's shadows suffocated him. He knew then, without a doubt, that what had been plaguing his nightmares these past few months was *real*. The ultimate nightmare, a creature the umbrae bowed to as their king.

If the sleepscape was a world of its own, a whole universe yet to be explored, then this, he knew, was its ruler.

And it wanted nothing more than to escape.

19

EMORY

THEY LEFT BY MIDDAY, WITH ASPEN GUIDING THEM INTO the woods, her mother's map of the ley lines tucked safely in her pocket. They were cutting across the spiral ley line to get directly to its center, where Mrs. Amberyl confirmed the door should be. After what happened with Bryony, they all thought it best to remain off the ley line, in case what had possessed her turned to one of them next.

Emory had thought Mrs. Amberyl might come with them, or maybe try to convince Aspen not to go. But it seemed she was finally trusting her eldest daughter to set off on her own. As they said their goodbyes, Emory couldn't help but overhear Mrs. Amberyl saying she wouldn't leave Bryony's side, and that was why she wasn't coming. She wondered if, deep down, Mrs. Amberyl was staying out of self-preservation. If watching Aspen go through the door would only break her heart further, thinking how she might not see her again.

"Don't sacrifice too much of yourself," Mrs. Amberyl said as she gripped Aspen tight.

Sacrifice: that was the only thing the High Matriarch knew was needed to open the door. Emory thought back to Dovermere and the ritual that the Selenic Order did around the Hourglass. A slice of their palm, an offering of their blood. Blood—which was a key element to their lunar magic. An unsettling thought came to her, but she dared not voice it. Not if it meant risking Aspen backing out or Mrs. Amberyl deciding she didn't want to grant Emory and Romie leave after all.

The deeper into the forest they went, the worse the rot became. Trees here were completely decayed, and the very air around them was putrid. Dead animal carcasses littered the ground, full of maggots. Flies droned around them like bad omens. Death lingered, and any magic that might have thrived here once seemed depleted now, affected by this blight.

"It feels like something is watching us," Romie said at one point, even though there was nothing but them and the rotting woods for miles around.

Aspen perked up at that, frowning. "You feel it too?"

A chill ran through Emory. "Let's just keep going." She sensed it too. Something looming near, like a predator on the loose. She thought of the demon that had possessed Bryony and couldn't help but wonder if it had escaped somehow, slipping into this world to claim them next.

With how on edge they were, making camp for the night in these dark woods seemed like the beginning of an all-too-real nightmare. Even with the fire Aspen built—painstakingly so, for every other piece of wood they found was rotted through—they couldn't help but jump up at the slightest noise, glancing over their shoulders to peer into the darkness at the edge of the firelight.

As they ate cheese and bread, Emory noticed Romie stealing glances at her. She'd been doing so all day, as if monitoring Emory's every movement.

"Okay, out with it," Emory snapped.

"What?" Romie asked with her mouth full.

"You've been staring at me like you think I might grow a second head or burst into flames."

Romie kept chewing quietly, as if delaying her response. "I guess I'm still trying to figure out why you didn't Collapse." Her eyes were trained on Emory's wrists and the bluish veins at her pulse point. "I saw the silver. You *should* have Collapsed."

It was Emory's turn to go quiet. She had been mulling it over all day, and the only explanation she had was this: "I think being on the ley line stopped me from Collapsing. Like it lent me some of its power or something."

"Or something," Romie muttered, voice laced with doubt. She eyed Emory with suspicion. "What about if you use magic now that we're off the ley line? Will it throw you over the edge?"

"I used Memorist magic yesterday and was fine."

Romie cocked a brow. "Fine? You threw your hands over your ears and looked like you were under the worst sort of torture. And it's not the first time you've acted so strangely after using magic."

So she *had* noticed. Emory sighed and decided on a sliver of the truth. "After the ley line, all that magic . . . it made me see ghosts."

"Ghosts."

"I figured I must have tapped into my Shadowguide magic and drawn them up. Or maybe I was imagining them. I'm not sure. But I swear, I have it under control."

"Do you?" A harsh laugh slipped from Romie's lips. "Tides, you don't even realize what you did."

Emory tried to fight the embarrassed flush that rose to her face. Suddenly it felt like she was back in the past, nothing but a mediocre Healer sulking in Romie's shadow. Except the stakes were higher now that she was a Tidecaller. An Eclipse-born who might Collapse at any moment just like Romie's father had. A pang of understanding hit her. Of course Romie was wary of her, after seeing the devastation her own father's Collapsing had brought on, and then seeing Emory nearly Collapse the same way.

Still, the lack of faith hurt her more deeply than she could say. She was compelled with a desperate need to prove herself capable, but fear kept her from calling on her magic here in these woods, so close to the ley line they were tracking.

Romie watched her carefully, expectantly. When Emory couldn't find whatever words her friend waited on, Romie's mouth thinned. She turned her back to the fire and said, "I'm going to bed."

They were so close, yet this rift between them seemed wider than it had been when they were worlds apart.

The embers of their fire were all but spent when Emory woke with a start. Soft cries punctuated the darkness, which Emory first mistook for the sighing of leaves in the wind, or the creaking of branches. But then she saw Aspen's face, illuminated in the dying light. Her eyes were open, tears staining her cheeks.

Emory lifted herself up on an elbow. "Are you all right?"

Aspen wiped furiously at her eyes. "Yes," she said in a clipped tone.

But just as Emory lay back down to give her some privacy, the witch spoke again, so soft she barely heard her. "She was the best thing in my life. It's all my fault. I should have known they'd come for her. I should have done more to protect her. I shouldn't have–I shouldn't–"

Emory's heart twisted as Aspen sobbed quietly. They both knew there was nothing Aspen could have done to prevent what happened to Bryony.

Emory wanted to tell her as much, but she remained quiet. She herself was well acquainted with guilt, so she knew such words wouldn't appease Aspen. Instead, she said:

"Before coming here, back in my own world, people died because of me. I've been carrying that guilt with me ever since. I think about the million things I could have done differently. I play out all the what-ifs in my mind. Sometimes I . . . I wish it had been me instead of them." She swallowed past the lump in her throat, surprised at her own admission. At how true it was. "But the thing I've learned, or rather the thing I'm *still* learning, is that we can't keep blaming ourselves for something we had no power over."

The words were spoken as much for herself as for Aspen. For so long, Emory had wished someone would tell her those exact words, absolve her from the deaths she carried with her, but the only person who had such power of absolution and forgiveness was herself.

Yes, it all started when she first went into Dovermere and unlocked her Tidecaller powers. But everything after . . . She couldn't have known her presence at Dovermere would draw Travers and Lia back to meet such cruel ends. She had done what she could to avoid the same fate for Jordyn, but she couldn't have predicted he would become an umbra.

She wasn't the one who drove the knife through Lizaveta's throat.

And as for Keiran . . .

She recalled that brief moment in the sleepscape when he was overtaken by the umbrae, when she might still have done something to help him. The desperate, pleading look in his eyes. The sound of her name on his lips.

Perhaps she should have saved him. Prevented one death, at least, from staining her hands. But she would not allow herself to feel guilt over this one. Not when helping Keiran would surely have meant the end for her. Not when his ghost still had her in a choke hold.

But then, she hadn't actually *seen* his ghost, or any other, the last time she called on her magic. Only heard them. Perhaps these ghosts of hers were only tied to her guilt, not her use of magic. Perhaps all it took for them to leave was for her to forgive herself.

Emory thought Aspen might have drifted off to sleep until she heard her murmur, "I don't blame you either."

20

ROMIE

THE FACT THAT ROMIE COULD NO LONGER FEEL THE dark presence in the sleepscape was more unsettling to her than Emory's complete ignorance of what she'd done on the ley line–the magic she'd leeched from Romie.

Romie had quickly recovered from *that* ordeal, plunging into such a deep sleep that night, she'd felt like a new person by morning. Her unease of Emory, though, had not been so quick to disappear. It was only Emory's apparent unawareness that stayed Romie's tongue, making her question if she'd imagined everything. And Romie was not one to *question* herself. Ever. But doubt wormed its way into her mind, encouraged by her refusal to believe Emory would have hurt her like that. At least not on purpose.

Maybe what she'd felt on the ley line wasn't Emory's doing at all, but the very demon she'd been fighting.

Its sudden exorcism from Bryony, Romie came to realize, coincided too closely with the absence of whatever had been looming in the dark between stars. She was beginning to think they were one and the same—just like the sleepscape and the astral plane. Which meant whatever had escaped could be following them now.

She could not have been more relieved to find the door when they did.

Even if Mrs. Amberyl hadn't told them where to find it, Romie would have known they were here by feel alone. They came upon a giant yew tree bigger than the one where the witches did their burials. It was partially uprooted, its roots on one side twisted in a way that called to mind a cyclone. A spiral of roots so old they were nearly worn smooth to the touch. They opened onto a hollowed-out tree trunk, the interior so dark they couldn't discern how deep it went.

Romie was the first to move toward it, throwing the other two a look over her shoulder. "You coming?"

An odd sense of déjà vu overcame her. She was suddenly on Dovermere Cove, putting on a brave face for the other Selenic Order initiates who would all perish in the Belly of the Beast. She shook the image away as the three of them stepped into the hollowed-out tree trunk. But as the darkness around them thickened, Romie realized she wasn't the only one having déjà vu. Next to her, Emory's breathing had become shallow, and Romie understood why.

The cold and the dark . . .

It was like they were back in Dovermere.

Light suddenly flared from a lantern Aspen held up.

Around them, the ghost of Dovermere instantly disappeared. This was no sea cave, with slick rock walls and mossy tide pools; this was packed earth and spindly roots and twisted vines, with cobwebs hanging every which way and clumps of odd-looking mushrooms growing along the walls.

They were in a cave below the yew tree that kept on going deeper and deeper, the ground beneath them sloping in a steep decline. They ventured down in silence, the solitary lantern illuminating the way. Romie gave a sidelong glance to Emory, who was watching the light in Aspen's hand with something like longing. As if she yearned to amplify it with her own magic.

But Emory abstained herself. No doubt realizing, like Romie, that they were at the very center of the ley line, where its power would be strongest.

Oddly enough, the air did not become colder or damper or thinner, as Romie would have imagined; instead, it grew warmer, to the point where rivulets of sweat began to form on her forehead.

Suddenly the ground evened out, and they found themselves in a larger cave with walls unlike any Romie had ever seen. Great columns of rock, hexagonal in shape and charcoal in color, were all jointed together, growing in length the closer they were to the wall, giving the impression of giant steps leading upward. Dotted all over the cavern were small, steaming pools set into the same odd rock formations, like primitive baths carved by time.

"These are basalt columns," Aspen said, running a hand along the wall. "They're formed from cooling lava."

"Like from a volcano?" Romie asked, looking around dumbfounded.

"Yes. From long, long ago."

Romie supposed that might explain the steaming waterholes and temperate air.

"Look." Emory pointed to one of the shorter columns along the far wall, where a silver spiral was etched into the rock's dark surface.

Exactly like the Hourglass.

Romie moved toward it, drawn to it like the water was to the moon, or bees to honey and leaves to sunlight and rain. This was it, the door to the next world. The way into the Wastes. It felt to her as if her pulse were beating to the rhythm of the song she swore she could hear now, and when she laid a hand on the rock, it beat louder in her ears. Warmth emanated from the column, comforting, inviting, *mesmerizing.*

Aspen pressed in close beside her, setting down the lantern at her feet. She looked just as entranced. "It calls to me," she whispered. "I can feel it in my bones, that this is where I'm meant to go."

"I feel it too," Romie said.

Their eyes locked. The song in Romie's soul soared to new heights. It felt momentous to have someone else feel what she'd been feeling for so long, to share this sense of destiny with another. It felt like everything had been leading them to this moment, this place.

Romie removed her hand from the rock. "Try opening it."

Aspen blinked at her. "How?"

"The door in our world opened at Emory's touch," Romie said, "with the magic contained in her blood. If this door is keyed to you—as it was to the witch in the story—then it must open with your magic."

Frustratingly, Clover did not go into detail on *how* exactly the witch got the door to open in *Song of the Drowned Gods*, stating only that each world's hero had the power to open their door.

Aspen pressed a hesitant hand against it. She stroked the grooves of the silver spiral, her frown deepening in thought. She began untucking her shirt from her skirt, her movements hurried, almost frantic.

"What are you doing?" Emory asked, voicing the question on Romie's mind.

Aspen lifted the side of her shirt to reveal her rib cage. The spiral scar on her skin was identical in size and style to the one on the rock. She pressed her rib cage to the column, fitting the symbols together.

Blood and bones and heart and soul.

All three of them held their breath. This had to be what opened the door. A scar born of the rearranging of Aspen's bones, a mark of her Sculptress's favor.

A witch-born key for a witch-world door.

But as seconds, then minutes passed, nothing happened. Aspen tried and tried again, slipping into scrying as she did so, using her magic however she could to try to unlock the door. But the column remained a column, the rock did not bleed into darkness, and the key they thought they'd found seemed to be no key at all.

Aspen gave a frustrated sigh. "Why is it not working?"

"Didn't your mother say there would be some sort of sacrifice required?" Emory asked. "The Hourglass didn't open for me alone. I'm not the only one who bled on it—every other Selenic Order member did too. What if their blood was also required to open the door? The blood of every lunar house made in offering to our world's door. A sacrifice needed for me to unlock it. Blood is tied to our magic. Bones are tied to yours. So if the same is needed here . . . maybe it's literal—your bones needed as sacrifice."

Aspen blanched.

"Are you suggesting we take an actual *bone* from her?" Romie asked. "How?"

And which one would she have to sacrifice?

But as Romie locked eyes with Emory, she knew exactly what she, too, was thinking.

The rib cage that wraps around the heart of the world . . .

The door required a rib bone.

Romie wanted to laugh at how outrageous the idea sounded. How on earth were they supposed to take a rib bone—or *any* bone—out of Aspen without hurting her? Romie was fairly certain Emory's healing magic would not go so far as to regenerate a bone. But if this was what was needed to open the door . . .

They all stared at each other in petrified silence.

"There you are."

The three of them spun at the haunting voice that rose behind them, the lantern shattering at their feet as one of them knocked it over—and stared at a face that was a nightmare itself.

21

BAZ

BAZ STOOD FROZEN WITH FEAR AS KAI THRASHED around, sputtering as if something were choking him.

"What's wrong with him?" Nisha asked in a panic.

It looked as though Kai was fighting an invisible demon, and Baz realized that might very well be the case. They were in the sleepscape, after all–the realm of dreams and nightmares. The same place Kai had been having a hard time distinguishing from reality, never knowing what was fabricated fear encountered in sleep and what was tangible out in the real world.

But this . . . Whatever unseen horror Kai was fighting against, there was no denying that his suffering was real.

Baz snapped out of it, recalling another time he'd seen someone he cared about falling prey to inexplicable magic. And just as he'd wound back time on the budding Tidecaller abilities Emory had unleashed the night Travers washed ashore, he pulled back the threads around Kai now, desperate to wind back time to before this nightmare started.

In the Belly of the Beast, it had been easy to call on his magic to open the door. As soon as he'd stepped close to the Hourglass, he'd felt the magic of Dovermere brushing against his, whispering lovingly in his ear. *Hello, Timespinner. We've been waiting for you.*

This power that permeated Dovermere had always felt vast and unknowable to him, yet so very familiar. It was the strangest thing Baz had ever known, stranger still, he thought, than the Tidecaller power Emory could wield or the fluttering he got in his stomach when he caught Kai's gaze sometimes. Inexplicable and wonderful and frightening all at once.

And so Baz had reached for the threads of time around the door, tugging ever so gently at the ones that made up the fabric of the Hourglass, this column of rock that was just rock until it unlocked and became a portal into realms of endless possibility. He had pulled away at the threads with the utmost concentration, the most delicate touch. As if he were a mechanic operating on the inner workings of complicated clockwork.

Pull. Untangle. Stop and start again until at last he had unraveled the mechanisms of the door, wound it back to the time it was unlocked and open to other worlds. It had felt natural, instinctive, as if his magic had been created for the sole purpose of tending to this door.

But now, as Baz reached for the threads of time inside the sleepscape, he found that time here was not what he was used to. It was more complicated than the threads bound to the portal. In fact, they were not just loose threads at all. Time was a tapestry of closely woven threadwork, patterns that were complex in a way he couldn't understand. An overlapping of color and sense and feeling and life and death and *everything.*

Time here was a language he did not speak, undecipherable and strange. Though it left him with the impression that it was something he had understood, long ago. A language he'd once heard and tasted and forgotten since.

The tapestry shifted before his eyes, something darker tugging at the edges of his vision. A sense of urgency gripped him. He reached for the thread he thought was connected to Kai and pulled it back, letting go of his magic as quickly as he could.

In a blink, Kai was no longer convulsing and choking on air, but standing beside Baz once more, as if the past few minutes had never happened.

Kai gaped at Baz with confused bewilderment.

"What was that?" Vera exclaimed.

Kai's eyes caught on a point behind Baz and all the color leeched from his face again, the same as it had done before.

"Brysden," he said in warning.

Baz whirled, hoping to catch sight of this nightmare that was starting all over again.

But where before the nightmare that came for Kai had been invisible, this one was decidedly not.

Three figures had just stepped through the rift still open to the caves beyond, joining them in this liminal space between worlds.

At first Baz thought them to be umbrae, and his hand reached for Kai's arm in a quiet plea. But the newcomers were not umbrae.

"I knew I'd find you here," said Artem Orlov.

Artem's expression was triumphant, and more than a little wild. His lip curled in contempt as his gaze slid from Baz and Kai to where Nisha stood. "Zenara. I can't say I'm surprised to see you with them. I always thought your loyalty to the Order was rather unconvincing, especially after the Brysden girl died." He smirked. "You and Virgil really thought you could fool me."

"What did you do to him?" Nisha asked.

At first the question baffled Baz. But then he finally saw who the other two coming up behind Artem were: The first was Virgil

Dade, an unsettlingly vacant expression in his eyes that could only mean Artem was using his Glamour magic on him. And the second, equally Glamoured, was a woman in her thirties whom Baz recognized as Freyia Lündt.

The Reanimator.

It dawned on Baz that Virgil and Freyia were carrying something between them: a stretcher, on top of which was a body bag.

"Set it down," Artem said, voice laced with compulsion. Virgil and Freyia did as he commanded without blinking an eye, setting the body between them on the path laden with stars. "That wasn't so bad, was it? You can talk now," Artem added as if in afterthought, waving his hand at them. "But no moving, no magic. That goes for all of you."

Baz felt the Glamour magic settle into him, rooting him in place. He couldn't reach for his magic now, no matter how hard he tried.

Virgil blinked rapidly, that vacancy leaving his eyes. His gaze found Artem's, full of fury. "I'll kill you for this," he said through gritted teeth. Then, to Baz and the others: "He's the one who broke the Reanimator out. He forced her to use her magic on Lizaveta, and now he's—"

"Don't you dare mention my sister's name!" Artem howled, getting dangerously close to Virgil's face.

A strangled cry that sounded like a laugh broke from Virgil's throat. "You killed her all over again."

"Artem, what did you do?" Nisha asked in a small, horrified voice. Her eyes darted from Artem to the body bag, no doubt realizing whose corpse was hidden inside.

A flicker of shame or maybe grief flashed in Artem's wild eyes. "I tried to bring Liza back." He looked at the Reanimator with disgust. "This Eclipse scum is Collapsed, so I thought her limitless magic would work. Seems it wasn't so limitless after all."

Freyia closed her eyes, a tear running down her cheek. "I

warned you it would not work. The dead are meant to stay dead."

Artem gave a manic laugh at that. "Explain to me, then, why you killed all those people so you could have corpses to experiment on."

"I *never* took a life that was not already dying, or so corrupt that it had no right to live," Freyia said fiercely. "Criminals and killers of the worst sort. The terminally ill, hours from death, to whom I could offer this small kindness, before . . ."

"Before bringing them back as soulless corpses?" Artem pressed. "Trying to play god and perfect this twisted, unnatural gift of yours. If the dead are meant to stay dead, why bring them back at all?"

Freyia swallowed hard. "I brought back my husband," she said in a barely audible whisper. "After he was murdered. He came back with his Reaper magic all wrong. It–he couldn't control it, and it got our son killed. I Collapsed trying to bring our son back, trying to fix my husband at the same time. My son came back an empty shell. My husband shriveled up from the inside, as if his own Reaper magic was killing him all over again. And it did kill him, for good this time. Then it was just me and my son, barely two years old and no livelier than a porcelain doll. I went on the run with him, unable to let him go. I thought maybe, if I perfected the Reanimation, if I tried it often enough that I managed to bring back someone the right way, soul and all, I could fix him too."

Freyia blew out a sigh. "But I was never able to. Even with the expansion of my Collapsing, I could never bring them back right. And my son . . . It seems the clock ran its course on this second life I'd given him, which was really no life at all." She fixed Artem with a hard stare. "So yes, I learned my lesson the hard way. The dead should stay dead. You saw what happened with your sister, and it won't be any different for your friend."

"It will be," Artem argued. He motioned to the starry expanse around them. "Here, the boundaries of the possible are expanded. Magic is endless. Your power won't be constrained to its usual restrictions. At least, that's what he believed. So you'll bring him back *fully*, soul and all. Not just an empty corpse."

The words made the hairs on the back of Baz's neck rise.

"Artem, who is that?" Nisha asked, eyes glued to the body bag.

Artem unzipped it in answer. Inside was not Lizaveta but another familiar face, deathly pale and horribly still, yet perfectly preserved, as if his corpse had been kept on ice.

Baz wanted to recoil but couldn't, kept rooted in place by Artem's Glamour. This had to be a nightmare, his worst fears drawn up by the umbrae he was certain lurked in the darkness, playing tricks on his mind.

He had watched Keiran Dunhall Thornby die in his arms, had gone to his funeral and watched as his body was buried six feet deep. Yet here Keiran was, still dead–there was no doubt about that–but perhaps not for long.

"You can't be serious," Baz said with bleak realization, shocked that Artem would go to these lengths to bring Keiran back. But as he looked at Artem, he recognized the deep grief there, and somewhere in his heart he felt sorry for him.

Artem was alone–his sister dead, his best friend dead. Those he'd called family, all gone.

Some of them gone because of Baz himself.

"This started with you, Timespinner," Artem said as if he'd had the same thought. "When your own Collapsing robbed Keiran, Lizaveta, and me of our families. Oh yes, I know," he added at Baz's bewildered expression. "I know it was you. Keiran had started to piece it together, and after I saw you open the Hourglass back there, I knew for certain."

A half-formed apology died in Baz's throat as Artem added, "If the Reanimator's magic can't bring him back, then yours will." His gaze slid to the Eclipse sigil on Baz's hand, lip curling in distaste. "At least you Shadow-cursed filth have your uses."

"You're pathetic," Kai said with a laugh. "No wonder you lost everyone around you. Lizaveta, Keiran, *Far*–"

"How dare you speak their names?" Artem was in Kai's face, looking like he wanted to throttle him. "I could argue this started with you, too, Salonga. The way you poisoned Farran's mind with this 'Tides and Shadow being equal' nonsense . . ."

"What are you talking about?"

Farran Caine–the boy Kai used to date when he was at Trevelyan Prep. Baz had only ever heard Kai utter the name *once*, but he remembered it acutely. And judging from the fury on Kai's face, it was still a sore spot for him.

"Don't act like you don't know," Artem spat.

"All I know is he chose you depraved lot over me, and look where that got him."

Artem's hand grabbed a fistful of Kai's shirt, the veins at his temple bulging out.

"Stop it," Baz said. "Please."

With a sneer, Artem let go of Kai. "At least I won't have lost *everyone*. Not once Keiran returns."

"Don't make me do this," Freyia pleaded.

But Artem looked at her and spoke in that voice laced with compulsion again: "Bring him back."

Powerless against his Glamour magic, Freyia knelt beside Keiran's corpse. Tears fell in earnest down her cheeks now, even as her expression became glazed. She was a puppet whose strings were being pulled against her will. They all were, forced to watch without being able to do anything to stop this perversion.

Baz half expected silver light to flood the sleepscape. But no silver shone beneath Freyia's skin, her Collapsing long since over. The only sign of her magic was the faint ripple between her and Keiran's corpse.

And then, impossibly, Keiran took a gasping breath, eyes

shooting open to stare at the dark expanse above him. Life was returning to his pallid features. He looked like he was waking from a nap, alive, alive, alive, and Baz thought Freyia might have actually succeeded this time.

He felt Kai's sharp intake at his side. "Something's wrong," the Nightmare Weaver said.

Baz saw it with his own eyes: darkness gathering above Keiran, hovering there as if in wait, becoming denser until it formed into claw-tipped hands that reached down to Keiran's face. Horror lined Freyia's features, and though she tried to wrench back from Keiran, from this creature of darkness, she couldn't do so under Artem's spell.

"What is this?" Artem barked, a note of fear disguised as annoyance in his voice. "What are you doing to him?" he yelled at Freyia.

"It's not me," Freyia gritted out. "I can't–"

"*Stop!*" Artem yelled.

Freyia wrenched away, falling backward as she was released from the Glamour, just as the clawed, shadowy hands gripped the sides of Keiran's head. The darkness spilled inside him. Keiran convulsed, and then–the darkness was gone, and it was just him. He sat up and stared at them, eyes unnaturally dark and sharp with starlight, rings of gold and silver around his pupils. And though it *was* Keiran, there was nothing of the golden boy of Aldryn in his expression, none of that carefully contained arrogance, that air of superiority disguised in charm.

There was something old and bloodthirsty in the curve of his mouth. A promise of death in the look he swept over them.

"Keiran?" Artem croaked. "Is it you, brother?"

Keiran craned his neck toward him in an unnatural motion. The golds and silvers in his eyes seemed to flare like dancing flames. Before Artem could utter another word, Keiran was upon him, moving with a kind of preternatural speed that no one should possess. He grabbed Artem by the neck, lifting him off his feet with a strength that couldn't possibly belong to Keiran.

Baz felt the compulsion's hold on him vanish. Artem must have lost his grasp on it as he fought against Keiran's choke hold, feet kicking wildly beneath him. Kai grabbed Baz's wrist with such ferocity it had him snapping his head toward Kai. He had never seen Kai look so afraid—other than earlier, when he'd been fighting his invisible demon.

"Tell me this is real," Kai said tightly. "Tell me I'm not seeing things."

"This is real." As fucked-up as it was, it was *real*—had to be.

"Okay." Kai blinked rapidly as if coming out of a trance. "Okay, then I suggest we run before that thing is finished with Artem."

Nightmares erupted out of the gloom between stars.

The umbrae were here.

They milled around Keiran and Artem, as if called by the darkness within Keiran or perhaps by Artem's fear as he screamed and sputtered, whimpering broken pleas to Keiran. If there was anything of Keiran left, he did not seem to recognize his friend as he squeezed the life out of him.

More umbrae manifested from the darkness, setting their sightless eyes on the rest of them, swiping for Virgil and Freyia first since they were closest to them.

"*Run!*" yelled Baz.

A few things happened all at once then.

Freyia blinked wildly past the tears in her eyes, a look of utter bewilderment on her face as she took in the horrors around her. She glanced at the darkness beyond the bridge of stars, ignoring Baz's plea to move. She simply stood there at the edge of the path, and though her face was stained with tears, there was something serene there, a sense of peace with herself as she looked up at them.

"I'm sorry for the pain I've caused," she said softly.

As if he knew what she meant to do, Kai moved toward her, yelling, "Don't!" just as Freyia threw herself into the void.

She plummeted into darkness and stars, to the death she had always defied, a few umbrae trailing eagerly after her.

At the same time, Keiran let go of Artem, who fell limply on the star-lined path, eyes turned unseeing toward the rest of them. Virgil came out of nowhere, throwing a punch at Keiran with a snarled, "You should have stayed dead!"

Keiran stopped Virgil's fist inches from his face and shoved him back with the strength of a bull. Virgil teetered toward the edge of the path, umbrae turning toward him gleefully. Nisha was upon Virgil in a second, helping him up, just as Kai shrugged off the umbrae around them as if they were nothing.

"Head for the door!" Vera yelled, motioning in the direction Kai had heard the song.

They had to make it through the next door, leave this place behind before that *thing* that was Keiran followed them out.

"Kai, let's go!" Baz pleaded.

But now Keiran had set his eyes on Kai, the gold and silver in them flaring ravenously again. Kai seemed rooted to the spot. The blood leeched from his face. Whatever he saw in Keiran clearly had him scared beyond all logic. Keiran moved toward him, slowly, as if savoring the Nightmare Weaver's fear.

Baz reached for the threads of time, willing Keiran to stop, and–

Oh.

The complicated tapestry of time burst into dazzling colors, as if the very fabric of time were changing, altered by this dark presence it was trying to reach for. Threads came apart and wove together again in dizzying patterns, wrapping around Baz until he was all tangled up in them. Baz tried to let go of his magic but found he couldn't, not as the threads pulled him away from his friends like he was a fish on a hook.

Someone grabbed his hand then, wrenching him free of this pull that time had on him. Baz blinked at Kai, who'd finally snapped out of whatever hold Keiran had on him. The Nightmare Weaver clasped Baz's hand tight as they both ran after the others down the star-lined path, toward a door none of them could yet see.

But there—the faint smell of earth and moss, so distinct that Baz nearly cried.

There is a world not far from our own where things grow wild and plenty.

The Wychwood. It was here, real, just out of reach.

Something wrapped around Baz and yanked him back, his hand tearing out of Kai's grip. It wasn't the umbrae or Keiran or anyone. Rather, it was time itself, pulling him toward its strange maelstrom of threadwork, as if whatever odd magic lived in this liminal space between worlds had other plans for him. Like it would not let him go where he wished.

Baz flung a hand out to the others—to Kai, who turned to him as Baz screamed his name.

The Nightmare Weaver's eyes widened, fear like Baz had never seen in him flooding his features. Kai's hand grabbed for his own again, fingers digging for purchase, gripping so tightly it hurt. The world around them squeezed in, sucking them backward. Baz and Kai held on to each other, their only tether to the here and now.

It felt to Baz like he was dying. Like his body was being splintered apart, pulled into a hundred different directions.

He wished then that Kai had not grabbed for him, that he would have stayed with the others so he could live.

"Let go!" Baz screamed, but Kai did no such thing. He only held on tighter.

They were going to die here together.

But then—the world expanded again as the strange tapestry of time crackled and burned and fizzled out.

Baz hit a body of water, the impact almost like he'd hit solid ground. He knew he was underwater only by how the force of it ripped him and Kai apart, and suddenly he inhaled a mouthful of salt water into his lungs, trying to scream out Kai's name.

Everything went black. Baz fought to catch his bearing, to discern what was up and what was down. What was real and what was not.

He broke the surface with a great gasp.

Strong arms were wrapped around him, and for a horrible moment, Baz thought he was trapped in that Tides-damned nightmare of his, back at the printing press to relive his worst memory.

But upon opening his eyes he realized he was out at sea, great waves trying to pull him under again. There was moonlight overhead, and seawater in his nose and mouth, and the arms around him weren't his father's but Kai's, holding him afloat.

"I've got you," Kai breathed. "I've got you."

Baz tried to turn around to face him, legs kicking wildly underwater. But an angry wave broke over them, and suddenly they were under again. When Baz emerged, he looked around frantically for the coastline, but it was all sea, all water everywhere, freezing and dark.

They were going to drown here.

"There," Kai said, pointing to somewhere in the distance, where Baz could barely make out a light along the shore.

They swam with everything they had, aided by the swelling tide. When they finally reached the shore, Baz heaved among the weeds and shells and silt. Kai lay panting beside him.

Wiping his mouth, Baz gave a puzzled look at the cliffside. They were on Dovermere Cove.

"How in the Deep are we back here?"

It was as if the sleepscape didn't want them to reach the next world, so it pulled them back to the one they had come from, depositing them on Dovermere Cove like all the bodies it had spat out before them.

The others were nowhere to be seen.

"I don't think we're on the same beach anymore," Kai said, a strange quality to his voice.

Baz frowned at him where he sat staring at the top of the cliffs. "What are you–"

But as he tracked Kai's gaze, the words died on his lips.

Kai was right. They weren't on the same beach, not exactly. It was Dovermere Cove, sure enough, but not the one they knew. For at the top of the cliff where Aldryn College stood, the old light-house that had all but crumbled to dust and had been out of service for decades now stood tall and pristine, a great beacon of light shining from it.

Kai met his gaze and spoke words that made no sense at all.

"I think we've gone back in time."

22

EMORY

EMORY MINDLESSLY REACHED FOR HER LIGHTKEEPER magic to keep the shattered lantern from plunging them into darkness, but even with the ley line beneath her feet, the light sputtered on dimly, as though there were no hope to cling to.

As if Keiran's ghost had snuffed it all out.

He'd emerged from behind them, swathed in shadows as if he were an umbra, pulled from the darkest recesses of Emory's nightmares. The shadows dissolved at his feet as he stepped closer, falling behind him like a cloak he was shedding, a train of lingering nightmares.

Emory gritted her teeth, bracing for the cacophony of whispers from the other ghosts to assault her ears. But it was only him. "I told you to leave me alone," she said aloud, uncaring of what the other two thought of her. "Why won't you leave me alone?"

"Em." Romie gripped her wrist tight, a tremor in her voice. "I don't think that's one of your ghosts."

It was only then that Emory realized both Romie and Aspen

were looking right at Keiran–at the ghost she alone should be able to see.

She faltered, a sound between a sob and a scream catching in her throat. Keiran smiled at her, and she wondered how she could have missed the unnatural black of his eyes, pupils ringed in gold and silver. And it *was* Keiran, this she was sure of–even if she hadn't been haunted by his ghost these past few days, she'd know his face anywhere, that chestnut hair, the sun-kissed skin, those thick-lashed eyes, still the same despite their odd coloring.

But that smile . . .

There was nothing of Keiran in that smile. No boyish dimples, only a tight-lipped line, cruel in its hardness. A slash of malice.

"How?" Emory breathed. "I watched you die." She'd watched the umbrae *devour* him.

Keiran tilted his head to the side, a hint of curiosity in his expression. "You did," he said, though it was almost formed like a question. His cold voice slithered unpleasantly over her, so unlike Keiran's own, but familiar in a way that had a horrible realization dawning on her. Keiran's smile widened. "But I am not him."

The shadows at his feet gathered, forming into a handful of umbrae that hovered behind him like sentinels. There was a flicker of motion, and then the umbrae were on them, clawed hands wrapping around their necks and arms to keep them rooted to the spot. Emory could feel Romie fighting against their hold, could hear Aspen's broken whimper as she, too, realized what stood before them.

The same demon that had slithered into Bryony's mind.

Keiran's attention went to Aspen, as if called to her by her cries, or perhaps by the familial bond she shared with Bryony, recognizing in her the power of a Sculptress-blessed witch. He advanced on her, steps slow and unbothered. His eyes shuddered as he breathed her in. "I can smell her on you."

"Please," Aspen whispered. "I'll do anything if you release my–"

Keiran's hand shot out and grabbed her by the neck, silencing her. His features darkened with hatred. "This is all your fault," he said to Aspen. "You deserved to be ripped apart, and I will ensure that you never be put whole again."

With unnatural strength, Keiran plunged a hand clean through Aspen's chest.

Aspen's eyes widened. Romie shouted *no*, the sound of it ringing in Emory's ears, tearing through her heart.

There was a horrible cracking and squelching sound as Keiran fished for something inside Aspen's chest. None of them had time to move before he ripped a blood-slick piece of rib bone out of her, and Aspen fell, lifeless, at their feet.

Emory watched in total stupor as Keiran walked up to the door and slotted the bloody rib into the spiral etching. It fit perfectly in the second outermost ring of the curved cavity.

The door accepted its sacrifice.

A breath blew through the grotto, making the fine hairs on Emory's arms stand to attention. Both the spiral and the bone erupted in silver light, and suddenly cracks of it ran along the basalt columns, shifting from silver to green to the rich brown of tilled earth, as if the woods themselves were trying to erupt from the columns. Spores of silvery green lifted from the striated rock, concentrating around the spiral, where they sprouted into a collection of strange fungi and moss and leaves that seemed to form a lock.

And yet the door did not open. Keiran pressed a hand to the lock expectantly, anger darkening his features when the door remained shut.

Emory felt Romie's hand brush against hers. She followed her line of sight to Aspen, prone and bleeding at their feet, and understood Romie's meaning: use Keiran's distraction to heal Aspen.

Blood poured out of the hole in the witch's chest, a wound too big and too swiftly administered for Emory to heal, if the deathly pallor of Aspen's face was any indication.

But Emory refused to have another death on her hands.

She willed whatever light she could into her, making it pulse bright enough to blast back the umbrae that held her and Romie, creating a protective dome around the two of them and Aspen. The umbrae shrunk away from the light, slithering back into shadows around Keiran, whose focus was on them now, the door still unopened behind him. Emory quickly willed Wardcrafter magic into the dome of light, hoping it would keep the demon at bay.

Indeed, his features grew dark when he found he could not approach them. "You cannot keep me out forever, Tidecaller."

Emory ignored him as she crouched at Aspen's side. Her usual ghosts had finally deigned to make an appearance, hovering around Aspen like a morbid welcome party. Travers, Lia, Jordyn, Lizaveta—all of them whispering accusations in her ear. All of them here except for Keiran.

"Can you save her?"

Romie's strained voice snapped her back to the here and now. There were unshed tears in her eyes as she crouched on the other side of Aspen.

Emory fought to block out the darkness pressing in. "I can try, but the ley line—"

A sliver of fear in Romie's eyes, then a steely tilt of her chin. "Do it," she said.

Emory didn't need to be told twice. She called on all the magic she could muster, throwing caution to the wind as she opened herself up to the power of the ley line that ran beneath them. She'd felt it growing in strength as they neared the door. The air down here sizzled with possibility, power. Begging her to take from it. And so she flung every bit of healing power she could grasp into

Aspen, all the while strengthening the protective dome around them.

Emory's magic assessed the damage, finding the spot where Aspen's rib bone had been ruptured, nearly piercing her lungs in the process. The witch's eyes were glassy, fixed above her unseeingly, but Emory refused to believe she was dead. And there *was* breath to her still, though her life force was faint and fading fast.

Distantly, Emory was aware of Keiran moving at the edge of her vision, but he could not get close to her and Romie and Aspen, not as Emory's magic flared brighter and more powerful around them, Healer and Lightkeeper and Wardcrafter blending together until she didn't know which was which, until it became something new entirely, fueled by the crackling energy of the ley line that flooded through her. She was suddenly aware of silver veins running along her arms as she ran her hands over Aspen, trying to mend the witch's bones. But again she felt invincible, feeling no impending sense of Collapsing.

"Please," she gritted out. "Please don't die."

Her blood felt like ice fire in her veins, the sort of burning cold that the stars themselves blazed with. She could feel her ghosts hungering for such power, could see that hunger echoed in Keiran's expression as he watched her, but she blocked it all out, focusing her attention on Aspen until her rib finally mended—*regrew* from nothing—and her chest stitched itself up and life returned to her face, her eyes.

There was no time to wonder at what she'd done as Romie suddenly fell limply at Aspen's side, her own face as white as a sheet, lips tinged blue as though from a lingering kiss from death itself.

"Ro!"

Panicked, Emory let go of her magic. All the light faded at once, the dome around them flickering out, her ghosts pressing in closer as if angered at being denied this feast of magic. Romie's eyes fluttered open as she managed a weak, "I'll be fine."

She was decidedly *not* fine, but before Emory could assess what was wrong, the umbrae pounced, flocking to Romie like moths to a flame. Emory was lifted to her feet as Keiran grabbed her by the back of the neck. Those unnatural eyes drew her in like a black hole. His other hand reached for her arm, and for a terrifying moment Emory thought he might rip her apart too. But he merely lifted her wrist to peer at the silver spiral on her skin. "Interesting," he said. There was something like bloodlust in his eyes. "I didn't think your kind still existed. But here you stand, the key to everything."

Emory reached for her magic again, but Keiran's grip tightened. "I wouldn't do that. Not if you wish to see the dreamling live."

He spun her around, keeping his hold on her neck as he moved to stand behind her, trapping her against his chest. Emory saw that Romie was being held by the umbrae, writhing in pain as they feasted on her fears. The color had returned to her face, at least—whatever happened before seemingly past—but fear gripped Emory all the same as she remembered Jordyn being turned into an umbra. She couldn't let the same thing happen to Romie.

"Please," Emory begged. "Let her go. I'll do anything."

Keiran grabbed her hand, and she watched in horror as the tips of his fingers elongated in shadowy claws, just like the umbrae. He sliced one across her palm, drawing blood, then shoved her forward so that she stood before the basalt columns, where the fungi and moss still formed a lock around the silver spiral and Aspen's rib.

His voice slithered in her ear. "Open it."

Emory suddenly understood why the door hadn't opened before—what it needed now.

Aspen's bone to act as sacrifice. And Emory's own blood to

unlock it–just as the four lunar houses had sacrificed their blood in Dovermere before she'd unlocked the Hourglass.

She remembered Baz telling her that eclipses were the perfect alignment of moon, sun, and earth. And if eclipses were what aligned all their worlds, made it possible to open the doors between them . . . her blood held all the power of that rare Tide-caller eclipse. It was a key in all the ways the door required it to be.

Given no other choice, Emory pressed her bloodied hand against it.

And the door unlocked.

Before her eyes, the columns rearranged themselves into an archway, through which she could glimpse the velvety, starry expanse of the sleepscape. She twisted around to look at Keiran, at Romie, who was still being feasted on by the umbrae, at Aspen, who lay prone on the cave floor, alive but barely conscious. Power still thrummed in Emory's veins, but she was grasping at straws trying to think of a way out of this.

"What are you?" she asked, staring at Keiran-not-Keiran, hoping to distract him from the magic she was reaching for–the light from the stars behind her, all the bright possibility of the sleepscape, hoping to use it to unmake the umbrae and whatever creature stood before her in Keiran's skin, the same way she'd done last time in the sleepscape.

His dark eyes flashed silver and gold. Shadows swarmed around him, as if in echo of her own gathering power. He opened his mouth to answer–and Emory unleashed herself.

The umbrae that held Romie erupted in brilliant silver light. Emory herself shone with it, veins rippling silver along her entire body. With the ley line coursing through her, she directed the power to Keiran, willing whatever dark force was behind his eyes to disappear as the umbrae had, but he was not so easily defeated. His gaze turned vicious. Emory amplified the blast, letting out a frustrated scream as Keiran remained impervious to her power, as darkness began to press in around her, her ghosts whispering in her ears again, goading her on, desperate for more more *more*.

"Stop this," Keiran said, seething.

But there was no stopping now. Her power tore through umbrae and rock and earth alike, until a grand trembling nearly shook her off her feet and part of the ceiling came undone, falling mere inches from her. She caught a glimpse of Romie's face–that deathly pallor returned despite the umbrae no longer there to feast on her–and wondered, with abrupt clarity, if this was *her* doing.

Suddenly Keiran grabbed her by the throat, as his ghost had in her dream, eyes aflame with something vicious. All the fight left her at his touch, her magic fluttering out like a candle, until all that was left was the darkness, the ghosts, the guilt. And Keiran's fingers tightening around her neck.

He was going to kill her.

A perverse part of Emory wanted to see what he might do to her–*wanted* to see him take revenge on her, punish her for having left him to be devoured by the umbrae.

"Do your worst," she said, feeling herself go limp in his grip. "It's what I deserve."

Her words made his features harden.

She might have imagined the darkness around her lessening, the whispers fading, the ghosts ebbing away from her in one swift motion as they drew into *him* instead. Before she could make sense of it, the sound of her name pierced through the groaning of the cave. Emory thought it might be the dream song spilling from the open door, calling her to the next world as it had brought her to this one. But no–it came from the opposite direction. And it was not a song at all but a voice.

Keiran's grip on her eased as he spun around to see the new-comer kneeling at the edge of one of the steaming pools, one hand dripping blood into the water and vines shooting from the other.

Nisha was here.

Nisha was *here*, and it was so impossible that Emory could only stare as the Sower commanded vines to knock Keiran against the wall and wrap around his arms and torso, binding him so he could not move. Virgil appeared at Nisha's side, along with another vaguely familiar girl, the three of them bruised and battered but alive, and real, and *here*.

"*Nisha?*"

This came from Romie, who had managed to pull herself up onto her elbows, face still blanched, but alive. Her look of absolute bewilderment would have been laughable in any other situation, but as Keiran fought against his bindings and the cave kept raining debris down on them, there was a sense of urgency that left no time for contemplating the hows and whys of their old friends being here.

"Those bindings won't hold forever." Nisha's face was strained as she fought to keep her hold on Keiran.

"Quick, through the door!" Virgil yelled, pulling a dazed Emory along with him as he ran toward the portal.

Emory snapped out of it at last. The vaguely familiar girl–Vera, Emory recalled–helped Romie up and went through the portal with her. Emory and Virgil gathered Aspen between them. Nisha didn't budge from where she still knelt by the pool, her concentration set on Keiran.

From the sweat beading down Nisha's forehead, the weakening vines, Emory could tell the magic was taking a toll on the Sower, fatigue already kicking in. "Go," Emory said as she took control of the vines, wove her own magic through them to reinforce the bindings with ropes of light and chains of darkness. "I've got it, Nisha, go!"

Nisha didn't need to be told twice. She took Emory's place

carrying Aspen, and went through the door with Virgil. As soon as they were through, Emory let go of the magic and flung herself with all that she had into the bleeding darkness.

The last image she had was of Keiran's eyes flashing that unnatural silver and gold.

The sensation of falling among stars. A rush of fear. And then her feet struck solid ground and she found herself back in the space between worlds, on a familiar starlit path.

Emory whirled toward the rift she knew would still be open behind her, willing the door to close, to lock, before that *monster* followed them.

But as the rift closed–becoming once again a marble door with roots climbing up its smooth surface, exactly like the door Emory and Romie had opened into the Wychwood–she realized the monster was already here.

Keiran moved with a speed that wasn't human, rushing past Emory with a snarl to chase after the others already barreling down the star-lined path.

Emory's magic crackled beneath her skin, eager to be let loose in this realm of endless possibility. She unleashed a blast of silver light toward Keiran. He whirled on her with a surprised look of pain. She blasted him again, making him move farther and farther away from her friends–and closer to the edge of the starlit path.

"Stop," he said angrily. Shadows gathered around him, and Emory saw claws begin to form in them, the umbrae come to help their master.

With a sudden thought, Emory plucked a star from the darkness above her the way Romie had done last time. She barreled into Keiran, pressing the burning star against his heart. He screamed out in pain. She closed her own heart off against it, despite the sound being more human than before, more like *Keiran* than before, and pushed the star harder against him until he fell to his knees with a grunt, trembling in pain.

Emory dropped the star at her feet, distantly realizing it hadn't burned her hand in the slightest, and *ran*.

She picked up on that Tides-damned song, the same one she and Romie had followed into the Wychwood, guiding them down the path. She caught up to the others just as Vera exclaimed, "It's here!"

The third world's door was solid gold.

It was a resplendent thing, a work of art. A border of sculpted gold depicting the wings of a great beast and, in its middle, a carved sunburst.

Emory pushed the door open, and just like last time, water spilled over the lip of the threshold. Glaring light had them all shielding their eyes as the third world Clover had written of opened wide to them.

This time when she went through the door, Emory was prepared, steeling herself against whatever waited on the other side. There was a feeling of falling, a heart-stopping moment where she thought she would break against the red-hued earth that appeared beneath her.

Emory landed with a painful thud on her back at the edge of what looked like a small spring. It was all she allowed herself to see before she spun around to catch a glimpse of the still-open door, a rift of dark stars open beneath a sandstone arch through which the spring ran. She hurried to shut the door with her magic and trap Keiran in the seams between worlds–but he slipped through the archway seconds before it closed, landing solidly on his feet as if he'd been doing this for centuries.

They stared at each other for a second that seemed frozen in time, his eyes more golden than black here, as if they had gobbled up the sun.

Keiran took a step toward her, then stopped, wincing in pain at the horrible burn on his chest, where she'd pressed the star against his heart. Shadows flickered dimly around him, then disappeared altogether, as if the umbrae that had clung to him vanished with the closing of the door. As if the power he'd wielded back in the grotto was all but spent.

When Keiran met her gaze, gone was the promise of violence. In its wake was a knot of confusion, an unbidden show of weakness, that left Emory wondering why she felt *bad* for him when he had just tried to kill them.

"What in the name of the holy fucking Tides is *that*?" Virgil shouted, pointing up at the sky—where great winged beasts blotted out the sun.

Emory could make out only their shadowed outlines from here, and though their eerie cries sounded distant, it was clear they were much larger than any bird should be.

A chill ran up her spine.

When she looked back at the arch where the door had been, Keiran was gone. But she knew it wouldn't be the last she saw of him.

PART II:

THE WARRIOR

WHEN TOL WAS A BOY, HIS HEART GAVE OUT.
He remembered the slow agony of it. The thunderous sounds of battle, the nauseating smell of sulfur and smoke and blood. Lying with the other injured, unable to move as the wound above his knee turned black and putrid from the rushed amputation he'd endured—his leg having been mangled by one of the eldritch beasts that attacked his village. A phantom impression was left behind by the missing limb. The healers, wherever they were, if they were still alive at all, would not reach him in time to set the wound properly.

Help did not come for him.

But Death did.

Death, Tol discovered, was a weather-worn woman with features like a hawk. She swooped down to him and rested a cold hand atop his feeble heart. Her mouth twisted to whisper something that Tol was too weak to make sense of. It sounded almost comforting, like the lullabies his mother would sing to him before bed, or the last words of comfort she spoke to him before Death came to claim her, too.

Tol thought of his mother as Death gathered him in her talons. It was easy to accept this too-quick end to his too-short life if it meant being reunited in the afterlife with his mother and father and sisters, his entire family ravaged by war.

The sound of beating wings enveloped him as Death carried him off. They were flying, Tol realized. How nice of Death to offer him such a gift—to give him a taste of this sweet freedom on the way to the heavens that awaited him.

What Tol did not realize was this:

Death was not here to claim his life, nor was she Death at all.

She was a woman indeed, with features more draconic than hawklike, and great golden wings with which to carry him to their destination—not the sunlit heavens above, nor even the dark chasms of hell below, but rather a place in between, where death could be transformed into life, hearts of flesh made into gold, and broken children chiseled and shaped into valiant heroes.

"Do you swear to follow the light, child?" the woman asked him, her voice a beacon cutting through the fog of death. "This oath, once taken, can never be broken."

At the time, Tol did not understand what such an oath meant. A small sound escaped him, neither consent nor refusal, but enough that the woman brought him to the legendary draconic forge where children like him, bound for death before their time, were made anew.

It was a rare gift, this marvel in alchemy that would turn his heart to gold and make him into something more than a boy. Here, he would become a draconic, a shifter like the woman herself, able to manifest wings and talons. This feat of magic and alchemy required the sacred flame of a dragon, a treasure not so willingly relinquished and ever more difficult to come by.

The first step was death.

Tol did not remember the moment his human heart gave out. What he did remember was the scorching heat and searing pain that followed.

It started in his no-longer-beating heart, a pain unlike any he'd ever known that traveled through his body like burning, molten liquid. He screamed as this terrible fire tore through his veins. It burned every inch of him from the inside out, molding him into something different, something bold.

This place was a forge, and he was the lump of metal being melted and molded and beaten and honed into what was to become a powerful, gilded weapon.

Such was how a draconic was born.

Tol was not the only one of his kind. The knights of the Chivalric Fellowship of the Light tried to save as many dying children as they could by gifting them this new life forged by dragon fire. Together, the children grew up in the legendary halls of this ancient, sacred order, learning to master their new forms—some of them, like Tol, having to relearn the use of their bodies with prosthetics for their severed limbs, for the strange magic of alchemy could not grow back human bones or cure human hurts. It only turned human hearts into hearts of fiery gold, gave human limbs the ability to sprout wings and grow talons, an echo of the almighty dragons to whom they owed this second life.

While the world was full of beasts—legendary monsters and eldritch horrors born of darkness, whose sole purpose was to sow terror and death—the dragons were divine, believed to be descended from the sun itself. The draconics were their disciples, trained in the arts of battle and alchemy and all things beastly. Their one purpose was to serve the land and protect its people from the eldritch beasts who sought to take away all light and warmth and heart.

Tol's formative years with his draconic masters were thus spent surrounded by children like him who had lost families and limbs and their own human lives to these never-ending eldritch wars. And yet, despite this shared history of theirs, Tol could not help but feel isolated.

He had been a strange boy in his first life, aloof and stubborn. But here he was a true maverick who always challenged the lessons of his draconic masters.

"Why do we slay the monsters instead of trying to mediate with them?" Tol would ask, to which the masters would answer that there was no mediating with the forces of evil.

"How do we know they are evil?" Tol would wonder, and the masters would scoff and say that the monsters were killers, and that taking a life was the definition of evil.

"Are the draconics not evil, too, then, for taking eldritch lives?" Tol would counter, and the masters would explain that their knighthood–this link they had to the dragons–meant they were meting out just punishment. That their slaying was not only reasonable but holy. They carried an ember of the divine sun within their hearts, and with it they would chase away the dark stain of these evil beasts.

The older Tol got, the more pointed his questions became. Some of the masters grew wary of him, seeing this rebellion in him as a challenge to their ways, an endangering of their order. Others, few though they were, thought it gave him the qualities of a leader. That he would make a fine general one day.

And though Tol did indeed have skill in battle, his heart lay in the alchemy of it all, not the fighting. He was endlessly fascinated by this transformation he had suffered through–even more so by the strange ability it had ignited in him.

To feel the emotions of others, both eldritch and draconic,

human and animal, was entirely unheard of. Tol could see the truth of their hearts, how their lives were tied together in intricate ways. He could feel those lives end, something he'd discovered upon slaying his first beast and feeling a part of him die with it. And, perhaps most curious of all, he could feel *her* in his mind.

Tol did not know who she was, or whether she was a person at all. All he knew was that when he took his first scorching breath as a newly born draconic, he did not take it alone. *She* was there, having also died and been remade. He knew that she lay slumbering somewhere in the depths of the earth, and that his heart was an echo of her own. His pulse beat to the rhythms of her steady breathing. Her mournful song resounded in the gilded chambers of his heart.

Sometimes, she shared with him glimpses of faraway places she had seen in her time, verdant forests and shimmering seas and snowy peaks so unlike the arid landscape Tol called home. Beautiful, peaceful places that did not know the endless war and death that stained this one.

"You have been touched by the Sun Forger," declared the woman who had saved Tol from the brink of death, whom he had come to see as a mother, when he confided in her about the existence of this strange bond. "You are light-blessed, my child."

And because there was weight to her words, to her title of Knight Commander, no one contested her declaration. Not even Tol. What else could this bond be if not divine? The godly Forger who had created the dragons from the fire of the sun itself. He bore her mark on his breastbone, a mark no other draconic could boast of, seared in gold on his tawny skin during his rebirth.

The Sun Forger's presence in him was the hope Tol clung to when life was too bleak to bear, when his loneliness was so unendurable that he thought he might die from it. But as the world grew stranger, darker, so too did his connection to the Forger. Suddenly the impressions he got from her were of decaying forests and uncontrollable floods and deadly avalanches, a dismal understanding that the world as they knew it was dying. His own corner of the world was bathed in blood and death. The more monsters the knights slayed, the more monsters appeared. As if slicing off the head of one beast made it sprout four more, each more lethal than the last.

Tol couldn't bear their deaths. He felt each one, saw the shining golden threads that bound them all extinguish, and knew in his heart that all this senseless killing was not the answer. Surely there must be another way—a *better* way. He brought it up to his masters again, but no one would hear him.

The knights' way was the proper way, he was told; there was no alternative.

The masters' answer to this growing darkness was to see their own ranks grow, and for this, they required more dragon fire with which to forge new draconics. But dragons were elusive, choosing to remain hidden in all the faraway, deep places of the world. And knights could only earn their heart-flame through acts of bravery, something that required time. Time they did not have.

But then, Tol had his bond with the Sun Forger, the source of their holy order. No one knew where she slumbered; rumors and folklore were all they'd had to go on for centuries. But if anyone could find her, persuade her to help their holy cause, it was Tol.

Certain he'd found the solution to all their problems, Tol rushed to the Chasm where he knew the Knight Commander was posted. The Chasm was many things: a prison for beasts and humans alike, the fighting arena where they were pitted against each other for sport, and below that, the alchemists' workshop where all draconics were made, a place only those who had mastered in alchemy could enter. Tol was called to it now by an overwhelming sense of wrongness, his feet guiding him to the site of his rebirth as if of their own volition.

The workshop was aflame. Shouts and screams echoed off the walls, and there was a distinct smell of burning flesh as robed alchemists and armored knights tried to appease a great, raging beast thrashing about the workshop.

No, not a beast—a *dragon*, eyes wild as it tore through its most loyal servants with fire and teeth and claws.

Tol didn't understand. There was no reason for a dragon to turn on those who venerated it.

Pain stabbed through him, felt from both the dragon and the draconics. Their suffering became his own. And just as he began to understand why one had turned against the other, just as a crack formed in the foundation of his world, threatening to bring down everything he knew, a pain like no other erupted inside him.

Tol fell to his good knee, his scream making the earth beneath him tremble.

When Tol was a boy, his heart had given out. And despite

all the unthinkable hurts he'd endured since, all the battle wounds his body had weathered throughout his draconic training, there had never been a worse agony than that first death and the painful remolding of his heart and body that followed.

Until this.

Tol felt that same pain again now, only tenfold. It was the pain of a life ending. A heart ceasing to beat. A sun forever setting, never to rise again.

Death had a certain taste to it, one that was easy to recall even years later. It filled his mouth as he screamed toward the heavens, scorched through his senses as he writhed on the ground, tore through his body like a raging inferno.

Tol thought his alchemized heart had finally given out. That the flame within its golden chambers had been snuffed out like the torches in a great echoing hall blown out on a sudden gust of wind. That he had been deemed unworthy of this second life, and now he would know true death.

But it wasn't his heart that gave out.

It was *hers*.

He felt the Forger die, their connection severing in the most horrid of ways. Tol raged and cried at the sudden emptiness within him. He wished his heart would stop with hers, because that would be a far better fate than having to endure her absence. He wanted to dig his own heart out, throw it into the very flames that had forged it, angry that it could feel so much pain.

When the dragon turned its attention to Tol, a dark promise of death in its eyes, Tol held his head high. This time, when he died, it would be for good. He gladly accepted this fate, knowing what he now knew.

He was too full of pain and grief to realize that the very heart he was mourning had started beating again, ever so faintly.

The world could burn for all he cared; he very much intended to burn with it.

23

BAZ

THE INCOMING TIDE HAD THEM SCRAMBLING FARTHER up the shore. Baz stared forlornly at the disappearing cave mouth. Panic seized him as he realized no one else had emerged from the depths after them. "Did you see any sign of the others?"

Kai swore in answer, running a hand over his wet face. "We need to go back. Make sure they're safe."

If the others hadn't been sucked into this same peculiar void that had pulled Baz and Kai through time, then the monstrosity that was Keiran's reanimated corpse might have already gotten to them.

And if that didn't do it, then the deadly magic of the doors surely would.

Baz quickly assessed himself and Kai. They showed no signs of withering away like Travers and Lia had. He could only hope the others would be just as lucky.

Kai suddenly shot to his feet and waded into the roiling waves.

"What are you doing?" Baz bellowed after him.

"We have to get back."

"But the tide's coming in."

"So use your magic to make it low tide again. We were so close . . ."

A wave broke against Kai, pushing him into Baz's steadying arms. Kai shoved out of his grasp, motioning to the cave mouth with angry determination. "The tide, Brysden. *Now.*"

"Are you hearing yourself? Look what using my magic just did!" He pointed to the beaming lighthouse above them. "I brought us *back in time.* Who's to say going through the door now will bring us back to our friends? To the *present*?"

Kai's jaw tightened. "We have to try."

"No. I don't trust my power right now, not for a second. What if using time magic here only makes things worse? I don't know the rules–I didn't know time travel was even *possible.* I just–I can't–"

His heart was beating erratically, painfully pounding against his chest. Breathing became a foreign concept as he gasped for air and felt his vision begin to blur.

"Brysden. Hey, breathe." Kai grasped his face between his hands, forcing Baz to look at him. His face was inches from his own, his fingers digging softly into Baz's skin, threading themselves behind his neck. "Just breathe."

Baz focused on the stars in Kai's eyes, the dark depths of them drawing him to a calmer place where he could breathe again. In. Out. Ebb and flow.

The sea barreled into them, making Baz lurch forward into Kai. He gripped a fistful of Kai's sopping-wet shirt to hold himself steady, feeling Kai's fingers digging into the back of his neck as he tried to do the same. Wordlessly, they pulled each other back onto the slender strip of shoreline yet to be devoured by the tide, where they fell back panting in the wet sand. Teeth clattering at the wintry cold seeping through them, they exchanged a weighted glance.

Kai's throat bobbed. He was the first to look away. "Let's start by getting out of these wet clothes. We'll come back when the tide is low and figure things out."

"Okay."

Kai's composure soothed Baz's frayed nerves. They would find their bearings while they waited for low tide, try to figure out *when* exactly they were—and why they were here to begin with—before attempting to open the door again.

They drew themselves up and started toward the secret stairs to the Eclipse commons before glimpsing movement behind the window.

Right. This wasn't their time. They couldn't exactly barge into the Eclipse commons.

They locked eyes again, the weight of the situation almost but not quite laughable. "Best we head to town, then," Kai said.

There was no denying they were in the past once they got to Cadence. The cobblestoned streets were illuminated by gas lanterns—not everlight—and lined with horse-drawn carriages instead of cars. A few people ambled in the night, each of them dressed in fashions that were at least a century behind the times. Three-piece suits and suspenders and floppy hats, crinoline skirts and tailored coats. They threw Baz and Kai odd looks, and Baz hoped it was because of their sopping-wet clothes rather than the fact that those clothes were much more modern than anyone else's. Entirely out of place.

They ducked into a busy tavern, hoping to fly under the radar and get something warm in them to fight off the cold seeping into their bones.

They didn't make it very far. A man barred their way in, saying a gruff, "Hands."

"E-Excuse me?" Baz stammered.

"Your hands. We inspect sigils here." The barkeep pointed to a sign behind him that read *No Unchaperoned Eclipse-Borne.* The backs of his hands were bare. No magic to declare.

Bile rose in Baz's throat as he understood what this meant. He felt Kai stiffen at his side. They didn't know what year this was, but if establishments like this one were asking their would-be patrons to show their sigils and putting up such signs, it was undoubtedly a dangerous time to be Eclipse-born.

Baz lifted his left hand even as every instinct in him screamed this would not end well. Kai did the same, holding his middle finger slightly higher than the rest as he did so, an angry storm brewing beneath his features.

The barkeep's eyes narrowed on their Eclipse sigils. He motioned to the sign again. "You're not meant to be here alone, lads. Off you go on up to the College."

"Sir," Baz protested, "if we could just–"

"I'll not have you here unchaperoned, and without damper cuffs at that. Has no one told you you're supposed to stay behind Aldryn walls during the Bicentennial? Come back with an escort and cuffs."

The Bicentennial.

They had gone back *two hundred years* in time.

Kai swore under his breath.

Some patrons were glancing their way. A rowdy, red-faced man bellowed, "Send the Shadow-stained away!"

Baz's stomach locked up as this earned murmurs of consent from those around him. This was not good. If they'd thought things back in their time were bad for Eclipse-born, this was so much worse.

"What seems to be the problem, Hayworth?" a voice intoned.

A young woman appeared at the barkeep's side. She seemed to be their age–and quite well-off compared to most folks here.

Her strawberry-blond hair was swept up in a chignon, a small hat with a feather pinned atop her head. She wore a long woolly skirt and a coat cinched at the waist, matching pieces the color of a deep emerald sea. The cream-colored shirt she wore underneath was lacy and high necked, and a small emerald pendant rested on her chest.

The barkeep seemed annoyed at her intervention, though there was a deference in him that hinted to the young woman's social status. "Respectfully, Miss Cordie, this is no business of yours."

The young woman, Cordie, put her hands on her hips, an air of defiance in her green-blue eyes. "And if I choose to make it my business?"

The barkeep looked nervous now. "These Eclipse-born are unaccompanied," he said defensively, "and have no damper cuffs to boot. You know the rules."

"Yes, I do in fact know the rules. The law allows establishments like yours to demand Eclipse-born be accompanied, sure enough, but the requirement of damper cuffs has been illegal for some time now, Hayworth. You know better than that." This was delivered in a conversational tone, her polite smile never slipping. The barkeep fumbled for words, but Cordie beat him to it, adding, "Honestly, Hayworth, you disappoint me. Can't you see these two are sodden wet and looking for a place to get warm?"

"I'm sorry, Miss Cordie. Rules are rules. I can't risk the Regulators bearing down on me now, what with the Bicentennial going on. You know they'll come down harder on all of us in these times."

"Then I guess we'll be taking our leave." She heaved a withering sigh. "Such a shame to think I'll have to find another tavern to patronize. You know how much I like to come here after a long day at the art studio. But I simply cannot abide by this sort of prejudice."

"Miss Cordie . . ." There was a note of desperation and regret now in the barkeep's voice; no doubt he was scared to lose a patron as well-off as she seemed.

"Good night, Hayworth." To Baz and Kai, she said, "Come along, gents."

Cordie pulled Baz and Kai through the door as if they were old friends and led them down the dark street. She laughed when they were out of earshot, studying them from head to toe. "Tides, you two are a *mess*. Did you fall to the bottom of the Deep?"

"I'm sorry—who are you?" Kai asked.

"Right, where are my manners?" The girl stuck out a gloved hand. "I'm Cordie. Third-year Aldryn student, House New Moon."

Kai gingerly shook her hand. "Kai."

Cordie offered her hand to Baz when Kai refused to say more.

"Er, Baz. House Eclipse." *Obviously.*

She arched an amused brow. "I can see that. Sorry about the barkeep. He has one foot still in the past, that one."

So do we, it seems, Baz thought.

"He's not wrong, though," Cordie continued. "The Regulators are going to be far more severe with their rules. Cadence is usually great for Eclipse-born, but with the influx of delegates from other countries, no one wants any accidents happening." She scoffed. "Still, I assure you that kind of hostility isn't a reflection of every student here at Aldryn. Some of us are much more accepting than others."

"Glad to hear it," Kai said flatly, like he didn't quite believe her.

Cordie looked the two of them over. "May I ask where you're from?"

Shit. Surely they couldn't say they were Aldryn students—not in *this* time, at least.

"Um—"

Kai's elbow dug into Baz's side, cutting him off. "Luagua."

Cordie's gaze flickered to Baz, and he knew she must be thinking he clearly did not look Luaguan. Before he could think of some excuse, she asked, "And did you swim here from Luagua, then?" Her tone was tinged with amusement. "Tides, you must be freezing. I assume the sea swallowed up your luggage, too?"

Kai chuckled. "Something like that."

Cordie clasped her hands together. "You'll be needing some clothes, then. I'll fetch you something to change into. I assume you haven't registered at the college yet?"

"Registered?" Baz echoed.

"You don't have your badges." At their blank expressions, she added, "For the Bicentennial. All of us are asked to wear them to indicate which college and country we hail from. See?"

She pointed to an enamel pin affixed to the lapel of her coat, which Baz recognized as Aldryn College's emblem: open hands holding up the eight phases of the moon, which formed a ring around a dagger that dripped blood onto an open book.

"Right," he said. "We, er, hadn't gotten around to it yet."

"Well, come with me, and I'll help you get sorted."

Cordie started up the road with a saunter.

"What are we going to do?" Baz whispered furiously as he and Kai trailed behind her.

"Pretend we're from the Luaguan school," Kai said under his breath. "Karunang College. It's the oldest one in the Constellation Isles."

Aldryn's campus looked, for all intents and purposes, the same as it did two hundred years from now. A registration table had been set up in the courtyard near the dean's office. They gave their names—Kai didn't seem to mind using his real surname, so neither did Baz—and said they were from Karunang College. When the clerk frowned at the fact that they were evidently not listed among the Luaguan students, Baz thought surely they would be kicked to the curb.

"We were last-minute additions," Kai said smoothly. "They probably forgot to add us."

The student did not seem to care for that logic. "You'll have to clear this up with your dean. I can't give you a badge until–"

Cordie stepped in. "Honestly, Theopold, where is your sense of hospitality?" She ripped the list from his hands and added both their names at the bottom before plucking two badges from the pile in front of the dumbstruck student. "They can sort this out after the opening ceremony." She looked at Baz and Kai with the tiniest eye roll before motioning for them to follow. Theopold was red in the face, looking dejected at having been so schooled.

Cordie led them to the Noviluna dorms. She fished an old-fashioned key out of her pocket and ushered them into a dark-paneled room. A large bed took up most of the space, its luxurious bedding–clearly not the typical school-issued kind–perfectly tucked in. The room was neat as a pin, in a way that almost made it seem not lived in. The books on the desk were perfectly aligned in order of their height, and the assortment of dip pens and steel nibs and ink pots was organized neatly next to a straight stack of writing paper. Even the wardrobe that Cordie opened hinted at order, the garments arranged by color and fabric.

"Whose room is this?" Kai asked, no doubt noticing, as Baz did, that all the clothes were menswear: shirts and trousers and cravats in rich fabrics and prints that hinted at luxury, shoes that were so polished they glimmered in the soft light.

Cordie gave a little laugh as she pulled things out of the wardrobe. "My brother's. Don't worry, he won't mind. He has far too many clothes anyway." She shoved past them to set the garments she'd selected into two neat piles on the bed. "Now, put these on, and we'll head to the opening celebration. We've already missed too much!"

Baz and Kai exchanged a look. "Oh, well, we'd rather just head to the Eclipse commons, if that's all right?" Baz said. "It's been quite a journey."

"Nonsense. You must come and meet everyone. I swear my friends are nothing like that barkeep. Besides, I can't escort you down to Obscura Hall myself, since it's warded to allow only Eclipse-born in. But I'll introduce you to Thames and Polina–they'll be your Eclipse classmates here at Aldryn." She motioned for them to hurry. "I'll be outside if you need anything. Oh, and you can leave your wet clothes here. I'll see that they're properly laundered and brought back to you."

As soon as Cordie shut the door behind her, Baz whispered, "What are we going to do?"

"Let's just go along with it. Tide's still high. No point hiding out here like wanted criminals while we wait to get back."

Baz grumbled at the thought of going to a celebration full of people, especially after just narrowly escaping the celebration that had turned sideways in his *own* time. Everything about this place set him on edge; he was afraid to breathe wrong, to say the wrong thing, to do something that might set his magic disrupting the laws of time more than it already had. But Kai was right; there was nothing else for them to do while they waited for the tide to recede.

They exchanged a weighted glance before turning their backs to each other. The sounds of Kai undressing made Baz's stomach flip, not unpleasantly. He focused on getting out of his own wet clothes and into these blessedly dry ones. The fashion of this century felt stiff compared to his usual cozy sweater and slacks: dress pants held in place by suspenders, a high-collared shirt with ample sleeves, a patterned waistcoat, and a thicker frock coat to fight off the wintry cold.

Walking over to the standing mirror adorned with a silver frame, Baz gave himself a disgruntled once-over, fumbling with the patterned cloth that he figured must be a tie. He caught Kai's reflection in the mirror, looking at him with an odd expression.

"What?" Baz asked.

"You're tying that ascot all wrong. Here." Kai stepped in front of him and deftly undid the cloth Baz had tied up askew.

Baz was profoundly aware of how little space there was between them. He could feel Kai's breath on his skin, feel the heat of his fingers through his shirt as they worked on the ascot.

Kai kept his attention on the task, and only when it was done did he lift his eyes up to Baz. "Suits you," he said in that low, midnight voice.

Baz grew lightheaded, his stomach aflutter with nerves at the fervor in Kai's eyes. He was trying very hard not to think how well the fashion suited *him*. "Where did you learn how to do this, anyway?"

"Saw it in a book once. Farran was obsessed with fashion history."

The admission cut between them like ripped fabric.

"Oh," Baz said awkwardly. "That's . . . useful."

Kai frowned at whatever he heard in Baz's voice. A soft knock came at the door, followed by Cordie's muffled voice asking after them.

Baz cleared his throat. "Be right there."

Kai seemed happy to pretend the past minute hadn't happened, concentrated as he was on getting the Karunang badge affixed to the lapel of his coat. Baz fiddled with his own badge. The Karunang emblem was beautiful: an owl unfurling its wings, with the moon phases curved above its head and an eclipsed sun beneath its talons. Baz pinned it to his coat, trying to persuade himself he wore it convincingly enough. That he could pretend his way through this whole night.

The Bicentennial's opening celebration was held on the banks of the River Helene. The last time Baz was here had been the fall equinox festival. He remembered the magicked everlight lanterns dangling from trees whose leaves had just begun to turn, the students gathered on wool blankets as the air filled with the thrum of magic and the scent of hot cocoa and fried dough.

Now the trees were bare, the earth dusted with snow, and the lanterns that lit up the bank were not everlight but the mundane gas kind that had long preceded the more modern invention. Students dressed in the same stiff formal wear that Baz and Kai had donned milled about, clouds of steam rising from their mouths as they exchanged laughter and bottles of brownish liquid. Near the frozen water's edge, students were setting off fireworks that burst above them in enchanted designs, illuminating the night with the colors of each lunar sigil–except for the gold of the Eclipse, Baz noticed.

Most people they passed gave Cordie amicable nods and friendly smiles; she seemed to be well-liked and had a kind word for everyone who greeted her.

"Oh, there's Polina," Cordie exclaimed as she spotted a girl who stood apart from the crowd, watching the fireworks with quiet awe from where she leaned against a tree. She was short and stocky, with dark, fluffy curls and an olive undertone to her fair skin. She and Cordie exchanged prim air-kisses.

"I thought you wouldn't show," Polina said in a gentle, barely audible voice.

Cordie squeezed the girl's hands, her expression turning fiercely protective. "Is everything all right? Did Thames leave you here alone?"

Polina shrugged. "He went off with your brother. I didn't want to intrude." She eyed Baz and Kai with shy curiosity, as if just now noticing their presence. Her gaze lingered on Baz, and a faint blush colored her cheeks.

Cordie pulled her toward them. "Polina, let me introduce you to

Baz and Kai, Eclipse students from Luagua. Polina is one of two Eclipse-born students here at Aldryn."

"That's two too many, if you ask me," a voice slithered from behind them. "Abominations, all of them."

There stood a young man who stared at Polina with such visceral hate, it almost made Baz want to cower the way she did now, ducking her head trying to make herself appear smaller. At his side, he felt Kai tensing as if for a fight. The student who'd spoken had slicked-back dark hair and a severe brow. He was flanked by two of his friends, both burly in stature and just as hateful in appearance. Their combative stances made it clear they were looking for trouble.

"No one asked you, Wulfrid," snapped Cordie. "Keep walking."

Gone was the polite manner with which Cordie had addressed the barkeep earlier. It was as if a wolf had broken free to replace her saccharine exterior, called to the surface by these bullies.

Wulfrid sneered at her. "Or what?" He made a show of looking around, his gaze flitting over Baz and Kai as if they were nothing before landing on Cordie again. "Not quite as invincible as you believe yourself to be when your brother's not around, are you?"

Cordie advanced on him with her hands fisted at her sides. The boy didn't even flinch. "Come on, then, Seer. Do your worst." When Cordie merely glared at him, he smiled with oily satisfaction. "You're a pathetic excuse of a lunar mage. Mingling with Eclipse scum. Next to no magic to speak of yourself. Everyone knows you're only here because of your family name."

Cordie's jaw worked, her eyes blinking rapidly. Wulfrid had clearly hit a nerve.

"I think that's enough."

This came from Kai, who was watching Wulfrid with barely leashed rage.

Wulfrid's attention darted to him—and the Eclipse sigil visible on both his and Baz's hands. His lip curled in disgust. "I can't believe they're allowing your kind to participate in the Bicentennial. You're a stain on our school's history."

"You'll be a stain on this snow if you don't walk away right now," Kai said, voice low and threatening. Like a beast prowling the night, he stepped closer to Wulfrid, towering over him by at least a head.

Wulfrid lifted his chin in defiance, but he couldn't hide the way his throat bobbed in fear or the faint tremor in his voice as he asked, "And who might you be to address me in such a way, Eclipse scum?"

Kai's smile was cold and unsettling. "Call me scum one more time, and what I'll be is your worst nightmare."

Whatever Wulfrid saw in Kai's piercing gaze was menacing enough to get him to back off. With a sneer, he motioned to his friends to follow him.

"Come on," Cordie said once they were gone, her eyes never leaving the back of Wulfrid's head. She grasped Polina's hand. "Let's go find Thames and—"

"I don't want to stay out here anymore," Polina said weakly, tugging back her hand and holding it to her chest. She looked pale. "I should have stayed in Obscura Hall."

"Wulfrid's a menace," Cordie argued. "Don't let him ruin our fun."

"You don't understand." Polina's voice was meek, quiet. "Wulfrid might be menace enough to say something, but plenty of other students share his opinions. I feel them staring. I know what they think of us."

Cordie looked like she wanted to press her friend further but didn't. There was a bleak sort of understanding in her eyes as she nodded, saying, "Of course. Let me walk you back to campus."

"No, really, you stay here. Enjoy the festivities. I can find my way back."

"We'll go with her," Baz chimed in. This earned him a beaming look from Polina and a raised brow from Cordie.

"Are you certain?" Cordie asked. "You only just got here."

"We're really tired after everything that happened," Kai chimed in, catching on to Baz's plan. "It'll give us time to get settled." More like time to prepare to slip into Dovermere as soon as the tide was low again.

Cordie looked only slightly dejected. "Well, all right, then. But oh, you *must* come to our salon tomorrow and meet everyone."

"What's this salon she was talking about?" Baz asked Polina as they made their way toward campus, the sounds of fireworks and laughter slowly dying behind them.

"It's this social justice club that Cordie's brother started," Polina said, cheeks warming as though unused to the attention. "A place for like-minded students to gather and discuss Eclipse magic, its place in the world, what we can do to fight against all these rules and regulations that limit our magic." She gave Baz a sidelong glance. "It's a wonder they even let Eclipse students come to the Bicentennial. As far as I know, you're the only ones who came. I know things are far better in the Constellation Isles. You're very lucky to study there."

"We are," Kai said with a note of fond yearning.

"There have been some strides made in Elegy in recent years," Polina continued, "but we've got a long road ahead still. These academic salons are working toward change. You'll see for yourselves tomorrow."

They hopefully would not *be* here tomorrow, Baz thought, his mind going back to Dovermere, the Hourglass, and the time magic he was trying very hard not to dwell on.

They found themselves going down the elevator to the same hall they'd left back in their own time. *This* elevator wasn't as rickety as it was two hundred years from now. It was pristine and shiny and went down smoothly. The wards let them through without a fuss, recognizing in them the power of the Eclipse.

But the inside of Obscura Hall made Baz stumble.

Gone were the fields of gold bowing toward the sea; gone was the willow tree that led into the commons. The elevator doors opened onto a path lined with round, glass lanterns all lit by the glow of fireflies dancing within. They were in an enchanted garden, with marble statues overcome with lichen and archways drooping with delicate flowers lining the path that sloped down toward a quaint stone cottage. The sky above them was dark, just as Baz's own illusioned sky had been.

"Is this your illusion?" Baz asked Polina. Obscura Hall was enchanted to reflect a scene from the most senior Eclipse student's memory.

Polina blinked at him. "How did you know it was an illusion?"

Shit. "Oh, we have the same thing at Karunang." Baz could only hope that was true–or that Polina would never find out otherwise.

Kai threw Baz a withering look that said, *Smooth, Brysden.*

Polina appeared unconcerned. "This is Thames's. He's a fourth year, I'm only a second year. You'll meet him tomorrow, I'm sure."

She opened the cottage door for them, and as they stepped inside, they found themselves in the commons proper. This corner of Obscura Hall was, by all means, the same as they'd left it that very morning, though much less threadbare. The sunflower wallpaper was pristine, gold filigree shining under the lamplight and the glow of the flames that crackled pleasantly in the fireplace. The sofas were in the same spots, bright reds and oranges and yellows, where in the present they were subdued shades of browns and rust. The curtains looked like they were the same, too, though not yet quite as moth-eaten.

"Up here are our dorms," Polina said, leading them up the stairs. "I'm in this room. Thames in that one. You can have your pick of the others." Her cheeks flushed as she met Baz's eye and said, "If you need anything, don't be shy to knock."

"Th-Thank you," Baz stuttered.

"Of course. Good night." Polina fluttered her lashes prettily at him before she disappeared inside her room.

Baz had the odd thought that she might have been *flirting* with him, though for the life of him, he couldn't see why. He met Kai's gaze. The Nightmare Weaver lifted an amused brow.

"Shut up," Baz muttered before heading back downstairs.

The two of them sat by the fire, waiting for Polina to fall asleep so they could slip out the secret door—which was still there, thankfully—and into Dovermere. If Baz were to close his eyes, he could almost imagine he was in the present. The sounds were the same. The smells. The sofa was firmer than he remembered, but with Kai here by his side, it still felt like home.

It hit him then that they had truly gone back in time, and he didn't know if he wanted to burst out crying or start laughing at this strange twist of fate.

"What do you think happened to them?" Kai asked, lost in the hypnotic flames. "Virgil, Nisha, Vera . . ."

"Keiran?"

"Yeah. Or whatever the fuck was wearing his face."

They hadn't had the chance to speak of it yet—of the fact that Keiran had been *revived* right before their eyes. Baz didn't know how to feel about it. Ever since he'd watched Keiran die, he'd been pushing all his guilt way down. Guilt at robbing Keiran of his parents. Guilt at being the reason why Keiran had done everything he'd done at all, because all of it had been to see his parents again.

He wasn't sure if Keiran had survived the sleepscape this time, but if he had, perhaps this could be a second chance for him.

But it wasn't really *him*, was it? There was so much they didn't know about Reanimator magic, so there was no way to tell how much of Keiran would be, well, Keiran.

And what if this soulless version of him wanted revenge?

What if, with all pretense of civility shed at last, Keiran meant to come after Baz?

Or Emory?

Baz felt the panic from earlier crawl over his skin again, his lungs constricting as he fought to remember how to breathe. "What in the Deep are we going to do?"

Kai met his gaze, the glow of flames from the fireplace dancing in his eyes. "We'll figure it out, Brysden."

The panic receded, as if the Nightmare Weaver were leeching away all his fears. That was what Kai's presence did to Baz. What it had always done, he realized. A soothing balm, a confidence booster. Someone to keep him grounded.

"I'm glad we're together, at least," Baz offered.

"Me too."

Kai looked unguarded, as if all the sharp edges he liked to arm himself with had suddenly been filed away. But the moment disappeared as Kai turned to the window, the cove beyond. "Let's just hope we don't get tangled in this mess any more than we already are."

24

KAI

A T LOW TIDE, THEY WENT OUT TO FACE THE CAVES ONCE
more, only to find that Dovermere, too, was different in this
time.

Kai and Baz wove through the network of tunnels and cav-
erns without incident, though with each step closer to the Hourglass, Kai grew more and more uncertain. He could tell Baz was
unnerved too. He'd gone completely quiet, his breathing coming
in shallow bursts as he no doubt assessed the risks of opening the
door again.

Before they could even reach the Belly of the Beast, they found
themselves stopped by a solid wall of rock.

"What the fuck?" Kai muttered.

Where the tunnel should have opened wider into the grotto that
housed the Hourglass, it simply came to a dead end. He and Baz
pushed and prodded at the wall with no luck. But if there was no
Belly of the Beast . . .

"Maybe the Hourglass doesn't exist yet?" Baz said, puzzled.

Kai's mind raced with possibilities. None of them made sense. "We can't have appeared here out of thin air. There has to be a door."

"I don't feel it," Baz said, frowning at the wall.

"Feel what?"

"The magic of Dovermere. Of the door. It . . . it used to whisper to me. Like it recognized my own magic. Like they were one and the same."

Kai realized he didn't feel anything either. He heard no song. Felt no pull.

There was *nothing*.

Baz swore, looking at Kai with wide eyes. "What if we're truly stuck here?"

If there was no Belly of the Beast, there could be no Hourglass. No door to the Deep.

No way for them to return to their time.

Kai refused to believe it. "Can't you just bring the door back?"

Baz gulped down on the fear he was clearly trying to keep leashed. In a quiet, broken voice, he said, "I don't trust myself to try."

"Brysden . . ."

"No, listen. I don't know if I alone did this or if it's Dovermere itself that brought us here. Either way, we don't know what my magic might do. Even if I were to make the door reappear, I don't know the first thing about how take us back to the present."

Kai had to admit he was right. "So what do you suggest?"

"Maybe I can find answers here. Another Timespinner who might have studied time travel? I don't know."

Of course Baz's answer to their problem would be Tides-damned *research*.

"This isn't a time we want to be stuck in, Brysden," Kai cautioned, thinking of Wulfrid. The encounter still slithered unpleasantly along his spine–how much Wulfrid reminded him of Artem, and all the bullies like him. "We'll need to be careful."

"I know." Baz scratched the back of his head in thought. "We'll need to be mindful of our actions too. Surely there are rules, ways that our being here might affect the fabric of time. What if we trigger something that changes the future–our present?"

Kai's mind hurt just thinking about it. "One thing at a time. First, let's get out of here before the tide traps us in. The rest we'll figure out together."

Kai was in the printing press again.

The nightmarish scene was as it always was: it was the printing press one minute, then Dovermere, then the sleepscape. Machinery and rubble. Crumbling stone and crushing waves. Darkness and stars that reached for the one person Kai could not bear to be parted from.

Again the scenes bled into one another. Again Kai called out to Baz, and when Baz twisted toward him, he braced himself to see his friend transform into that towering umbra crowned in obsidian. Braced for the creature he had glimpsed in the sleepscape to speak in that tongue again, beckoning Kai to open the door.

But none of that happened. Baz only stared at him–not the real Baz, but an imagined one plucked from Kai's own nightmares–his features unchanged. There was no crowned umbra, making Kai wonder if it had left the sleepscape entirely. He had *seen* it go into Keiran's revived body. Maybe that meant it would no longer plague Kai's nightmares.

What happened next was worse than the umbra:

On Baz's neck appeared deep bruises, imprints of Kai's fingers. Behind his glasses, his brown eyes pinned Kai with accusation.

"I wish you were the one to have disappeared," the nightmare Baz spat, "instead of her."

Her. Romie, Emory, it didn't matter who he meant. It was all the same in the end.

Kai moved backward out of the prison of his own fears, scrambling to jump into another nightmare, any nightmare, just not his own.

A different sort of darkness called to him. He stepped into a nightmare that felt inexplicably safe, if nightmares could be called that at all. He felt the same tug as when he'd glimpsed Emory before, as if a glittering ribbon of stars had been pulling him to her.

Someone was there, but it wasn't Emory. It was a young man, a boy around his age, though Kai couldn't see his face as he leaned over a body lying in a pool of blood, shoulders shaking with quiet sobs.

"Hello?" Kai asked, his voice sounding distorted in his ears.

The boy did not seem to hear him. But another appeared from behind the first. He had fair skin and a wiry frame, with floppy chestnut curls. He stepped in front of the crying boy and looked straight at Kai from behind thick, half-moon glasses.

"You shouldn't be here," he said.

There was a shove, hands pushing him out–

Kai awoke with a gasp.

There was no confusion this time. He knew he was awake, knew the young man who'd pushed him out of the nightmare was real, because he *recognized* him. Not his face, but his magic. The way Dreamers could recognize each other in the sleepscape, acting like beacons to one another.

Except this had been no Dreamer.

It was another Nightmare Weaver.

25

ROMIE

WHERE THE WYCHWOOD HAD BEEN DAMP FORESTS and rotting earth, the Wastes were dry and barren. This came as no surprise to Romie, who by now had memorized most of *Song of the Drowned Gods* in a way that would make her brother proud.

This world is a forge. Brutal and scorching and full of finely crafted things.

And brutal it was, by the looks of it—though nowhere near as scorching as Romie would have thought. Perhaps the chill that ran through her was only from the residual effects of whatever Emory had done to her back on the ley line. But her strength had returned enough now that she could draw herself to her feet and marvel at the world around her.

They were in a strange red-hued desert full of eroded, domed cliffs and rugged mountains as far as the eye could see. All around them sprouted giant cacti and odd trees with twisted, bristled branches. The winged beasts that had momentarily blotted out the sun were gone, and so too was the monster who'd worn Keiran's face. Still, Romie was left with the eerie impression of being watched.

This place was too open, too wide. And if it was anything like Clover's book, they could expect more beasts where those came from.

Romie swept a gaze over the others, still catching their breath. Nisha was right beside her. Their eyes locked.

"Are you real?" Romie asked, scared to know the answer. Scared that she might still be under the torture of the umbrae.

Nisha cupped Romie's cheek, eyes shimmering with unshed tears. "I'm real."

Romie sagged against her with a quiet sob, all the vulnerability she'd never dared to show erupting out of her. She had no fight in her left to hide it. To act the part of the brave Dreamer.

Out of the corner of her eye, she saw Virgil Dade swallowing Emory in a tight hug. Emory clung to him, her rapid blinks indicating she was trying hard not to cry. Romie couldn't help but wonder at the bond that had formed between them in her absence.

Virgil held Emory at arm's length then, looking her over with a somber expression. "Are you all right?"

Emory nodded, though she looked dazed, uncertain. She glanced down at her hands like she was searching for signs of silver in her veins, the same way Romie was. But it was just like last time. Emory *should* have Collapsed–had seemed right on the verge of it, if her silver veins had been any indication–but hadn't.

Romie left Nisha's side to kneel over Aspen. The witch was still unconscious, her clothes a torn, bloodied mess around her middle, but the wound was closed in such a way that it almost had Romie wondering if she'd imagined Keiran plunging his hand through her chest.

Romie caught Emory's gaze. "Will she recover?"

Emory hugged herself. "I think I managed to undo the damage."

She stared at the archway where the door had been, her face white with horror. "Virgil, please tell me that wasn't really Keiran."

Virgil sighed. "You're not going to like this, but yeah, it sort of was."

"How?"

"Artem Orlov got a Reanimator to bring him back from the dead." The acidity in Virgil's voice as he explained the particulars of how that had happened made it clear he was disgusted with such a perverse act of magic. "I told Artem reanimation would come at a cost. Interfering with death like that, even for someone who's Collapsed . . . A person can't come back wholly themselves. That might've looked like Keiran, but he came back without his soul intact, that's for sure."

"If he had one to begin with," Nisha mumbled.

Emory looked like she wanted to say something but didn't. Romie knew what she was thinking: that whatever had taken hold of Keiran was not human. Those eyes . . .

They mirrored those of the demon who'd possessed Bryony.

"You said someone who's Collapsed," Romie said with a frown. "You mean the Reanimator who brought Keiran back?"

"Yeah."

"And that kind of unchecked power didn't kill all of you?" Romie choked out.

The others looked at her as if she'd grown three heads.

Virgil smacked his own head. "Shit, that's right, they don't know."

"Know what?" Romie snapped.

"About Collapsing. Turns out it's not the curse it's made out to be, not really. It gives Eclipse-born limitless power, and most seem to be able to live with it if they can escape the Unhallowed Seal." He nudged Emory. "So you don't need damper cuffs or any of that shit if you Collapse while we're here. If Baz and Kai can handle it, so can you."

The ground tilted beneath Romie's feet. "What did you just say?" Her pulse stuttered as Virgil and Nisha exchanged a look. *"Did Baz Collapse?"*

It was the other girl who answered–Vera, if Romie remembered her name correctly, having met her once before at the Veiled Atlas when she was looking for answers on Adriana Kazan. "He's been Collapsed ever since that incident at your father's printing press."

The words were slow to sink in. "No. That would mean . . ." Romie took a step back. "My father's Collapsing got people *killed*."

"Your father was never the one who Collapsed," Nisha said gently. "Baz was. Your father took the fall for him."

Romie breathed out a disbelieving laugh. "We're talking about *Baz*. My recluse of a brother. The guy who's afraid of using even the tiniest speck of magic."

"You've been gone for quite a while, dream girl," Virgil said. "Your brother's kind of a badass now."

"Tides, *that's* how he was able to stop my Collapsing," Emory said suddenly, staring off into the middle distance. "Back in Dovermere, when we were fighting against Jordyn-turned-umbra . . . That kind of power . . ."

"It could only come from someone who's Collapsed," Virgil finished for her. "If you want more proof, take the magic Kai used in Dovermere to fight the umbrae. I mean, *we* were passed out around the Hourglass at the time and didn't see it, but from what we heard, it was pretty incredible."

Emory frowned. "I kept wondering if I'd imagined it, but . . . How did Kai even have access to his magic? He had the Unhallowed Seal."

"Baz took it off," Vera said. "He used his own Collapsed magic to revert time, make it so that Kai never got the Unhallowed Seal. Which means Kai now also has limitless magic."

Limitless magic.

Romie locked eyes with Emory. A silent exchange passed between them. This could explain Emory's apparent inability to Collapse, because maybe she already had. But Emory shook her head and said, "That's not what this is. I haven't Collapsed."

"What if you did?" Romie pushed back. "If Baz never knew he Collapsed, maybe it's the same for you." To the others, she asked, "After they've Collapsed, does their blood run silver every time they use magic in really big ways?"

"No," Nisha said. "The silver only stays for the duration of the Collapsing itself, a few days tops. Then it's back to red."

Emory gave her a look as if to say *See?* But Romie couldn't shake this feeling that something was off. She wanted to trust Emory's grasp on her magic, but she couldn't deny the kernel of fear that had taken root inside her ever since that night in the Wychwood with Bryony—maybe even before then.

It wasn't only the silver she'd seen running along Emory's arms as she used her magic. It was the way Romie had *felt* when Emory used all that power to cast the demon out of Bryony, and again in the grotto to unmake the umbrae—as if a conduit had been opened between them, and Emory were siphoning all of Romie's power to her.

Emory couldn't be limitless if she was stealing power from someone else.

Romie turned away from Emory, shutting out that awful word—*Tidethief.* "If Baz and Kai have this limitless magic, why are they not here? In fact, better question: How are *any* of you here?"

"We came to get you," Nisha said. "Both of you."

"But mostly you," Vera added matter-of-factly to Emory.

Emory's brows shot up. "Me? Why?"

"Things are really bad back home," Virgil said. "The tides have been all out of whack for months now, coastlines are flooded—"

"Wait—*months*?" Emory interrupted. "We were only in the Wych-wood for a few days."

"That can't be right. You went through the door months ago. We just celebrated the solstice."

"But . . . I swear, it's only been eleven days for us. How is that possible?"

Romie felt just as puzzled as everyone else looked. Could it be that time flowed differently in each world? If so, how much more time would elapse back home while they kept going toward the sea of ash?

"Best we not open that can of worms, I think," Virgil said with a forced, frenetic laugh. "Point is, the Regulators think the Eclipse-born are rising against the world at *your* request, Em. I know, ridiculous, right? They think you're the Shadow reborn. So we need you to come back and show them you're not, well, evil."

"How did they even find out I'm a Tidecaller?"

"Someone in the Order must have talked," Nisha said. "Artem, most likely."

"The bastard," Virgil muttered darkly.

"But how are you all *here*?" Romie pressed, ignoring the little voice in her head that wondered if Emory actually *was* the Shadow reborn. "How did you even get the Hourglass to open?"

They shouldn't have been able to cross through worlds, not without Emory's Tidecaller blood. Not without being themselves a key—which they were decidedly not.

"Baz reversed time back to when the door was open," Nisha explained. "Limitless power, remember?"

"As for how we survived the journey across worlds and didn't end up like those students who washed ashore last year . . ." Vera produced a compass that hung from her neck. "My theory is we have this thing to thank for that."

"Where did you get that?" Emory exclaimed. "That's–that was my mother's."

"Yeah." Vera shifted uncomfortably. "Adriana Kazan, right?"

"How do you–"

"A long story for another time. The important thing is, I think this compass grants those of us who *aren't* keys safe passage through worlds."

"We don't know that," Nisha said.

"How else do you explain us three still being alive? Those students last year died because they didn't have what it takes to travel through the sleepscape: Emory's Tidecaller blood."

Emory blanched. "You think they'd have survived if they'd had the compass with them?"

Vera nodded. "Protection against the absolute weirdness that is the space between worlds." She fiddled with the compass, eyeing Emory. "Adriana left this with you, right? Then she disappeared, and we know she somehow made it through the door, since she left the epilogue there for *you* to find." She pointed to Romie at that. "Maybe you Dreamers are made of different stuff than us and that means you're able to withstand the sleepscape longer without the compass's protection. I don't know. But without this thing guiding us, I don't think we'd have found the Wychwood door. It pointed us right to it, and then to the *next* door once we were in the Wychwood."

"And what about Keiran?" Emory asked.

"I thought we'd have to fight him once we realized he'd slipped through the door with us," Nisha said, "but he suddenly didn't seem to care about us. He slipped right through our fingers, disappearing into shadows. We hoped that might be the last we saw of him until we followed the compass and found him at the next door with you."

"Okay, back up," Romie said, her head hurting. "You got *Baz* to open the Hourglass, watched a Reanimator bring Tides-damned Keiran back to life, then managed to find us in the Wychwood thanks to Emory's lost mother's compass." She ticked off every statement on her fingers, each more ludicrous than the last. "Where is Baz in all of this?"

The three of them exchanged looks that unsettled Romie.

"Is he all right?" Emory asked in a small voice, echoing Romie's thoughts.

"He's fine," Virgil said with forced confidence.

"We don't know that," Nisha corrected him.

Romie felt her nerves fraying. "Someone had better tell me where my brother is or I swear—"

"We lost him in the sleepscape," Nisha relented with a sigh. "Him and Kai."

"What do you mean you *lost them*? Are they—*alive*?"

"We don't know."

Romie felt dizzy. For a moment, it was as if she were back on the ley line having all her energy drained, or in the sleepscape with stars swirling around her, making her wonder where was up and where was down. Her world was tilting on its axis. First Keiran coming back to life. Then Aspen nearly dying, Emory's apparent inability to Collapse despite using scores of magic, and the suspicion that she was leeching power from Romie. And now Baz . . .

No. He couldn't be dead. Romie refused to even consider it.

"There was this kind of . . . opening," Vera explained. "Almost like another portal forming within the sleepscape. It sucked Baz and Kai right in. One minute, they were with us, and the next, they were gone."

Pulled into another door. Forced down another path.

"I'm sure they'll be fine." Virgil's feigned cheeriness convinced no one. "They probably just ended up somewhere else in the sleepscape, right? Or maybe back in Dovermere. Anyway, with both their Collapsed powers, I've no doubt they can do just about anything."

Romie clamped down on the worry that was threatening to pull her under. Virgil was right—he *had* to be, because she refused to believe her brother was gone.

"We should settle in for the night, wait for your friend here to wake up," Vera said after a long silence.

The day was rapidly fading around them—*too* rapidly. The moon already hung low in the sky despite the sun still being out, tinting the world in hazy hues of orange and purple. An eerie sound pierced the quiet, a faraway beast, perhaps, like the mythical ones the warrior fought in Clover's book.

Romie shuddered. "Let's just hope whatever's in this world lets us live till morning."

"And that Keiran doesn't come back to finish us off," Virgil added. "I hope he gets his eyes plucked out by those giant-ass birds. He deserves every bit of pain after what he made you go through, Em."

"What he made us *all* go through," Emory said, her cheeks tinged pink as Virgil threw an arm around her and gave her a playful kiss atop the head.

"Yeah, but you especially," Virgil said. "Playing with your heart like that . . . You were always far too good for him."

"I swear if we'd known what he intended to do, we would have told you," Nisha chimed in, squeezing Emory's shoulder.

Emory very pointedly ignored Romie's stare as the pieces suddenly fell into place.

It wasn't just that Emory, like the rest of the Selenic Order, had been oblivious to Keiran's true intentions. Something had happened between the two of them. Something Emory had been keeping from Romie after swearing there would be no more secrets between them.

Hurt and betrayal seared through Romie. As she watched the familiarity between the three of them, it struck her that these people *she* had gotten close to in secrecy last year, these friendships she'd made outside of Emory . . . they weren't hers alone now. Emory had as much of a claim on Virgil and Nisha as she did, perhaps even more after what they'd all gone through. And Emory was the one keeping Romie out of the loop now, giving her a taste of her own medicine with this vital piece of the puzzle that she'd hidden from her.

It made sense, of course. Romie should have put it together before, but she'd been too caught up in everything else to see what was so obvious now. She supposed in the grand scheme of things it didn't matter whether Emory and Keiran had been more than what Emory had let her believe, but it was the lying that bothered her.

Because if Emory had lied about this, what else was she keeping from her?

As Emory and Virgil looked over Aspen, and Vera ventured out to forage for some kind of edible plants, Romie volunteered to find firewood–or anything they could burn–along with Nisha. With the sun rapidly going down, the desert had turned frigid, something Romie hadn't thought possible in a world that Clover described as a forge, full of warmth and sunlight. But then, the sickness Mrs. Amberyl had foreseen plaguing this world did involve a dimming sun, a world plunged into darkness.

Romie barely noticed the silence that fell over them as they walked away from the others, her thoughts still intent on Emory. She snapped out of it only when Nisha nudged her gently. "Everything all right with you?"

Romie mustered a smile. "Of course. Why wouldn't it be?"

"I'm pretty sure you were about to pass out when we found you back in that grotto," Nisha said, unconvinced. "And I don't know. You seem preoccupied."

Romie couldn't help the rush of feelings that came back to her at this reminder that Nisha could always see right through her.

And Tides—Nisha was really *here*. It hit Romie all over again as she took her in. Nisha looked just as she remembered—better, even. Long lashes fluttering prettily against her high cheekbones. Those dark eyes she could get lost in. Black hair unbound, tucked over one slender shoulder. The disparity between the outfits they each wore was almost laughable: Nisha in a fine-knit sweater tucked into wide-legged corduroy pants complete with dainty brogues, and Romie in a lacy high-neck blouse and ample skirts that were at least a few centuries behind the fashion back in their world.

"I just can't believe you're here," Romie breathed. She wanted to reach out and touch Nisha, to solidify that this wasn't all a twisted dream. But she didn't, reminded of how they'd left things before Romie had slipped through the Hourglass. She swallowed past an unpleasant tightness in her throat. "I thought I'd never see you again."

Nisha smiled timidly at that. "Does that mean you're happy to see me?"

"Are you kidding? Of course I'm happy to see you. You traveled across worlds for me . . . and Emory," she added quickly. It dawned on her that Nisha might have moved on from the brief romance they'd had, that she might have come here only for the friendship she'd made with Emory and not for the feelings she'd once had for Romie. After all, Romie had messed things up between them, isolating herself in her search for the epilogue, losing everything and everyone she cared for in her all-consuming pursuit of destiny.

"So what's bothering you, then?"

Romie chewed on the inside of her cheek. She wanted to let it all pour out of her, how it had felt like Emory was leeching from

Romie's power when she stood on that ley line, how betrayed she was that Emory had lied about Keiran. How she couldn't yet bring herself to voice her suspicions that Emory might indeed be a Tide-*thief*, as the slur went.

Instead, Romie said, "Remember when you last found me in the greenhouse?"

"Before your initiation?" Nisha asked, taken aback.

Romie nodded, smiling fondly at the memory. The greenhouse had always been *theirs*, and it was no wonder that Nisha had found her there before Romie slipped through worlds. Nisha had told her the time and place she was expected at Dovermere for the Selenic Order initiation, and though she hadn't explicitly told Romie *not* to go, Romie remembered her worry.

"You told me to be careful," Romie said. "And I . . . you left before I could say anything, but I remember swearing to myself that I'd see you on the other side. That if I made it through the initiation ritual and survived Dovermere, I'd come back and make things right between us."

Nisha's eyes blazed as if they housed the remnants of the fading sun. "I remember hoping for the same thing."

"Do you think it's too late now?" Romie asked, heart in her throat, skin hot at the intensity in Nisha's gaze. She wasn't sure where this blatant honesty was coming from—maybe it had something to do with nearly dying at the hands of a demon wearing a resurrected Keiran's face and her own best friend's magic. But if she didn't ask now, she wasn't sure she'd have the courage to later.

"No." Nisha stepped closer to her. "I would have waited for you however long it took."

"That won't be necessary."

Romie wasn't sure who made the first move, but suddenly they were kissing, Nisha's hands laced behind her neck, and Romie's tangled up in her silky hair. Romie lost herself in the warmth and familiarity of Nisha's lips, transported back to before, to the early days at Aldryn College when everything had been exciting and new. When she'd been falling head over heels for Nisha, sneaking kisses in the greenhouse, just a normal girl doing normal girl things. Before the Order had sucked her in, before the song had snuck into her dreams, before the hunt for the lost epilogue had consumed her whole.

Romie clung to this moment of normalcy, the utter bliss of Nisha's kiss. It was like nothing had changed between them, even as everything was changing around them.

The rest of her world might be imploding, but this, at least, was something to hold fast to.

26

EMORY

EMORY WAS CHOKING ON LUNAR FLOWERS.

Black narcissus and indigo hollyhocks and white orchids and purple poppies grew between her lungs, sprouted up her throat, their roots sinking deep into her heart, draining all the blood from her veins and marrow from her bones. Before her stood her ghosts, whispering in her ear:

Tidethief.

Your fault.

Everything you touch crumbles to dust.

A hand touched her arm. With a gasp, she jerked awake to find Virgil leaning over her, face shadowed in concern. "Bad dream?"

Brushing the base of her throat, Emory blinked around her in confusion. The two of them were the only ones awake; it was barely dawn, and freezing with the absence of the sun.

"Must have been," Emory muttered. The flowers weren't real. Her ghosts weren't here. For now, at least. Peering at Virgil, she said, "I see ghosts whenever I use my magic. In sleep and in waking."

"Ghosts?" Virgil looked around as if he could make them out in the dark. "Anyone I know?"

Emory shuddered. It felt like both Keiran and Lizaveta were here, hovering unseen between them.

Virgil seemed to feel it too. He sat down next to her. "You know, I did try to stop the Reanimator from bringing Keiran back. But even she had no choice. We were all under Artem's compulsion."

"Why did Artem want to do such a thing to begin with?"

"Grief made him irrational. He tried it with Lizaveta first. He thought the Reanimator might have been able to bring her back properly with her boosted-up Collapsed magic, but obviously it failed." Virgil threw a pebble in the dead embers of their spent fire. "Now Lizaveta is gone for good, and Keiran's possessed by whatever the Deep that was."

Unshed tears gleamed in Virgil's eyes, making Emory's heart twist. It felt surreal to have him and the others here. The last time she saw him, he was lying at the foot of the Hourglass, knocked unconscious by Keiran and Lizaveta's combined power. And now he was here, sitting beside her in this strange world, dealing with the same profound grief and betrayal she was still trying to untangle herself.

"I'm sorry about Lizaveta," she murmured, remembering how close the two of them were. "She was . . . nice."

Virgil snorted. "Don't lie. She was a total bitch to you." He patted her hand. "But I do appreciate the sentiment. I hope her soul can find peace. Keiran's can burn, for all I care."

His words sounded halfhearted, as if he couldn't quite forget that Keiran had been his friend. The same way Emory couldn't forget what he'd been to her before the end.

The question left her lips before she could think twice: "Were you in love with her?"

"Liza?" Virgil considered it. "You know, it's funny. I never hid my interest in her, and she never exactly discouraged it, either. We'd kiss sometimes at parties whenever she felt ignored by Keiran or was trying to get his attention. I knew I was an option she kept in her back pocket. But I would have taken any crumb she gave me and called it affection, just on the off chance that she might one day fancy me back. Even knowing what she did, what she was willing to do to her friends . . ." He caught Emory's eye, a sad smile touching his lips. "Those feelings don't just go away overnight, do they?"

Emory knew exactly what he meant. She'd thought she was in love too. With someone who claimed to care for her, only to use her.

The same way you used Baz, a voice in her head said.

With Baz's face in mind, she cleared her throat and asked, "So it's true what you said, about the Collapsing curse not being real?"

A nod. "I'm telling you, Em, they're completely fine–minus a few hiccups with Kai's magic, but he's still new at the limitless-power aspect of it all. But Baz . . . he's formidable."

Emory had no trouble believing it. Because, despite all of Baz's lessons about how dangerous it was to Collapse, the effortless control he had over his magic couldn't be overlooked. Emory had always marveled at it, the ease with which he wielded such a vast, unthinkable power. The way he'd stopped *her* from Collapsing, something that should have been inevitable, irreversible. And Baz had turned back time to stop it without even coming close to Collapsing himself.

She should have known. The irony of it was almost laughable. How Baz had kept himself from using magic in fear of Collapsing, when all this time the thing he feared had already happened, leaving him to sit on this untapped well of depthless power.

"How is he, really?" she asked, the ache in her heart almost too much to bear as she thought of how devastated Baz must have been when he'd found out the truth. Because if Baz had been the one to Collapse in his father's printing press, then that meant *he*, not his father, had killed Keiran's parents in the blast.

"Like I said, he's become a total badass. Between coming to terms with his Collapsing, presenting his case against the Selenic Order and the Regulators for harnessing silver blood, harboring fugitives—it's a lot, but it builds character, you know?"

The thought of Baz doing anything illegal drew a smile from her. "I hope he'll be okay, wherever that portal brought him." She was glad to know that Kai was at Baz's side, remembering how fiercely protective of Baz the Nightmare Weaver had been when she met him at the Institute.

"This is all so messed up," Virgil breathed. "If only we had a bottle of alcohol . . ."

Emory shot him a look. "The sun isn't even up yet."

"Precisely. It's still partying hours."

Virgil gave her his signature smile. Emory could almost imagine they were back on Dovermere Cove, sitting around the bonfire where they'd first met. Except Keiran and Lizaveta were gone, and everything was irrevocably changed.

Movement caught her eye as Aspen sat up, looking around in a daze.

"How are you feeling?" Emory asked, handing Aspen a gourd of water that they'd filled at the spring. The witch's face was haggard, but her wound at least seemed entirely healed. She nearly emptied the gourd in one go.

"Surprisingly well, considering my brush with death. I think I actually *did* die for a second." Aspen looked at Emory intently. "You brought me back. How?"

"Healing magic, remember?" Emory didn't mention how it had taken much more than that.

Aspen hugged herself as she looked toward the horizon, where a dim sun was making its way up. "It feels like I've been here before," she said. "I've seen this landscape through Tol's eyes. Which means he's *real*."

"Could you find him through scrying?" Emory asked with sudden inspiration. "Maybe he could help us find this world's key."

"The warrior from your story," Aspen whispered, her eyes bright with an emotion Emory couldn't place. Her jaw set in determination. "Let me try."

They watched as she sat cross-legged on the red-hued earth, face tilted up to the sun, eyes going milky white as she sank into her scrying. Emory wondered what her tether might be–if she needed one at all, given the uniqueness of her ability–before she noticed Aspen's hands fisted in the dirt.

By now everyone had awoken and was watching Aspen quietly. Emory tried to catch Romie's eye, but her friend was either very focused on the scrying or pointedly avoiding her.

They all jumped when Aspen gasped out of her trance and scurried to her feet, nearly backing into the remnants of their fire.

"What happened? What did you see?"

"I'm not sure. Some strange beast's mind, I believe . . ." Aspen frowned. "The astral plane feels so different here. I couldn't find my way. This will be more difficult than I thought."

"So how are we going to find this key, then?" Virgil asked.

"Not sure about the key, but *this* should lead us to the next door." Vera produced the compass. "Just like it did in the Wychwood."

"Can't exactly open the door without a key."

"Thank you, Virgil, I know how doors work," Vera quipped. "Where do you suggest we go? The desert stretches on in every direction with no end in sight, and we're all hungry and thirsty and tired. We can at the very least start walking in the direction of the door and hope for the best."

Emory found herself agreeing with Vera, hiding a smile as Virgil grumbled something under his breath. They ventured out shortly after, following the direction of the compass. Emory couldn't help but notice Romie and Nisha walking closely together, all secret smiles and brushing hands. A pang of jealousy hit her, fueled by the way Romie had been ignoring her since they'd gotten to the Wastes. It was like they were back in their first year at Aldryn, with Emory watching her best friend slip through her fingers.

Except maybe this time Romie was justified. After what happened on the ley line . . .

No. Emory wouldn't let herself think of that. She picked up the pace to walk beside Vera, who led the pack and was studying the compass like her life depended on it.

"How did you know Adriana was my mother?" Emory blurted out. She herself hadn't even known her mother's true name until Keiran told her, right before he died.

Adriana Kazan.

Luce Meraude.

Mother, sailor, liar.

"Baz told me," Vera stated, eyes darting away from Emory's.

"Baz knew my mother as Luce Meraude, not Adriana Kazan."

A beat. Then: "Adriana was my aunt." Vera chanced a look at Emory. "That makes us cousins, I suppose."

"Oh."

Emory let that knowledge sink between them. *Cousins.* She had never known family outside of her father, who was an only child, and his parents, who had died when she was young. Her mother had been a mystery, but now here was something concrete, a living piece of her family tree, someone who shared her blood.

"She disappeared years ago looking for Clover's epilogue," Vera continued. "Set out from Trevel and sailed across the seas to find it." She frowned at the compass in her hand before holding it out to Emory. "You should have this."

"Keep it," Emory said, trying to hold back the bitterness from her words. "It was never really mine to begin with."

Just like her mother. This woman she had never known, who'd had an entire family to love and be loved by, people to remember her long after she was gone. People who knew her when Emory never would.

Adriana Kazan–the real woman, the person behind all the mystery–seemed to belong to everyone but Emory. She had only ever known her mother as Luce Meraude, the sailor. A storybook character that her younger self could fantasize about, a fabricated persona she was free to dream up in her mind.

That person belonged to no one but the sea.

There wasn't a single version of her mother that was hers, and holding a damn compass wouldn't change that.

Emory stopped dead in her tracks, stumbling as a familiar energy hummed beneath her feet.

Vera steadied her. "What's wrong?"

As the others caught up to them, Emory's eyes went to Aspen. "Do you feel that? It's like the ley line in the Wychwood."

Aspen tilted her head, as if listening to the air and the earth, hoping to learn their rhythms the way she'd been attuned to the Wychwood's. "I think I'd be powerful enough to scry here."

Romie tensed, looking between the two of them like she was ready to tackle them off the ley line if she must. "Don't you think it'd be best to keep the scrying off the ley line? After what happened to Bryony . . ."

But Aspen seemed undeterred. "I'm not my sister. Besides, the thing that possessed her is already possessing another."

Keiran.

Before anyone could stop her, Aspen plopped down on the ground and grabbed fistfuls of dirt. She let the red earth fall from one hand to the other, watching it as if the motion were hypnotizing. And perhaps it was, because her eyes grew filmy again, indicating she was scrying.

Emory's heart raced. There was an odd tingling at her fingertips, a hunger in her that had nothing to do with her empty stomach. She could *feel* Aspen's magic as it worked, smell its sweet, earthy scent. It called to her in a way she didn't understand.

She watched mesmerized as Aspen's eyes jumped unseeing from side to side. And when they stopped moving, Aspen gasped–and Emory along with her.

Emory was no longer seeing the world as she had a second earlier. Gone was the barren landscape and her friends, gone was the feeling of weak sunlight on her skin. She was in a dark tunnel, standing guard outside what looked like a cell. She wore golden chain mail, and a sword hung at her hip. This wasn't *her* body. It was corded with muscles she didn't have, had suffered through hurts she'd never known. The heart beating in her chest felt *heavy*, made of something other than connective tissue and fibrous muscle. Something warm and bright and magical.

A monstrous growl shook the walls.

Emory stumbled as she returned to her body. She was again looking at that barren land, and her friends' concerned faces. They weren't looking at her, though–they were looking at Aspen.

"That wasn't Tol," the witch said with a frown. "I felt him near, but something's blocking me from him."

Emory's heart pounded as she tried to make sense of what happened. She had *seen* this, just as Aspen had. She'd felt this undeniable pull toward Aspen, her *magic*, and then she was scrying along with the witch. How could that be possible? She was a Tidecaller, able to draw on *lunar* magics, not magic from other worlds.

This ley line was doing something to her. Could it have opened her up to other kinds of magic? She could feel the residual power from Aspen on this very spot, could feel it traveling beneath her feet like a live wire calling her name, begging her to grab hold of it, use it as her own.

Her friends' chatter grew distant. Emory had to get off the ley line or she felt like she might burst. The scorching heat expected of this world was only mild at best, yet she was sweating profusely, something electric traveling in her veins. There was a darkness pressing in all around her now. Emory took a few stumbling steps, trying desperately to get off the ley line.

"Em, you okay?" Virgil called out behind her.

Before she could answer him, Emory fell, her vision going dark.

She did not know that falling into unconsciousness would involve *actual* falling. But that was the sensation she got, interminable and heart-lurchingly fast. Then at last everything stopped.

She was in the sleepscape again, or rather, it looked like she was *beneath* it. She stood in utter darkness, solid obsidian under her feet, and above her was a black expanse filled with stars that hung threateningly low. It was, Emory realized, as if she'd fallen *past* the bridge of stars and into this darkly glittering pit.

"Hello again."

Emory whirled at this voice she knew too well. The demon wearing Keiran's face stood behind her. He smiled at her with the unsettling mannerisms of Keiran, all cool confidence and ease, nothing like the murderous demon she'd faced off against in the grotto.

"What did you do to me?"

"So quick to cast blame." Keiran-not-Keiran tutted. "You're the one who fainted. I merely called your consciousness here."

"And where is *here*?" She threw a wary glance around her. "What is this place?"

"It is many things and nothing at all. It is liminal. A seam between time and space and planes of existence."

"The sleepscape."

"Not quite. A little pocket that exists at the edge of it, if you will."

Emory hoped that meant neither of them was corporeal—that he couldn't hurt her here. The memory of his fingers wrapped around her throat made her retreat a step, bracing defensively. "If you're going to kill me, go on with it."

Heat flared in the depths of his eyes. "I am not going to kill you."

The *yet* dangled unspoken at the end of his sentence, evident in the cruel tilt of his mouth.

Emory swallowed past the tightness in her throat. He looked so much like Keiran, but she knew it wasn't him, couldn't be.

"Tell me what you are," she demanded, affecting a bravado she did not feel in the slightest.

"Isn't it obvious?" Keiran-not-Keiran stepped toward her, shadows swirling in his wake. She tried not to flinch as he appeared to tower over her. "I am that which dwells in the dark between stars," he said, and his voice echoed oddly around them. "How disappointing that one such as yourself can't put it together."

Emory's pulse raced. "But you're not an umbra."

"Don't insult me. The umbrae are mere nightmares—echoes of consciousness, fear given form." His eyes narrowed to slits as he took her in from head to toe. "You took a horde of them away from me a while back. I felt it, the moment their blackened souls vanished from the sleeping realm. The same way you got rid of those that were with me yesterday." He cocked his head to the side. "What did you do to them?"

She tilted her chin up. "I set them free."

Keiran watched her with faint amusement, but there was something else hiding behind his eyes, a sort of wonder bordering on anger that Emory couldn't begin to understand. "I have not felt that kind of power in a long time," he said. "Do you even know what you could do with it? The things you could accomplish. The doors you might open."

Emory's mouth went dry. The question felt so much like *Keiran* that for a second, she got lost in his gaze, in his words, in the alluring quality of his voice. She couldn't help it. It struck something within her, got under her skin. And Tides, she hated herself for it. Hadn't she been in this same position before? Listening to Keiran's promises, fooled by his lies, drinking it all up like she was a faithful servant worshipping at the altar of some dark, powerful god. He had appealed to her thirst for power, her search for significance, and she had bent to him so easily, she should have been embarrassed for it. But at the time, nothing had felt so right. And all it did in the end was lead to a heap of hurt and death.

Emory wouldn't let herself get swayed like that again.

"I know enough," she said, willing iron into her voice.

"Do you, now? And yet you are leading the pieces of her to the godsworld without knowing what it will do. You call yourself Tidecaller, but you don't even know what that means."

Emory refused to let him get under her skin, even as a million questions came to mind. "Tell me what it means, then."

"Are you always this demanding of your betters?"

"My *betters*?"

"I imagine it's that death wish of yours. I seem to recall you saying it's what you deserve." He drew so close, she could see all the unnatural details of his eyes. The outer ring of pure obsidian, the golds and silvers around his pupils that flared brighter, almost molten, as he held her gaze. "All that potential, and you would so carelessly let it sputter out?"

Emory did not dare to answer. She felt dizzy with fear, her pulse racing to a painful throb.

Keiran stared at a spot behind her. "Perhaps you'll get your wish after all." Then, lowering his mouth to her ear: "If I were you, I'd run."

He gave her a shove, and then she was being pulled up into

consciousness again, the strange, dark world around her dissolving. Emory opened her eyes to the red-hued desert. Hands were shaking her, and for a panicked moment Emory thought the demon had followed her here. But it was Virgil's face she was looking up at, Virgil's voice that pierced through the fog of her mind.

"Run!"

A horrible screeching sound had them both putting their hands over their ears and looking up at the sky.

Where a great winged beast stretched its sharp talons toward them.

KAI

K AI SPENT THE REST OF THAT FIRST NIGHT SEARCHING the sleepscape for the other Nightmare Weaver. He couldn't find him, not a single trace, because the boy had either woken up or somehow managed to block Kai out. The sun was rising when he finally gave up. By some twist of fate, Kai had found himself in his old room, a small comfort he clung to. Though he sorely missed the quote and stars he'd painted on the ceiling.

Throwing on the same clothes as yesterday, Kai opened his door to voices drifting up from downstairs. Baz was there, nursing a cup of coffee. Polina sat on the counter next to him, watching him with the same doe eyes that hadn't slipped Kai's notice yesterday.

"I forgot to ask what your alignment is," Baz was saying.

Polina seemed flustered at his attention. "I don't much like talking about it. People . . . they tend to judge me for it."

"People are terrible." This drew a smile from Polina. "You don't have to tell me if you don't want to."

"I'm what they call an Enshriner. I can extract memories and bind them to objects." She ducked her head. "Memories from corpses, that is."

Kai nearly stumbled on the last step. He'd never heard of such an Eclipse alignment before–it was like a grim play on Memorist magic.

Polina caught sight of him and gave him an awkward wave. "Hello. Sorry if we woke you."

Kai's gaze slid right past her to another Eclipse-born, who had his head buried in a book. He recognized him immediately. "So you're the asshole who shoved me out of the sleepscape."

Baz choked on his coffee, giving Kai a reproachful look. Kai didn't care about the lack of manners. Neither did the other Nightmare Weaver, apparently, whose mouth lifted in a sheepish grin.

"Sorry about that." He took his half-moon glasses off–they hung from a chain around his neck–and peered at Kai. "You gave me quite the fright last night. I've never encountered another Fear Eater before."

Fear Eater? The name struck something familiar in Kai. He vaguely remembered reading about the history of magical terminology, how some Eclipse alignment names had changed over time, given their rarity. "I prefer Nightmare Weaver myself," he said. "And you're the first I've encountered too."

"Nightmare Weaver. I like that." The boy put out his hand. "I'm Thameson Caine, though I go by Thames."

Caine.

Like Farran.

Kai felt Baz's eyes on him. It was too early to deal with such strangeness. He shook Thames's hand, ignoring the million questions burning on his tongue. "Kai Salonga."

"We were just about to head out to the Eclipse salon I was telling

STRANGER SKIES —— 271

you about," Polina said as she slipped off the counter and grabbed what looked like a pastry.

"We promise it's not as boring as it sounds." Thames slid his glasses back on. "And we'd love to hear from a Luaguan's perspective, I'm sure."

As they followed Thames and Polina out of the commons, Baz sidled up to Kai and whispered, "You okay?"

Kai tore his gaze from the back of Thames's head. "Yeah. I just can't believe there's another Nightmare Weaver." And that he was the ancestor of a boy Kai had once thought he loved.

"What was that about him shoving you out of the sleepscape?"

"I'll tell you later." Kai gave Baz a sidelong look.

"What?" Baz fussed over his appearance. "Did I spill coffee on myself?"

Kai smirked at his distress. "You managed to get the tie right this time."

Baz touched the ascot around his neck, cheeks burning as if the memory of Kai doing it up for him last night made him nervous. "Yeah, well, we need to blend in, right? Maybe this salon will give me some insight on past Timespinners."

"Let's hope so."

28

BAZ

THE SALON HAD ALREADY STARTED BY THE TIME THEY arrived. Cordie spotted them at the door. She motioned for them to come stand beside her. Everyone around them was listening enraptured to a student speaking with such conviction and poise, it was no wonder there were so many people here.

The student presently had his back turned to them. He stood in the middle of the room, with the gathered crowd forming a circle around him. His shoulder-length hair was perfectly coiffed, and his clothes seemed finer than what the typical student wore, with an added flair that made him look ahead of his time.

"All magic is born equal," the student was saying. "Every facet of this system that governs us is part of a larger equation, and to disregard a single one of those facets is to let the whole system fall apart. There is no moon without a sun. No seas without shores. No dreams without nightmares. No Tides without their Shadow counterpart. No successful party without an Illusionist there to give us all the best—if not chaotic—night of our lives."

Laughter erupted from the crowd at whatever inside joke this was. The student slowly spun around to look at everyone, his voice growing serious again as he said, "There is no lunar magic without Eclipse magic, and to think otherwise is not only folly; it puts us *all* in danger."

He turned around fully then, giving Baz a good look. If everyone around them was mortal, then he must be a god. His features were delicate and fine, blond hair curling around his chiseled jawline, and his eyes were a striking shade of blue-green. They were like sea-foam, like turquoise waves spilling on white sand, or the cloudy hues of sea glass.

And they were staring right at Baz.

Recognition struck, and Baz nearly gasped at the impossibility of it.

Because here was a man he never thought he would ever get to meet. A face he'd seen only in paintings and books and his own imagination. A name he'd seen printed on the cover of his favorite book time and time again.

Standing before him was his literary idol, the brilliant mind behind *Song of the Drowned Gods*.

Cornus Clover.

Here. In this time.

It was impossible—yet so was traveling two hundred years into the past, and here they were, and here Clover was, and none of it made sense. Baz caught Kai's gaze as Clover turned from them and kept on with his speech. Kai's mouth hung agape in what had to be a mirror of Baz's own bewildered expression.

"Did you realize–"

"No." Kai swore under his breath, the hint of a chuckle in his voice. "This can't be real."

A student next to Kai shushed him, drawing their attention back to Clover.

". . . the heinous brutalities that those who suffer the Unhallowed Seal are subjected to," Clover was saying. "And now, some Institutes have started employing Purifiers to try to expel the evil from those who have Collapsed."

"As they should," a loud voice boomed.

Everyone turned toward the disturbance. Wulfrid and his two friends from last night stood at the door, their faces etched in disdain.

Clover seemed undisturbed by their interruption, clasping his hands smoothly behind his back. "Care to share why you think so?" he asked conversationally. "Go on. I'm sure we're all very curious to hear a Purifier's perspective on the matter."

"All Eclipse-born are corrupt," Wulfrid said with righteous fury, "and those who Collapse are even more so, because they have succumbed to the Shadow's dark, sacrilegious curse. It is as the Tidelore faith says: Eclipse-born carry the stain of the Shadow who brought the Tides to their doom. They are ruination, a plague upon our world, and you are no better by associating with them."

Tidelore. Baz had read all about it when he was helping Professor Selandyn with her research on the Tides and the Shadow. Those of the Tidelore faith believed in the myth that portrayed the Tides as good and the Shadow as evil—a faith that was no longer prevalent in Baz's time, even if the general sentiment of it remained. From the sounds of it, it was still relevant here.

"So it is religion that shapes your perspective," Clover said, nodding his head sagely.

He sounded as calm and assured as if he were debating whether the sky outside was blue. As he spoke, Baz was reminded of what Jae always thought of Clover, that he was a fervent criticizer of these religious zealots. Jae would be pleased to know they'd been right.

"Surely you must know that Tidelore is only that: *lore*," Clover continued. "Like any myth or fable, it is told in a myriad of ways and paints the Shadow in different lights depending on who does the telling. Those of the Constellation Isles believe the Shadow to be on equal footing with the Tides. Heroes, both. You'd be hard-pressed to find a Luaguan who agrees with the sanctioning of these Purifying *exorcisms*, for lack of a better term."

"What do I care what Luaguans think?" Wulfrid spat. "Faithless heathens, just like you. Spewing your criticism of our faith and siding with these Shadow-stained abominations." He eyed Thames and Polina at that, then Baz and Kai. He glowered at Kai, clearly still angry that their last encounter saw Kai having the last word. "The world would be better off if you all went back to the Deep where you belong."

The cruel malice in his remark had Kai tensing. Before a fight could ensue, Clover smoothly stepped in.

"That's enough," he said in that unaffected voice. "I suggest you take your leave now, friend."

Wulfrid went rod straight, face still red with indignant fury, but he did not challenge Clover's suggestion. Instead, he immediately left, leaving his two friends to give each other a puzzled look before following him.

It was almost as if Wulfrid had been commanded to leave against his will. Which would be impossible . . .

If Clover were not a Tidecaller.

Baz and Kai exchanged a knowing look as people around them began to whisper among themselves. No one seemed to suspect what just happened—that Clover might very well have used *Glamour* magic to get Wulfrid to leave. Clover himself didn't seem fazed by the situation. He simply righted his waistcoat and waited for silence. When he had everyone's attention again, he swept a hand toward the door.

"*This* is what we're fighting against. People who hide behind their Tidelore faith, thinking themselves justified in their hatred of Eclipse-born. If people like him had their way, no progress, however small, would have been made at all. This is why the fight for Eclipse-born justice does not concern Eclipse-born alone but *all* of us." He gestured to the back of the room. "Please, sign our petition to have Purifying practices against Eclipse-born banned from the Institutes. Your voice is needed in this fight. Thank you."

As students started moving toward the designated table, Clover sidled up to Cordie. He squeezed her elbow in greeting, a twinge of concern visible beneath his courteous mask. "He's getting bolder."

"You shouldn't have confronted him like that," Cordie whispered. "Wulfrid's family is well-connected within the Tidelore faith. They could destroy everything we're working toward."

"They won't." Clover turned his gaze on Baz and Kai with a smile. "Where are my manners—you must be our guests of honor. My sister's told me all about the two drenched Eclipse-born she had the pleasure of meeting last night. I'm glad you could join us." He extended a hand to Baz. "Cornelius Clover."

Reality sank in as Baz looked between Clover and Cordie—his *sister*!

And here Baz was shaking his favorite author's hand, the very same hand that'd put pen to paper to create the fantasy world of his dreams, the characters he'd called friends all his life, the story that had spoken to his soul from its very first line. Cornus Clover, whose personal journal and the lost epilogue he would one day become famous for were tucked into Baz's breast pocket, waterlogged and all but ruined until he deemed it safe to fix them with his time magic.

Impossible. All of it.

"N-Nice to meet you," Baz stammered. "I'm Brysden. Baz—Baz Brysden." Unsure of how to address this legend come to life—whose fancy clothes he was *wearing*, he realized with no short amount of embarrassment—he awkwardly added, "Uh, sir."

Clover threw his head back and laughed. "Please, call me Cornus." He extended a hand to Kai next, a twinkle in his eyes as he took in his Eclipse sigil.

"Kai Salonga." Kai had scores more poise than Baz did. "That was quite the speech you gave. I didn't know they'd started doing that. With the Purifiers, I mean."

Clover's mouth thinned. "Yes. I'm afraid the Regulators here are easily influenced by Tidelore leaders." He righted his waistcoat, face darkening with disgust. "They believe like Wulfrid does that Eclipse-born are corrupt, but the *real* corruption lies within the Institutes and Tidelore temples. Small-minded, fearmongering fools, the lot of them."

He gave Baz and Kai a sad smile. "Cordelia told me what happened last night. Not the best way to welcome you to our corner of the world, is it?"

For a moment, the name did not register. But as Cordie muttered something about the barkeep, it hit Baz. Cordelia–*Delia*. That was the name Jae had said was mentioned in Clover's journal, a sister referred to as Delia.

Cordelia Clover. The forgotten sibling.

"That's why Cornelius started these salons," Cordie was saying, face full of pride as she watched her brother. "He's setting an example here at Aldryn, to radicalize the students into doing everything in their power to help our Eclipse counterparts and tear down unjust barriers and prejudices."

"We students are the voice of our generation. We owe it to ourselves to use that voice to its full might. Hopefully it will carry to the rest of Elegy and beyond. Helps that some of us have quite the pull with authorities," Clover added with a wink.

The solidarity between everyone here was evident. Thames

and Polina mingled with the other students, and barring what happened with Wulfrid, there was none of the animosity they'd encountered in the tavern when they first arrived. This level of acceptance and camaraderie felt . . . it felt, in some ways, beyond even their own time.

"It's amazing," Baz gushed. "Truly, I've never heard of anything like this."

Cordie gave him a funny look. "Hasn't it always been like this in the Constellation Isles?"

Baz fumbled at his blunder. "Er, yes, well, I–"

"He's a recent transplant to Luagua." Kai stepped on Baz's foot in a way that said, *Shut up before you ruin this.* "Hasn't been there long enough to understand we're much more accepting of Eclipse-born."

"Where are you originally from?" Clover asked.

"Here, actually," Baz said, deciding to opt for the truth rather than a blatant lie. "Well, Threnody, that is."

"Must have been quite the shock to move to Luagua."

"It was, yes. In the best way, of course."

"Can I ask what prompted you to become invested in all of this?" Kai asked Clover, pointedly eyeing the New Moon sigil inked on his hand. "You're not Eclipse-born yourself. So why go to all these lengths?"

There was no brusqueness in his tone, just genuine curiosity. But Baz heard the insinuation behind his question, inviting the possibility of this simple fact–that Clover was New Moon–being false.

Clover seemed genuinely taken aback. "Does one need a reason to be invested in the well-being of their friends, their peers, their fellow humans? If someone is struggling in front of you, do you not reach out a hand to help them?"

"I find that most people will only help their own," Kai answered, "and won't bother with those they consider other. Unless there's something in it for them."

Clover made a contemplative sound. "What a cynical outlook to have. But then, I am a Healer; perhaps I can't help the naive sort of compassion that comes with the territory."

Healer. Surely if Clover had used Glamour magic earlier as Baz suspected, he had to know this was a lie. The research they'd found in Keiran's ledgers pointed to Clover being born on the same rare ecliptic event as Emory, meaning he would indeed have been *born* a Healer, but might have unlocked the true nature of his magic– his Tidecaller abilities–after having a near-death experience.

The sound of the clocktower suddenly droned in their ears. Students started leaving, waving goodbye to Clover and his group of friends.

"Good luck at the opening challenge this evening!" one of the students called out to Clover.

"You're participating in the Bicentennial?" Baz asked, reminded of the fact that *he* would have been competing in the Quadri challenges in his own time had he not magically found himself two hundred years in the past. That is, if Drutten and the Regulators hadn't ruined everything.

"I am," Clover said with pride. "This evening is just an introduction of sorts to the *real* games that will follow."

"My brother," Cordie sighed. "Any chance to show off."

Clover gave her an indulgent smile before eyeing Baz and Kai. "Will you be partaking in the games?"

Baz laughed nervously. "I don't think that'd be wise."

Not when the Bicentennial was supposed to have been the deadliest event in Aldryn's history, the reason why the whole premise of the centennials had changed afterward.

"I'm afraid my particular ability wouldn't translate so well to these games," Kai said.

"And what ability might that be?"

"I'm a Nightmare Weaver." Kai jerked his chin at Thames, who'd just appeared at Clover's side. "I'd say I'm the one and only, but it looks like I'm not quite so original here."

Thames gave a sheepish smile at that. Clover clasped him on the back of the neck. "If you're anything like our Fear Eater, I've no doubt we'll get on marvelously."

The words were clearly directed at Kai, but Clover didn't take his eyes off Thames as he spoke. Thames beamed at him, his whole demeanor changing. It was like Clover was the sun and Thames was a plant coming alive in the light.

The intimacy in Clover's lingering touch on Thames's neck had Baz darting a look at Kai. It made him think of that charged proximity between them as Kai fixed his tie, and the unwarranted twinge of jealousy he'd felt upon discovering Thames's last name was *Caine*. All those memories it must have brought up in Kai . . .

"What about you, Baz?" Cordie asked. "What's your ability?"

"Oh, uh–I'm a Timespinner? I can manipulate time."

Clover's expression turned eager at that. He let go of Thames. "With such talent, you *must* participate in the Bicentennial."

"I couldn't, really."

"Stop pestering him," Cordie said to her brother. To Baz, she added, "I'm not one for all this academic fanfare myself, but I'm told the best part comes *after* the challenges."

"And what is that?"

"Yes, what *is* that, dear brother?"

Clover's mouth tilted up, his pale turquoise eyes glinting with mischief. "A group of us will be throwing an . . . *exclusive* party after the first real challenge later this week. You'll have to come and see what it's like for yourselves." He leaned closer to them and whispered, "Be sure to dress your best."

Cordie laughed at Baz's deer-in-the-headlights look. "I forgot your belongings are at the bottom of the sea! Not to worry, I can give you the name of the best tailor in town."

"It's just that, uh, we don't–"

"All of our money's at the bottom of the sea too," Kai offered smoothly.

"Then it'll be on us," Clover said. At Baz's protest, he added, "Please, I insist. Every man should own a good suit." He gave a pointed glance at the clothes on their backs–*his* clothes. "And more than a single outfit."

It felt odd to accept all these handouts, even though the Clover siblings offered them so casually as to make it clear that money wasn't an issue.

"I was headed into town now, if you care to join me?" Cordie suggested.

Her brother frowned. "Don't you have class?"

"Only later this afternoon. Thought I'd head to my studio in the meantime."

Clover's jaw tightened in disapproval. He said nothing more on it, though, only smiled at Baz and Kai. "Well, I'll leave you in my sister's capable hands. *I* have classes all day and a study session before the event. See you tonight?" To Cordie, he added, "Give the tailor my best."

Cordie seemed taken aback by something in his voice. A faint blush crept up her cheeks, but she blinked and it vanished. "Come along, gents."

Baz was loath to part with Clover in case this all turned out to be a fever dream and he never got to see his literary idol again. But he and Kai followed Cordie into town, with the promise that they'd see Clover later at the opening challenge.

Cordie, they learned, was an artist. She had a studio in town, no doubt paid for with her family's deep pockets, where she came to get away from "rigid curriculums and pompous students," as she put it.

"I plan on going to art school after this," she told them, a dreamy look in her eyes. "Somewhere in Trevel, perhaps."

Baz was a tad envious of that dream. A normal life away from magic.

After getting suits that fit them perfectly at the tailor's, they parted ways as Cordie went to her studio. Baz and Kai returned to Obscura Hall, unsure what students from visiting colleges were supposed to do while at Aldryn. If they kept to the warded walls of the Eclipse commons as much as they could, perhaps no one from Karunang or otherwise would ask questions about them.

They found a quiet corner of the illusioned gardens to sit in, making sure neither Polina nor Thames was around before they finally spoke.

"We just met Cornus Clover," Baz said. "The scholar on the shores himself."

"Do you think he's started writing it yet?" Kai asked, equally awed.

"I don't know." He'd been wondering the same thing. Clover was meant to have written *Song of the Drowned Gods* during his time at Aldryn College, so surely he must have started if he was in his last year of undergrad.

Baz took out Clover's journal, completely ruined and illegible after Dovermere spat him in the Aldersea with it in his pocket. The epilogue tucked into its pages was equally spoiled. Baz knew he could save both journal and epilogue, turn back time to before they were waterlogged, but he hadn't dared use his magic yet.

"Just try it," Kai said, as if reading his mind. "If we're pulled through time again, at least we can say we met Cornus Tides-damned Clover in the flesh."

"I don't know . . ."

But Baz had to admit his earlier trepidation felt unwarranted. If they were stuck here, he'd likely have to rely on his magic at some point. And there was no safer place to test it out than Obscura Hall.

He pulled on the threads of time, bracing for the worst. But time was as it always was here, nothing like the complicated tapestry he'd encountered in the sleepscape. In a blink, the pages in his hand became legible again.

Still, the journal's cryptic pages sparked no answers about the situation they were in. Not a clue on how to get back to their time nor how to access other worlds.

But if what Alya and Vera believed was true—that Clover had actually lived through the events of his own book, the scholar in the story—then perhaps Clover could lead them to a door, since the one they knew of did not yet exist. Maybe his being a Tidecaller meant he would somehow *create* the door they so very much needed to get home. Maybe the door didn't exist before he first opened it—and if that was the case, they needed to be there when he did.

Baz's plan to find out more information about Timespinner magic seemed somewhat pointless now. What they needed was to find out more about *Clover*. It felt too serendipitous a thing for them to have traveled to this time specifically, as if fate wanted them to come face-to-face with the man who started it all.

Clover was the answer.

29

EMORY

EMORY AND VIRGIL DUCKED OUT OF THE WAY WITH SEC-
onds to spare, sharp talons just barely missing them. They
scurried behind a spindly bush as shrieks and shouts assailed
their ears, both human and otherwise.

They were under attack.

The sky was blotted out by what looked like giant ravens with
feathers so black they appeared blue, beaks and talons that could
rip them apart in a second, and big eyes that were entirely too
alert and intelligent. But while the top half of their bodies was
ravenlike, the tail end resembled that of a snake, feathers giving
way to gleaming black and blue scales, the point of the tail scored
with viciously sharp, slightly hooked spikes.

One such tail arced downward through the air above Emory. She
barely avoided getting impaled, the tail landing between her and
Virgil and making dust cloud up between them. Their wide eyes
landed on each other for a fraction of a second before the beast
lunged for them again, great wings flapping to keep it hovering

above them. Its tail came down once more, but this time Emory had the good sense to call on her magic, an easy thing to do with the ley line crackling beneath her.

Whips of light and shadow and spindly vines extended from her hands, lashing at the beast's tail as it tried to fly higher. The threads curled around the tail, and she *pulled*, forcing the beast toward the ground. It shrieked in frustration, beating its wings harder to get free.

Angry now, it lunged right at Emory.

"*Look out!*" Virgil shouted.

Emory fell back, her magic sputtering uselessly as the beast's beak came for her neck.

Keiran-not-Keiran's words rang in her ears. She was going to die here.

But the beak stopped inches from her face. There was a squelching sound and a spray of bluish-black blood as a blade pierced through the monster's head, right between the eyes.

The beast fell limply at Emory's feet. In its place stood a woman in golden armor pulling an actual *sword* out of the beast.

A *warrior*. Just like in Clover's story.

Others similarly armed fought the remaining beasts, golden armor and golden swords and golden wings glinting in the sun.

Emory thought surely she must be imagining things, but as the woman who'd saved her shot into the sky after one of the beasts, there was no denying what she was seeing. The warriors had *wings*. Great wings like that of a mythical dragon, nearly as big as the ravenlike creatures'. They sprouted from their backs, accommodated by holes in their armor. The muscles and tendons and veins seemed made of the same solid gold as their armor, but the membrane was ethereal, shining like spun sunlight.

Emory watched in awe as the woman circled one of the beasts in the sky, a dance of black feathers and golden armor, talons and swords. The woman's eyes flashed golden like they were the sun itself as she plunged her blade through the beast's open beak, then sliced its head clean off, baring her teeth in a feral snarl that made her seem more beast than human herself.

A shriek pulled Emory's attention away from the slain raven beast plummeting toward the ground, just as Nisha was pulled into the sky by another one of the monsters.

"Nisha!" Romie yelled, reaching for her with desperate hands.

One of the warriors flicked a golden dagger at the beast. It found its mark in the bird's chest, and the monster shrieked in pain, letting go of Nisha as it tried to flap its way to safety. Before Nisha could impale herself on the sharp rocks beneath her, a winged man caught her, breaking her fall, and deposited her safely at Romie's side.

With the rest of the monsters slaughtered, the half-dozen winged warriors landed around Emory and her friends. The woman who'd saved Emory took off her helmet, revealing short, gray-streaked hair and sandy skin deepened by sunspots and fine lines, markers of a seasoned warrior.

She pointed her sword at Emory. "What business have you here, travelers?"

Emory held up her hands. "I—we're just trying to find our way."

"No one is supposed to travel in these parts without a guide to fend off the eldritch." She eyed their strange array of clothing with curiosity. "Have you no weapons? No belongings?"

"We lost them," Emory said. "Please, we only want to get to safety."

The woman's gaze caught on her tattooed hand—the dark moon wreathed in silver narcissus. An instinct Emory didn't understand had her tugging on her sleeve to hide it.

Aspen's words drew their focus: "That crest—you're the draconics, aren't you? The sacred knights who defend the land from these beasts."

Aspen was looking at the woman's armor with recognition that could only come from what she'd seen through Tol's eyes. The crest was a stylized dragon curled on itself in a circle, eating its own tail.

The woman dipped her chin in a solemn nod. "We are the Chivalric Fellowship of the Light, at your service." Seeming to decide they weren't a threat, she sheathed her sword. "It's a good thing we found you when we did. These are strange times, I fear. May the Sun Forger protect us all from the Night Bringer's rise."

Before Emory could ponder why those words made the hair on the back of her neck rise, movement at the corner of her eye caught her attention. Two men without wings or armor or blade had joined the knights. One was middle-aged, dressed in a hooded robe the color of sandstone that contrasted with his rich brown complexion. The other couldn't have been past thirteen and was dressed in a simple, belted tunic that fit loosely on his lanky frame. He held a massive tome under one arm, and with the other he tugged at the robed man's sleeve to whisper something in his ear.

The warrior woman raised a brow. "Does your page have something to say, Master Bayns?"

"Apologies for the boy stepping out of line, Knight Commander," Master Bayns said with a hard look at the boy, whose fair cheeks flushed a deep pink as he bowed in apology. "He says he saw that one using . . . er, well, *magic*."

All eyes slid to Emory. A few knights inched their hands to their weapons. The woman who had been called Knight Commander frowned at her. "Magic?" she echoed. "I saw no such thing. Is that true?"

Emory caught the subtle shake of Aspen's head. They could rely only on the witch's knowledge of this world at this point and hope that what she'd gleaned helped them survive it.

"I'm sorry, he must be mistaken," Emory said with an apologetic smile. "No magic here. It must have been one of those ravens."

She hoped none of them could feel the Glamour magic she laced through her words, willing them to believe her. Willing them not to see the moon phase tattoos and silver spirals that marked her and her friends as other. Darkness pressed in, the ley line trying to pull her under. The page looked at her from beneath his lashes. His furrowed brow made it seem like he knew what Emory was doing, but he remained silent.

"They are called *corvus serpentes*," the robed man said of the strange beasts. "We will be sure to add this magic of theirs to our bestiary. Make a note of it, will you, Page Caius?"

"Yes, Master Bayns." The boy half-heartedly scribbled something in the tome he carried.

"Come, the city isn't far," the Knight Commander declared.

"City? What city?" Virgil exclaimed, looking around pointedly. "It's desert for miles around!"

"You have to know where to look, young sir." The woman pointed toward the ridge of mountains in the near distance. It had been cast in shadows before, but with the dim sun now higher in the sky, the light revealed a city that seemed carved from the stone itself, red-hued like the ridge it was tucked against. "Welcome to Heartstone. The draconic city of light."

Heartstone was a fortress, but more than anything it was a work of art, a marvel in architecture, full of sweeping arches and massive pillars, buttresses and vaults carved with intricate scallop patterns that called to mind the scales of a dragon. The city was built on three levels that rose to nearly the full height of the ridge, each level decreasing in size the higher it went: busy streets lined with markets and trades greeted them on the bottom level behind the large, carved gates that opened onto the city; on the second level were housing facilities and places of worship, an oasis of calm full of quaint gardens and fountains; and at the very top was the mighty citadel where the draconics oversaw the city and trained their young.

"Only the draconics are allowed up there," Aspen whispered as they were led through the streets, pointing at the looming citadel.

Indeed, everywhere around them were people who appeared as human as they did, though dressed in a fashion that felt centuries behind the times. Tunics and doublets and dresses adorned with leather armlets. Capes and cloaks held in place with bejeweled brooches. Men who wore bonnets and floppy hats, and women who wore circlets that cut across their foreheads and ornamented headdresses and colorful kerchiefs. None of them had dragon wings sprouting from their backs, but then again, neither did the knights who were escorting them through the city—not since they had made their wings *disappear.*

It had been the oddest thing to see. Those golden, ethereal wings there one second, and gone the next. Like a candle being blown out.

"If you know so much about this place," Emory whispered to Aspen, "that must mean Tol is here, right?"

Aspen gave her a knowing glance before clearing her throat, calling the Knight Commander's attention. "We're looking for someone. A draconic like you who goes by the name of Tol."

The woman paused. "You know Anatolius?"

"He's . . . a friend."

The woman's face hardened. "I'm afraid he is indisposed at the moment." She stopped before a charming inn, motioning them inside. "You may stay here for as long as you need. We see plenty of displaced people come through these parts, so please, make yourselves at home. There is food inside, and clothes will be brought to you shortly." At this, she eyed their curious clothing again, though abstained from commenting on it.

She made to leave, but Aspen stopped her with a concerned frown. "Pardon me, but would it be possible to get in touch with Anatolius? It's just I haven't seen him in so long, you see."

A pause. Then: "Are you an acquaintance from his old village?"

"Yes," Aspen said, and Emory herself nearly believed her for how honest she sounded.

The Knight Commander bowed her head, mouth downturned with sudden sadness. "Then I truly hate to be the bearer of bad news. Anatolius has broken his most sacred oath and turned his back on the light." Her throat bobbed with emotion. "For this, he has been sentenced to death."

Aspen faltered, all the blood leeching from her face. "No, that can't be."

"I'm sorry."

"Please, if I could see him . . ."

"You can see him at the Chasm, the arena where he is to fight to the death in two days' time," the woman said in a clipped voice. She gave a curt bow at the waist, golden helmet tucked beneath an arm. "Good day."

The rest of the knights followed her at once. Only the young page, Caius, hesitated, his green eyes trained on Aspen, as if he wanted to say a word of comfort. But a sharp command from Master Bayns had him following.

"What are we going to do?" Aspen lamented. "I can't let him die."

Emory stared after the retreating knights, tempted to call on her Memorist magic to peruse their minds. But after what happened on the ley line, she abstained. "Let's start with getting changed and fed, and we'll go from there."

As they settled into the quarters the innkeeper brought them to, Romie took Emory aside, dragging her to the small balcony overlooking the city streets below.

Romie crossed her arms. "What in the Deep was that back there with you fainting on the ley line? And if you lie to me or say it's nothing," she added quickly before Emory could utter a word, "I swear I'll shove you off this balcony. No more secrets, remember?"

Emory shied away from her gaze. "I think being on the ley line allowed me to access Aspen's magic. I saw what she saw when she scried."

Romie's eyebrows shot up. "Is this the first time it's happened?"

A nod. "It was like this overload of power inside me. And when I passed out . . ." She heaved a sigh. *No more secrets.* "Keiran appeared to me."

"What?"

"He pulled me into this space that looked like the sleepscape." She frowned, remembering how Keiran had told her to run before pushing her out of that odd state of consciousness. She told Romie as much, and though she couldn't exactly bring herself to say it'd felt like he'd *saved* her, Romie seemed to deduce as much.

She scowled. "Let's not forget he tried to kill Aspen and attacked us with a horde of umbrae. You can't trust him."

"I didn't say I trusted him."

"Well, he *is* wearing your ex-lover's face."

Here it was. The real reason Romie had pulled her aside.

Emory felt anger and guilt warring with each other. "This is exactly why I didn't tell you about me and Keiran. I knew you'd judge me."

"Judge you? Tides, Em, I couldn't care less who you fall for."

"Ouch," Emory said.

"No, not like that—of course I care to *know* these things, but I'd never judge you for it. And I get it. Keiran was charming and mysterious and, let's face it, gorgeous as hell. He had the whole college fawning over him, not just the Selenic Order, and not just you." Romie fixed her with a hard stare. "But I'm mad that you kept this from me after we *just* promised each other no more secrets."

"Like you're so transparent?" Emory bit out. She knew she was in the wrong here, but Romie's words only made her angrier. "This whole thing started with *you* keeping secrets. For a whole year, you drew away from me, lied to me, made me feel like I was losing my best friend. And when I *did* lose you, I fought like hell to get you back. You don't get to fault me for a few secrets now. Not when half the things I had to do to get you back are things I'm not proud of. Things I wish I could take back."

"I never asked you to do anything for me."

"Of course not. Rosemarie Brysden never asks for help, does she? And why would she ever need help from her useless Healer of a friend, anyway?"

"Well, you're definitely not a useless Healer anymore."

The vehemence in Romie's words stung. "You still see me that way, don't you? This meek girl you had to speak for half the time, the girl who hid in your shadow."

"That's not—"

"I've changed, Ro. I've had to step up and take charge while you were gone, and you know what? I like who I've become. Someone who's not weak or mediocre, but powerful."

"And where does that hunger for power stop?" Romie asked, her voice dangerously low now, trembling with an unknown emotion about to erupt. "When you Collapse? When you hurt one of us?"

Emory let the words settle between them. "You can't stand it, can you?" she said softly, heart aching with the realization.

"What?"

"Me being more powerful than you. Being a Tidecaller, having access to all these magics . . . it's what *you* always wanted. And you can't stand the idea that I'm the one who got this power, not you."

Hurt flashed across Romie's face. "Is that really what you think of me?"

"Well, isn't it the truth?"

"No. The truth is I'm *scared* of you, Em. Because while you're using all this glorious power that makes you feel oh so special, you don't even realize that you're hurting *me*."

"What are you talking about?"

"The ley line? Didn't you notice the effect it had on me when you used your magic? You were leeching power from me. It felt like I was being drained of blood, of magic, of *life*, because that's what you've become, Em. A Tidethief."

The word was like a stab to the heart. Emory shook her head, denying the accusation, despite suddenly recalling how Romie had looked on the ley line, how she herself had wondered if she were hurting her.

"Tides, you can't even admit it." Romie scoffed, wiping angrily at her eyes. "I guess you have changed."

With that, she stormed off, leaving Emory behind with a bitter taste in her mouth.

30

ROMIE

E MORY'S WORDS BURROWED INTO HER, AND THOUGH
there *was* some truth to them–because yes, fine, Romie *had been*
a tad jealous of Emory's power, but that was before experiencing
firsthand how dangerous it was–the fact that Emory believed she
would stoop so low as to let that jealousy come between them hurt.

Romie had already apologized about the secrets she'd kept at
Aldryn. She wasn't one to dwell on past mistakes. She was more
than willing to move on, go back to how things were before everything went to shit, if only Emory took responsibility for *her* part.
But Emory still didn't seem to grasp what she'd done.

"You okay?" Nisha asked as Romie barged into the room.

Romie had never been so happy to see her. Unlike Emory, Nisha at
least seemed more than content to go back to the way things were.

Needing an outlet for all these silly feelings, Romie related her
conversation with Emory. She expected outrage on Nisha's part,
or at least for her to take Romie's side. But Nisha merely bit her lip,
looking uncertain.

"Don't tell me you agree with her?"

"She did go through a lot."

"So did I," Romie argued. "I had to watch my friends slowly go mad in the sleepscape. I watched Travers and Lia disappear without knowing where they'd gone. I saw Jordyn turn into an umbra in front of my very eyes."

"I know," Nisha said placatingly. "I'm not saying what you went through was any less hard than what Emory did."

"Then what are you saying?"

"That maybe everything you went through changed you. Both of you. People grow apart. That doesn't mean they can't find their way back to each other."

Nisha gave her a knowing look, the hint of a smile lifting her mouth. It broke through Romie's defenses until she was rolling her eyes playfully at her, hiding a smile of her own. "Do you have any other sage advice for me?"

Nisha made a show of thinking it over. "Actually, yes."

"Oh?"

"Come closer."

Romie shuffled closer, raising a brow.

"I said closer."

The gleam in Nisha's eyes finally registered. Romie smiled, leaning in for a kiss–and jumped back as Aspen's voice rang out.

"Romie, do you– Oh, sorry."

Aspen's worried expression had Romie on high alert. "What is it?"

"I still can't find Tol through scrying," the witch said, full of devastation. "This whole thing doesn't add up. From what I know of him, Tol would *never* break his oath. He might have had a bit of a rebellious streak in him, but these people saved him. They're his family. His oath to the light is his purpose."

"We should ask questions around the city," Nisha suggested. "Find the answers that the Knight Commander wasn't keen to share. Like what's this Night Bringer she spoke of? And the Sun Forger?"

"The Sun Forger is their goddess," Aspen said. "The Night Bringer, though, I have no clue." She worried her lip. "Is there no mention of this in that book of yours?"

Romie shook her head. "There are warriors in *Song of the Drowned Gods*, sure enough, but they never sprouted *wings*."

"Although the warrior of the story did confront a dragon," Nisha supplied. "Surely one of these draconic knights has to be the key we're looking for."

Romie caught Aspen's eye at that, a thread of understanding unfurling between them. She didn't want to be the first to voice this suspicion growing in her mind, so she was thankful when Aspen said, "I think the key might be Tol."

"Because of this connection you share?" Nisha asked. Romie could hear the doubt creeping into her voice.

"Yes, but it's more than that. This song you and I hear," Aspen said, looking at Romie, "I don't think it calls us *only* to other worlds. I think it calls us to each other. This kinship I felt when you arrived at the Wychwood, this same kinship I feel toward Tol . . ."

"It's like there's an echo of the song in our souls," Romie said quietly, recalling this thrum of familiarity, of *rightness*, she felt whenever she encountered Aspen in dreams, or when she'd seen her transform into Tol as she scried. There was a profound sort of magic in whatever bond they shared. If Romie was the girl of dreams and Aspen the witch, it stood to reason that Tol was the warrior.

She wondered, not for the first time, why she didn't feel that same bond with Emory, the scholar. But she shut away the thought once more.

Romie, Nisha, and Aspen slipped away into the city that evening while the others bathed and ate. Someone had brought them clothes that made them blend in to the busy streets. There was a grim undertone to Heartstone, something that seemed to make its inhabitants skittish and tense.

Romie couldn't help but note how many cats roamed about–her heart lurched at the thought of Dusk–though she seemed to be the only person here with any sort of affection toward them. Merchants shooed the cats away from their stalls, mothers hugged their children close and cut to the other side of the street to avoid walking past them. None of the cats looked feral. They were simply *there*, watching the world with keen eyes.

And so were the owls.

As the sun dipped past the horizon, the winged creatures were suddenly everywhere, perched atop arches and buttresses. Owls big and small, with feathers ranging from snow white to ink black. The sight of them seemed to chase away most people from the streets, and those who remained were quick to light torches and lanterns, as if scared of the dark.

"For people who live in a world full of terrifying beasts, you'd think it would take more than cats and owls to spook them," Romie remarked.

"They fear the Night Bringer's creatures," someone said behind them.

Romie spun to find the young page who'd been with the draconics–Caius, she recalled–sitting on a rampart with a book he was writing in. Torchlight made his strawberry-blond curls glow orange.

Romie peered at the inside of his book. He'd sketched an owl on one page, the drawing surprisingly accurate, and a cat on the other. Both animals were surrounded by tidy handwriting listing their characteristics and behaviors. "You seem to have quite the interest in them," she noted.

"I have an interest in *all* creatures. Most of them are feared because people simply don't bother trying to understand them."

Caius shut his book with an air of self-importance. "Which is why *I* want to master as a sage. Master Bayns says my personal bestiary is already far more complete than those of most squires he's taught."

"What exactly is a bestiary?"

Caius looked at her like she was a particularly odd monster. "Why, it's only the Fellowship's most sacred weapon. A compendium of all the eldritch beasts we encounter. A map of the evil that needs to be purged by the light."

Romie didn't think a *cat* warranted such vitriol. When she said as much, Caius laughed.

"It's not so much the cat itself that people fear, or the owl. It's what they represent." He reopened his bestiary to a page where he'd drawn a creature that had the body of a black cat and the head of a gray owl, with great wings spanning either side of it. "*Panthera noctua*. The Night Bringer's emblematic beast."

Romie exchanged a wary glance with Nisha and Aspen. "Why do they fear this Night Bringer so much?"

"Rumor is he has returned." Caius frowned at them. "Don't *you* fear the evil deity who destroyed the Forger?"

"Of course we do. We just, er, haven't heard the story in so long. Would you tell it to us?"

"Welllll," he said, stretching out the word, "as you know, the eldritch beasts, like the ones we saved you from today, were born of the underworld, ruled over by the Night Bringer. And the dragons that we draconics owe our magic to were descended from the heavens, created by the Forger, who gobbled up a piece of the sun, took its heat within her heart, and spilled it into fiery mountains across the land to give birth to the sacred dragons. So the Sun Forger's magic–the power of the sun itself–lives on in both the dragons and draconics like me. But something happened to the Night Bringer and the Sun Forger, and they disappeared from the world, leaving behind their respective beasts. Pitting eldritch monsters against us who are Forger-made."

Caius pointed at the sky. "Only recently has the sun started to burn less and less every day, the nighttime pressing in earlier than it should and stretching on past when is normal. Strange things have been happening all over, like the warmth and light of the sun has been slowly diminishing. The eldritch are growing bolder, more volatile, in the dark."

"Hence the rumors about the Night Bringer's return?" Nisha guessed.

A nod. "We were returning from a nearby village when we crossed paths today. The whole place was ravaged by the same *corvus serpentes* that attacked you."

Romie squinted at him. "If you're a draconic, where are your wings?"

Caius gasped like she'd uttered the worst swear word imaginable. "Pages and squires aren't allowed to unfurl their wings outside of the training citadel. Only the masters may shift as they please."

"Are knights masters as well?"

"Of course. There are three masteries: knighthood, sagehood, and alchemy. We pages and squires study all three before mastering in one. Knights are the warriors, sages are the keepers of the bestiaries, and alchemists are our makers, trained in the secret art of draconic forging."

"And Tol?" Aspen asked with quiet hope. "What is he?"

Caius's endearing enthusiasm sputtered out at that. "Tol was still a squire, but favored to become an alchemist soon." He cast wary glances around them. "I heard you asking the Knight Commander about him earlier."

"Do you know what happened to him? Where they're keeping him?" Aspen asked.

"We're not allowed to speak of draconics who've broken their oath."

"But you know where he is."

"Maybe." He eyed them with suspicion. "What do you want with him?"

"We just want to speak with him before he's . . ." Aspen swallowed back her emotion. Tears welled in her eyes. "I knew him a long time ago, before he came here to be a draconic. I would give anything for a chance to say goodbye."

Caius considered. "I'll be at the Chasm the day of the execution, like all pages and squires. I might be swayed to point you in the right direction before the fighting begins . . . if you agree to do something for me in return."

Romie begrudgingly admired his cunning. "What do you want?"

"Master Bayns and the Knight Commander don't believe me, but I know for a fact that *corvus serpentes* have no magic, at least not the kind I saw your friend using earlier." Caius's eyes went bright and eager. "I want to see that magic again, if only to know I was right."

"And do what with that knowledge?" Romie asked. She didn't like the tight grip Caius kept on that bestiary of his. Emory wasn't an eldritch beast, but her magic, dark as it already was, might not go over well in this world.

"I swear it's only to satisfy my own curiosity." Caius worried his lip, glancing at Aspen. "Tol has rare magic too. They say he's light-blessed. Favored by the Forger."

If Caius was implying Emory might also be light-blessed, Romie doubted he would run to his masters claiming she was evil. Then again, if a death sentence was what awaited one of their own, someone blessed by their goddess at that . . .

She certainly didn't think Emory was anything close to *light*-blessed, but she kept that thought to herself.

31

KAI

"**B**RYSDEN, COME ON, IT'S NOW OR NEVER."

Baz had been staring at the lock for the past minute, face tinged green with worry. You'd think he was about to commit the biggest crime of his life.

They were standing in front of Clover's dorm, and though the corridor was empty, what with everyone still in class, it wouldn't stay that way for long.

With a groan, Baz lamented, "Why did I let you talk me into this?"

"It was *your* idea!"

"I wasn't being *serious*."

"Then why are we here?"

Kai had to admit, when Baz suggested they break into Clover's room to find something that might help them make sense of this mess, he'd laughed. Surely it had to be a joke. But with Clover otherwise occupied for the day, the opportunity was too great to pass up on.

If anything, Kai just wanted to know if Clover had started writing *Song of the Drowned Gods*. There was no doubt in his mind that Baz burned with the same curiosity.

With a mumbled "I'm going to the Deep for this," Baz finally unlocked the door with his magic. He winced as if he expected to be struck down for pulling on even the tiniest of time's threads, but just like earlier, nothing happened. Obviously.

"I'm not sure we should–"

Kai gave Baz a light shove inside before he could finish his thought. "Just make it quick." Kai remained in the doorframe, keeping one eye on the corridor.

"I don't even know what to look for," Baz grumbled as he leaned over the desk, careful not to disturb anything. "There's schoolwork . . . bloodletting instruments . . ."

Kai snickered. "To keep up appearances, I guess."

"Oh!"

Baz held up a familiar leather journal–the same one he had in his pocket, though nowhere near as threadbare. Baz carefully flipped it open. His brow creased. "There's nothing in here. Other than his name on the first page and this"–he held up a flattened four-leaf clover that had been pressed in the pages–"it's completely bare."

Maybe Clover *hadn't* started writing *Song of the Drowned Gods*, though the timing made little sense to Kai. This was Clover's last semester at Aldryn; surely he must have at least started brainstorming the book that would propel him into literary stardom.

"Wait . . ." Baz put the empty journal back in its place and reached for a small, dark book crammed between two larger volumes. "This is *Dark Tides*. How–"

Voices echoed down the hall. Baz nearly jumped out of his skin. Wide-eyed, he strode to the door, book still in hand.

"Brysden," Kai gritted out. "Leave the book."

Baz swore, rushing back to the desk. Something seemed to hit him as he glanced between the book in his hand and the door. Outside, the voices were growing louder.

Suddenly the world went quiet.

It took a moment for Kai to understand what had happened as Baz started to flip through the book instead of putting it back, looking like he had all the time in the world to do so.

Which he did–because he'd stopped time.

They might as well have been the only two people left in the world, everything around them frozen except for them. All Kai could do was stare at Baz as this indescribable sense of pride and wonder swelled inside him.

Having seemingly found what he was looking for, Baz slammed the book shut and put it back. He pushed a still-mesmerized Kai out the door, brushing his abdomen as he did. Kai sucked in a breath. Their eyes met as the click of the door's lock sounded.

"Get ready to run," Baz said.

Time resumed with a whoosh of sound. And then Kai and Baz were running down the corridor, eager to leave the scene before anyone could see them.

There was no real sense of impending urgency, but their adrenaline propelled them forward all the same, breathless laughter ripping from their throats. They'd just broken into Cornus Tides-damned Clover's room–and thanks to Baz's magic, no one would ever be the wiser.

When they reached the empty courtyard, they toppled onto a frost-dusted bench, still wheezing with laughter.

"Okay. What did you find?"

Breathless, Baz said, "Doors to the Deep. I figure if Clover's read about them in *Dark Tides*, he has to know about the Hourglass, right?"

Kai had never read *Dark Tides* himself, but both Romie and Baz had become enthralled by it–especially with its epigraph, which even Kai knew by heart at this point.

There are tides that drown and tides that bind,
tides with voices not all kind,
moon-kissed tides with pitch-black eyes,
and those that dance 'neath stranger skies.

Baz leaned in excitedly. "I found an underlined passage about doors to the Deep that I must have missed before. It mentioned portals that carry you *on the tides of time*–the authors used those words specifically."

Kai frowned. "Wasn't *Dark Tides* published after Clover's time?" It was written anonymously, and since Clover had brainstormed an early version of the epigraph in his own personal journal–a journal he had yet to write in, apparently–they'd speculated whoever authored *Dark Tides* must have taken the epigraph from him.

"I thought so too," Baz said. "I guess not?"

"What are you two doing out here in the cold?"

Kai and Baz twisted around to see Clover smiling at them.

Shit. How much of that had Clover heard? Students had appeared all around them, heading from one class to the next. Judging by the textbooks in Clover's arms, so was he.

"Just enjoying the fresh air," Kai said, plastering on a smile. "Thanks again for the clothes–Cordie was great help picking out all the best styles. We're grateful to you both." He elbowed Baz. "Aren't we?"

"Y-Yes," Baz stammered. "We'll pay you back as soon as we can."

Hopefully they'd be long gone before that.

Clover waved a nonchalant hand. "Please, it's my treat. And you can keep the ones you got from my closet." He winked at them. "They suit you."

Kai felt his skin prickle, hoping he didn't know they'd just gone *back* to his room.

32

BAZ

THE FIRST BICENTENNIAL CHALLENGE SAW PARTICIPAT-
ing students divided into teams of four, each member repre-
senting a different lunar house. Their respective tidal alignments
were written on badges pinned to their shirts. Clover, whose
badge read *Healer*, was on a team made up of an Amplifier and
a Memorist from Aldryn College, as indicated by their school
badges, and a Soultender from Ilsker College, the more illustrious
of Trevel's two magical establishments (both of which paled in
comparison to Aldryn, according to academic snobs).

Sixteen teams sat at tables that had been pushed into the middle
of the assembly hall. The gathered crowd of students and professors and foreign dignitaries alike stood along the walls of the hall,
craning their necks for the best view. Baz, Kai, Cordie, Thames,
and Polina had managed to find spots at the front, right next to
Clover's table. Clover winked at them with a confident smile, his
eyes lingering on Thames.

Aldryn was playing host to five other colleges. Karunang was the only school from the Constellation Isles, with the largest number of students present. "Easier for us to blend in," Kai noted. Not all its students were participating in the games; most of them were in the crowd, along with someone Baz assumed was their dean–a short man with a graying beard who wore a navy silk tunic embroidered with the emblematic Karunang owl in silver and gold thread. Some students wore similar clothing traditional to Luagua, while others were dressed in fashions more common to Elegy and Trevel.

Then there were the two rival Trevelyan colleges, Ilsker and Sevstar, with as many students between them as those from Karunang alone. On one side of the assembly hall was the Ilsker crowd, all of them dressed in burgundy robes thrown over their straitlaced suits and gowns. The emblem pinned to their robes depicted a wave weaved through with the eight phases of the moon, curved around a droplet of blood. On the other side of the hall were the Sevstar students in similar robes of teal, their emblem a quill and dagger over a spiral conch. The rival deans, two pompous fair-skinned men in stuffy cravats and refined suits the colors of their respective colleges, glowered at each other from across the room.

And finally, two tiny groups from the Outerlands: Fröns, a college found in the frozen north, and Awansi, hailing from the far southern plains. The Fröns dean, a pale, austere-looking woman in a fur-trimmed robe, stood with one of her students in the crowd; only two more were participating in the games proper. They were recognizable by their white frocks adorned with intricate silver buttons, and their delicate emblem that portrayed the four lunar flowers sprouting from the pages of an open book.

The Awansi students–the four of whom all seemed to be participating in the games–wore kaftans in colorful, patterned fabrics, their emblem composed of the eight moon phases connected by geometric lines and symbols, with a blazing sun in the middle. Their dean, a woman with rich dark brown skin wearing a kaftan threaded with beads and patterns that echoed the Awansi emblem, smiled proudly at her students from the sidelines.

Each participating team received a specific moon phase and time of day–these were written on a sign at their respective tables, and each set was different. At first no one knew what these meant, until a student moderator from Aldryn explained that the teams would need to solve a problem using only the magic at their team's disposal *without* resorting to bloodletting, which meant they needed to find a way to work around the specific lunar and tidal circumstances of their table.

"For example," the moderator said, "if you've been given a full moon at an ebbing Lightkeeper tide, and the problem you must solve is, say, finding your way on a treacherous path in the dark without slipping and falling to your death, how do you use the magic at your team's disposal to succeed? There is only one rule: bloodletting to access your magic outside of the particular lunar and tidal alignment set you've been given is not permitted. You have an hour to solve your challenge. Good luck."

"Wait, that's it?" Baz asked Cordie. "This is all the games are?" This sounded a lot like what Aldryn had planned for the Quadricentennial–not a dangerous event with the potential to end in death.

"This is only a warm-up to the real games they'll face over the next month," Cordie explained. "It's a way to give *some* insight into what the actual games will require."

Clover's team was given a complicated ward to break through as their problem. But none of them were Unravelers, and none of their abilities, even if they *had* been allowed to use bloodletting, would be able to decipher the ward.

Baz's gaze traveled to the other tables, his brain working to make sense of this as if he were participating himself. Though if that were him up there, he'd most definitely let panic overtake him with all these eyes on him. But in the anonymity of the crowd, things were easier and plainer to see. Which is why, about twenty minutes in and with multiple dead ends encountered in his head, the solution finally came to him.

"They have to help each other," he said under his breath. "To show that magic is collaborative."

He might have imagined the way Clover caught his eye at that very moment, as if he'd heard him—or read his mind. Clover looked around at the other tables' sets of lunar and tidal alignments. The same realization seemed to dawn on him. He stood up, chair grating so loudly on the floor it made everyone jump. Clover ignored his teammates' confused looks—and the scowl that Wulfrid, who was also participating, gave him from where he sat at a nearby table. Clover made his way to a team whose set of lunar and tidal alignments read *New Moon, Rising Healing Tide.*

"I'm guessing your problem requires some sort of healing?" Clover asked them.

"Yes," a girl from Sevstar College said warily. "But none of us are Healers."

"No, but I am." Clover pointed to a Karunang boy whose badge read *Unraveler.* "And you're what *my* team needs to solve our problem."

"And?" the boy said gruffly.

Clover smiled. "There's no rule against switching teams."

The boy blinked, then shook his head. "That would be cheating. I'm no cheater."

"No, he's right," the girl said. "There is only one rule: bloodletting isn't permitted. If there's only the one rule, then anything else goes."

The boy still looked uncertain, though he seemed to reconsider when the nearby teams started whispering among themselves and looking at the other tables' placards, having clearly overheard this exchange and wondering if they should go for it themselves.

Clover made a shooing motion with his hand. "Go on. We wouldn't want them to solve it first, would we?"

The boy darted toward Clover's group. Clover sat down at his new table and read over their problem. He quickly solved it. The moderator declared his new table the winners, and the crowd burst into applause.

Kai shouldered Baz. "You're the one who should be up there."

"You know me." Baz shrugged. "The limelight's not where I shine."

"I pity those who don't get to see you shine in the shadows."

Baz met his gaze, unsettled by the intensity in it, the sentiment behind his words.

Before he could respond, the moderator called on Clover. "Since you were the first to solve this challenge's riddle, you have earned yourself a small advantage for the actual games. The lesson here was that of collaboration. Over the next month, you will have to solve a series of *real* problems such as these. The first leg will require you to be in pairs. The details will be given to you by our dean of students in a few moments. But before that . . ." Turning to Clover, he said, "You get to have first pick of your partner. Who will it be?"

Clover made a show of thinking it over as murmurs rose all around him, everyone speculating on what the challenge would entail and who might be his best pick. At last Clover declared: "I choose Baz Brysden of House Eclipse."

Baz felt the ground tilt beneath him as confused and shocked whispers filled the assembly hall. Clover met his gaze with a wink. "If he feels up for it, of course."

The moderator gave a nervous laugh. "An Eclipse-born, you're sure?"

"Yes."

"But . . . there is no Baz Brysden here among those who signed up for the games," the moderator said, looking over a list of names. "There is no Eclipse-born on here at all."

Clover lifted a brow. "Did you really expect any of them to sign up when we all know the sort of hardships your administration would have put them through if they did? The extra measures you would have them take to restrict their magic? The vitriol they would face from fellow students?"

The moderator sputtered as he tried to come up with an answer. Clover spared him as he continued: "It was a hard-fought battle for Eclipse-born to even be allowed to *come* to the Bicentennial, much less partake in its games. After two centuries of this college denying them the same opportunities as the rest of us, you can't fault them for their mistrust now. Baz Brysden is one of only two foreign Eclipse students who decided to brave coming here despite our strict rules. If he wishes to take me up on my offer, then perhaps he can show you all that Eclipse-born are nothing to fear—and that indeed they might just surpass us all."

His eyes found Baz again. "Do you accept?"

Baz's instincts screamed at him to refuse, to not make any ripples in this time he did not belong to. He didn't want to involve himself in these games he knew would become deadly.

But Clover's words dislodged something in him. He thought of everyone back in his own time—his father, Professor Selandyn, Jae, even Rusli—who were fighting against Drutten and the Regulators and everything that Baz had been forced to run away from.

Maybe this was his way to fight for the Eclipse-born. To make even the tiniest sliver of difference in the world.

If he could influence the future in this small way, help better things for Eclipse-born, for those he loved, by showing his control and strength here, now, two hundred years in the past . . .

He had to do it.

"I accept," Baz heard himself say before he could think twice about it.

"Well . . . but the list . . ." sputtered the moderator.

"Nothing in the rules states that students cannot sign up for the games later on," Clover argued.

"He's right," someone in the crowd said–a professor, from the looks of her.

"Dean de Vruyes . . ."

"He is right," the dean repeated with a note of finality. "We will allow the addition of the Eclipse-born student."

The moderator looked between the dean of Aldryn and Clover and Baz. Finally, he scribbled a name on his list and cleared his throat. "Very well. Cornelius Clover, House New Moon, Healer, will be paired with Baz Brysden, House Eclipse . . . Pray tell, what is your alignment?"

"Timespinner," Baz said, thankful his voice did not crack.

The moderator's eyes widened. Whispers rose in the crowd, a ripple of awe and fear that made Baz want to disappear.

But he'd made his bed and now he had to lie in it. Perhaps he should have been more scared about using his power here, given how badly Eclipse-born were still seen in this time, but for some reason, this just lit more of a fire inside him. A desire to prove to the world that Eclipse-born were good–that those like Wulfrid who feared them only set them back.

Baz caught Clover's eye. At the very least, this was an opportunity to get close to him, see what Clover knew about the Hourglass.

But he had to wonder: Why had Clover picked him of all people?

He wanted to take it all back when he noticed Karunang students whispering among themselves, and their dean watching Baz like he was trying very hard to place him. Because of course, none of them had seen him before. Of course, they would all know he was a fraud.

His racing thoughts were interrupted as Dean de Vruyes took to the podium to address the assembled students. She had that same air of quiet authority that Dean Fulton had.

"Students from Aldryn and beyond, I'd like to officially welcome you to Aldryn College's Bicentennial celebrations," the dean said. "This year's much anticipated games will revolve around knowledge, the very foundation of our school. You may know of Aldryn's famed library beneath the college, which houses our world's most ancient and precious texts. The Vault of Knowledge contains books older than all our colleges, scrolls that predate our magic, tomes in languages that no scholar has any memory of. These precious gems of knowledge are kept safe behind intricate wards. Very few people ever get to set foot in the Vault, other than Aldryn professors and a selection of acclaimed scholars from around the world." The dean smiled. "But now is your chance to gain access to such exclusive knowledge."

Murmurs ran through the crowd, silenced again by the dean's raised hand as she continued: "The wards that guard the Vault have been there since the founding of the college. Whoever succeeds in breaking through them will be given lifetime access to the Vault. Such is the premise of the Bicentennial's games."

Excitement only grew at that. Baz looked at Kai with a quizzical expression. "The college is condoning its students *breaking in to* the Vault? That's just . . . so wrong."

Kai's smile was wicked; he was clearly pleased with such rule-breaking behavior. "This is going to be fun." He smirked at Baz's shocked face. "For me."

Baz was a rule-follower through and through. But if the school was allowing this . . .

The dean once again managed to get the students' attention. "You will have a month to successfully break through the wards. The first step of the games will be a scavenger hunt across Aldryn's four libraries, where you will seek information that will prove invaluable in getting past the wards. This scavenger hunt will be held in a few days. You have until then to find a partner. Whether or not you remain with said partner after this first step will be up to you. You can choose to merge teams or even to go solo. But as you saw here today, collaboration is often key."

The dean swept a somber gaze over the assembly hall. "Now, I must warn you, the wards around the Vault are not to be taken lightly. Breaking through them is not as easy as getting an Unraveler to undo them like a locksmith picks a lock. The wards are tricky and complicated and designed to keep the most ambitious and cunning of magical thieves out. There is but one way to break through them, and this is what you will have to figure out. A single misstep *will* get you harmed or, worse, killed."

The words fell so heavy on the assembly, you could have heard a pin drop in the resulting silence. "I urge you to think twice about your participation in these games. Knowledge and power are worthy ventures, but they can make or break a person, and these games are serious business. You must ask yourselves what you are willing to risk for knowledge. Tread lightly."

"I guess we know why they cancel the games after this year," Kai muttered.

Deadly wards. This was what Baz had foolishly agreed to participate in.

But if the Vault held such knowledge, maybe there was something in there about time travel. Something that could help them solve all their problems once and for all.

33

KAI

KAI WAS IN THAT SAME NIGHTMARE AGAIN.
Printing press, Dovermere, sleepscape. Machinery and stone and swirling stars.

Again he noted the absence of the crowned umbra, and he knew it had left for good.

Again the scene dissolved around him, and he was called to a different sort of darkness, a nightmare not his own. He saw the same two people, one sobbing over a body in a pool of blood, the other hanging back at the edge of the scene.

Except this time, they were no strangers. This time, Kai knew the bespectacled Fear Eater who watched the other was Thames, and in the other boy, he recognized the fine features of Cornelius Clover.

And this time, Kai saw the face of the body he was cradling.

It was Cordie.

"I'm sorry," Clover was saying, rocking his dead sister gently back and forth. "I'm so sorry."

Kai understood that he was in Clover's nightmare. His worst fear laid bare: to lose his sister.

Thames watched the scene with heartbreaking empathy. The Fear Eater rested a hand on Clover's shoulder, murmuring something Kai didn't hear. Clover broke down in Thames's arms as the darkness of the nightmare slowly ebbed into Thames.

It reminded Kai of all the times *he* had gone into Baz's nightmares, sitting quietly with him as the printing press fell to ruins around them. Absorbing that darkness for him.

And suddenly someone else was by Thames and Clover's side. At first Kai thought it was Cordie, revived—but this girl's blond hair was a shade different, her eyes darker, and with a pang Kai realized it wasn't Cordie at all but *Emory.*

A million questions surged to his lips as faint silver threads appeared between Clover and Thames and Emory. As if the stars themselves had drawn pathways between their souls.

Kai blinked, certain he was seeing things. He must have moved toward them, because Clover's attention snapped to him with sudden awareness. "You're not supposed to be here," he said.

The nightmare trembled around them. Darkness pressed in. The body that Clover leaned over was no longer his sister's but a mound of faceless corpses that deteriorated before their eyes. Clover clawed at his face as he, too, started succumbing to whatever dreadful affliction this was, his flesh tearing away from his body like ash billowing on a putrid breeze and dissolving into the growing darkness around them.

An unnatural, ravenous darkness that grew into elongated limbs and sharp claws.

The umbrae were here, ruthless with a hunger unlike Kai had ever seen from them. Emory disappeared, blinking out of the nightmare like a star. Thames braced against the umbrae, absorbing their darkness as much as he could while yelling at Clover to *wake up*, that none of this was *real*.

Clover's veins rippled silver, and though Kai knew this was only a nightmare, he didn't trust what a Tidecaller's imagined Collapsing might do in a place like this. Clover wasn't waking up, and more umbrae were swarming in, too many for one person to fend off.

Kai didn't think twice as he rushed toward the umbrae. Their attention shifted to him. They flocked to him instantly, yet Kai did nothing, waiting for them to get closer . . .

"What are you doing?" Thames yelled at him.

"Getting them away from you."

With the umbrae pressed tight around him, Kai pulled them with him into waking.

He opened his eyes to a dark room that grew darker still with the appearance of the umbrae. Kai struggled against them, willing them to disintegrate as all nightmares *should* when pulled into reality, but they did no such thing. This was not the time for his Collapsed magic to be stubborn.

"*Sleep*," he said, throwing the full force of his magic into that one word, like he had back in Dovermere right after Baz had taken the Unhallowed Seal off his hand. The umbrae at last seeped away into the dark, just as Kai's door burst open, revealing a panting Thames. Wide-eyed, Thames watched the umbrae disappear.

In the silence that followed, they stared at each other.

"How in the Shadow's name did you do that?" Thames asked.

Kai tried for an unbothered shrug. "I . . . have a hard time controlling what I bring out of the sleepscape sometimes."

If Thames suspected Kai was Collapsed, he didn't say anything except, "I've never seen that kind of power before."

"I'd gladly trade you for it." Kai smirked. "These umbrae are a pain in my ass."

"Are they always so ruthless in the nightmares you visit?"

"No. Are they in *yours*?"

"Never."

A suspicion formed in Kai's mind. The umbrae were attracted to *power*, to new magics especially. Whatever he'd seen between Clover, Thames, and Emory . . . those silver threads . . .

There was a bond there. Some kind of link between them. And with both Clover and Emory being Tidecallers, it didn't surprise Kai that the umbrae would be so intrigued.

"Who was that girl with you?" he asked.

"Girl?" Thames echoed, raising a brow. "There was no girl."

Kai didn't push him, wondering if he had seen Emory at all. Reality and sleep fusing together again.

It made no sense that he should still be able to see her in his sleep when two hundred years separated them. But this wasn't the first time he'd found her so inexplicably. When he'd been at the Institute, he'd somehow ended up in her nightmares despite his magic being put to sleep. As if this connection they shared knew no limits.

"You and Clover . . . Do you often find yourself in his nightmares like that?"

Thames seemed flustered. "His nightmares are stronger than most people's. And we're very close, he and I, if you catch my meaning. So yes, I often drift to him in sleep."

A certain bespectacled Timespinner came to mind. Kai asked, "Do you trust him?"

"With my life." His expression softened. "If this is about the games, I assure you Baz is in good hands. If anyone can make it past these wards, it's Cornelius."

Because he's a Tidecaller, Kai thought. He wanted to trust him, but Clover reminded him of Farran—more so than Thames did. The Fear Eater might have the same last name, but the similarities stopped there. Clover, on the other hand, had the same idealistic fervor that Farran once had. Ideals Farran had abandoned at the first sign of hardship, the same way he'd abandoned Kai.

What Artem had said in the sleepscape came back to him.

The way you poisoned Farran's mind with this "Tides and Shadow being equal" nonsense . . .

Kai had been racking his brain trying to figure out what Artem meant by it. Had Farran had a change of heart, in the end? Had he regretted siding with people who'd seen all Eclipse-born as vile?

All pointless questions, really. Farran had broken more than Kai's heart. He'd shattered Kai's trust in anyone who claimed to stand with Eclipse-born. The reality was, they all folded when things got hard.

Clover, he knew, was different. He was Eclipse-born himself—a Tidecaller at that. Having to hide his nature meant he had more to lose than any of them, yet he still chose to put his neck out for his fellow Eclipse-born, when the safer approach would have been to not associate with them at all. That earned points in his favor, Kai supposed.

But he couldn't be too cautious. Not where Baz was concerned.

34

EMORY

"LET ME GET THIS STRAIGHT: YOU WANT ME TO *SLOW down your heart*?"

"Precisely."

Virgil looked at her like she'd grown a giant raven's head and serpent's tail.

"You have Reaper magic," Emory explained again. "You can technically stop my heart. What I'm asking you to do is bring me to the brink of death, just to the point where I pass out."

"Okay, first of all, I've never done anything like that before. And second, how do you know I won't accidentally kill you? Don't put that on my conscience, Em."

"You won't kill me. I trust you."

Virgil huffed a laugh, rubbing at the back of his head. After her disastrous talk with Romie, Emory had come to him with this plea for help. She needed to contact the demon again. And if it took *fainting* to reach him, then she would find a way to make herself faint.

"Why is it so important to talk to him?" Virgil asked. "He's gone. We shook him off. I hope a giant raven-snake plucks his eyes out. Bottom line, he's not our problem anymore."

Emory shook her head. "We haven't seen the last of him. He's after something, and I want to know what it is." And most importantly, he knew things about her magic—things she needed to understand.

Especially if Romie was right about hurting her on the ley line.

Virgil sighed, looking at the ceiling. "To think you were an innocent once, not so long ago, and we were the ones corrupting you to do dangerous deeds."

"I'm not that girl anymore," Emory snapped, thinking of her conversation with Romie.

"Oh, I know you aren't." He flashed her a sly grin. "You're far more fun."

"So you'll do it?"

"Let the record show that I still think there's a safer way to do this, but . . ." He threw his hands up. "What can I say? I'm an enabler. A proud supporter of terrible decisions."

Emory grinned at him. "I know. That's why I came to you."

Virgil clutched at his heart.

They set up in a well-appointed living room, Emory lying down on a divan so she wouldn't fall flat on her face. Virgil slashed his palm and bled into a bowl of water, bloodletting to call on his Reaper magic.

"Ready?" he asked.

"Ready."

"When you see dear old Keiran's ugly face again," Virgil said, "punch it for me, will you?"

"You'd have to show me how to throw a punch first."

Virgil gasped in mock offense. "Do these hands look like they've ever thrown a punch? I'm insulted. Go ask one of those winged weirdos. They're the buff warriors. I'm just the pretty face."

He was indeed a pretty face to look at as her heart slowed. Emory felt herself slipping into oblivion, and then she was falling through the strangeness of the sleeping realm.

Keiran-not-Keiran was there waiting for her like last time. The golds and silvers in his eyes flashed as he sized her up.

"I see you survived the eldritch in one piece," he remarked.

She couldn't tell by the tone of his voice if he was pleased by this or not.

"You knew those beasts were about to attack us," Emory said, "yet you were in here with me. How can you be in two places at once?"

He made a vague motion with his hand, looking bored by the question. "The same way a tree exists both above and below, feels the air and the earth in equal parts. The same way your magic can be more than one thing at once, and so much more if you'd let it."

"You seem rather preoccupied with my magic for someone who tried to kill me."

The corner of his mouth lifted. "When I truly mean to kill you, Tidecaller, you'll know."

So that was how it would be. Veiled riddles and not-so-veiled threats.

Emory studied him. "What do you want?"

Her question seemed to unsteady him. Almost as if he hadn't considered it before. He quickly regained his composure and said, "Wanting is such a pathetically mortal thing. I'd forgotten how dreadful it could be until I stepped into this." He motioned at himself–at Keiran's body, which was not his own.

Emory couldn't stop herself from asking, "Is any part of him still there?"

Dark satisfaction played on Keiran's lips at whatever he saw in her expression. "Would you like him to be?"

He advanced toward her, and it took everything in her not to flinch away from him. *He can't hurt you here*, she thought to herself, hoping desperately that it was true.

"Would you like me to tell you that I can taste his memories of you? How deeply he cared for you. How eager he was to tell you those three little words you yourself chose to keep trapped in your throat at the last." He reached out a hand to brush her hair in a motion that was so very Keiran-like, she stood rooted to the spot, unable to extricate herself from his hypnotizing gaze. "How shocked he was that you'd let him die, in the end."

This snapped her out of it. Emory wrenched herself away, disgust roiling in her stomach. "He deserved it." She struggled to keep her composure as she forced out the words. She wasn't going to let him use her shame like a knife, plunging it right through her heart.

Keiran hummed pensively. "Perhaps." He cocked his head to the side. "The way he saw it, he believed he was going to make you into something more powerful than what you already are. A formidable vessel to house the power of gods." His eyes darkened. "Funny how that works out. He was so very wrong, but still, he would have gone to the ends of the universe for you."

"That's not . . . He didn't care about me. He just *needed* me. Used me."

"And paid the price for it with his life."

There was an appreciative note in his words that unsettled her. But he was right.

Emory thought of Baz—how she had done to him exactly what Keiran had done to her. Used him when she needed him, when it suited her. She didn't deserve his forgiveness. Not when she herself could never forgive Keiran.

She wanted to believe she was nothing like Keiran—that she would never let herself become him. Someone who was willing to sacrifice his friends. Someone so deluded he'd thought he was doing the right thing, that he was going to save her by eradicating everything that she was.

But maybe she'd already started down that path.

"How does it feel," the demon said, voice low and sinister, "to get retribution against someone who wronged you?"

Emory thought of Keiran's ghost, of his hand around her neck, his silent promise of keeping a choke hold on her even in death. And now here he was, plaguing her still.

If surviving him was retribution for what he'd done to her, it didn't feel like it. It only made her feel hollow.

"Is that what you're after?" she asked. "Retribution?"

"Retribution. Vengeance. It's what I'm owed."

"For what?"

The gold and silver around his pupils blazed in a way that promised violence. "Everything that was done to me and mine."

Emory took a step back despite herself. "Who are you? Tell me your name so I can stop thinking of you as Keiran."

"I have had many names," he said, "none of which I care to remember."

"Then you won't mind if I call you demon."

"Said in such an endearing way? I insist." He looked her up and down. "But enough about me. I'd rather talk about what *you're* after. Have you found the heart yet?"

The heart—this world's key.

Emory's own heart stumbled. If he got to the key before they did . . .

She felt the dawning of consciousness pull at her, beckoning her back to herself. Before she could be swept away from this strange place, she said, "If you hurt my friends again, I'll kill you."

"I'm positively *trembling* with fear," he deadpanned.

"I'm serious."

"Oh, I don't doubt it. Though, from what I've seen, you seem to be doing a fine enough job of hurting your friends on your own. Careful, there. A Tidecaller's power is a double-edged sword, as I'm sure you know."

She glimpsed a wry smile on him before the scene dissolved, and she was pulled up through the darkness and into the light as she regained consciousness.

It was a jarring thing to have those last words ringing in her ears as she opened her eyes to find not only Virgil staring at her but Romie, Nisha, Aspen, and Vera too. There was another face in their midst, that of the page they'd met earlier that day, looking at her with wide, eager eyes.

"Can we see some magic now?" Caius asked, making Emory very nearly wish she were back in that strange in-between space with the demon.

35

BAZ

B AZ QUICKLY LEARNED THAT AGREEING TO BE PART OF THE
games meant he and Kai could no longer afford to be invisible.

The morning after the opening challenge, they were accosted
in the quad by the Karunang dean. They braced for the worst—
surely he would call out the fact that they weren't actually
Karunang students—but the dean only greeted them with a warm
smile.

"Mr. Brysden, is it?" He wore another silk tunic, this one a deep
plum with gold-threaded stars. "I wanted to touch base with you,
see if you need anything now that you'll be in the games."

"Um." Baz's confusion was mirrored in Kai's eyes. Surely the
dean had to know they were frauds. "Is it . . . is it all right that I
signed up?" he asked cautiously.

"I admit I was surprised when you agreed to it," the dean said
with a chuckle, "but I couldn't be prouder. The first Eclipse participant in these games, a Karunang student? I wouldn't dream of
having it any other way." He glanced between Baz and Kai. "The

two of you should be in class, though. Participation in the games does not excuse my students from their schoolwork."

Indeed, all foreign students had to follow a regular Aldryn schedule while they were here, their class attendance mandatory for this to count toward their own studies back home.

"Now off you go," the dean said as the clocktower bell tolled. "And if you need anything, anything at all–please know I'm here for you both. I won't stand for mistreatment of my Eclipse students."

An hour later, Baz and Kai filed into a classroom in Pleniluna Hall, having worked out a schedule that would allow them to remain close to Clover. Indeed, Clover sat alone in the very top row of the lecture hall–all gleaming white walls and vaulted white ceiling. He didn't appear to see them as they climbed the stairs to join him, his pen gliding in a frenzy as he wrote in a familiar journal.

One that clearly *wasn't* blank.

"These seats taken?"

Kai's question had Clover casually sliding the journal away from view, but not before Baz saw the pages once more go blank. Some kind of Wardcrafter magic against prying eyes, maybe?

Clover smiled up at them, motioning for them to sit. "Please."

Baz took the spot next to Clover. "What are you writing?" He forced himself to sound casual and not like the absolute gushing fanatic he felt like.

"A bit of this, a bit of that," Clover answered vaguely. "I like to dabble in different things. There is nothing more alluring than a good story. It's why I enjoy this class so much."

As if on cue, a professor turned to them from where she'd written *THEOLOGY* on the blackboard. "For those of you joining us from other colleges, welcome to our advanced theological studies. I'm Professor Aurora Hoyaken. Let's discuss the Tides and the Shadow, shall we?"

A current of excitement ran through Baz as he recognized the professor's name. She was one of the authors of the book he'd gotten out of the Vault for Professor Selandyn at the beginning of the school year, *The Tides of Fate and the Shadow of Ruin: A Theological Study into the History of Lunar Magics.*

Professor Hoyaken started her class off by disclosing that theology was not science, and as such no single belief should be regarded as incontestable fact. This had a familiar face sneering. Wulfrid launched into a self-righteous monologue about why the Tidelore faith was the only one that made any sense in explaining the origin of their magic.

"That guy's really starting to piss me off," Kai muttered darkly.

"See, this is why I reject the small-minded views of our modern Tidelore faith," Clover intervened, drawing the class's attention and Wulfrid's irritation. "It seeks to erase so much rich mythological history. To truly understand the relation between lunar and ecliptic magics–both the dichotomy that exists and the unity that *should*– one can only benefit from looking at every facet of the mythology that surrounds the origins of such magics. What common thread can be found in these stories? Who was doing the telling, and how did their portrayal benefit them?"

"And what have you found?" Professor Hoyaken asked with keen interest, while Wulfrid rolled his eyes, sulking in his seat.

Clover leaned back in his chair. "What I find particularly intriguing is how every myth paints the Tides and the Shadow as being *products* of gods, of entities much bigger than them. The predominant myth here in Elegy supposes the Tides were given their power by a benevolent moon divinity. The Constellation Isles also believe the Tides were blessed by a moon goddess, and that the Shadow was cursed by a sun god. Magicless folk in the northern Outerlands tell tales of the Tides and the Shadow being sent here by a vengeful death god to tempt humans with sinful magic and lead them astray from the rightful path of life. On and on it goes, all these myths that color our history sharing this one commonality of powerful gods and higher powers. And yet, none of us has ever worshipped such gods. Only the Tides and the Shadow."

"What does that make them, then, if not deities?" Professor Hoyaken asked.

"Oh, I believe they were divine in their own right," Clover said, face alight with the same sort of passion that Baz was used to seeing in Professor Selandyn and Jae Ahn. "Not gods in the way most people seem to paint them, but perhaps *messengers* to such gods. Intermediaries between us mere humans and the higher powers we owe our creation to."

"That's blasphemy," Wulfrid spat, earning a few nods of agreement.

"It's academic speculation," Professor Hoyaken corrected, "and it's precisely the point of this class. Do go on, Mr. Clover."

Clover leaned forward excitedly. "Well, the question then becomes: If the Tides and the Shadow are gone from our shores, if we are to believe our magic became limited and splintered between lunar houses and tidal alignments after their disappearance, could these mightier gods be the reason why? Did they call back their messengers to wherever they came from? Could they have not liked how involved the Tides and the Shadow were in our human lives, granting magic to everyone and anyone who asked, and so they decided to limit our magic by depriving us of our would-be deities?"

"All intriguing questions indeed," Professor Hoyaken said. "Thank you for your insight, Mr. Clover."

Clover gave Baz and Kai a bashful smile as the professor moved on with her lesson. "Apologies," he whispered. "I tend to get carried away with these sorts of theories."

Baz waved him off. "I know some people who share your fascination." Selandyn and Jae would have loved debating theories with him.

Kai remained quiet, eyeing Clover with something cold and skeptical that Baz didn't understand.

When class ended, Clover asked them about the other classes they would take, looking pleased that their schedules aligned. He spoke of the next Eclipse salon he would be holding and the party that would take place after the first leg of the games, and the normalcy of the conversation had Baz forgetting everything except a single thought: that he was classmates with his literary idol. That he was walking in the hallowed halls of Aldryn with a legend, and somehow, they were *equals*. Peers.

"Why did you call on Baz to be your partner?"

Kai's blunt question brought Baz back to reality. There was that guarded look in his eyes again, like he didn't trust Clover. He'd blocked their path as they made their way to their next class, the cold air blowing through the frigid cloisters nowhere near as cold as the tone of his voice.

"Ah, I wondered when I was going to be reprimanded for that," Clover said with a penitent wince. "In all honesty, I heard Baz solving the first challenge's riddle." His eyes met Baz's. "You're clever. I like clever. And your magic . . . I'd heard of Timespinners before, but they're so rare. A gift like that will likely prove useful in this game of ours."

"This isn't a game for us," Kai snapped before Baz could get a word in edgewise. "You might have nothing to lose, but you dragged Baz into this, and he's Eclipse-born. It's different."

Clover sobered at that, his brow creasing. "I would never do anything to put a fellow student in harm's way. *Especially* an Eclipse-born."

"But you did. The moment you said Baz's name, you put a target on his back."

Baz shifted uncomfortably. "Kai . . ."

"Is this about the nightmare of mine that you stepped into last night?" Clover didn't sound reproachful; he sounded ashamed.

Kai quirked an eyebrow. "You mean the one where everyone around you died?"

Baz blinked at Kai. This was the first he was hearing of this.

"My nightmares tend to get fairly gruesome at times, yes," Clover conceded. "When you witness death, especially as a child . . . it scars you. I hold tight to those around me because my worst fear is losing them. I put my neck out for the Eclipse-born because I know what it's like to—"

"You might have compassion for the challenges we Eclipse-born face," Kai interrupted, "but it's not the same as experiencing them firsthand. You will never understand what it's like for us because you're not like us."

Clover opened his mouth as if to contest that fact but caught himself. Baz realized what Kai had been trying to do: he'd baited Clover so that he'd show his hand—admit to being one of them. Eclipse-born. Eclipse-*formed*. An identity he had to live with in secret.

"What I'm trying to say," Clover maintained, "is that I will not do anything to jeopardize Baz's safety. You have my word."

"Good." Kai smiled at him in a way that scared most people. "As long as we're all on the same page."

Baz found himself unable to concentrate during their next class. He kept replaying Kai's insinuated threat to Clover. That intimidating smile, the protective stance—all for Baz's benefit.

He didn't think Clover deserved such distrust from them. But he found he didn't mind this protective side of Kai—that in fact, he enjoyed it.

That night, when they were alone in the illusioned gardens, Baz and Kai speculated over the dean of Karunang's apparent belief that they really were students of his. It was hard to believe he would have such little awareness of his charges that the sudden appearance of two Eclipse-born students wouldn't even cast the slightest of doubt.

"I suppose we should be grateful," Baz said with a shrug.

Kai wasn't so convinced. "I don't like it. Clover asking you to be his partner, the lack of pushback from the dean . . . It all feels too convenient. We need to be careful."

Baz's stomach was aflutter again thinking of Kai's earlier protectiveness. "What was this about Clover's nightmare?"

He listened, horrified, as Kai recounted the scene he'd witnessed in Clover's sleep and the umbrae he'd pulled out of it. If Clover was dreaming about *Collapsing*, there was no doubt in their minds that he'd unlocked his Eclipse magic.

"There's something else." Kai fiddled with a blade of grass. "I was waiting for the right moment to tell you, and I'm not even sure it was real, but . . . I think I saw Emory in Clover's nightmare."

Baz's heart stopped. "How . . ."

"I keep seeing *Thames* in Clover's nightmares too. It's like I drift to them in sleep without even trying, the same way it was with Emory before." Kai gave Baz an assessing glance. "You know, I always wondered why *your* nightmares called to me more than others. For a while, I thought . . . I don't know. That there might be something magical to our connection. But maybe there isn't."

"Okay," Baz said with a confused chuckle, trying not to be hurt by the comment.

"No, I mean, what we have—it doesn't *need* some weird magical explanation. You intrigue me, Brysden. You always have, ever since I first stepped into that printing press nightmare of yours. You're not like anyone I've ever met. And maybe that's why I can't get away from you. Why I always end up in your mind like a damn moth to a flame."

Baz didn't think he could bear it if that was all Kai saw him as: a mind full of repeating nightmares and deep-rooted fears that he found interesting in a purely academic way. A project to work on as he kept pushing further into Baz's psyche to understand his fears.

"I'm not some experiment for you to decipher," he said, the bite of anger to his words taking him by surprise. Why was this bothering him so much?

"I'm explaining it all wrong. What I'm getting at is this dream-bond I have with Clover, Thames, Emory . . . I think *that* has a magical explanation. It's like our souls call to one another in sleep, a pull that can't be ignored." Amusement lifted the corner of his mouth. "And just so you know, there's nothing about you *to* decipher. I can read you like a Tides-damned book, Brysden."

"Is it a good book, at least?"

"The best."

Baz felt suddenly warm despite the coolness of the illusioned gardens. Still, something Kai had once said to him darkened his thoughts. *It's always the quietest minds that hide the worst sort of violence.*

"Did you know, on some level, that I . . . that I'd killed those people?" he asked.

Kai flinched. "Why would you think that?"

"Maybe that's why you've always been drawn to my nightmares. Because of how horrible they are. Because of how horrible I am."

Kai's mouth thinned in an angry line. "You know I've seen truly terrible minds, souls darker than the dark between stars." His midnight voice sent shivers up Baz's spine. "You're not one of them, Baz."

They locked eyes. The sound of his first name on Kai's lips sent butterflies swirling in his chest. If it were anyone but Kai, Baz might think he was saying this only to make him feel better. But Kai wasn't one for lies or sugarcoating the truth.

Baz cleared his throat, trying not to sound too desperate as he asked, "Could you try reaching Emory in the sleepscape again?"

A pause. A thousand emotions winking in and out of Kai's eyes. Then: "I'll try."

Baz looked up at the night sky, reminded of the time he'd watched shooting stars with Emory in the greenhouse.

The memory conjured strange feelings in him now. He thought suddenly how much like a shooting star Emory was. Brilliant and awe-inspiring when it raced through his life, but momentary. A fleeting thing that could never truly be known in full. Even when they'd shared this massive secret between them—the knowledge of her being a Tidecaller and everything it entailed—it had never really felt to him like they were on the same team. She'd shared this one secret with him, sure, but how many more had she kept from him? How many half lies and veiled truths had she spoken, knowing his feelings for her would push him to believe whatever tapestry she weaved?

The stars above him were still. Baz preferred them this way. They were reliable in their stillness, just like the boy sitting beside him.

Baz studied Kai's reflection in the moonlight. How different he was from Emory. Here in the uncertainty of their predicament, he felt like he and Kai were on the same page. That they were in this together, secrets and all. And he realized it had always been this way between them. Sure, Kai might have kept things from him, but it was always to *protect* him, whereas Emory had always had ulterior motives.

Kai caught his gaze and arched a brow. "What?"

"Nothing," Baz whispered. When he looked up at the stars again, all he could see in them was the pattern of Kai's eyes.

36

ROMIE

ROMIE FOUND TOL IN DREAMS.

It was an easy thing to follow the vibration of that song, pulling her right to him. She knew instinctively that it was the key in him calling to her soul. Why she felt that connection to him, to Aspen, and yet not to Emory, was beyond her, and not something she wanted to ponder here in the sleepscape.

Tol's dream was warmth and sunlight, the feeling of hugging someone you love. He was sitting around a large meal with people Romie assumed were his family. A mother, a father, three sisters. There was laughter and love so deep it made her miss her own family with a sudden excruciating pang.

Tol turned to Romie. She recognized him as the young man she'd seen when she'd found Aspen scrying in the sleepscape. His face was like the golden glow of dawn on those sandstone formations they had traveled through, and the eyes that met hers were a striking shade of topaz. Where before he'd had shoulder-length, dark hair, his head was shorn now, as she imagined all prisoners' must be.

And the muscles on him—he truly looked the part of the warrior, a weapon forged by this fiery world.

"Anatolius?"

Something flared in his molten eyes. "No one but the draconic masters calls me that."

"Tol, then?" Romie took a tentative step toward him, not wanting the dream to get away from them. "I'm Romie. I'm a friend of Aspen's. She sent me here to give you a message."

He frowned. "Aspen?"

Right—Aspen could see through *his* eyes, but he wouldn't have felt her presence in his mind. He wouldn't know her name.

"A friend of Caius's."

"Caius," Tol repeated with recognition.

"We need you to hang on, all right? We're getting you out of there."

Confusion grew thick around him. "I don't understand." The dream shifted in a way that told Romie this was too much for him, that reality was seeping in again and he would soon be pulled out of sleep.

As the dream began to dissolve, the only words Romie could think of were those of *Song of the Drowned Gods*. "Patience," she called out to him. "Take heart."

And then she was in a different dream, in a mind she would recognize anywhere.

Emory's dream was more of a memory: three kids running barefoot through fields of gold, laughing their way to the shore, dancing with a flock of gulls. Romie watched as the younger version of herself pulled a young Emory up from where she sat with Baz, and the two of them ran into the water, laughing and shrieking as waves crashed around them.

There was nothing sad about the memory. But Romie was hit with a sense of melancholy so poignant she wanted to cry. She met

Emory's eyes—the real Emory suddenly standing next to her, not the dream one—to see them wet with unshed tears.

"Do you think we can get back to that?" Romie asked.

Emory didn't reply, only rested her head on Romie's shoulder. In silence, they watched the dream together, letting the gulls carry their burdens for a time.

Suddenly Emory lifted her head, brows knit together in confusion as she peered at something in the distance. "Is that . . . ?"

Romie hadn't noticed the darkness pressing in at the edges of the dream. And she certainly hadn't noticed *him* there.

"Kai?"

37

KAI

IT TOOK KAI TWO DAYS TO FIND EMORY IN THE SLEEPSCAPE. It wasn't for a lack of trying. He simply couldn't feel her there, which he assumed meant she was awake, since she didn't show up in Clover's nightmares either. He'd never sought her out this way before, had always simply found himself in her nightmares without knowing how he'd shown up there in the first place. He'd started to believe he'd imagined the whole thing.

Until the night before the games started. As soon as Kai drifted to sleep, he was like a magnet being pulled along the starlit path by a great force field, a thread tugging on his soul. This was different from the song, but similar too. Familiar in a way Kai didn't understand.

When he found her, she wasn't surrounded by ghosts like she'd been last time. In fact, she seemed almost peaceful.

And at her side was Romie.

"*Kai?*" The Dreamer gaped.

Emory glanced between the two of them—and at the shining

threads that bound her to each of them. One flowing between her and Romie, the other between her and Kai. "Please tell me this is real," she said, in such an echo of Kai's last nightmare that he had to remind *himself* that this was real, this was real, this was *real*.

"Looks like it," he said.

Romie nearly bowled him over as she threw herself at him with what he could only describe as a Tides-damned *squeal*. "I can't believe it's you!"

"Didn't realize you'd missed me so much," Kai wheezed under her tight embrace.

"Shut up and hug me."

Around them, the scene glitched, flickering between a sunlit beach and the gloom of a familiar cave. As if going from dream to nightmare.

"This makes no sense," Emory said with a laugh as she looked from Kai to Romie to the shifting sleepscape around them. Kai could tell her grip on reality was slipping. "I don't . . . I need to wake up."

"No, hey, *wait*." Romie grabbed Emory by the shoulders, forcing her to look at her. "This is real. See?" She put Emory's hand on Kai's shoulder. "Kai and I are in *your* subconscious. If you wake up now, I don't know if we'll be able to get this connection again. So take a breath and concentrate on staying *asleep*."

Emory blinked at her hand on Kai. She snatched it back as she realized he *was* real. "How is this possible when we're worlds apart?"

"There's more than worlds separating us now." Kai wanted to laugh at the absurdity of their situation. "Baz and I are stuck in time. Two hundred years in the past, to be exact."

"*What?*" Romie gasped. "How?"

"No idea."

"When the others said you disappeared, we thought maybe . . ." Emory's eyes were bright. "But you're *alive*."

"Wouldn't be here otherwise."

Romie gave a breathy laugh of relief. "Thank the Tides for that."

Kai frowned. "When you said the others–you mean . . ."

"Nisha, Virgil, Vera," Romie said. "They made it through the sleepscape and found us in the Wychwood. We're all in the Wastes now."

"So it's all real, then?" Kai asked, unable to hide the wistful note in his voice. "The other worlds, everything?"

Romie brimmed with excitement. "Yes, it's all real."

A part of Kai was jealous he wasn't there to see it. He and Baz were the biggest fans of *Song of the Drowned Gods* that he knew, and here Emory and Romie were, getting to live through the real-life version of it.

Their meeting Clover seemed to pale in comparison.

"It's not all good, though," Emory said, putting a damper on Romie's excitement.

Kai raised a brow. "You're traipsing around in Clover's worlds. How bad can it be?"

The girls exchanged a look. It was Romie who answered: "Things here are a bit more dire than what Clover's book portrays. The worlds are dying. We're going to the sea of ash to heal them."

Dying worlds–just like Professor Selandyn had read about in Clover's journal.

"It gets worse." Emory peered at the darkness. "Something escaped the sleepscape and tried to kill the key from the Wychwood."

The crowned umbra who'd gone into Keiran's reanimated corpse. Kai looked for it in the folds of darkness around them, but again couldn't feel it anywhere.

What he *did* feel were the umbrae pressing in. Romie seemed to notice it too, this sense of foreboding that permeated the sleepscape. She swore, face blanching, no doubt at the thought of being made an eternal sleeper. "We need to wake up." She squeezed Kai's hand. "Tell my brother I miss him, okay?"

The Dreamer winked out like a star, and then Kai and Emory were alone in the dark.

Emory turned pleading eyes on him. "Don't tell Baz about this."

Kai wanted to *strangle* her for suggesting such a thing. "I warned you I'd make your life a living nightmare if you fucked him over, do you remember that?" At least she had the decency to look ashamed. "Unlike you, I don't spend my time hiding things from him and using him for my own gain."

"This isn't–look, you and I both know he'll worry himself to death."

"He's stronger than you give him credit for."

"You're right. But–shit."

The darkness was suffocating now. It became harder for Kai to hold on to the connection.

"Wake up," he gritted out. "Now."

"You'll come back?" Emory asked, full of hope. "Whatever this is, we can–"

Kai opened his eyes. He pushed the bedcovers back, his first thought being of barging into Baz's room to tell him what just happened.

He stopped with his hand on the doorknob as Emory's words slid against the walls of his mind.

The games were starting tomorrow. Baz needed to stay sharp. Focused.

And maybe Emory was right. Maybe it was best Baz didn't know, at least not until Kai could make sense of things.

You're just protecting him, he told himself. *He'll understand.*

Kai went back to bed, the sting of his own betrayal churning in his gut.

38

BAZ

BAZ HADN'T QUITE REALIZED JUST HOW FAR BACK IN time he'd gone until confronted with the library classification system of the period. The cataloging of titles felt confusing and impractical; had it not been for Clover, he would never have found what they were looking for.

"*A Brief and (Mostly) True Historie of Elegyan Hauntings* by Porpentious Stockenbach," Baz read with a raised brow as Clover pulled the title off the shelf. "How are ghost stories supposed to help us with the wards?"

Clover looked just as dubious as he thumbed through the large book, which didn't seem very brief at all. "Perhaps the next clue is in here?" He read from the table of contents. "'Life Beyond Death' . . . 'Damnation, Purgatory, and the Eternal Soul' . . . Ah yes, surely 'The Phantom Animals of Stonehaven Farms' will help us solve this mystery."

Baz grinned at Clover's sarcastic tone. "Definitely."

Each team had been given a single clue to start the scavenger hunt: the name Porpentious Stockenbach, which had led them to the Noviluna library after Clover determined that the late author had been a Shadowguide. From the looks of it, they were the first team to have solved it.

Baz peered over the wrought iron railing of the second-story gallery that overlooked the main floor of the library, where a few students studied quietly at the long tables. A chill ran through him. He'd never liked the foreboding gloom of the Noviluna library, with its austere black marble and dark-stained wood that mimicked the cold of a winter's night. He liked it even less as he spotted Wulfrid and his teammate—a tall, burly boy from Fröns College, judging by his white frock and flowery badge—making their way up to the second level. The two boys who always followed Wulfrid around like helpless pups were not far behind, they too having signed up for the games.

"Looks like we're not the only ones who figured it out," Baz said in warning.

Clover's jaw tightened as he noticed the approaching participants. He eyed the book, then the shelf, searching for whatever clue they needed next. Baz was about to suggest he stop time while they figured it out, as they weren't allowed to actually take any of the clues from the spots they found them in. But Clover merely put the book back on the shelf, a curious smile tugging at his lips.

"What are you—"

"Trust me." Clover spun to meet Wulfrid's seething glare. "Gentlemen," he said with a curt nod. "Best of luck to you."

Wulfrid narrowed his eyes at them and spat an insult as they brushed past him.

"Where are we going?" Baz asked when they were out of earshot.

"Crescens library. The clue wasn't *in* Stockenbach's book—it was what sat next to it. *Conversations with Plants: The Magickal Landscaping of Aldryn College.*"

"That doesn't sound like something that belongs on New Moon shelves."

"Precisely."

The brightness of the Crescens library was a welcome change from the gloom of Noviluna Hall. Wintry sunlight filtered through the domed glass ceiling and high windows. Baz noted the absence of music; whatever Wordsmith magic made the library alive with ever-changing instrumentals back in his time must not have been invented yet.

The musty smell of books mixed with the green scent of the plants that grew all over the conservatory-like library reminded Baz of the greenhouse Romie had spent all her time in. With a pang, he found himself missing her.

Clover beelined to an alcove between two pale-wood shelves, where ivy grew thick on the wall around a series of paintings depicting Aldryn College in different lights and periods. Among them was an old, framed map of the college a few years after its inception. A silver placard underneath read: *Aldryn College grounds designed by Wordsmith Florien Delaune, founder of Crescens library.*

"'Founder of Crescens library' . . . ," Clover read aloud, frowning at the placard.

Baz could see the wheels turning in his head. "I'm assuming the next clue should bring us to the Pleniluna library?" he said, unsure of what to look for. He felt useless with Clover doing the brunt of the work.

But Clover beamed at him like he'd solved the mystery of the world itself. "Of course! The founder of Pleniluna library . . . perhaps they were a Wardcrafter, the very one who might have erected the wards around the Vault."

With nothing else to go on, they headed to Pleniluna Hall. Whereas the Waxing Moon library was reminiscent of a tranquil conservatory, the Full Moon library spared no expenses in its lavishness. It was the biggest library on campus, downright palatial with its winding staircase and four stories of stately shelves and ornate columns. It was dressed all over in white marble, with glistening silver chandeliers and gold filigree brightening up the space until it almost hurt to look at.

Clover tracked down the librarian in charge to inquire about the library's founder. As they waited for an answer, Baz spotted Wulfrid and his allies hurriedly making their way up the stairs, gleeful looks on their faces.

Baz and Clover exchanged a look just as the librarian came back to them with their answer: "Lutwin de Vruyes," she said. "He was a Purifier, founded the Pleniluna library . . . and, ah, he wrote a volume titled *Purifying Practices Against Evil.*"

She eyed Baz nervously. It was easy to guess what *evil* referred to here.

At Clover's insistence, she pointed them in the book's direction on the third floor. Every floor here was dedicated to a Full Moon tidal alignment, starting with Soultenders on the first floor and ending with Lightkeepers on the fourth.

Wulfrid must have easily figured it out, being a Purifier himself. They crossed paths while he was on his way down, a smug smile on his face as he told Baz, "Enjoy the very pertinent reading, Eclipse scum."

If Kai were here, Baz was certain he'd shove Wulfrid down the stairs.

Clover did a better job at hiding his anger than Kai would have, but Baz felt it simmering off him as he grabbed the book in question off the shelf. "I can't believe they included such a book in the scavenger hunt. They could have picked anything else, but they had to go for something that got a rise out of us." His eyes flickered to Baz. "Out of you," he corrected himself. "I'd understand if you hated me for roping you into this."

"No, of course not—it's fine, really. Let's just find the next clue and make sense of all this before Wulfrid does."

"Fair enough." Clover thumbed through the book, grimacing at whatever he saw there. "It's mostly theories on exorcisms of spirits and . . . certain supposedly dark forces. Best you don't look at this. Lutwin de Vruyes was decidedly *not* an ally of the Eclipse-born." Disgusted, he put the book back. "At least the dean is more open-minded than her ancestor."

Baz frowned. "Most of the clues so far concerned the library founders and the general history of Aldryn. If each clue's supposed to bring us to the next library . . . isn't *The History of Aldryn* shelved in Decrescens library?"

Clover lifted a brow. "How do you know that?"

Right. Only an Aldryn student would know that, and Baz was supposed to be from Karunang. He was saved from coming up with a lie as two more groups of participants appeared at the top of the stairs completely out of breath. The first duo gave Baz a friendly nod—two Karunang students who, just like their dean, did not look the slightest bit suspicious of Baz. The second duo, two girls wearing the burgundy robes of Ilsker College, gave him a wide berth, eyes catching fearfully on the Eclipse sigil on his hand.

Clover motioned for Baz to follow him. They quickly found their way to the Decrescens library. Baz's nerves stilled as he stepped into this place he knew by heart, its eclectic opulence making him feel right at home.

The History of Aldryn was mandatory reading for first-years even in Baz's time. There was a whole shelf dedicated to it here, with multiple battered copies that freshman students would borrow for their coursework. And the shelf stood right beside the entrance to the Vault.

Baz eyed the laurel-leaf-crowned marble busts on either side of the slender archway that led down into the Vault. Back in his time, the wards did not reach this far up; he still remembered the silver door at the bottom of these stairs, wrought with intricate motifs of the Tides, that unlocked to let in those lucky enough to peruse the Vault. Here, though, the wards started at the archway, where a similar silver door now stood.

"Could the wards around the Vault be tied to the other libraries?" he wondered aloud.

"Perhaps." Clover grabbed two copies of *The History of Aldryn*. "If the wards were erected when it was built, we might learn something about them in here."

They found a quiet corner to peruse the large history book. Baz could barely concentrate. There was a certain magic about being in *this* particular library with *this* particular person, seeing as how it was said to be where Clover wrote his fabled manuscript.

By now most teams had made it here and were all doing the same as them. Baz and Clover didn't find anything about wards specifically, but they did find the names of each library's founder. All four of them had been prominent members of society whose money had gone into building the school. Each of their names was associated with the library of their respective lunar houses. The founder of the Noviluna library was Hilda Dunhall—Baz tried not to scowl at the name. Then there was Florien Delaune, who'd founded the Crescens library; Lutwin de Vruyes, who'd founded the Pleniluna library; and Suera Belesa, who'd founded the Decrescens library.

"Does it say anything about a founder for the Vault?" Clover asked.

"Not that I can tell. Looks like there's no name attached to that one. Maybe it was a collaboration between the other four?"

Clover tapped his fingers against the table pensively. "None of them were Wardcrafters, though. Hilda was a Shadowguide, Florien a Wordsmith, Lutwin a Purifier, and Suera an Unraveler."

"So none of them could have erected the wards," Baz said, deflating at this dead end.

"No. Still, we should read up on each of the founders, see if something about them leads us to information on the wards–and the Wardcrafter who must have created them."

A sudden, disquieting hush fell over the library. The air turned cold, colder still than the wintry Noviluna library, as an unnatural wind blew through the shelves, ruffling loose pages on tables and making the hair on Baz's neck stand to attention.

Then a bloodcurdling "Help!" pierced the quiet.

Clover was out of his chair before Baz could even think to move. Students were flocking toward the sound, which came from the entrance to the Vault–where one of the Ilsker girls from earlier was on the floor, screaming as blood poured out of her eyes and ears.

"What happened?" Clover asked, taking charge of the situation.

The girl's partner knelt beside her bleeding friend, face pale as she said, "She tried to break through the wards. Thought she could do it with her Unraveler magic, but it must have triggered a curse."

Indeed, the silver door to the Vault seemed to have come alive, lines of shimmering light running through its surface. That unnatural wind blew again, and Baz could have sworn the lanterns flickered and grew dim, as if death lingered in the air.

"It hurts," the bleeding girl moaned, "it–"

Blood spurted from her mouth. She was choking on it, drowning from the inside.

Clover looked around him in a frenzy. "Quick, I need blood-letting instruments–"

To try to heal her, Baz realized. Something he could do with his Tidecaller magic *without* bloodletting, though not without blowing his cover.

The girl was going to die choking on her own blood before then.

Baz did not hesitate as he pulled on the threads of time. He willed the blood to go back into the girl's veins and reversed the damage done to her body, returning it to a time when it had not yet been afflicted by whatever curse this was. In a matter of seconds, she was completely fine. The blood that had marred her skin and darkened her burgundy robes was gone. The library became nice and warm again, the lanterns glowing strongly. The lines of white light on the door dimmed, becoming simple grooves on a silver door, as if the wards had never been triggered at all.

"Thank the Tides," the girl's partner exclaimed, drawing her in for a hug. "You're all right."

The Ilsker girl blinked in confusion at the door, then at herself. "I don't understand. The wards were killing me, and now . . ."

Clover met Baz's gaze. "I believe you have our Timespinner to thank for that."

Everyone turned to Baz, who was suddenly very aware of the Eclipse sigil on his hand. The girl looked at him through tears. "Thank you," she murmured. Her friend helped her up, and she planted a kiss on Baz's cheek, mindless of the gasps from the gathered students at the impropriety of the gesture. "You saved my life."

Clover started clapping, and all of a sudden, everyone in the library was following suit, beaming at Baz. There was no fear in their eyes. Only gratitude and something like awe.

Baz felt all the blood rush to his head. The dean had been right: these games were not to be taken lightly.

39

EMORY

THE CHASM WAS NAMED AS SUCH BECAUSE THE FIGHTING arena had been built in a gaping crevice in the red-hued mountains, only a short distance from Heartstone. Rows upon rows of seats were carved in the stone all around the pit where the fighting would take place. The arena was full of spectators come to watch these gruesome fights to the death that pitted all manner of criminals against eldritch beasts as punishment for their crimes, which Caius had told them was a main source of entertainment here in Heartstone.

The stands were full of children and adults alike, chattering excitedly about the kinds of monsters they would see today, as if they were coming to watch a highly anticipated play or acclaimed opera. Some even placed bets on how long the fights would last. Beneath it all, though, was a grim current of sorrow and confusion and anger and fear.

Never had the people of Heartstone seen an oath-breaking draconic, squire or otherwise. In their eyes, this was the Night

Bringer's doing. Evil seeping into the ranks of the Fellowship of the Light and corrupting the purest of hearts.

"The oath we take before being remade into draconics is sacred," Caius had explained to them. "It is a magical vow we make to the dragons whose flame is used to turn our hearts to gold, swearing to uphold the light with this power they lend us. To break this oath is to forsake your life. Tol's alchemized heart is now tarnished by the dark. Over time, his heart would slowly lose its magic and eventually kill him. This is quicker, at least."

As Emory glanced around the fighting pit below—noticing an oval patch of dark-stained dirt she realized was old, dried blood—she wasn't sure which was worse: a slow, agonizing death, or one that was to be made into a bloody spectacle.

The event started off with a ceremonial jousting match between two draconic knights. One was dressed in elaborate golden armor emblazoned with the Fellowship's crest of the dragon eating its tail. An ouroboros, Caius had called it. The other knight wore what could only be described as a costume: their golden armor was painted with black and blue motifs of moons and stars, and their helmet was made to look like an owl's head. The silver crest on their chest was of a half-owl, half-cat beast.

The symbol of the Night Bringer.

It seemed silly at first to see the two knights take to the pit in what was clearly meant to be a practiced routine, the crowd booing and jeering at the knight portraying the Night Bringer. The two opponents wielded bejeweled javelins that looked more suited to hanging in a museum than drawing actual blood, and when they bowed at the waist to each other, they were the picture of politeness.

Until they unleashed themselves.

It had been one thing to see the draconics' wings flicker out like candles after they'd fought the *corvus serpentes*; it was something else entirely now to see their wings *appear*. One second, the two knights looked perfectly human, and the next, their bodies were engulfed in ethereal golden flames that started at their heart and coiled around their armored limbs without singeing. Their wings took shape at their backs, as if created from the flames—which sputtered out when the draconics unfurled their wings to their full length, the golden membrane glinting in the light.

They flew off the ground and attacked each other in swoops and swerves, javelins arcing through the sky. This wasn't a battle to the death, Caius had explained, but a show of skill, an act that would inevitably see the favored golden knight prevail over the Night Bringer's champion.

But Emory wouldn't be here to see the outcome.

Taking advantage of the crowd's focus on the jousting, Emory left the stands with Romie and Aspen, but not before throwing one last look over her shoulder. Virgil gave her a goofy-smiled thumbs-up that made her want to laugh despite the utter seriousness of what they were attempting.

They'd decided it was best that Virgil, Nisha, and Vera stay here while Emory, Romie, and Aspen headed for the cells where Caius had told them the prisoners were held. It was only meant to be Emory and Aspen at first—both their abilities being needed in their plan to break Tol out—but Romie had insisted she join them.

"I'm the only one Tol has actually seen," she argued, after telling them she'd managed to find Tol in a dream. "Might help convince him he can trust us."

They descended the hundreds of steps to find the lower levels of the stands occupied by young pages and squires and the draconic masters they trained under. Caius spotted them and stood at once, brandishing his small fist toward the jousting knights, and shouted at the top of his lungs: "Down with the night!"

"Let shine the light!" came the crowd's eager, earsplitting response.

Again and again the crowd shouted the chant, the distraction allowing Emory, Romie, and Aspen to slip unnoticed through the door that led into the prison.

"Left," Aspen instructed as they came upon a fork in the corridor. "There will be a guard fifteen feet away."

The witch had spent the day before scrying into every mind she could find, mapping out the prison through its guards' eyes. Emory herself had tried to be of some use by prodding into a few minds, but just like the witches' minds had been closed off to her Memorist magic, so too were the draconics'. The nausea she'd been left with afterward made her want to give up on Memorist magic for good.

Now Emory had a different sort of power at the ready–the blood in her veins singing in elation at being used–so that when the guard saw them, her Glamour worked its magic before he could even look surprised.

"You never saw us."

They hurried past the guard as his expression became blank, his eyes seeing right through them. Emory's pulse quickened at the ease of this power. Again and again they used this same trick on the guards they passed as they traveled deeper into the prison built below the Chasm, until the air grew thin and sweltering, and a familiar energy crackled beneath their feet.

Emory paused, the force of the ley line nearly knocking her out.

Its addictive pull beckoned. Her eyes widened in equal parts horror and elation as they found Romie's, whose brow was knit in confusion. "What is it?"

A low, grumbling noise suddenly filled the corridor. Then a roar.

"I'm assuming they keep the eldritch beasts down here?" Romie asked, face blanching.

"No." Aspen frowned. "The eldritch are kept on the other side of the prison."

The sound came again, though it was less of a roar, more of a whimper. The ley line in that direction felt more powerful than it did here. Emory couldn't help moving toward it, ignoring Romie and Aspen calling after her.

She stopped dead in her tracks when she reached the end of the corridor. Hand braced on the wall, she stared into the chamber before her, trying to make sense of what she was seeing.

The chamber was immense, more like a grotto than anything. Torches cast long, dancing shadows on the ground. Odd instruments lined the walls, as well as several doors leading to smaller chambers. One of them was open, revealing what looked like a surgical table. Like some sort of laboratory.

People stood chanting a low, humming tune around the center of the grotto. Red-robed sages, one of whom she recognized as Master Bayns. Knights in golden chain mail. And an aging man in a rich, gold-threaded white doublet who held a peculiar-looking glass jar.

The whimper came again from the massive *thing* in the middle of the chamber. A *dragon*, so large it looked like it could engulf the entire grotto, dark scales gobbling up the light from the torches. Its wings were tucked close to its sides, and around its neck and feet were thick metal chains. It moaned in pain as one of the knights jabbed its flank with a wicked metal poker. A faint trickle of bright, golden flames shot from the dragon's mouth, and the aging man caught the flame in the jar, which he hurried to stopper.

"Keep it close," a woman Emory hadn't noticed said to him. "We'll have new youths to use it on soon."

The Knight Commander.

She turned to the corridor and froze when she saw Emory looking into the chamber. Her jaw tightened, her hand immediately going to the sword at her hip. "You were not meant to see that."

Before Emory could pull up her magic, the hilt of a blade hit her on the head.

She fell into darkness, past the stars of the sleepscape, and found herself again before the demon.

His eyes were ablaze with fury as he grabbed her by the throat. "I smell them on you," he said, seething. "You're with them, aren't you? The blood, the bones, the heart—"

"Let go of me!" Emory yelled, clawing at his wrist to try to loosen his grip.

His fingers only tightened around her neck. There was a cruel tilt to his mouth. "We'll see each other soon, Tideca—"

Emory gasped as she found herself back in her body, her *real* one. The impression of Keiran's fingers around her neck lingered, and for a moment she thought he had reappeared with her into consciousness as rough hands shoved her unceremoniously to the ground. She grunted in pain as her palms split open on the rock beneath her.

Far gentler hands were on her then, forcing her to look into someone's eyes. Romie's eyes.

"You okay?" Romie asked.

"What—*ow.*" Emory touched the wound on her head, wincing in pain. Her fingers came away bloody. "Where are we?"

"They threw us in the Tides-damned cells," Romie said, slumping to the ground at Emory's side. Aspen stood over them with an air of total abandon.

Through the fog of pain, Emory tried to make sense of their surroundings. They were indeed in a large, dark, damp cell with five other people. Prisoners, she realized, bare-headed, hard-eyed, sallow-faced men clothed in ill-fitting breeches and threadbare shirts.

Without thinking, Emory healed both the wound on her head and the gashes on her palms. The darkness that had been lingering at the edges of her consciousness pressed in fully then, her ears assaulted by slithering whispers and her vision swarming with bloodied lunar flowers looking to choke her–

"It's you."

The utter awe in Aspen's voice, the bright note of hope that rang through it, pierced through Emory's darkness, enough for her to realize who the witch had spoken to.

At the other end of the cell, sitting straight-backed and confident despite the death that awaited him, was a young man with molten eyes, his naked torso corded with muscles. There was a band of dark metal around his neck, like a fetter, which none of the other prisoners had. His draconic wings were nowhere in sight, but Emory knew who he was nonetheless, because the spiral symbol on his chest atop where his heart was could mean only one thing.

Tol.

Aspen's face was full of wonder as she took him in, this person she had come to know through his own eyes and had probably never truly *seen* unless through a reflection.

"Who are you?" Tol didn't seem to recognize Aspen at all–and why would he, when she'd only ever been this presence in his head that he couldn't even feel?

Aspen's shoulders sagged, her expression dimming as she must have come to the same realization. When she spoke again, she became the High Matriarch's daughter once more, cold and aloof. "Apologies. My name is Aspen, and this is Romie and Emory. We came to free you."

One of the older prisoners snickered at her. "What a piss-poor job of that you did."

The rest of the prisoners laughed darkly. But there was a spark of understanding in Tol's eyes as they landed on Romie. "You were in my dreams."

"Told you we were coming." Romie gave an apologetic shrug.

"Unfortunately, we ran into some unexpected trouble. Did you know they have a *dragon* chained up out there?"

A muscle feathered in Tol's jaw. "That dragon is the reason I'm in here."

"Because you broke your oath to it?"

"That oath is a farce," Tol spat. "Did you see what they were doing to it? The draconics who have the dragon chained?"

"They were taking its flame."

A grim nod. "Taking by force what is supposed to be given *freely*. The Knight Commander, the masters–they lied to the entire Fellowship. They make us swear fealty to the light, tell us we owe our second life to the dragons who have blessed us, the dragons we *revere*, when the dark truth of it is, those dragons are captured, beaten, *tortured* to give up their sacred heart-flame. Our alchemized hearts are not earned; they are stolen." He looked disgusted with himself, like he wanted to tear his own heart out. "We are made of the worst sort of violence."

"Don't despair, lad," one of the prisoners said with false cheer. "All your misery will end soon enough."

"Can you not shift into your draconic form to overpower the guards?" Aspen asked.

Tol motioned to the metal band around his throat. "Prevents me from shifting."

An unpleasant feeling came over Emory at how much it resembled the damper cuffs used back home to nullify Eclipse magic. Her own magic still throbbed beneath her skin, the darkness clamoring at the edges of her mind. She dug her nails into her palms, savoring the small hurt, praying for the darkness to stay away.

"There has to be another way out of here," Romie despaired.

"No one gets out of the Chasm alive, girl," the same prisoner said gruffly. He pointed to a scar running down his pale cheek and neck. "If we survive the eldritch, we're thrown right back into our cells to await the next fight. All we can do is pray we make it another day. Except your friend here. They'll make an example out of him, to be sure."

"Why?" Romie asked. "Because you found out the truth of how draconics are made?"

"Yes." Tol's face darkened. "I tried to free the dragon, unable to stand by what the masters were doing to it. And now they see me as a threat to the sanctity of the Fellowship."

Just then one of the walls started to pull up in a great metallic clamor. The sunlight that spilled into the cell felt too bright after such darkness. Outside, someone was turning a lever on the outer wall, lifting the grate to unveil the arena. The prisoners dragged themselves up to their feet, the more seasoned of them holding themselves at the ready, almost as if they looked forward to the fight.

Tol winced as he stood, favoring his right leg as though his left were injured. He wobbled slightly, and Aspen was instantly at his side, lending a solid hand.

"Your leg–will you be all right to fight?" Aspen whispered.

They exchanged a weighted, knowing glance.

"I'll be fine," Tol answered at last, composing his features into that of a fearless warrior. "The damp just exacerbates it, is all."

He took a few steps forward, each one steadier than the last, and came to stand next to his fellow prisoners. It was only then that Emory noticed the skin at his ankle, which peeked out from under his pant leg, was not skin at all, but gold. A prosthetic.

As the grate finally came to a metallic stop, Emory saw that a similar door had opened on the opposite side of the fighting pit. The inside of that cell was dark, and she could only imagine what manner of horrible beast would emerge from it.

Fear wired through her as draconic knights in gilded armor

came into their cell and roughly pushed the prisoners out into the fighting pit–including Emory, Romie, Aspen, and Tol.

Romie fought against the guard who was pushing her. "You can't do this to us. We didn't do anything!"

Her pleas went ignored. There was a moment of confusion in the crowd as they made sense of these three girls in plain clothing standing amid the prisoners. But then the crowd exploded in shouts and cheers and eager applause.

They were ready for a spectacle, no matter what.

Emory tried in vain to find the rest of her friends in the crowd. At her side, Romie was swearing under her breath, while Aspen hovered near Tol, as if he were the sun toward which she gravitated, ready to catch him should he fall.

The ground beneath their feet shook. A low, terrifying grumbling came from the other side of the pit. Something moved in the darkness within that open cell, making the ground shake again and the crowd go wild with anticipation. Two yellow eyes gleamed in the dark.

And then the creature stepped into the arena.

If Emory had thought the *corvus serpentes* was monstrous, it was nothing compared to this one.

It looked like a giant bear, with thick gray fur that spiked to wicked points along its spine. Its feet alone were each roughly the size of a small horse. And on its head were crimson antlers that curved in all directions, each tip ending in a bladelike point.

"An *ursus magnus*," Tol breathed, eyes wide.

The creature let out an earth-splitting roar as if in recognition of its name. The grates on both sides of the arena shut with a thudding metallic sound, trapping them in the arena.

"We're completely screwed, aren't we?" Romie muttered.

One of the prisoners charged against the *ursus magnus*, fists raised in defiance, a scream bellowing out of him. The bear pawed at him with a resounding growl, sending him flying toward the other end of the arena, his body slashed and spilling too much blood.

The *ursus magnus* worked itself into a frenzy then, charging at them. Tol screamed at them to run, and they barely missed getting mauled by the creature. Yipping sounds suddenly met their ears as several smaller creatures emerged behind the bear. They were foxlike in nature, their reddish fur tipped in black flames, embers following in their footsteps. Their eyes glowed dark like coals as they stalked the prisoners.

Romie screamed as one of them jumped right at her throat.

Emory reacted without thinking, drawing on the only magic that would be quick enough to save her friend. The fox didn't even have time to cry out in pain before it fell dead at Romie's feet, eliciting a broken cry from Tol–as if he'd felt the beast's pain as his own.

Romie's wide eyes met Emory's, shock and gratitude and fear warring on her features as the weight of what Emory had done settled.

She had slain the beast. Killed it with Reaper magic.

Blood pounded in Emory's ears as her breathing came in quick, shallow successions. *She* had done that. Had killed a living thing without blinking, had felt its heart in the palm of her hand and silenced it without an ounce of hesitation. Remorse didn't come, not as another fox pounced toward her, and again she reached for the Reaper magic that could end all of this right now–

"*No!*" Tol shouted, coming between Emory and the fox.

Heart jumping to her throat, she pulled the death magic back just in time, letting it fizzle out inside her. The beast's teeth closed on Tol's forearm, black flames blaring around its maw. Tol grunted in pain and tried to shake it off, finally managing to send it scurrying away with a yelp.

"Why did you do that?" Emory snapped. "I had it!"

Tol whirled on her, face full of anger. "The eldritch aren't our enemy."

"They're trying to kill us!" Around them, the other prisoners were fighting for their lives against the beasts, two of them already dead. With a cry of triumph, one of the prisoners managed to hurt a fox, which fell to the ground, its leg broken.

Tol stumbled and grabbed hold of his own leg, as if the pain were mirrored in him. "There has to be another way to do this," he lamented.

The earth shuddered as the gate the eldritch had come out of blew off its hinges.

A collective gasp rippled through the crowd before they erupted into cheers again as beasts of all kinds charged into the fighting pit, each more terrifying than the last: feral boars and horned wolves and three-eyed deer, and more of those *corvus serpentes* that took to the sky.

Following in their wake was another sort of horror, one which Emory knew all too well.

A dozen umbrae slithered out of the dark. In their midst was the demon wearing Keiran's face.

The arena devolved into utter chaos as the eldritch monsters attacked the guards and whatever prisoners remained ran for their lives to escape the umbrae. The crowd broke into genuine screams of fear now, realizing this wasn't part of the fight; the *corvus serpentes* swooped over them, grabbing whoever they could in their talons.

Two frightful words swept the arena like a tidal wave:

Night Bringer.

Something clicked in Emory's mind as she looked to Keiran–who was heading straight for Tol, those blazing eyes flaring bright with murderous intent. And she knew then, without a doubt, that Tol was the key.

And the demon would rip his heart out.

Emory unleashed herself. A blast of light surged out of her with a deafening boom, blasting back eldritch and umbrae and the demon himself, yet leaving her friends and the draconic guards and the remaining prisoners untouched. Dark satisfaction seized her as she watched Keiran's body hit the arena wall, as he pulled himself slowly to his hands and knees, visibly hurt.

She could end them all right here. The ley line burned through her, crackling seductively as it lent her its strength, powered her up as it sought to make her *invincible*.

"Em."

Romie stared at Emory's arms, the silver rippling in her veins.

Around them the beasts had already recovered from Emory's blast, and they were *angry* now. They mauled the remaining prisoners and jumped into the stands to have their fill of spectator blood.

Keiran drew himself up and set his murderous gaze on Emory, the umbrae swirling around him like a protective second skin. His focus was torn by Tol as the draconic picked up a discarded golden sword and arced it down on the demon. The demon was quicker. He sidestepped the blow with lethal speed and produced a shadowy sword of his own, blocking Tol's next attack.

"He's going to kill him," Aspen said, staring horrified at the dance of gold and shadow.

Emory grabbed hold of Romie, pretending not to see her friend flinch as the silver in her veins flared brighter. "You have to go. I don't want to hurt you, but I—I can't—"

All that power whispering in her ears, illuminating her veins, searing through her soul . . . It was a swelling river inside her, and she was a dam bound to break. There was nothing she could do to stop it.

"Emory! Romie!"

Their heads snapped toward the sound of their names to find Virgil, Nisha, and Vera running across the fighting pit toward them.

The *ursus magnus* jumped between them with a growl, spittle dripping from its open maw as it headed straight for Emory's friends.

Romie's grip tightened around her wrist. "Do it!" she screamed, eyes wild.

The dam around Emory broke.

She blasted back the demon and the beasts once more, erecting a barrier between them and her friends. It wouldn't last. She opened herself up to all the magics around her, to the three bright spots that called to her like lodestars: the power in Romie's blood and Aspen's bones and Tol's heart, all of them *demanding* to be used. She drew the magic into her, and instinct propelled her into the mind of the giant bear.

Emotions and senses and wisps of dreaming overcame her as she felt everything the *ursus magnus* had ever felt. The freedom it had once known. The daily torture it underwent under its captors. The terror and death it was forced to instill.

She laced this new magic coursing through her with the power of Glamours, influencing the bear's mind to do her bidding, pushing it in the direction she wanted it to go. She extended this magic to the other beasts too. All at once, the eldritch stopped fighting the prisoners and bystanders—and turned instead on the guards. The draconics who had captured and tortured them into submission.

"Heretic!" one of the draconics yelled, pointing at Emory with pure terror before the *ursus magnus* trampled him.

They thought she was aligned with the Night Bringer, even as bright, silver light emanated from her. Still Emory did not feel on the verge of Collapsing. Power coursed through her like a river unleashed and filled her with elation. Only a small, weak voice in her mind made her think to check on her friend. Romie was on her knees, face drawn and pale, lips gone colorless as if all the blood in her had left. At her side, Aspen writhed in pain as her bones *broke*, her arms and legs snapping at unnatural angles and rearranging themselves under some invisible torture.

And where Tol stood before the demon, he suddenly dropped his golden sword to the ground and clutched at his chest, doubling over in pain.

Leaving himself undefended for the demon to rip his heart out.

"No!" Emory screamed through the rush of power, trying desperately to let go of it, to shut the conduits open between her and these other magics she was tapping into, these three *lives* she felt vibrating in the palms of her hands, but she couldn't, and now the darkness was pressing in, lunar flowers in her mouth and sprouting from her lungs, ghosts tearing at her clothes and shouting in her ears–

"Em, behind you!"

Virgil's warning came a moment too late. Emory had barely begun to turn when she caught the glint of golden armor, a blade arcing down toward her, and knew death, at last, had found her.

Except it didn't.

For a second, she was too stunned to realize someone had jumped in front of her, taking the death blow that had been meant for her. More stunned still to realize who it was.

The demon held her at arm's length, fingers digging into her biceps, a pained, surprised expression on his face as he looked down at the sword tip protruding from his middle.

He met her gaze, and for a moment that seemed suspended in time, everything was clear. All the darkness Emory had been drowning in vanished, as if drawn into the demon, silenced by his touch, chased away by the shifting light of his eyes. She could feel the magic she'd been leeching from Romie and Aspen and Tol slowly returning to them as her own blood faded from silver to red and the ley line beneath her quieted.

It felt like when Baz had saved her from Collapsing, except Emory knew this had nothing to do with time, and everything to do with the demon who had taken a sword for her. As if he were a stopper on her magic, a balm against this twisted, uncontrollable, deadly side of it.

Time resumed as the sword was pulled out of the demon's middle, making blood splatter. But instead of crumpling to his death, the demon moved with lethal speed, turning to tear the sword from the knight's hands. With it he sliced their helmeted head clean off their body.

He looked every part the demon he was then, a thing of death and darkness and blood. With movements that were too grace-ful to be human, he heaved himself onto the *ursus magnus*'s back as the beast bounded toward the blasted gate. But Emory saw the way he clutched his middle, the wince of pain as he gripped the beast's back. And the face that looked at her over a shoulder, deathly pale.

The demon might not be human, but Keiran's body was. And with a wound like that, Emory knew he wouldn't last for much longer.

Her gaze cut to her friends, worry and guilt warring inside her. Tol was picking himself up, looking winded but fine. Aspen had stopped writhing in pain, her limbs unbroken, set in all the right angles. And though Romie had regained some color, she looked at Emory with an ashen, defeated expression. As if saying, *You see now? This is what you are.*

Tidethief.

And she was right.

40

ROMIE

ROMIE WAS DYING. SHE COULD FEEL HER BLOOD TURN
to ash, the magic fade from her veins, the song in her soul go
quiet—a silencing she knew was mirrored in the witch and the
warrior at her side, for in this moment, their pain was her own,
felt through whatever conduit had been opened between them by
Emory. A Tidethief stealing all their magics.

And then the pain stopped. Romie watched Emory through
bleary eyes, standing with the demon, the two of them entwined
in darkness. As if whatever passed between them was stronger
than Emory's grasp on the ley line, strong enough to sever her
connection to Romie and the others.

Romie was still trying to make sense of it when Nisha was suddenly at her side, helping her to her feet. Virgil yelled at everyone
to get up and *move* as more draconic knights swarmed the arena.

"Where are we supposed to go?" Vera yelled in despair.

"Through there." This from Tol, who was helping a white-faced
Aspen up with one hand, the other gripping a bloodied sword. He

jerked his chin to the blasted gate through which the demon and his beast had disappeared.

They made their way into the dark tunnels but quickly had to hide as the clink of armor followed closely at their heels. Tol pulled them into a shadowed alcove just as voices rang out in front of them.

"This trail of blood leads toward the city. It must be the Night Bringer's. Both he and the *ursus magnus* were bleeding profusely when last seen."

"Follow it," the Knight Commander said. "The Night Bringer can't have gotten very far. I want him captured–*alive*."

"What about the escaped prisoners?" a man's voice asked.

"I'll find them myself," said the Knight Commander. "The Night Bringer's followers will get what's coming for them."

The Night Bringer's followers. They really thought they were allied with that murderous demon after all that?

Once the sound of receding footsteps faded, Tol gestured for them to follow him.

"Wait," Aspen said, frowning in the opposite direction. "Isn't that the way out? The other way will lead us back to the dragon."

Tol looked at her with a quizzical brow, no doubt wondering how this girl he'd never seen before, who was clearly not a dra-conic knight, knew the ins and outs of the Chasm. He shook his head, taking an insistent step in the direction he'd started in. "I can't leave the dragon here to suffer more torture. You can all stay here or head for the exit, but this is what I have to do."

He bounded off before any of them could protest. Aspen met Romie's gaze, the desperation in her eyes also felt by Romie. They couldn't lose sight of Tol–of this world's key.

There was no debate as everyone followed Tol. But Romie stopped as she realized Emory was heading the opposite way. "Em–*where are you going*?"

Emory had trouble meeting her gaze, her eyes sunken with shame. "There's something I have to do. I'll be right back, I swear."

Before Romie could stop her, Emory disappeared into the shadows, using Darkbearer magic to cloak herself. Romie had half a mind to pursue her, but after what happened in the arena, she wasn't overly eager to be near Emory. Not when there was a risk of her tapping into Romie's magic again.

With a frustrated sigh, Romie followed the others.

They found their way back to the chamber where the dragon was being kept. The group of sages and alchemists and knights that had tortured the beast were no longer there, but the dragon was. It appeared to be slumbering, the band around its neck connected to five massive chains tethered to the circular wall of the chamber.

"That's a dragon," Virgil panted. "We are standing in front of a Tides-damned *dragon*."

"Yes, Virgil, we can all see that," Romie said between her teeth. "Now lower your voice before it decides to burn us to a crisp."

The dragon lifted its head weakly as Tol approached it. It tried to shuffle backward, no doubt scared of people after what it had endured, but the chains kept it rooted in place.

"We're not here to hurt you," Tol said. He sheathed his sword and held his hands up to drive his point home. "Remember me? I was here the day they captured you. I wouldn't fight you. And when the guards took me, I promised you that if I survived this place, I'd find a way to get you out of here, do you not recall?"

A low sound rumbled in the dragon's throat. Its pale golden eyes blinked slowly as it took Tol in, as if gauging whether or not it could trust him. It inhaled deeply, and Romie felt Nisha sidling closer to her, no doubt as scared as she was that they were about to be incinerated by dragon flame.

You smell of her, a voice said in Romie's head.

"It's speaking to us," Virgil muttered. "The dragon is speaking to us in our heads."

Judging from the others' reactions, they had all heard it too.

This dragon has a name, the voice said with a tinge of annoyance, and Romie swore she heard a huff coming from the dragon. *You may address me as Gwenhael.*

Its voice was lilting and soft, not at all like Romie expected from such a colossal creature.

"Gwenhael." Tol bowed slightly at the waist, pressing a hand against his heart. "My name is Tol. I was made a draconic years ago, unbeknownst to me that this was how dragons are treated."

Your alchemy masters guard their secrets well. It was not always this way. Once, we dragons gave our heart-fire willingly to those who were worthy of our power. But your Fellowship of the Light has since sullied this sacred offering. They imprison those of my kind and torture us to give up our heart-flame, all so they can create more of you.

"I know," Tol said, dejected. "Had I been aware of this earlier . . . The Fellowship wanted me to seek out more of your kind. I fear things will only grow worse now that the Night Bringer has risen."

I remember the days of the Sun Forger and the Night Bringer. They were formidable, designed as mirrors, two sides of a scale. Light and dark, night and day, creation and destruction, beginning and ending. Not better or worse, but equal.

"What happened to them?" Romie asked.

Something changed between them. Where they had once existed as peaceful allies, they became ruthless foes. Death followed in their wake. Eldritch were pitted against dragons. The world became a battlefield, scorched in fire and blood. When the Night Bringer and the Sun Forger looked at the destruction they had wrought and realized they were to blame for it, all they felt was remorse. So they forced each other to venture into the underworld, where they would slumber in exile as penance for what they had done.

The world started to heal without them in it. But now it has started all over, an evil spreading across the world like wildfire. They say the Night Bringer has risen. But if the Sun Forger still slumbers beneath the earth, there is an imbalance in the world, and this chaos that is unfolding can only be stopped by waking the Sun Forger. Restoring balance.

Romie and Nisha exchanged a glance. This sounded eerily like the myth about the Tides and the Shadow and how they'd been sent to the Deep.

"I'm afraid the Forger is dead," Tol said mournfully.

Dead? Gwenhael echoed. *Why do you say such a thing?*

"I'm light-blessed. Touched by the Forger," Tol explained. "I've always had a connection with her, and I felt the moment her heart stopped. It was right here, on the day the knights chained you and threw me in a cell for breaking an empty oath."

Romie glanced at Aspen, wondering if he was confusing the witch's presence in his mind for this connection to the divine. Aspen's heart had stopped only a few days ago, when the demon tore a rib from her chest, right before Emory healed her back from the brink of death.

The Sun Forger cannot be dead, the dragon said. *I feel her energy in this very room.*

Confusion and hope warred on Tol's face. "How can that be?"

She lives on in you.

"But I can't feel her. Not like before."

That band around your neck is like the one around mine. An old magic used on dragons and draconics and eldritch alike to sever us from our makers' magic. That is why you cannot shift into your draconic form, and why I cannot regenerate my heart-flame and burn my way to freedom.

"If the Forger is alive," Romie said, a suspicion forming in her mind, "can you tell us where to find her?"

I do not know where she slumbers. But there are those who might. Those who follow the old ways and uphold their vows to the dragons they serve. If you free me, I can take you to them.

"These chains are unbreakable," Tol despaired. "Made by the alchemists out of the most solid metals."

"Is there any water nearby?" Virgil asked. This earned him several confused looks. He rolled his eyes at them. "For bloodletting, obviously. Any metal can r–"

The sound of a sword being unsheathed had them turning to see the Knight Commander. Her armor was stained dark with eldritch blood. She looked at Tol with disappointment. "I should have known this is where I'd find you. I see you haven't come to your senses, even after all this?"

Tol practically shook with anger. "After you proved the Fellowship to be rooted in brutal lies and dishonor, chained me up for stumbling on the truth, and sent me to my death for breaking a binding magical oath that never existed, to beasts that are supposed to be *sacred* but instead are tortured?"

The Knight Commander sighed. "I always feared that empathy of yours would get us here one day. But I gave you the chance to live, Anatolius. You chose to side with beasts instead of your own family. You rejected the Fellowship's way, so its secrets must die with you."

Tol seemed to fight back angry tears. "What kind of family treats their own like that?"

"A strong one. A family that knows their enemy well and will do anything to triumph over it." She held up her sword. "If you don't stand with us, Anatolius, then I'm afraid you stand against us."

Tol's sword remained limp in his hand. "You were like a mother to me. I don't want to fight you."

"Then I'll leave you no choice."

There was a lethal flash of gold as the Knight Commander pounced and Tol's blade just barely lifted in time to meet hers. Movement caught Romie's eye. Virgil was kneeling next to a puddle of water at the dragon's foot, either because he had a death wish–

Or because he was calling on death itself.

Before their eyes, the chains holding the dragon rusted through until they became completely withered. With a deafening, bellowing roar, Gwenhael snapped its neck up, the chains breaking–*dissolving*–as easily as a pile of ash might disappear on a sudden wind.

And then the dragon lowered its mouth to them, white-hot flames building at the back of its throat.

41

BAZ

"I DON'T LIKE THIS."

"The fact that you, Basil Brysden, are going to an actual party? Or the fact that said party goes against the rules?"

"Both."

Baz caught himself staring at Kai again as they wound their way through a darkly lit Decrescens library. The navy tailcoat and patterned waistcoat he'd gotten at the tailor fit him like a glove. Kai didn't wear the ensemble the *proper* way–his black neck cloth was draped lazily around his neck, his golden chains peeking out from his partly unbuttoned shirt–but this small act of fashion rebellion made him all the more dashing.

Baz, on the other hand, hadn't felt confident enough to play around with what he'd been given. He felt awkward in his own dark copper tailcoat and golden waistcoat, and though the satin neck cloth felt nice and cool against his skin, he couldn't help but feel stifled. Or perhaps that was just his nerves.

He was still reeling from the near disaster with the wards earlier, uneasy now in this library he'd always felt at home in. But Clover had insisted they come to the secret party he was throwing—which really wasn't so secret at all once he'd invited every single student participating in the games, even Wulfrid and his friends.

"Like I'd want to mingle with you depraved lot," Wulfrid had spat at him. He'd gestured to himself and his three companions. "While you're having your little fun, *we'll* be working on unraveling the wards."

Clover had shrugged. "Suit yourselves."

Baz and Kai finally found the stained-glass window Clover had told them to look for. Whereas most of the windows in the Decrescens library depicted poppies—the lunar flower associated with House Waning Moon—this one showed a colorful bouquet of all the house flowers: black narcissus, indigo hollyhocks, white orchids, purple poppies, and a singular sunflower. It was in an alcove at the very back of the library, tucked away in a spot Baz couldn't remember ever coming to. The faint moonlight that shone through the window hit a large painting on the adjacent wall, which showed a wizened Quies weaving a tapestry of shimmering thread that looked like stardust.

"This is ridiculous," Baz said with a laugh. "If there was a secret room hidden in here, we would know about it, right?"

"One way to find out." Kai leaned in toward the painting and whispered, "Velleity."

For a second, Baz thought the password Clover had given them held no magic at all. But then the painting melted away like liquid silver, transforming into a dark-stained door with a silver waning-moon-shaped knob.

Baz and Kai stood transfixed before it. All these years of haunting the Decrescens library, and Baz had not once heard a single rumor of this.

The door opened onto a smaller library—though still too large for something that was hidden in the walls–all gleaming dark wood and arched ceilings. Its shelves weren't lined with books. At first Baz thought they might have been vials of water meant for bloodletting, but he quickly realized they were various bottles of alcohol.

The scene unfolding before them was lavish and exuberant. People drank and chatted and kissed and danced, so careless and free it felt like stepping into another time, or another world entirely. There was none of the stuffiness and decorum of the period. Students mingled in an extravagance of styles and costumes with curious arrays of feathers, furs, hats, and jewels the size of small planets. Some were dressed like Baz and Kai, just as others were barely dressed at all–girls scantily clad in short frilly dresses and boys in sheer shirts that would make people in Baz and Kai's own time blush.

Jaunty music played, produced by a quartet of finely dressed musicians wearing elaborate powdered wigs and a large amount of rouge on their cheeks. Baz swore he could see the bright reverberations of notes in the air coming from their instruments, some kind of Wordsmith magic, no doubt.

A girl wearing nothing but a bejeweled leotard came up to them, offering them drinks on a golden tray. They were a bright green color, with a rim of salt or sugar around the glass and a decorative crystal flower floating on the surface.

"Yeah, I'm going to need something a bit stronger than . . . whatever that is," Kai said with mild disdain.

The girl smirked at him. "Suit yourself. And you?"

Baz grabbed a glass, in part not to offend the girl, but mostly because he thought he might need a bit of liquid courage. Plus, he liked the color, the flower, how innocent it all looked.

One sip had him entering a fit of coughing. His throat was on fire. "Tides," he sputtered, not complaining when Kai grabbed the glass from him and took a curious sip of his own, "what's *in* this?"

"It's absinthe," a laughing voice said behind them. "Not for the faint of heart."

Clover stood behind them. He wore an all-white suit that looked dramatic and over-the-top with a frilly collar and ample sleeves, his waistcoat adorned with fine-threaded golden accents that shimmered in the light.

"Welcome to our secret library turned ballroom," Clover said with a smile.

Baz shielded his eyes as a sudden flash flooded the room.

"What is that?" Kai asked, taking the words right out of Baz's mouth as they stared at a big contraption, behind which stood a student who had the machinery pointed at a smiling, clearly posing couple.

"A new invention," Clover explained. "They call it a camera. The light captures our likeness on these silver plaques, you see." Clover clasped them both on the shoulders. "The three of us should take a photograph together to mark our new friendship, don't you think?"

Panic seized Baz. If this photograph persisted through time, it would be proof to any future eyes that he and Kai had been here. In a time not their own. But before they could refuse Clover with some made-up excuse, he'd dragged them toward the photographer and was making introductions.

"This is Reynald Delaune, brightest Lightkeeper of our generation." A lazy smile. "Pardon the pun."

Reynald chuckled. Then his eyes went wide as he took Baz in. "You're the Timespinner who saved that Ilsker girl earlier!" He grabbed his hand, shaking it fervently. "Bravo, truly. That was incredible."

"Oh, uh, thanks?"

It was only then that Baz noticed the eyes on him, the friendly smiles thrown his way. Like everyone's hostility toward him being

Eclipse-born had vanished since he saved the girl from the deadly wards. His lungs expanded as a pleasurable warmth spread through him. He felt an unusual sense of pride. He felt, for the first time, like he didn't want to hide from a crowd.

Reynald had Baz and Kai sitting next to each other, their knees slightly touching, while Clover stood behind them, a hand clasped on either of their shoulders. The posing process was rather long, and Baz couldn't help but think, *I am taking a photograph with Cornus fucking Clover*, a thought he knew for certain must be echoed in Kai's mind. He only hoped this photograph would remain lost to history.

Baz hadn't realized his knee was bouncing nervously until Kai applied gentle pressure on it. The light touch only sparked another sort of nervousness in him, not entirely unpleasant.

"Say *velleity*," Reynald singsonged before the flash drowned their vision in white.

"What does *velleity* mean, anyway?" Baz asked Clover once they were done with the process.

Clover smirked. "It means a desire that is not strong enough to be acted upon. A bit of a joke among us, you see, because that is the exact opposite of what these parties are. It's what society expects of us, to not act upon our desires, at least not in ways that would tarnish our family images or such things. Same with the college. So many rules, so much decorum to follow. But here . . . here, in these private soirees, we get to indulge and be free."

"There you are!" Cordie was suddenly beside her brother, weaving her arm through his. She looked glamorous in a lacy dark-green gown that fit loosely around her body, flowing like the waves of a deep, dark sea. She had on satin gloves the color of seafoam, and her hair was done up in an artful mass of curls. "Monopolizing our guests, are we?"

"I'm not monopolizing anyone."

"Not anymore, you're not." She turned with a dazzling smile to a young man Baz recognized as the tailor they'd gone to to get their suits. "I wanted to introduce you to *my* guest."

All the warmth leeched from Clover's smile. "The tailor, Cordelia? Really?"

"His name is Louka," Cordie said tightly, throwing her brother a look that said *behave.*

Louka held his hand out to Clover. "How d'ya do," he said in his easy lilt. "Thanks for inviting me."

Clover raised a brow. "I certainly did no such thing. I think it's best you leave."

"Cornelius . . ."

Someone in the crowd called for Clover over the loud music. Clover gave his sister a look that said *we'll talk about this later,* before he slipped on his charming smile again and left.

Louka looked baffled. "Did I say something wrong?"

Cordie leaned against him. "Not at all. My brother's just . . . over-protective. Let's forget him and have our fun." She looked at Baz and Kai pointedly. "And why are you two not dancing?"

Baz made vigorous hand gestures, teetering backward. "Oh, no, I don't—"

"Come on, Brysden." Kai surprised him by pulling him toward the dance floor after Cordie and Louka. "A little fun won't kill you."

Baz looked forlornly in the crowd for Clover, wishing he could have stayed with him rather than being forced to *dance.* He was usually more of a sit-and-watch type of person. In fact, he was more of a stay-in-his-dorm-room-and-not-come-out-at-all person, so this was all quite overwhelming.

The song that was playing was fast-paced and energetic. The four of them copied those around them, moving as they did, laughing together as they butchered the steps—well, as *Baz* butchered the steps. He was all two left feet and uncoordinated movements, while Kai and Cordie and even Louka seemed to have a natural knack for it. But oddly enough, Baz couldn't find it in himself to be the slightest bit embarrassed. Here he was surrounded by so many people, and he didn't care, because he was with Kai, and they were laughing, and everything in him felt light for the first time in what felt like forever.

As the fifth or sixth song ended–Baz had lost track–Cordie fanned herself, cheeks flushed and face glowing with sweat. "I need to sit." When Baz made to follow her and Louka, she said, "Please, stay, enjoy yourselves. We'll be right back."

Baz wasn't so sure about that as he spotted Clover coming up to Cordie, his mouth tight. They exchanged words. She seemed to yell something at him in anger before grabbing Louka and heading for the door.

"What do you think that's about?" Kai asked, leaning in to be heard.

"No idea."

The music had slowed, and couples formed around them, dancing closely. *Intimately.* Baz palmed the back of his neck, his cheeks warm from the exertion. "Should we grab a drink?"

But Kai seemed to have a different idea in mind. He offered Baz his hand, brows shooting up. And maybe it was the one sip of alcohol he'd had or maybe it was this high he was riding, but Baz took that hand without a moment's hesitation. Kai bowed to him in a ridiculous way, to which Baz answered in kind, laughing.

It started out this way–as a joke, with the two of them smiling giddily, taking turns twirling each other around in an overly dramatic fashion.

But then something changed. The air between them became charged as their gazes met and held. Baz's stomach dropped. He couldn't make sense of the sudden racing of his heart or the warmth of his blood. He averted his gaze to focus on his feet, even though he didn't want to–because, Tides damn him, he *liked* look-ing at Kai, and he liked how he felt when he was around him.

The realization came to him with no small amount of confusion, especially as his gaze flickered up to Kai's again, and something swelled in his stomach at how close they were. He didn't under-stand what was happening. Except . . . hadn't it always been there? This thing between them that felt like more than friendship alone. A sense of kinship Baz had always struggled to describe.

And now . . .

"Brysden." Kai nudged him at his sudden change. "You all right?"

"I–yeah, of course." But Baz let go of Kai as the slow song came to its end and the music picked up speed again. "I think I need to have a sit, though," he said, clearing his throat. "All this dancing."

He tried not to dwell on the look in Kai's eyes–disappointment, perhaps. The start of a melancholy storm.

"May we cut in?"

Clover and Thames had joined them, looking as breathless as they were from dancing. They made quite the pair, with Clover dressed all in white and Thames in dark crimson, the same golden threads mirrored in each of their outfits. It took a moment for Baz to realize Clover's hand was extended toward him.

"Oh, well, I–"

"If Kai doesn't mind, of course."

"What?" Baz sputtered, laughing nervously. "Kai's not–we're not–"

"We're just friends," Kai said with an easy smile. "Baz can dance with whoever he likes."

Just friends. The words sliced through him like a knife.

"Although, didn't you say you needed a break?" Kai asked.

Baz thought it sounded like a challenge as Kai's dark eyes held his.

"I could use a break if you want some company," Thames chimed in. He looked about as uncomfortable in this party scene as Baz felt. "We can leave these two to their dancing."

"Wonderful," Clover said jovially, pivoting to Kai with a crooked smile. "Shall we?"

Baz watched them take to the dance floor, where they seamlessly settled into the quick rhythm of the dancers around them. He was still trying to figure out what had just happened as he followed Thames to the drinks table. His gaze kept drifting to where Clover and Kai danced. Too close, he thought bitterly. And did Clover really have to lean in to whisper so intimately in Kai's ear?

"Cornelius is like that with everyone," Thames said with a placating smile.

"Like what?"

"A shameless flirt. It used to bother me, too, at first."

"I'm not—this doesn't bother me. Like Kai said, we're just friends."

He tried not to read into the knowing look Thames gave him. There was an air of melancholy to him that had Baz thinking Thames wasn't as unbothered by Clover's flirtatiousness as he made himself out to be.

Desperate to change the subject, Baz pointed to a wet patch on Thames's suit. "You've got something there."

Thames looked down at the stain. "Must have spilled some wine," he said with a laugh that sounded forced. "I best go clean it up . . ."

Baz was left to himself, sitting forlornly on a divan with no one to talk to. He thought he saw Kai's eyes linger on him at one point—as Kai leaned into Clover, suggestively enough that even Baz understood he was flirting with their Tides-damned literary idol. It was almost as if Kai were trying to make Baz jealous.

But no, that couldn't be right. Kai wasn't interested in Baz that way . . . was he?

Thames's words wormed into his mind. Maybe he *was* bothered by all this. And that left him more confused than ever.

The thing about Baz was this: he scarcely ever noticed his own attraction to people. He was aware of beauty conventions, sure enough, and appreciated features that were striking and visually interesting to his eye. But he recognized beauty more so in the way that an artist looked at picturesque scenery or a sculptor studied the human form so they could replicate it in the most perfect of ways. Physical attraction manifested rarely in him, and only if an emotional connection was there to begin with–or sometimes even just a fabricated one, the hope of an emotional bond, when Baz would imagine himself sharing intimacy with a person and feel an inkling of desire as a result.

But such thoughts scared him, and so he rarely if ever acted on them. Emory had coaxed out that side of him, and though it had terrified him to ever act on his feelings, it had also felt right to do so when he finally had.

Kai, on the other hand . . .

Baz wasn't sure what to think. But he couldn't keep sitting here doing nothing. Suddenly the party was too much, so he slipped out of the secret room to seek solace in the quiet of the library. He was surprised to find Cordie sitting on the floor, her face stained with tears.

"Hello." She patted the spot beside her. "Welcome to the pity party."

Baz joined her. "Where's Louka?"

"Gone. My brother had me send him home."

"Why?"

"Non-magical folk aren't allowed on campus. If anyone were to find out I brought him here . . ."

"I thought the point of tonight was to bend the rules. *Velleity* and all that."

Cordie gave a dramatic sigh. "Some rules are more ingrained in us than others, just like some desires are not meant to be acted upon." She gave him a wobbly smile. "What brings you out here?"

"I'm not one for parties and crowds."

"Neither am I. Well, not *this* type of crowd, anyway. The lavish parties, the magic . . . That's always been Cornelius's world, not mine." She bit her lip as if considering whether to keep talking or not. "Can I tell you a secret?"

"Of course."

"I'm not very good at magic. Ever since I enrolled at Aldryn, there have been particularly vicious rumors about me, students saying I'm *undeserving* of my spot at such a prestigious college because I don't have enough magic to study here. Cornelius thinks me associating with those who don't have more than the tiniest speck of magic only fuels such rumors."

"I always thought it unfair that colleges only admit those they deem magical enough," Baz said. "Magic manifests differently in everyone. Someone's gift might be more subtle than others', but if they want to study the theory behind it, they should deserve a place here as much as anyone else."

Cordie looked at him fondly. "Louka would agree with you. He's always wanted to study here. But I doubt colleges would soon change their minds on the matter. It would destroy their entire model."

She was right—two hundred years from now, things were still the same.

"What my brother doesn't understand is that I don't care about those rumors," Cordie continued. "I don't care about fitting into academia. I want to live out there in the world, free to do what I want, to paint when I want, to be with who I want. But that's not what *Cornelius* wants for me, so here I am."

"Do you not get a say?"

A harsh laugh. "My brother and I have spent our whole lives glued at the hip. Mingling with the same people, working toward the same goals. I love him, and I know he's only trying to protect me, but Tides, does it ever feel suffocating at times." She frowned, staring into the distance. "Do you ever notice how sometimes, the people we're closest to don't know us at all? They see the version of us that they want to see and don't bother knowing the version of us that *we* want to be."

"Yes," Baz breathed, thinking of everyone who'd ever wanted him to be different than what he was, more adventurous and self-assured. His sister. Emory. Even Kai, on occasion. His mind lingering on the Nightmare Weaver, he added, "But sometimes they see the good in us when we can't."

Cordie made a small sound of contemplation at that.

"Does the rest of your family live nearby?" Baz asked. It couldn't hurt to do some subtle digging into the Clovers.

"We don't have any family left."

Baz startled. "Oh. I'm so sorry."

"It's fine. Cornelius and I have been on our own for a long time. Our parents died when we were still toddlers, and whatever relatives they had are either unknown to us or long since dead. My brother has been managing our family estate for as long as I can remember." She eyed him with curiosity. "What of your family?"

"They're not alive either."

It was the truth, in a way. They were not *yet* alive—would not be for nearly two centuries.

A sad smile touched Cordie's face. "It's funny. My brother and I have everything we could ever possibly need and more, and I'm so grateful to him for being my blood, my protector, my dearest friend. But I don't think he's ever yearned for family the way I do. He seeks kinship well enough, and I don't disagree that family can be whomever you choose. Like you and Kai, for example. The bond you share, this feeling of . . . home in a person."

Baz blushed at the insinuation.

"Sorry, I don't mean to presume," Cordie said.

"No, it's fine." She was right, after all.

"Those bonds are precious. Though I cannot deny that I have this deep yearning for something *more*." Cordie sighed, eyeing the art adorning the wall across from them. "Do you paint? You look to me like you have an artist's soul."

"Painting, no, but I do like to draw."

"You should come with me to my studio sometime. I have charcoals and sketchbooks and all sorts of things. We could have ourselves a quiet artists' afternoon."

"I'd like that."

Baz found he enjoyed Cordie's company. She reminded him oddly of his sister. She had that same effortless magnitude, the bright fervor of someone who dared to dream.

And apparently she couldn't hold her liquor.

Without warning, Cordie doubled over and was sick all over the floor.

She looked up at him aghast, face tinged green. "I don't know what's come over me. I barely had a sip all night."

"Maybe we should get you to your room," Baz said, giving her an awkward pat on the back–grateful *he* hadn't had more than a sip of that absinthe.

42

KAI

D ANCING WITH CORNELIUS CLOVER PALED IN COMPARI-
son to dancing with Basil Brysden.

There might have been a time when Kai would have loved nothing more than to receive such attentions from someone like Clover, all suave and confident and intoxicating. But his mind now was full of Baz. The way everything and everyone had seemed to fade around them until it was only the two of them, slow dancing in an empty room, so close it would have been the easiest, most natural thing to lean in for a kiss.

It'd been impossible not to think of it, not when Baz had looked at him the way he had. Like he was finally realizing what Kai had been waiting so long for him to grasp.

But then Baz seemed to second-guess the whole thing and retreated into himself again.

Moment ended. Illusion shattered.

Kai thought dancing with Clover might make Baz jealous. But his heart wasn't in it. And when he could no longer spot Baz in the crowd, he just felt angry at himself for driving him away.

Just friends. What a fucking lie.

But maybe that was all Baz would ever want them to be.

Kai hovered at the edge of a group of students sitting enraptured as they listened to Clover speak. They hung on his every word, making Kai wonder if it was just Clover's natural charisma or his use of Glamour magic. Kai was barely paying attention to what was being said, silent and sullen as he nursed his glass of absinthe.

When Baz finally reappeared, their eyes met from across the room. Time seemed to stop, the world narrowing to just the two of them again, until a pair of students accosted Baz, no doubt to praise him for his stunt with the wards. Baz looked uncomfortable at the attention, fiddling with his silk tie like it was hindering his breathing. At last, he managed to slip away and join Kai.

"Where were you off to?" Kai asked, trying very hard to keep his voice casual. Like he wasn't completely unmoored without him.

"With Cordie. She got sick, so I offered to bring her back to her room." Baz's eyes cut to him. "Did you and Clover have fun?" There was something prying in his words, underscored by what sounded like accusation. Or something else. "He seemed quite, uh, taken with you."

"You jealous, Brysden?"

"What if I am?"

Kai nearly choked on his own saliva, so taken aback was he by Baz's honesty–the brazenness of this simple admission. Kai prided himself on not being surprised by much. People were predictable, for better or worse. And though Baz's timidity and inability to gauge some of Kai's cues sometimes–okay, most of the time–frustrated him, Kai had grown to find it endearing.

But this . . . this, he did not expect.

He found himself searching Baz's gaze, feeling completely

disarmed. Kai realized how close they stood. That if he reached out a hand, they could be in each other's space again, like when they'd been dancing, or when Kai had fixed Baz's tie. But for the life of him, he couldn't tell if that's what Baz wanted.

"There he is, the man of the hour!"

Clover's exclamation had them both pulling apart. Clover dragged Baz away from Kai and into the middle of the crowd. He swept a hand to the gathered students. "Your admirers would love for you to regale us with the details of how you saved Ms. Arnavois here from the wards."

The girl in question batted her lashes at Baz. "I can't thank you enough, truly."

"How does it feel to reverse time like that?" another girl asked, twirling a curl around her finger.

Kai resisted the urge to roll his eyes. What was it with these girls fawning over Baz in this time?

"Tell us how you did it!" another student demanded.

A flush crept over Baz's neck. "Oh, well. It all happened so fast . . ."

"But such quick thinking on your part."

"It was nothing, really."

Clover put a hand on Baz's shoulder. "You're far too modest. Everyone who was there saw how brilliant you were."

To everyone's delight, Clover recounted how Baz had saved the girl from the wards. He painted a glorious picture, his voice rich with the cadence of a storyteller. Even Baz clung to his every word.

But Kai saw through him, right down to the truth of what Clover was.

He was a collector. He surrounded himself with individuals he deemed interesting. Rarities and oddities he acquired like an antiquarian collected invaluable artifacts. And then he threw these parties to revel in his collection.

It was why he didn't care much for Kai; he already had a Fear Eater in his entourage and didn't need a second. But Baz . . .

Timespinners were about as rare as Tidecallers, and so of course Clover had to add him to his collection. And look how much clout and glory this newest addition was bringing him.

Kai noticed Thames at the edge of the crowd, staring at Clover and Baz with something like longing or jealousy. Kai felt for him. It was clear that Thames craved Clover's affection, and if he had to constantly see Clover chasing after the next rarity . . .

He wondered if the Fear Eater grew tired of only ever being loved in the shadows.

43

EMORY

EMORY KNEW THE TRAIL OF BLOOD WOULDN'T LEAD the knights to the Night Bringer. At first she wasn't sure *how* she knew this, but as she moved away from her friends, she felt it. A tug inside her, calling her forth. A sense of calm in the chaos.

There was also blood on the floor leading away from the more obvious trail left by the *ursus magnus*. It led to a dark, damp cellar, the door to which was ajar. Emory slipped inside, and there was the demon, as she suspected. Hiding in plain sight after duping the knights into believing he had left. What his plan might have been, Emory didn't know. He looked like an injured animal come to die, slumped as he was against the wall, his hand clutching the bloody wound in his middle, his face drawn and pale.

Still, he managed to give her a withering stare. "If you've come to finish me off, I'd rather we get on with it."

Emory hovered by the door, keeping a careful distance even though she was fairly certain he couldn't hurt her in this state. "Tell me who you are."

He laughed, a wet, sinister sound. "Did you not hear them clamoring for my head? I am the villain they made me. The Night Bringer that darkens their world."

"But that's not all you are, is it? You said you had many names once."

"And I said I did not wish to recall them." He coughed up blood, wincing in pain.

Emory pushed off the door. "Fine. I was going to offer to heal you, but never mind. I hope that body rots with you inside it."

"Wait." Keiran studied her. "Why do you insist on this when I suspect you already know the answer?"

Because it was *impossible*, she thought. Because she needed to hear him confirm what had already taken root in her, what felt inevitable now that she'd seen the influence he had on her magic, the way every dark thing in her quieted in his presence.

The words he'd told her when she'd first fainted echoed in the chambers of her mind: *I am that which dwells in the dark between stars.* Words she'd pondered ever since.

And as the demon looked at her now with Keiran's face and those unnatural eyes, she knew her suspicion had to be true. Black and silver and gold. They were the eyes of the Sculptress's demonic counterpart, of the Night Bringer who'd destroyed the Sun Forger.

Of the first eclipse to shadow the world and bring the Tides to their ruin.

"You're the Shadow," she said.

His head tilted back against the wall as a faint, knowing smile played on his lips. "In the flesh." A wince of pain. "Well, not quite."

Emory's heart raced. All this time, she'd had it wrong. He was no demon. He was *divinity*. The first Eclipse-born to ever walk the earth. The deity she owed her very magic to.

"How can this be?" she asked. "You're supposed to have been sent to the Deep–the sea of ash. Wherever our souls go when we die."

A storm brewed in his eyes. "No. I was imprisoned in the sleeping realm, banished to the seams between worlds with no way out. Severed from my own body, my true form. Then this empty vessel came along," he said, motioning to Keiran's failing, bleeding body, "dead and useless to me until life was breathed into him again as if by some miracle. In his body, I could disguise my way out of the sleeping realm. So I seized my chance and slipped from my prison back into the world of the living." He coughed up blood again, pressing a hand to his wound.

"If you're the Shadow," Emory said, "why are you so . . ."

"Fragile?" he provided with a gruff laugh. "I forgot how useless mortal bodies are."

"Could you not jump into another body–a stronger one?"

One that didn't stir such complicated feelings in her.

"What a brilliant idea I couldn't possibly have considered already," he said wryly. "Let me muster up all the power at my disposal and saunter into another vessel like it's nothing."

A bloody cough drove his point home.

"I'm assuming that means you also can't vanish into shadows or travel through that liminal space of yours?" Emory asked, unable to keep the gloating out of her voice.

He glared at her. "So long as I wear your dead lover's vulnerable skin, I am doomed to remain half myself, my abilities fading with his strength." At her visible flinch, a cruel smile lifted his mouth. "Did I hit a nerve?"

Emory didn't give him the satisfaction of a reply. It was ironic, she thought, that the thing Keiran hated most should be what possessed his body. He had wanted to make Emory a vessel for the Tides to bring about the destruction of all Eclipse-born, only for him to be made a vessel for the one who had created Eclipse-born in the first place.

She didn't want to imagine what the full might of the Shadow's power would be if he were in his true form. Clearly, Keiran's body didn't care for the divinity inhabiting it.

"Now, I believe you mentioned healing me."

Emory considered him. How weak he appeared, not the demon or the deity or even the once-confident boy whose face he wore, but a revenant. She wondered how long the Reanimator's magic would last—if perhaps there was an expiration date to this reanimated corpse slowly deteriorating with the Shadow trapped inside it.

"Maybe I should leave you here to die," she said. "You tried to kill my friends, after all." Even though he'd saved *her*.

"Friends," he repeated gruffly. "If you knew what those friends of yours carry, what *she* did to your kind, you might not be so quick to protect them."

"She?"

"The Tides. The Sculptress. The Forger. The Celestials. If I have many names, then she has more. Like me, she is but one deity echoed across worlds. But when she splintered herself into pieces to keep her magic alive, those pieces of her lived on in those marked by her favor. Blood, bones, heart, soul. Always yearning to be put back together. That is what lives on in your *friends*."

The pieces of her he had tried to kill.

You deserved to be ripped apart, and I will ensure that you never be put whole again.

Emory stepped back from him as realization hit. In the myth she knew, the Tides were said to have left their shores to trap the Shadow in the Deep after he sought to take power from them. Whatever truth there was to the story—a story that existed across worlds, just told through a different lens, with differently named gods—it was clear the Shadow wanted revenge. That he would stop at nothing to destroy the pieces of this multifaceted deity who had trapped him. Pieces that called to each other through a song they alone could hear.

A song Emory no longer heard. At least, not in the same way that Romie and Aspen and Tol heard it.

All this time, they'd thought Emory was the scholar on the shores–the blood to Aspen's bones and Tol's heart and the guardian's soul. To Romie's dreaming, that fifth part the epilogue mentioned. Yet Romie was the one who shared an inexplicable bond with the other keys, not Emory. Romie was the scholar on the shores who'd first heard the song to other worlds, not her. And it was Romie who had true lunar magic–the power of Quies, the Waning Moon Tide, running through her veins–while Emory was a product of the eclipse. Of the Shadow.

"I don't have a piece of her in me," she said with bleak realization, more to herself than to the Shadow. "I'm not a key."

"You're a Tidecaller. That means you alone have the power to turn a key in its lock, and so much more you don't yet know."

Tidecaller, Tidethief.

But it wasn't only the Tides Emory had stolen from. The magic that had called to her on the ley line had been the power of the Tides and the Sculptress and the Forger, pieces of a single deity entrenched in the friends whose life force she had gorged herself on.

She assessed the Shadow. "Is that why you saved me back there?" Because her magic made her *his*, perhaps a weapon he might use against his rival.

He seemed disgusted at the reminder. "A moment of weakness on my part, influenced by this miserable mortal's lingering feelings for you."

"I don't believe you." Whether a part of Keiran remained alive or not in there, she doubted he would have cared whether she lived. "You didn't just take a sword for me. You saved me from myself–from what the ley line does to me. How?"

"Maybe I *should* have let you die, if only to save myself from these incessant questions."

"You need me alive." For what, she wasn't sure yet.

"And it looks like you need me to control your magic. Heal me, and I might find it in myself to help you."

And damn her, she considered it. He was the Eclipse god, after all—did she really want to make an enemy of the entity she owed her magic to? He alone seemed to keep the darkness that came from her magic at bay. He alone might help her understand her Tide-caller power and how it related to the keys. The very keys whose magics she kept tapping into every time she stepped on the ley line.

Voices suddenly rose outside the cellar—too close for comfort. Emory held her breath as she listened.

"Sir, the blood trail was a decoy. We found the *ursus magnus* but not the Night Bringer."

"Did you slay the beast?"

"Of course."

"The Night Bringer can't have gone far with that wound he suffered. Search the Chasm."

It would be only a matter of time before someone spotted the blood that led to the cellar. Emory already had one foot out the door when the Shadow growled, "You cannot leave me here like this."

She stopped, considered. She did need him. But she couldn't trust him not to hurt her friends.

Nor could she stand to keep hurting them herself.

"Over here!"

A golden-armored knight had spotted her and was barreling toward the cellar, his sword at the ready. Emory made a dash for it, but not before sending a wave of healing magic toward the Shadow. The last she saw of him was his surprise as he glanced down at Keiran's mending body.

He could deal with the knights on his own.

So long as he was alive, she could find him in the liminal space, get answers from him there. She could only hope he wouldn't be able to get to her friends.

A dragon's roar rent the tunnels, making the entire Chasm shake with the force of it. Emory ran toward it, recognizing it as the direction Tol had said they were going. She picked up the pace as she heard someone scream and knew it was one of her friends, suddenly hating herself for having left them behind in the first place. She got to the dragon's cell in time to glimpse white-hot flames spewing out of the dragon's mouth, the heat nearly knocking her back.

The beast seemed larger than it was before, and she realized it was no longer chained to the walls. The ceiling above it had come down, letting in a curtain of sunlight. She spotted a glint of golden armor scurrying away from the flames. Swords clashed as Tol fought the Knight Commander at the edge of the inferno. The rest of her friends were nowhere in sight, and she feared they might have gotten caught in the dragon's flames or trampled beneath its feet or stuck under the rubble from the collapsed ceiling.

"Emory!"

Relief and confusion swept through her. The voice came from the dragon's back–where Romie, Aspen, Nisha, Virgil, and Vera all sat astride it.

It is time for us to go now.

Emory blinked incomprehensibly at the voice in her mind. Tol suddenly rushed to her side, sword still in hand, the Knight Commander knocked out on the floor behind him. "Don't fight it!" he screamed.

Before Emory could make sense of his words, the dragon's talons closed around her and Tol.

Then it jumped toward the skies, unfurling its wings to carry them off to freedom.

44

BAZ

FOUR STUDENTS WERE DECLARED MISSING WHEN NO one could find Wulfrid and his friends the day after the party. A librarian found blood near the Vault's entrance, in the same spot the Ilsker girl had nearly bled out. And because it couldn't possibly be her blood, since Baz had reversed time so she never bled at all, the worst was presumed by everyone.

The four students must have tried getting past the wards while everyone was at the party–the same party they had vehemently refused to attend, wanting to focus on the games instead. Dean de Vruyes conducted a search of the Vault, then the campus at large, but there was not a single trace of them except for the blood in the Decrescens library.

Grim gossip swept the college.

"They can't possibly have vanished into thin air from blood loss."

"The dean did say the wards were deadly . . ."

"Are they really going to let the games continue after this?"

The answer to the latter, apparently, was yes. Which was why

Baz found himself in the Decrescens library with Clover, poring over their research as if nothing had happened—except everything felt different now, the stakes much higher. The library was busier than usual, as if students were irresistibly drawn to the gruesome site.

All Baz could think of was how, if these disappearances weren't enough to stop the games, this was only the beginning of what would forever alter the college's centennial celebrations. The thought almost made him want to quit.

Clover caught him staring off toward the Vault's archway again. "Could you not turn back time to make them reappear?"

Baz scrunched his nose in thought. "I don't think so. Too many unseen variables. That kind of magic . . ."

"Right. We wouldn't want you to Collapse."

Baz gave him a weak smile. "Right."

"I guess if that's out of the question, then so is using your magic to undo the wards entirely?"

Baz blanched. "We're dealing with sentient, murderous wards. I'd rather not find out what they might do to someone trying to cheat their way past them."

"Quite right. Best we stick to our research, then."

It seemed they couldn't escape the topic of death even in that.

"Listen to this," Clover said as he pored over *The History of Aldryn*. "'It is worth noting the inexplicable deaths that taint the college's history, especially those that took place in its four libraries. This goes back to the construction of said libraries, during which all four founding members died under mysterious circumstances before the college first opened its doors. Following this, multiple students suffered similar fates over the years. There are those who speculate they were killed over possession of rare, powerful books which were subsequently transferred into the Vault for safekeeping.'"

Baz stared at him, horrified. "You think students were killed over knowledge?"

"Perhaps they found books that contained things they weren't supposed to lay eyes on. Books that *should* have been locked in the Vault but might have been misplaced."

Baz thought of the copy of *Dark Tides* he'd found in Clover's room. In his time, he'd had to get permission from the dean to check it out of the Vault. But if Clover had a copy of it now, perhaps the book was not yet considered a title worthy of being kept behind wards.

For Clover's sake, he hoped it wasn't one such misplaced book that the wards might kill for.

"This is interesting," Clover added as he kept reading. "'The deaths linked to Aldryn's libraries have sparked unfounded theories and curious superstitions due to the nature of the holy ground the college was built on.'" He frowned. "Holy ground? Do we know what Aldryn was built on?"

"Oh! Yes, wait, I think I saw something here . . ." Baz rifled through an old history book of Elegy that he'd only skimmed, thinking it irrelevant since it was older than the school itself. "It says nearly a millennia ago, there was a temple here, built in the name of the Tides and the Shadow. It eventually crumbled to ruins."

"If they built the college on the ruins of a sacred temple . . . Maybe whatever holy power remained seeped through the foundations of Aldryn and affected other magics, like the wards." Clover drummed his fingers on the table. "I'm sure the fact that Aldryn sits on a ley line only adds fuel to the fire."

"A *ley line*?" Why did that sound so familiar?

"A source of power that runs beneath the sea. Some scholars theorize the reason why the landmasses and islands that make up our world are laid out to form a great spiral is that they're built on this vein of pure power. A spiral-shaped magical thread, if you will, that feeds off our magic, and vice versa."

"So we've got murderous wards, sacred grounds, magical power lines, and deadly books." Baz pinched the bridge of his nose, feeling like they were right on the brink of something, but still not close enough to see how it all fit together. "Remind me again why we're doing this?"

Clover smiled. "Knowledge is power."

Baz found himself wishing Professor Selandyn were here; she would certainly agree with Clover. The two of them would get along well.

"What we've yet to figure out is how the wards were even created in the first place," Baz said with a defeated stare at their pile of research. "None of these founders were Wardcrafters. Surely the person who put the wards in place had the only magic capable of doing so."

Cordie suddenly appeared, joining them at their table. "Found anything interesting?"

"Are you asking out of politeness," Clover asked, "or genuine interest?"

"Politeness, definitely."

Cordie winked at Baz, making him laugh. "If you two are done for the day, I wondered if I could borrow Baz for the afternoon."

"Me? Whatever for?"

"I promised you a quiet artist's afternoon at my studio, did I not?"

She looked well recovered from the other night. When Baz mentioned as much, her smile grew tight, eyes flitting uncomfortably to her brother. "That night was a blur. Must have been the drink. Now come along, we're losing precious light."

Clover squinted at her. "You're not going to see that tailor again, are you?"

"Of course not." There was a hard edge to her placating smile.

"You made your feelings on the matter quite clear. *That* part of the night I didn't forget."

Cordie's studio was on the upper floor of a tavern Baz had been to before, known in his own time as the Veiled Atlas, though here it was named the Emerald. He remembered in vivid detail all the portraits of Clover that hung in the room he'd dined in with Vera and Alya. All the baubles and paintings that looked like they'd been plucked out of *Song of the Drowned Gods*, which the Veiled Atlas believed to be a true story Clover had lived through.

Evidently, there were no such things here now.

Gauzy curtains framed tessellated windows that let in wintry light, and glossy floorboards speckled carelessly with paint creaked beneath their feet. A myriad of canvases–both finished and unfinished–leaned against the tapestried walls, and a lone velvet divan that seemed far too expensive and entirely out of place sat in the middle of the studio.

Being here was a welcome distraction from the Bicentennial. In a new sketchbook gifted to him by Cordie–since the one his mother had given him for the solstice had been left in his own time–Baz tried his hand at charcoals while Cordie worked on a large canvas she wouldn't let him see.

"It's a strange one," she said, frowning at her work. "Not sure what it's supposed to mean yet."

The way Cordie spoke of her paintings made it sound like she was letting some higher power guide her hand. When Baz said as much, she laughed. "That's not far from the truth, I suppose. Sometimes inspiration hits me in a way that can only be explained by my Seer magic."

Baz raised a brow. "Your magic tells you what to paint?"

"In some ways, yes. It's always a surprise to see what I might work on next. An impression I got from someone I crossed in the street, or a crystal-clear image of a scene that came to mind with no context or explanation. I'm not good at deciphering these psychic visions I get, but translating them on canvas helps some. Mostly I just think they make for pretty paintings that tell intriguing stories."

"And the one you're working on now?"

Cordie bit the top of her dirty paintbrush, squinting at the canvas. "Like I said, I'm not sure yet."

If the disparate artwork strewn around the studio was any indication, it *was* a pretty eclectic collection, ranging from ultra-realistic portraits to abstract works of colorful shapes. No two pieces were done in the same style, as if every vision she got also inspired a different artistic approach.

"Do you not sign them?" Baz asked, noticing none of them had a distinct signature.

Cordie shrugged. "I can never quite bring myself to sign the ones that were inspired by visions. They're not *my* visions, after all."

"They're drawn by your hand, though. You make it yours by giving it life."

Cordie hummed pensively. "Maybe you're right. But I like the mystery it adds."

They worked in comfortable silence after that. Baz found his stride, and his confidence, with every stroke of charcoal. The hours passed like they were nothing, until suddenly the light coming in was low and muted, cutting large shadows across the paint-speckled floorboards.

A knock at the door made them both jump.

Cordie's face was flushed with excitement as she set down her brush. "I'll be just a moment."

She let out a little squeal as she opened the door and leaped into Louka's arms. So much for promising her brother she wouldn't see him again. Their hushed voices drifted through the crack in the door, and Baz busied himself with whatever he could think of to give them privacy. As he put away the charcoals he'd been using, he caught a glimpse of Cordie's current painting out of the corner of his eye. Intrigued, Baz stepped around the easel to look at it.

His jaw fell to the floor. For a second, he thought he'd stepped into one of his nightmares—not the printing press, but another that followed him like a shadow. Keiran, dying in his arms. The haunting image of him in Dovermere, lying in a pool of sea-foam and blood, was painted on the canvas.

Perhaps it could have been any young man that was depicted here. He was featureless enough done in this particular style that Baz couldn't pinpoint anything that was distinctly Keiran-looking. But with his hands folded neatly on his chest, the water and sea-foam and blood pooled around him, the blood that ran down his mouth and the wound in his middle . . . it was a perfect replica of Keiran's death.

And with what Cordie had just admitted to him . . .

Did she know where this particularly gruesome vision came from? How it was linked to Baz?

"Sorry about that," Cordie said as she came back into the studio, cheeks flushed and eyes shining. "Please don't tell Cornelius. Louka was just . . ." She wavered when she saw him looking at her painting. "What do you think?"

"It's . . ."

"Morbid, I know." Cordie came to stand beside him, folding her arms as she studied her work. "But there's something strangely . . . peaceful about it, don't you think?"

"I suppose." Baz was too close to the situation to see beauty in it. But he couldn't deny Cordie's talent. The dark, muted colors, the loose brushstrokes, the intricate details. It made for a fascinating piece. Haunting, yet undeniably alluring.

"Do you have any idea where you might have picked up on such a vision?" Baz asked, even though he was terrified to know the answer. He tried to keep his tone unaffected, light.

"No clue," Cordie said as she busied herself with cleaning her brushes. "When I paint things like this, I like to think I take away the pain of such memories from their bearers. Otherwise, what's the point?"

The words felt a little too pointed, and Baz had to wonder if she knew that *he* was the bearer of this particular memory. But Cordie didn't seem preoccupied with such things. In fact, her mind seemed elsewhere entirely as she closed the studio up for the day, her countenance withdrawn. It made Baz wonder if she'd broken things off with Louka after all.

As they walked up the hill to Aldryn, Baz thought maybe Cordie was right. Maybe painting such a gruesome thing in such light would give Kieran's memory a sense of peace–something he might have been robbed of when Artem brought his corpse back to life.

Maybe, in time, it could do the same to alleviate the shame Baz carried.

He eyed the cliffs below, the crashing waves that the cave mouth swallowed. And suddenly it hit him, why ley lines had sounded so familiar when Clover had brought them up: he'd read about them in *Dark Tides*.

Ley line. A vein of power that ran beneath the sea. A thread upon which all manner of curious rifts were said to have opened.

Like the door to the Deep that he and Kai had come through. The one that no longer seemed to exist in this time.

PART III

THE
GUARDIAN

THERE WAS A CRUEL SORT OF IRONY TO BEING BORN a musical prodigy in a world that demanded silence, but such was Orfeyi's curse.

The world had not always been so quiet. It was full of song once, when music had been a way to invoke the divine—a token of worship, an oblation made to the Celestials who ruled the skies. Different songs, whether sung or hummed or played in any way, shape, or form, called on different gods from this great pantheon. The Celestials were fascinated by music and would bestow blessings upon those who created it, magic both big and small depending on the skill of the musician.

By this logic, Orfeyi should have been highly favored by the gods. But the Celestials were gone, and to make music now was to tempt fate. To gamble with death.

So silence reigned.

But everything was music if one paid close enough attention. When Orfeyi was a boy, he would sit for hours by the fjord his village sat upon and listen, enraptured, to the orchestra of sounds around him. The water, the wind, the birds, the grass. The buzz of insects and the faint tremor of the earth shifting beneath him. He learned music without ever holding an instrument, simply by closing his eyes and tuning in to the song of the world. He would fancy himself its conductor, guiding the notes with his very soul.

Yet his hands yearned to hold an instrument. His voice begged to be heard.

Once, his mother caught him humming to himself while they tended to their small flock of sheep. She gripped his arm so hard it left a mark, though nothing was quite as scarring as the fear in her eyes.

"You must never sing," she warned in a frantic whisper, "or the Soulless One will come steal your song."

The Soulless One was said to be the reason for the Celestials' demise, the rogue deity who brought down an entire pantheon. If anyone was careless enough to make music now, it was the Soulless One who answered, and he was no benevolent god.

"What would happen if he took my song?" Orfeyi asked, his already pale face blanching to a deathly pallor as his imagination ran wild with the worst scenarios: the Soulless One ripping out his vocal chords, smashing his hands so he might never play an instrument, taking his hearing so he would never again hear the music of the world.

"Music is not tied to voice or hearing." His mother tapped the center of his chest. "It resides here. If the Soulless One were to take your affinity for music, you would stop feeling it in your soul. And a soul without song is no soul at all."

Orfeyi resisted the urge to sing after that–until, years later, his mother fell ill. Death waited at her bedside, laughing off all the would-be cures Orfeyi brought his mother in a desperate attempt to save her life. Nothing worked.

So one desperate day, Orfeyi decided to tempt fate and sing.

His song was an imploration to the gods, a plea for them to save the person he loved most. Thunder rumbled in answer, as if in punishment for breaking the silence of the world. A vicious storm erupted, the skies going dark and blue with veins of lightning, and raging winds shook the peat-and-stone house Orfeyi and his mother lived in, tearing off the roof over their heads in a violent gust.

The Soulless One was coming, but Orfeyi remained undeterred, singing ever louder. And perhaps because there had never been a more beautiful voice or a more moving melody, the heavens split open. A shaft of brilliant light pierced through the dark to shine upon the peat-and-stone house. The prodigious singer within felt his soul expand as the Celestials answered his song. Miracles danced at his fingertips. He cupped his mother's wan face in his hands, pressed his forehead to hers, and with one final note, sung health back into her.

Lightning shot through him. Orfeyi went rod straight, head tilted up to the angry sky. Forks of blue and white entered his open eyes and ears and mouth and coursed through him, burning, burning, burning.

He couldn't hear anything. Then he stopped feeling. And finally, he became nothing.

Death's claim on Orfeyi, however strong, was not meant to last; the Celestials had other plans for him. He woke to find root-like scars running all along his skin from where the lightning had burned him, a sign of the Soulless One's fury at not being able to steal his song.

"My marvelous boy, my sweet angel." His now-healthy mother beamed at him. "You are Godstouched." She brought a mirror to his face so he could see the spiral-shaped brand that had appeared on his forehead. The mark of the Celestials who had answered his song and saved not only his mother's life, but his own.

Word of what Orfeyi accomplished spread across the village

and well beyond the fjord. He was proclaimed the champion who might finally defeat the Soulless One, whose anger now darkened the world with storms that raged in near permanence. Orfeyi gladly accepted this role. His soul soared with purpose as he set off toward the Godsgate, the ancient seat of the Celestials' power. If anyone could sing this pantheon of gods back into existence, it was he.

His journey was a lonely one—had to be, for only those who were Godstouched were allowed up the perilous mountain range where the gate stood—but Orfeyi did not mind. He filled his days with song, plucking at the strings of the golden lyre his people had gifted him before he left. It was a beautiful instrument, one that had survived all these years of silence since the Celestials' fall, and playing it felt more natural than breathing.

The skies above still stormed, but the Soulless One did not come to steal Orfeyi's song. In fact, the more music he played, the more his connection to the Celestials grew. They shared with him visions of what had been and what could be, of people he had never seen but whose souls echoed his own. They showed him what would be needed to defeat the Soulless One and lent him strength as he weathered storm and snow and cold.

When Orfeyi reached the Godsgate, his body was weary but his faith remained unshaken. He was elated to find the others like him already there—the pieces of the whole they would rebuild together—and the one who could bridge the gap between them all. The Tidecaller. The opener of doors. The bridge between worlds.

But darkness walked alongside this Tidecaller, and Orfeyi knew it would be their unmaking.

45

BAZ

AT THIS POINT, BAZ SHOULD HAVE BEEN UNFAZED BY all the minor rule-breaking he'd been coaxed into, but there was something particularly upsetting about sneaking past the nighttime librarian in charge of enforcing the newly imposed curfew that shut down access to the libraries after dark.

Baz understood the need for such a curfew–it was the college's way of preventing other students participating in the games from ending up like the Vanished Four, as they'd been dubbed–but this warred with his deep-seated belief that libraries should be accessible at all hours of the day. What was he supposed to do with all his burning questions? *Ignore* them until the morning? Not a chance.

Sneaking into the Decrescens library might make him feel like a common criminal, but this couldn't wait.

Thankfully, the librarian on duty seemed otherwise preoccupied. In fact, there was no one at the front desk at all, though Baz and Kai did hear footsteps echoing in the aisles–the librarian making their rounds, no doubt.

They hunkered down in the Unraveler section, where works on arcane magic were usually kept. Surely ley lines would be mentioned in one of these books, and Baz had a hunch the information would help them make sense of everything.

"The authors of *Dark Tides* thought doors to the Deep were dotted along a spiral ley line, right?" Baz whispered. "And Dovermere has always been believed to be sitting on the innermost part of the spiral. The most *powerful* spot. What if we did something to disturb the ley line while we were in Dovermere? A rift opened up, pulling us through time. If we can map out the ley line, find another time rift . . ."

"We could go back to our time," Kai finished, understanding lighting his eyes.

A sound made them both snap their heads up. Baz was distinctly aware of how close he and Kai were. They held their breath as the librarian appeared farther down the aisle. She walked past them without glancing their way.

Shoulders slumping in relief, Baz resumed his perusal of the shelves.

"What are we looking for exactly?" Kai asked.

"Anything that has to do with arcane magical sources, tidal influences, geographical anomalies. . . ."

Kai reached around Baz, breathing into his space as he pulled a book off the shelf. "Something like this?"

Baz found it hard to concentrate on the title with Kai standing so close. He finally managed to make sense of the letters, which read *The Sacred Spiral of Rebirth: Influences in Art, History, and Magical Theory.*

Baz clutched the book to his chest, beaming at Kai. "*Exactly* like this."

There was a charged moment before Kai stepped back, craning his neck to see if the librarian was nearby. He motioned that the coast was clear. They tiptoed their way through the library, and stopped as they came upon the archway that led into the Vault.

The door was open. Someone was coming up the narrow stair-case beyond. The laurel-leaf-crowned marble busts on either side of the door let the person through like it was nothing.

Cornus Clover stopped dead in his tracks as his gaze locked on Baz and Kai.

"This isn't what it looks like," he said.

"Really?" Baz exclaimed, mind blank with incredulity. "So you *haven't* found a way around the very wards we're trying to break through?"

"Not exactly," Clover hedged. He glanced nervously around the library. "We should speak somewhere else–"

"You're going to tell us what you're up to right here, right now," Kai said with a dangerous edge to his voice.

Clover sighed, readjusting his vest and sleeves. Baz had never seen him so out of balance. "The truth is," he said, "that I am part of a select group of students who have express permission to go into the Vault. The wards don't prevent me from going in and out of it as I please."

Kai laughed in disbelief. "Then why the hell are you even partici-pating in the games?"

Baz's thoughts exactly. All the research he'd done with Clover . . . Why would he have bothered?

"Because," Clover said, "while the wards may not keep *me* out, they are keeping something hidden *from* me. There is something in the Vault that no one has access to–not any student or profes-sor or even the dean, I suspect. I believe the wards' main purpose is to keep this thing hidden from everyone."

"And what might this thing be?" Baz asked, his curiosity piqued.

"A door."

Something prickled along Baz's spine. "A door to where?"

Clover shrugged, but there was something feigned about the

nonchalance of the gesture. "That's what I mean to find out. This is the reason I joined the games despite already having access to the Vault. I believe the only way to unveil this door is by breaking through the wards."

"How did you know the games would involve breaking in to the Vault to begin with?" Baz asked. "They announced it after you'd signed up."

"I had it on good authority."

Pieces started to put themselves together in Baz's mind. "This group of students you're part of," he said slowly, "it's a secret society, isn't it?"

Clover lifted a bemused brow. "And why would you think that?"

"Exclusive access to the Vault?" Kai said, picking up on Baz's train of thought. "The very seat of knowledge hidden behind deadly wards? Sounds like something the Selenic Order would be involved in to me."

Clover's eyes sparked at the name, but he said nothing at all.

Kai gave a jerk of his chin to Clover's hand. "Show us your wrist."

"What?"

"Your right wrist. Show it to us."

Clover seemed utterly confused now as he pulled his sleeve up. There was no silver spiral there to mark him as a Selenic, yet he had all the makings of someone who'd be involved in such a secret society. The best connections, the prestige, the grades.

With an unsettling realization, Baz thought Clover had all the same attributes that Keiran had had, even if they were nothing alike—or maybe he was only refusing to see the similarities.

"Say I am part of this secret society," Clover said as he pulled his sleeve down. "This, of course, would mean I am silence bound. Something I'm sure you understand more than most."

The meaning behind those words was clear. He knew they were hiding something too.

Baz and Kai exchanged a knowing glance, unsure how to tread here. This door Clover sought had to be the Hourglass. If it was hidden by wards in this time, it would explain why members of the Selenic Order didn't have spiral marks, because they wouldn't hold their rituals in Dovermere—might not know the Hourglass existed at all (if it even *did* exist in this time). It surely wasn't accessible through the tunnels of Dovermere. Could there really be another way in through the Vault?

Like the Treasury—the Order's seat of power, so to speak—that Nisha and Virgil had told them was in a secret grotto carved beneath the Vault.

"I want to be honest with you," Clover said earnestly. "But I need assurances that this will stay between us. And for that, I think it's best we drop this veil of secrecy between us, yes? These riddles we speak in are only impeding our trust."

"Okay." Kai crossed his arms. "Then talk, Tidecaller."

A slow smile spread across Clover's face, as if he were pleased that they'd discovered his utmost secret. "Only if you admit to being from the future."

"You knew?"

"It was easy enough to guess, once I overheard you talking about time portals, a concept pulled from a book you snuck into my room to find." There was no accusation in his voice, only mild amusement. "Besides, you're not exactly the first ones I've met."

Footsteps sounded in the dark, growing louder as they neared.

"Shit," Baz said. "The librarian."

He readied his magic, planning to stop time so they could slip out unnoticed, but Clover lifted a hand to stop him. "It's all right. She won't tell on us."

Kai shot daggers at him. "I swear if you Glamoured her—"

"I did not Glamour her. She's a willing participant in this venture."

His smile grew as the librarian appeared behind them. "There's my favorite Dreamer."

"Don't flatter me, Cornelius."

Baz turned and froze as Emory stared back at him.

"What are these two doing here?" she asked Clover.

The unfamiliarity of her voice—the light accent behind it—rattled him out of thinking it was Emory at all. She looked so much like her, but the more he stared at her, the more evident the differences became. The blue of her eyes not as stormy. The blond of her hair lighter than Emory's, and the texture much curlier. She was shorter than Emory, curvier than Emory, her face rounder and mouth thinner. She appeared a few years older, too, but all her features echoed Emory's in some way, so much so that Baz was certain she must be an ancestor of hers.

The girl lifted a bemused brow at his open-jawed stare. "Have I got something on my face?"

"I–I'm sorry," he stuttered. "I thought you were someone I knew."

Tides, even the way she looked at him with that guarded expression was so very much like Emory.

"You're the Dreamer I saw in Clover's nightmare," Kai said with a frown. "Aren't you?"

The girl he'd believed to be Emory.

"I really hoped you hadn't seen me there," she said with a grimace. Her eyes flitted to Clover as if to gauge his reaction. When he simply shrugged, she added, "Neat trick with the umbrae, though. Thames can't stop talking about it."

"Sorry–who are you?"

She stuck her hand out to Kai. "I'm Luce. Luce Meraude."

Everything shattered inside Baz's brain, but the world kept going around him. Luce said something to Kai that he didn't catch–because that was *Luce*, and Tides, it couldn't be the same Luce that Baz knew of, because how could Emory's mother be here, two hundred years in the past?

No. This had to be a different Luce Meraude, an ancestor that Emory's mother might have looked to for inspiration when forging her new identity.

Kai's voice snapped him back to himself as he asked, "Is your real name Adriana Kazan?"

Never one to beat around the bush.

Luce gave Clover a puzzled look. "Have they confirmed . . . ?"

Clover dipped his chin. "Yes."

"And they know about me?"

"I was just about to tell them."

She frowned at Kai. "How do you know that name? Not even Cornelius knows it."

Tides—it *was* her. It made no sense, but the truth was all there, in every line of her, in all the ways she resembled Emory. A relative indeed—though not so distant at all.

Emory's mother was here, standing in front of him. By the looks of her, she couldn't be much older than he was himself. Which meant either she hadn't given birth to Emory yet or she had before somehow ending up *here*.

"We know your daughter, Emory Ainsleif," Baz admitted, taking a chance that he was right about this. "Or we *will* know her, in the future. Time travel is all very confusing."

Luce didn't even bat an eye at the admission. "How far back did you travel from?"

"Two hundred years from now."

"One hundred and eighty-one years for me. I just gave birth to my daughter a few months ago. In the future, I mean. If you know her . . . How old is she in your time?"

"She's nineteen. Studying in her second year at Aldryn College."

"Nineteen?" Tears glistened in Luce's eyes. She gave a soft, strangled laugh. "Tides, that's only a few years younger than I am now."

Sudden fear fell on her face, etching worry in every line. "Her magic—has anything . . ." She bit the inside of her cheek, stopping herself from saying something she shouldn't. "Is she a good Healer?"

Baz had the impression she knew *exactly* what Emory was. She must know—she'd been the one to forge Emory's birth date, after all, so that Emory could be believed to be a Healer instead of the Tidecaller she really was.

"She's a fine Healer," Baz decided on saying, haltingly. "Though I wouldn't say it's her . . . defining ability?"

Luce watched Baz with keen eyes. Before she could say anything, they heard a noise coming from the hall.

"We shouldn't be talking about such things out in the open," Clover said tightly.

"How about in there?" Kai pointed to the painting behind which hid the secret party room.

And so it was that they found themselves there, in the disquieting emptiness of a hidden ballroom. Three people plucked out of time and the would-be author this had started with, all of their secrets filling the spaces between them.

"All right." Kai crossed his arms, looking every bit the Nightmare Weaver. "Talk."

46

KAI

"HOW IS IT THAT YOU'RE HERE IN THIS TIME?"

Kai tried not to overanalyze the emotion behind Baz's voice as he stared wide-eyed at Emory's mother.

"I came through a time rift, of course."

Luce–Adriana; whatever the fuck she wanted to be called–said it like it was the most mundane thing.

"You mean Dovermere?" Kai asked.

"No, not Dovermere. Mine was off the coast of Harebell Cove."

"*That's* what I felt," Baz exclaimed, looking at Kai with wide eyes. "Remember when we found that weird cavern on the shore at Henry's lighthouse? There was something about it that felt so similar to Dovermere. Like whatever magic lived there was the same." He turned to Luce. "Is it still here in this time?"

"The rift I came through isn't. I mean, the cave is there–I tried going back as soon as I got here–but whatever magic powered up the time rift in *my* time doesn't seem to work here." She tilted her head. "Does yours?"

"The door in Dovermere isn't there," Kai said. He turned to Clover. "Though I suppose that's what you're trying to unveil by breaking through the wards?"

Clover's eyes gleamed. "This door of yours . . . did it by any chance lead elsewhere than through time? Other places, perhaps?"

"Maybe," Kai hedged. "But I suspect you already have an idea."

"I believe this door was hidden behind wards centuries ago after the Tides and the Shadow left our shores, by the very secret society I am now part of. The Selenic Order, we call ourselves. Keepers of all the hidden knowledge here at Aldryn. Though you already seem to know about us."

"We're acquainted, yes. In our time, the Order's run by murderous, Eclipse-hating pricks, so you'll understand our distrust now that we know you're a part of it."

"I assure you, that's not the case here."

"Do they let Eclipse-born join their group?"

"No. But that's in part why I joined in the first place. You see, the thing about being a Tidecaller is that no one ever suspects what I can do. The dreams I can walk into, the futures I can glean, the memories I can read. All of it is done in the comfort of secrecy, without anyone ever the wiser. The Selenic Order doesn't know what I am. No one does except for the people in this room, plus my sister and Thames, of course. Being part of the Selenic Order gives me leverage, a voice where other Eclipse-born struggle to be heard. Do you think the college would allow those academic salons of ours to take place, or Eclipse-born to partake in the Bicentennial, if I did not know whose strings to pull?"

"Congratulations on doing the bare minimum," Kai deadpanned, unfazed by Clover's speech.

"It's no coincidence the both of you have inserted yourselves so easily here," Clover continued. "If it weren't for my Glamouring the

Karunang dean and all its students, your ruse would have been up before the first challenge ended."

"And we're forever in your debt."

The biting sarcasm had Clover clenching his jaw. "Have I done something to offend you, Kai?"

Kai caught Baz's pointed glare and decided it best not to unravel that thread. "No, please, go on."

"The seat of the Order's power is below the Vault," Clover said, "in a grotto we call the Treasury. That's why I'm granted access to the Vault. The entire Selenic Order is. The Treasury is the place we gather to hold rituals to the gods."

Clover eyed Baz. "This research you and I have been doing into Aldryn's history has led me to believe that the Selenic Order existed long before the school, before even the temple it was built on. They were the original devoted followers of the Tides and the Shadow. They knew of the doorways between our world and the Deep and all the realms in between, and were allowed to travel through them. Until these doorways were sealed forever shut.

"They then took it upon themselves to become the guardians of these doors. They built their temple to the gods over the Treasury to keep this secret safe behind wards and the aura of mystery and power that has always permeated this place, thanks to its proximity to Dovermere. And when the temple eventually crumbled into oblivion, what remained of their order built this college atop its ruins, creating the Vault as the perfect front to hide the Treasury.

"But what started out as a sacred order tasked with guarding the secret of the door to other worlds eventually became more about power and prestige. The members of the Selenic Order were the founders of Aldryn College. They shared access to the Vault with only a select few students, the brightest and most brilliant of them, who became part of the Order themselves. The door was all but forgotten, a mystical thing that might have once explained the origins of our Order, but no Selenic has been concerned with such a thing for a long time now. Until me."

"But how do you know about the door if it's supposed to be a secret?" Baz asked. "If it's lost to time and wards?"

"I've always had an affinity for Seer magic. It has allowed me to see things that are impossible, things others might think are folly for their strangeness. But I've always known the truth: that I see glimpses of other worlds. Possibilities of what might become in each one, and the universe at large. These visions have allowed me to acquire *some* information on these worlds, but not enough and, most importantly, not how to travel through them. One thing I know for certain is that they're all connected through the realm of dreams."

Clover inclined his head to Luce. "Thames and Luce have been helping me map it out. We've concluded the sleeping realm is laid out in a giant spiral, and these worlds are points along it. Our world sits on the outermost ring of the spiral, and every world after sits a bit closer to the center of the spiral: the Deep, where the Tides and the Shadow disappeared to. A world ruled by the very gods who created them. A world that will fall to ruin if what I saw comes to pass."

There is a world at the center of all things where nothing ever grows . . .

Kai locked eyes with Baz and knew he was thinking the same thing. *The sea of ash.*

"I have seen the bleak future that awaits us," Clover continued, expression grim. "A future beyond yours that heralds the extinction of all magic—of life itself. Surely you must have noticed in your time that there are fewer and fewer eclipses? Possibly other odd goings-on as well?"

Kai thought of the tides being out of whack, of what Drutten himself believed: that all of this was due to the appearance of a Tidecaller. *The Shadow reborn.*

"I believe the only way to prevent such an apocalypse is to bring the Tides and the Shadow back," Clover said, "by petitioning the higher gods to restore magic to what it once was."

"We've heard all this before," Baz said weakly. "From someone in our own time who . . . who wasn't good." A generous way of describing Keiran Dungshit Fuckby. "He sought to bring back the Tides, but for that, he thought he needed a vessel. Someone who had the capacity to hold all the Tides' magic in their veins."

"A Tidecaller, yes." Clover sounded unsurprised. The words Selandyn had translated from his journal came to mind: *A Tidecaller must rise. Open the door. Seek the gods. Restore that which lies at the center of all things.*

Clover drew himself a bit taller. "If that is the fate that awaits me, I'm willing to accept it. If it means saving the world . . . as well as Emory."

Confusion muddied Kai's thoughts. By the look on Baz's face, he was just as lost.

"What does she have to do with this?" Kai asked.

"Everything," Luce said in a tremulous voice, closing her eyes as if to keep back tears. She blew out a long breath. "It's why I'm here, why I left my time to seek Cornelius in the past. He's not the only one who's seen this vision of the future."

"So you Dreamers have the gift of prophecy now?" Kai quipped.

"Dreams were once believed to be messages from the gods, you know," Clover mused. "Dreamers were seen as messengers between the mortal and divine realms, taught to interpret these dreams and translate them into waking. One foot in the concrete world and one foot in the sleepscape. A dead art, but I wouldn't be so quick to discount the prophetic nature of dreams."

Luce nodded. "*My* dreams were always full of stars and song, a voice that was not one but many, calling me to my destiny. I felt certain I was hearing the Tides. In my most vivid dreams I felt them being splintered, ripped apart, pulled into oblivion. I was suddenly driven by this need to avenge them. I wanted–*needed*–to put them back together, and I knew that Dovermere was the answer. So I sailed toward it. Then my boat capsized in Harebell Cove. One thing led to another, and I suddenly found myself pregnant with Emory."

Luce worried her lip. "It quickly became a difficult pregnancy, and my dreams turned . . . strange. All I heard in them was a song out of tune, screeching as if in protest at the life growing inside me. I tuned it all out. I *wanted* this child, but I couldn't deny the impression of impending doom that followed me everywhere. When Emory was born on a rare eclipse, I sought a trusted Seer friend of mine to tell me what she saw in Emory's future. She saw the same vision of apocalypse as Cornelius did . . . and that if Emory's true Tidecaller nature were ever unlocked, it would bring upon this ending of worlds.

"I knew Cornelius had also been a Tidecaller in his time, so when my friend saw his and my daughter's fates entwined, I had to seek his help. If anyone might save my daughter, it had to be him. So I hid the truth of Emory's birth, hoping it would keep her safe, hoping she would remain a Healer forever, like Clover was believed to have been. I left her with her father and found the time rift in Harebell Cove. I'd been studying ley lines in depth by then and guessed correctly that this cavern I'd found when my boat first capsized was indeed a door to the Deep, one that would carry me on the tides of time. And here I am."

Luce gave Clover a fond smile. "When I told Cornelius my story–a woman from the future claiming to be his distant descendant, asking for help saving her daughter from a nebulous vision . . . I was certain he would have me thrown into the Institute."

"Little did she know I'd seen her coming," Clover said. "Our goals aligned the moment she told me of this vision. *My* vision foretold Emory would indeed unlock her powers, and that with them she would burn the worlds to ash."

"Emory wouldn't do that," Baz said fiercely.

"Perhaps not willingly, no. But this is what I have seen: Emory unlocking her Tidecaller nature, going on a quest through perilous worlds to wake the Tides . . . and becoming so consumed with power that everything turns to ash."

Baz was shaking his head. "Emory wouldn't let that happen."

"She won't ever have to," Luce said. "Not if Cornelius succeeds."

"If I wake the Tides myself–and not just the Tides but the Shadow, too–then magic can return to what it once was. Balance can be restored. I can take this on myself, in this time, so that Emory never has to. If I succeed, it will change the future for the better. For *everyone*, including Eclipse-born. But first we need to open the doors between worlds–and we need to break through these wards to find *our* door."

Kai had to wonder if this was a hopeless endeavor; if the future could be changed at all, or if all their fates were already predestined. He saw the determination in Baz's eyes and knew it wouldn't matter to him. *He'll do anything for Emory*, he thought, perhaps a bit too bitterly.

And Kai would go along with it, because *he* would do anything for Baz.

When the four of them stepped out of the secret room, Baz slipped, nearly going down before Kai reached out a steadying hand.

"What the–"

The floor at their feet was wet. In front of the Vault's archway, four bodies in sopping-wet clothes were laid out in a neat row, limbs unnaturally straight and hands folded on their bellies. Their pallid faces stared unseeing toward the ceiling.

Kai recognized Wulfrid among them, glassy-eyed and blue-lipped. As if he'd drowned on dry land, drained of all blood, and the wards had finally spat him and his friends back up again.

47

ROMIE

ROMIE WAS USED TO SEEING THE MOST ABSURD THINGS in dreams, but none of them came close to riding on the back of an actual, real-life, fire-breathing *dragon*.

They flew away from the Chasm and Heartstone, the red-hued barrens beneath them moving at a dizzying speed. The dragon landed in the middle of a crop of odd rock formations that looked like teeth, jagged in parts and smooth in others, forming dark crevices that would be hard to get through if they were on foot. A few shrubs grew between them, as well as those odd, spindly-looking trees. But otherwise, it was as barren as the rest of the land.

The sun was setting, casting the world in soft purples and blues. Gwenhael perched itself at the top of the rocks, spreading its wings wide as it lavished in its freedom.

The Golden Helm will come, it said to them. *They will have been alerted to our presence by now. They have eyes everywhere.*

The words were said in a placating way, but only succeeded in putting everyone on edge. Tol sat atop a rock opposite the dragon, sword balanced on his knee as he kept an eye on the horizon. His draconic wings were unfurled after Virgil had rusted off the metal band around his neck that prevented him from shifting. Romie saw Aspen eyeing the wings with pure wonder, and maybe something else too.

As everyone settled around a fire that Gwenhael generously lit for them, Romie heard Virgil asking Emory where in the Deep she'd disappeared to back there. Emory had the good sense to look remorseful, even if she made no apology.

"You went after the demon, didn't you?" Romie guessed.

The way Emory avoided her gaze confirmed it well enough.

"He's not exactly a demon," Emory said. "He's the Shadow."

The world tilted beneath Romie's feet and didn't stop as Emory recounted what she'd learned. The Tides-damned Shadow himself was after them, and Emory wasn't the key they thought her to be, and Romie and Aspen and Tol apparently each carried a piece of the Tides, the Sculptress, the Forger—the singular deity found across worlds—inside them.

"If you're not our world's key," Romie said, "then that means the Hourglass didn't open with *your* blood but mine."

Emory nodded. "He said my Tidecaller blood is what's needed to fit each key into their lock. That's why the door in the Wychwood didn't immediately open with Aspen's bone. It needed my blood to activate it."

"Then how were you able to open the Hourglass a second time when I was in the sleepscape?" Romie asked. "And each time the door opened to let Travers and Lia and Jordyn through. You would have needed *my* blood as key."

Emory seemed at a loss. "I don't know."

"Maybe once a door is unlocked, Emory can open it at will," Nisha suggested.

"Hold on," Virgil said, pinching the bridge of his nose. "How do we even know for sure that Romie's our world's key?" He pointed to Aspen and Tol. "They have a spiral mark. But so do all of us." He pointed between himself, Romie, Emory, and Nisha. "Does that mean anyone who survived the Selenic Order ritual can be a key?"

"Romie's the only Selenic who hears the song," Emory pointed out. "And there's the connection she shares with Aspen and Tol."

It would explain why Romie heard an echo of that song in the witch and the warrior. The Tides, the Sculptress, the Forger—whoever she was, she was pulling on the three of them, trying to bring the pieces of her back together. Romie's blood, Aspen's bones, Tol's heart.

Still, Virgil's question stuck with her. She couldn't make sense of why, in their world, the entire Selenic Order was marked with the spiral, yet only *she* appeared to be the key. While in the Wych-wood, only one witch per generation was meant to bear the Sculptress's mark and the title of High Matriarch that came with it—which meant Aspen must have something that Bryony and Mrs. Amberyl did not possess, if she alone was her world's key.

And Tol . . . Romie looked at the spiral mark burned on his breastbone, visible beneath the jacket Virgil had graciously lent him. Like a brand that had healed over time.

"How did you get that?" Romie asked him.

"It's the Sun Forger's mark. At least, that's what the Knight Commander had me believing. The mark appeared when I was remade into a draconic."

Death and rebirth. Just like Romie had nearly drowned in Dovermere. Just like Aspen had survived being buried alive. Even Emory, though she may not be a key, had lived through a near-death experience to unlock her Tidecaller abilities—and maybe with that came the ability to turn keys in locked doors.

Romie studied her friend. "Did the Shadow have anything to say about what happened on the ley line?"

Emory couldn't meet her gaze.

"Wait, what happened on the ley line?" Nisha asked.

Romie pursed her lips, waiting for a reply from Emory that never came. "You have nothing to say to that? No apology for the power you took from me and Aspen and Tol, or the fact that the Shadow saved your ass–and ours in the process by severing your connection to the ley line?"

"What in the Deep are you talking about?" Virgil snapped.

"She's a *Tidethief*," Romie gritted out. "Every time she's been on a ley line, I've felt her sucking out all the magic from my veins, turning my blood to ash. Only this time she did it to Aspen and Tol too."

"Is that what I felt?" Tol's brow furrowed. "I thought my heart was going to stop."

Aspen looked at Emory with disbelief. "My bones breaking–that was you?"

This at last had Emory meeting their gaze, her eyes bright with unshed tears. "I'm sorry. I didn't know how to stop. I don't even know how I did it in the first place. It's like the ley line opens this conduit between us that I can't avoid and don't know how to close."

Romie crossed her arms. "I guess it makes sense that the Shadow would be able to stop it for you, since you owe him your Tidethief magic."

"Will you stop calling her that?" Virgil snarled. "She never *stole* anyone's magic back at Aldryn."

"What about Travers and Lia? They died when Emory called them back through the door after suffering some odd reversal of their magic, didn't they?"

"Romie, come on," Nisha said. "That wasn't Emory's doing."

Romie blinked at Nisha, hurt that she wasn't siding with her on this. Romie didn't *want* to believe Emory would do any of this either, but the facts were all there, and the memory of her magic being drained was too close to the surface of her mind for her to ignore it.

"It's only the keys, I think," Emory chimed in at last. "And only when we're on a ley line. Which we're not at the moment, don't worry."

"Still. Probably best you don't use any magic from here on out."

"You think I don't know that?" Emory snapped. "I don't want this to ever happen again. That's why I went after the Shadow. He knows things about my magic that might help me control it."

Romie raised a dubious brow. "And how do you suppose you're going to get his help? He wants to kill us, Em. You can't trust him. He might wear Keiran's face, but he's the *Shadow*. The reason the Tides disappeared. And not just the Tides but the Sculptress and the Forger too. He's the evil at the source of all this. You should have let the monster die."

Emory flinched at that. "I never pegged you for someone who bought into the whole 'Eclipse magic is evil' thing."

"That's not what I'm saying."

"Isn't it? You've been afraid of my Tidecaller magic ever since you found out about it."

"Can you blame me?" Romie yelled with a laugh bordering on tears. "My whole life has been shaped by Eclipse magic going wrong. My dad, Baz, now you. I just—I can't do it anymore."

They're here.

All of them turned to where Gwenhael perched. The dragon had lifted its head, alert to something only it could see in the inky night that had fallen.

There was movement in the dark, and before they knew it, Tol had his sword pointed at two women armed to the teeth. They wore gilded chain mail beneath rust-colored surcoats that bore a crest similar to the Fellowship of the Light's—an ouroboros, though this one featured both a gold dragon and a black winged beast that called to mind the *corvus serpentes*, all twisted up together. Leather baldrics were slung across their chests, leaden with a brutal assortment of knives.

And from their backs sprouted wings exactly like Tol's.

"You're a long way from Heartstone, draconic," the younger said with a voice rough like stone. She had umber skin and long tresses that fell to the middle of her waist, and she looked to be around the same age as Romie. Her eyes cut to Gwenhael with thinly veiled suspicion. "We have not seen a dragon traveling freely with the likes of your order for a long time."

The draconic and his friends freed me from the Fellowship of the Light, Gwenhael said as it moved to stand behind Tol, the gesture at once threatening and protective.

"Deserters?" the other warrior exclaimed with a raised brow. She had the same rich tone as the younger one, short-cropped hair, and must have been in her forties. She narrowed her eyes at Tol. "What made you break your oath to the Light?"

"Gwenhael." Tol motioned to the dragon. "I found the alchemists torturing it for its flame. I didn't know this was the alchemists' method, capturing dragons and taking their flames against their will. They sentenced me to die because I opposed them. We escaped with Gwenhael."

"Impressive," the younger warrior said, though her eyes were hard and untrusting, and she did not lower her sword. "Or maybe that's what you want us to believe in the hopes that we lead you to more dragons you can imprison?"

"That's not—" Tol started.

"Maybe that's also why there's a company of knights at your back," the girl continued, "lying in wait while you weasel your way into our midst."

A muscle feathered in Tol's jaw. "I can assure you we're not with them."

I vouch for the draconic, Gwenhael said. *Is my word as dragon not enough to convince you?*

"Forgive us," the older woman said with a reverent bow.

The younger one seemed reticent to show such deference, if only because she couldn't tear her gaze from Tol.

"We are of course in your service, mighty Gwenhael," the older woman continued. "But you will understand our distrust of the Fellowship of the Light. Too often have they captured dragons whose freedom it was our duty to safeguard. The Golden Helm will not fail again."

"What is the Golden Helm, anyway?" Tol asked.

"Your masters really tell you nothing, do they?" quipped the youngest. "The Golden Helm are knights-errant, loyal only to the dragons. Those who haven't been captured and tortured and killed by *your* Fellowship." She spat on the ground at Tol's feet.

"Ivayne," warned the older woman, just as Gwenhael emitted a low growl.

The girl glared at Tol. "We were the original draconics. Those to whom the dragons *chose* to give their heart-flame. *Our* oaths are truly sacred because they were made to the dragons themselves. Unlike your Fellowship. Thieves, the lot of you."

"Trust me, no one hates their methods more than I do," Tol said, lowering his sword. "But it's not like I was ever given a choice. That's how the masters trick us. They find us as children on the brink of death and turn us when we're too delirious to know what we're agreeing to. They claim to want to save us, but really, they only seek to add numbers to their ranks."

The older woman finally lowered her sword, considering Tol. "What is it you're after, then?"

"We seek the Sun Forger. Gwenhael told us you might know where she slumbers."

Ivayne laughed. "Even if we did know, what makes you think we would tell a supposed deserter of the Fellowship and his strange companions?"

If the Golden Helm truly serves all dragons, then you must share this secret with me if I request it of you.

The women exchanged a glance.

"Look," Tol said, taking a step toward them, "we just want–"

Both women thrust out their swords in warning. Tol stepped back immediately.

"Careful, draconic," the older one said, eyes ablaze.

Something had come loose from her tunic, dangling from a chain around her neck. Romie blinked in recognition.

"That compass," she said. "Where did you get that?"

It looked exactly like the one Vera had–the compass Emory's mother had left her.

"What is it to you?" asked the older woman.

Vera pulled on her own chain to reveal the identical compass.

The two women lowered their swords at the sight of it. The older one strode up to Vera and examined her compass. "You're part of the Veiled Atlas?"

"Yes?" Vera replied uncertainly.

The Veiled Atlas–the cult that believed Cornus Clover had truly gone to the other worlds he wrote about. A truth that was becoming more and more plausible. Did this cult exist here as well after Clover passed through?

"You must be Travelers, then," the woman said. She looked between them all. "Who of you bears the Traveler's mark?"

"You mean this?" Romie lifted her sleeve so the silver spiral on her wrist was visible. "Most of us here have it."

"But not all of you are keys."

"That would be the three of us," Romie said, pointing between her, Aspen, and Tol. There was no reason to hide the truth now.

The older woman put a hand to her heart. "Apologies, then. If

you're keys, we're at your service."

"*Mother*," Ivayne whispered furiously, clearly unconvinced.

"How do you know about us?" Romie asked.

"The Golden Helm knew of Travelers, once, when the doors between realms were still open and keys were not needed. We've been waiting for you ever since. You seek the Forger to save our world from the darkness that has befallen it, yes? It was like this, long ago, after the Forger and the Night Bringer vanished and the doors were shut."

"Those are but stories," Ivayne snapped.

"Every story has a morsel of truth," her mother said. "We'll bring you to the place where the Forger was rumored to have gone, where the door to another realm once stood. We call it the Sunforge, an old mountain surrounded by rivers of fire, so inaccessible and hostile it has not been visited by any human as far as memory serves." She studied them, then the dragon. "But if Gwenhael agrees to escort us, we may just find our way."

I accept, Gwenhael said, lowering its head.

48

BAZ

BAZ STARED BLANKLY AT THE DYING EMBERS IN THE Eclipse commons, wondering what in the Tides' name he'd gotten himself into. He wasn't sure what was more upsetting: Clover and Luce having visions of Emory bringing about the end of the world, or the four missing students they'd found dead–*drowned*, from the looks of them. And drained of blood.

These games felt suddenly ludicrous to him. No wonder the Tricentennial had been canceled–and their own Quadri hadn't fully reinstated the games.

"Say Clover actually brings the Tides and the Shadow back," Kai mused on the sofa beside him. "What would that mean for us? History would be completely rewritten. The world we knew might no longer be the same."

Baz ran a hand over the nape of his neck as he pondered all the rules of time travel they did not yet know. So much could go wrong. He didn't want to believe Emory could do what Clover and Luce had seen. But if they *were* right–and if there really was a way for them to prevent all of it–Baz couldn't leave Emory's fate up to chance.

"I guess it's just a risk we have to take," he said at last.

Kai didn't look so convinced.

"Do you not trust Clover?" Baz asked.

"I have a hard time trusting anyone."

"We have him to thank for keeping our Karunang cover intact."

"Which he clearly did to fit his own agenda. But I guess he does make some compelling arguments." Kai met his gaze. "I know you're deeply invested in Emory's fate, but–"

"This isn't just about Emory," Baz countered. "If Clover succeeds, it might fix *everything*. It would make the world we know a better place for Eclipse-born."

Baz's family might still be intact, his father never having gone to the Institute if the world were a safer, fairer place for Eclipse-born. Baz himself might never have Collapsed.

He would never have *killed*.

He thought about Cordie's painting. All that guilt he carried, all the darkness that had followed him since that day at the printing press . . . If Clover changed the future, they would no longer be his to carry.

When he looked at the embers dying in the hearth, he imagined his guilt burning to ash with them.

If only it were that simple.

News of the students' deaths swept the college like a grim tide. Over the next few days, Cordie tried to get Clover and Baz to abandon the games as other students had. But they remained undeterred.

"Delia doesn't know about any of this," Clover had told Baz and Kai, asking them not to breathe a word to his sister about doors and prophecies and this quest of his to change the future. Baz felt bad about lying to her, but he understood. Clover simply wanted to protect her.

The same way Luce had wanted to protect Emory.

As he and Clover sat in the Decrescens library late one afternoon, he watched Luce and Kai disappear into the secret room to try and map out the sleepscape together. It still hadn't hit him fully that this was Emory's *mother*. There had been a moment, upon first meeting Luce, where Baz had hated her at the thought of her leaving an infant Emory behind. But now he understood *why*.

He was pulled from his thoughts as a couple of Awansi students in bright kaftans passed their table, whispering about the deadly Vault and its victims. Baz glanced at the warded archway and blanched, the image of those four bodies still imprinted on his mind.

"You know, the strangeness of their deaths had me looking into the founders again," Clover said, noticing his stare.

"Oh?"

"The founders didn't just mysteriously die right before the college opened its doors. They died within the *same* month, in the exact order of their moon phases—on a day corresponding to their respective lunar phases."

"There's no way that's coincidental." Baz thought of Travers and Lia and Jordyn, called back through the door—to their deaths—on their respective moon phases. New moon, then waxing, then full. Romie might have been next on the waning moon. There was a connection to be made here.

"There's something else I wanted to show you," Clover said. "Now that you're aware of the Selenic Order, I can tell you the founders were part of it. And not only that—their names appear on a signed agreement by the first eight members of the Order as we know it today, dated the very year Aldryn College was built."

Clover produced a familiar journal that sent a jolt of excitement through Baz. He flipped it open to pages that were blank again . . . until they weren't. Ink appeared out of thin air, the pages full of Clover's tight handwriting.

Clover gave him a crooked smile. "A bit of Wardcrafter magic I built into the pages. To keep unwanted eyes from . . . sensitive information."

So Clover *had* started writing in his journal—and from the looks of it, it appeared nearly as complete as the one Baz had with him.

Clover pointed to a list of names he'd scrawled in the margins. "See here, the founding members of the Selenic Order: Dunhall, Delaune, de Vruyes, Belesa—the four library founders themselves—plus Dade, Esedenya, Caine, Orlov."

A chill ran down Baz's spine at the familiar names. "Do you know if one of them was a Wardcrafter?" If they found the person who'd erected the wards, maybe they could understand how to get past them.

Clover tapped the last name on the list. "Elisava Orlov. Appointed as the first dean of Aldryn. This further proves the Selenic Order is behind the wards, as I suspected."

Baz frowned. "But how does it explain the deaths of the library founders?"

"That I don't know yet."

Baz stared at the journal, a thought crossing his mind. "What exactly has Luce told you about . . . well, *you*? The legacy you leave behind."

Clover leaned back in his chair with a knowing smile. "You mean the famous writer I am to become?" He chuckled. "She didn't tell me more than that. We both agreed it would be best she keep such information from me. Seeing the future is burden enough as it is without knowing every detail of what my life is to be—or what death has reserved for me. I'd like to retain *some* agency. Besides, if we are to change the future, perhaps my story is meant to be rewritten."

Clover ran a fond hand over his journal. "Though I must say writing stories has always been a passion of mine." He smiled at Baz. "Maybe one day."

"I hope so," Baz said. "Your stories . . . they mean a great deal to a lot of people."

He didn't know if he could bear a world in which *Song of the Drowned Gods* might never have existed.

"Have you seen Luce and Kai?" Thames appeared at their table as they immersed themselves back in their research. "We're supposed to meet."

Clover jerked his chin toward the secret room, barely lifting his head from his book. "They seem to have started without you."

Baz caught the jealous glint that flashed in Thames's eyes–the way he hovered as if hoping Clover would say more, or look at him, or acknowledge him in any way at all–before he shuffled his way to the secret room.

Baz leaned in toward Clover. "Wait, Thameson *Caine*–his family is part of the Selenic Order?"

Clover nodded. "He would have been, too, were he not Eclipse-born." He stared after Thames with affection. "I couldn't bear the thought of being in the Order without him, so I pulled some strings with the Tidal Council–that's the heads of our Order. Thames may not be an *official* member, but he is given all the privileges of one. As he rightfully deserves." He eyed Baz. "I'm guessing the Order's rules against Eclipse-born members have not changed in your time?"

Baz shook his head. He was in the middle of telling Clover about the spiral marks that the Selenic Order members obtained during their initiation ritual when the library shook with such force, books toppled off their shelves. The trembling came and went in the blink of an eye, leaving students utterly confused.

Baz looked toward the Vault's entrance, bracing for the worst.

But there was nothing there, its marble sentinels unmoved. The disturbance came from farther down, in the alcove that led into the secret room, where shadows emerged from a now cracked painting.

The kind of shadows that only came from nightmares.

49

EMORY

THEY SET OFF TOWARD THE SUNFORGE THE NEXT morning, hiking their way through the hilly desert while Gwenhael took to the skies, keeping a lookout for the Fellowship who had followed them from Heartstone. Their two Golden Helm escorts—Ivayne, the youngest, and Vivyan, her mother—were familiar with these parts and knew how to avoid being seen, by both draconic knights and eldritch beasts who might be roaming around.

Ivayne was relentless in asking them questions about their respective worlds, at first sounding like an interrogator, but eventually succumbing to her curiosity enough that she lost a bit of that hard exterior. Her mother regaled them all with stories throughout the day, tales of the first dragons and the knights-errant that served them.

At one point they came upon a rocky mound that *moved*, the rock itself shifting and groaning until a stony giant was staring at them. Tol brandished his sword, and Emory had her magic at the ready despite vowing not to use it. But Ivayne and Vivyan told them to stand down.

"It won't harm us," Vivyan said.

"But it's an eldritch," Virgil argued.

"Yes, and not all eldritch are out for blood, contrary to what everyone believes." Vivyan bowed at the waist in front of the stony giant, whose responding groan sounded like the splitting of the earth itself. But it made no move to hurt them, merely watching them as they passed by it. Tol was mesmerized and spent the rest of the day listening to Vivyan speak of the rule of balance, and how the Golden Helm upheld this by protecting both dragons and eldritch alike.

They spent the next few days going over all the myths about their respective gods and the origins of their magic, trying to piece together how it all connected, to find all its common threads to weave a tapestry they could make sense of. In her mind, Emory kept going back to *Song of the Drowned Gods*, in which the heroes were lured to the sea of ash thinking they would free the drowned gods, only to be trapped there in their place. Surely if most of Clover's story was playing out now in real life, chances were they, too, were walking into a trap.

But there was no convincing Romie and the others of this.

"I hear the song clearer every day," Romie argued. "So do Aspen and Tol. The Tides, the Sculptress, the Forger . . . Putting the pieces of her back together is the answer to the worlds dying."

"How can we be sure?" Emory asked. "If she's anything like the drowned gods, then that means she's luring you all to her."

"She has a point," Nisha said. "The heroes in Clover's story felt certain they were following their destiny, and they ended up being played in the end."

"So you think we should believe the Shadow instead?" Romie bit back. "Need I remind you that in the book, the drowned gods were keeping a dangerous beast trapped in the sea of ash? Obviously referring to the Shadow." She pursed her lips at Emory. "Maybe he's the one luring *you* into some ulterior plan of his."

The comment stung more than Emory cared to admit, probably because there was some truth to it. She'd learned her lesson with Keiran and would never let herself be *lured* by anyone again. But she couldn't deny this drive she had to understand the Shadow and this bond they shared. Why he alone seemed to have the power to soothe her magic—magic she hadn't let herself touch since the Chasm, even though they weren't traveling on a ley line.

The pressure building in her veins was becoming unbearable. Not even bloodletting soothed it.

Emory wanted answers. When she got Virgil to make her faint again, hoping to find the Shadow in that liminal space of his, nothing happened. He wasn't there. In fact, there hadn't even been a *there*. One minute she was conscious, then it was oblivion, and finally she came to.

It was almost like the Shadow's magic was being blocked. The same way, perhaps, that Tol's ability to shift had been blocked by that damper around his neck.

It remained like that every day. A terrible inkling settled in her gut, later confirmed by Gwenhael.

The Knight Commander leads the company following us, the dragon said. *She and her knights have captured the Night Bringer.*

Emory wanted to kick herself. She had left the Shadow to fend for himself against the knights, thinking he'd be strong enough to escape them after she'd healed him. How long would the Knight Commander let him live? Could the Shadow even be killed, or would he survive Keiran's death to find another vessel?

"You want to go after him, do you?" Virgil asked her, as if reading her mind.

And though she *did*, Emory couldn't possibly do that to her friends. Not when they had a door to find–a door they needed her to open.

But the idea haunted her like one of her ghosts. The pressure in her veins protested at her abstinence from magic, and Emory could only imagine what might happen if she stumbled upon a ley line–the kind of destruction she would unintentionally wreak on the keys if all this unused power inside her came out.

She had to fix it before it was too late.

That night, she found herself in a familiar, idyllic dream. Chasing waves and seagulls with Romie and Baz. Laughter and salt spray and the sighing of tall grass in the breeze. The real Romie wasn't beside her like last time. In fact, she hadn't visited Emory in dreams since the Chasm, as if she were afraid Emory might hurt her even here.

A tear rolled down Emory's cheek as she watched their younger selves in this moment of levity. She'd do anything to get back to that.

The skies grew dark. The gulls fell, suddenly flightless, shattering on the sand, swallowed by the roiling waves. Emory watched her younger self dissolve to ash along with Romie and Baz. The scene gave way to a dark expanse full of stars, and Emory turned to find she was not alone.

"It's you again," she breathed.

50

KAI

"IF ANOTHER LIBRARIAN OR, TIDES FORBID, A *PROFESSOR* finds out I'm practicing magic with Eclipse-born students in secret, I'll get fired." Luce grimaced. "Or worse."

"Wouldn't enrolling as a student have been easier?" Kai asked with a raised brow. They were getting settled in the secret library room, waiting for Thames to come and map out the sleepscape with them.

"The school year was already underway when I got here, and it would have involved documentation I didn't have and couldn't exactly forge. Applying for an open librarian post seemed the easiest way to stay close to Cornelius." Luce smiled to herself. "When I first met him—as a librarian, that is, before I told him the truth of who I was—I introduced him to a book I'd brought with me from my time. *Dark Tides*."

"I'm familiar with it." It made sense now, why they'd found that book in Clover's room—a book believed to have been published after his time.

"So you know the strange topics it touches on," Luce said. "I thought it was the perfect way to ease into my big revelation, because, well, *Hello, I'm your four-times-great-granddaughter from the future* sounds like something I'd get locked up for."

"So is being a Tidecaller."

Luce gasped with mock affront. "Are you suggesting I could have used my ancestor's secret magic as a bargaining chip to save my own ass? Where's your loyalty?"

My only loyalty's to the four-eyed nerd currently studying with your ancestor, Kai thought with a wry smile. This, thankfully, he kept to himself.

"It's funny," Luce continued. "I have all this knowledge of *Song of the Drowned Gods,* but I can't say anything to Cornelius about it. And I have all these preconceived notions on what his life should look like, yet the reality is so much different. So much less . . . *mythical.* He's powerful and magnetic, sure, but he's just a man, after all. Makes me think *Song of the Drowned Gods* is nothing but a fictional story."

"I thought you Veiled Atlas fanatics were supposed to believe Clover actually went through other worlds."

"Who's to say he still won't? If his dreams are any indication, he *has* seen these other worlds he'll end up writing about one day. A verdant wood. An arid land full of beasts. A mountainous peak." Her eyes sparked as she said, "If we manage to go through the door, we might just see them for ourselves."

A thought crossed Kai's mind. "You had a compass-watch of some kind that had the Veiled Atlas initials carved into it."

"You know about that?"

"You left it with Emory, so yeah. What I don't know is what it's supposed to do."

"Nothing. It's broken, just a family heirloom that got passed down to me. I left it with Emory so that she'd have a piece of me to hold on to, should anything ever happen to me."

Like going back in time and being absent from her daughter's life for nineteen years.

"Well, it's not exactly broken, just so you know," Kai said. "It seems to work when you bring it into the sleepscape."

Luce's eyes were bright with stars. "I still can't believe you've stepped into the *actual* realm of dreams."

"I imagine you will too, if you're meant to leave the epilogue there for us to find."

"*What?*"

Kai realized his blunder at Luce's wide eyes. He and Baz hadn't told her of the epilogue yet. Kai reached for the folded page in his pocket. He told her how he and Romie had found it in the sleep-scape. "We believe you're the one who put it there. Or *will* put it there, I guess." Though Kai supposed any one of them could be the one to leave it in the sleepscape while they were here in the past—if they found a way back through the Hourglass, that is.

Kai handed Luce the epilogue without thinking. She reached for it like it was a mythical thing, and it might as well have been—she had spent years trying to find it, sailing across the seas in search of it. And here it now was, in her hands, for the very first time.

Luce frowned as she reached the end of the epilogue, eyes glistening with some emotion Kai didn't understand. "This Dreamer friend of yours . . . you told me she's friends with my daughter?"

Kai nodded. "She and I searched for the epilogue together. We found we could go farther in the sleepscape together than alone." A thought occurred to him. "I saw her and Emory in the sleep-scape. I've been able to slip into Emory's nightmares even though we're worlds and centuries apart."

The revelation didn't seem to faze Luce in the slightest. "I experienced the same thing with Cornelius. When I was still in my time, I'd get glimpses of him in my dreams."

"When I saw you and Thames in Clover's nightmare, there were these threads between you. Not between you and Thames–but tying both of you to Clover." Like they were three points of an incomplete triangle, with Clover as the connecting tether. The same way it had been with him, Emory, and Romie. "I think there's a connection between Tidecallers and us Dreamers and Nightmare Weavers. This sort of dream-bond that allows us to contact each other in sleep, no matter what limitations might hinder us."

Luce looked him over, slow realization dawning. "If you can connect with Emory . . ."

"I could warn her. Tell her of this vision you and Clover saw. And you could come with me, if you'd like to meet her."

Emotions seemed to war behind Luce's eyes. At last, she said, "On one condition: you don't tell her who I am."

Kai thought that was ridiculous; she looked so much like Emory, there was no way she wouldn't put the pieces together herself.

"Should we get Baz to come with us?" Luce asked, motioning to the door.

"Baz?"

"He's close with Emory, isn't he?"

"Yes . . . but he's not a Dreamer."

"Oh, I know that. But *my* specialty is taking things into the sleep-scape. I've been known to do a few buddy-sleeps in my time."

Buddy-sleeps. Kai had heard of the practice–Dreamers bringing non-Dreamers along with them in the sleepscape, guiding their sleeping consciousness to follow theirs. It was banned back in his time, too many non-Dreamers having been lost that way and becoming eternal sleepers.

As if reading his concern, Luce added, "I'm quite talented, I assure you."

Kai didn't doubt it. He was more concerned about the promise he'd made Emory last time. About Baz finding out he'd spoken to her and kept it from him. "I think it's best if only the two of us go."

Luce's smile was eager. "All right, then, nightmare boy. Let's set sail through the dark."

They found Emory more easily than Kai had on his own.

Perhaps it was Luce's presence that made it so easy to navigate the stars and the darkness, amplifying this bond between him and Emory.

"It's you again," Emory breathed when she saw him. There was no struggling with reality this time; she knew, as he did, that this was real. She only frowned in confusion as she caught sight of Luce hovering behind him. "Who's she?"

"A Dreamer," Kai said. "I needed the boost to find you again."

He kept his promise not to divulge anything more, though judging by Emory's lingering gaze on Luce—and Luce making no attempt to hide the emotions on her face, lips parted in awe, unshed tears glistening like stars in her eyes—he suspected the truth was plain enough to see.

"Did you tell Baz about this?" Emory asked.

Kai's jaw tightened. "No. And he'd have my head if he knew I was here now." He really needed to stop making all these promises. He was the Nightmare Weaver, not the Tides-damned Keeper of Everyone's Secrets.

"Thank you."

Kai studied her pale features, the sallowness of her face. "Are you okay?"

Emory turned her face up to the stars above. "Things are really bad, Kai." Her voice broke. "I keep hurting everyone around me, and I'm scared that I don't know how to stop. Romie's right: I really am a Tidethief. And if I keep going like this, I'll lose her all over again."

Kai met Luce's eye. How the hell were they supposed to tell her now? And what good would it do, really, if Clover succeeded at changing history?

"Just . . . hang in there, all right?" He only now noticed the darkness gathering at the edges of the sleepscape, the tendrils of it flitting to Emory, as if called by her turmoil. "You're not alone in this."

She huffed a sad laugh at that. "I am, though. I have to be. Otherwise, I'll end up hurting them all, one way or another. I always do."

The darkness around them rearranged itself so that they were in the Belly of the Beast, surrounded by all the students who'd flung accusations at her the last time they were in this same nightmare together. Except now the students were cadavers, a pile of them laid out at Emory's feet. Rotting lunar flowers grew from their empty eye sockets and between their blue-tinged lips. And then there was Romie, turning white as a sheet and withered as a leaf as all the blood left her veins. Beside her, a girl Kai didn't know, her bones breaking at gruesome angles until she was a heap of nothing on the floor, and a boy who clutched at his heart and fell to his knees as the light left his eyes.

"See?" Emory said, watching as everyone around her turned to dust. "They'll all die because of me. I'm cursed." She made a strangled sound, a feverish look in her eye. "Maybe I'm Shadow-cursed."

"Shadow-cursed?" Kai echoed. "Emory, did you Collapse?"

"Kai . . ."

He spun at Luce's voice to see a horde of umbrae had found their way in—and one of them had its claws around Luce's throat.

Looking to take the Dreamer's soul.

"No!" Kai reached for Luce, hoping he wasn't too late as he absorbed the umbrae into him. "We need to wake up now."

Luce clung to him weakly, face drawn, but she was still here, still herself. She glanced back at Emory, who stared at them wide-eyed, tears running down her cheeks. The umbrae steered clear of her, as if she were one of them.

"*Wake up,*" Kai growled.

And she must have, because suddenly he and Luce were back in the library–along with the darkness that Kai had brought back with him.

51

EMORY

STARS FOLLOWED EMORY INTO WAKING. ABOVE HER, the desert sky was a tapestry of fiercely burning constellations, but its beauty did nothing to chase away the stain of the night-mare she'd emerged from. The corpses. The lunar flowers. The keys becoming ash. The umbra sinking its claws into a Dreamer whose face was all too familiar and entirely impossible.

Enough of this. She needed to face this darkness inside of her—confront it at the root.

Gathering some provisions, she tiptoed away from her sleeping friends and the slumbering dragon. Ivayne and Vivyan were circling the perimeter of their camp, as they always did, but Emory would find a way to evade them, too.

"Where are you going?"

Emory's heart rose into her throat. She turned to see Vera watching her from where she perched on a small boulder at the edge of camp, an arm tucked lazily beneath her head as if she'd been stargazing. There was no judgment in her voice, not even surprise, just faint curiosity.

"I have to find the Shadow," Emory whispered, willing her to understand.

Vera didn't say anything for a second. "You know they'll be furious with you, right? Leaving when we're so close to the next door. A door we need *you* to open."

"I can't go near it until I get my magic under control." If it was anything like the Wychwood, they could expect this world's door to be on a ley line too. She wouldn't risk hurting the keys again.

At Vera's silence, Emory thought for certain she would go alert the others. But Vera only lifted the compass-watch from where it hung around her neck and extended it to Emory. "Take it. This way you can meet us at the Sunforge."

Emory's suspicion about who she'd seen in the sleepscape with Kai grew as she looked at Vera, but she pushed it back, not ready to open that can of worms just yet. She grabbed the compass and lingered, uncertain of what to say. Sudden guilt stabbed through her as she thought of how she'd been keeping Vera at arm's length, overwhelmed by the fact that they were *cousins*. Vera had been nothing but gracious, giving Emory the space she needed to process this on her own. And now this. Another kindness Emory didn't deserve.

"I'm sorry," Emory said, hoping those small words conveyed everything she couldn't bring herself to say. She vowed to herself she would give Vera a proper chance when she came back. "Tell Romie she can reach me in dreams."

52

BAZ

THEY FOUND THE SECRET LIBRARY ROOM COMPLETELY engulfed in shadows, as if Kai had brought back the entire sleepscape from his dreaming. Thick vines of lunar flowers climbed along the walls, spreading like wildfire even as they decomposed, turning black and putrid.

Then Baz saw the cadavers.

They were piled at Kai's feet where the Nightmare Weaver stood with Luce, trying to fend off the umbrae that formed from the gathering shadows and drew tighter around them. Baz thought at first they were like the reanimated corpses Kai had pulled from Freyia's dreaming, but these were clearly lifeless, with rotten lunar flowers sprouting from their empty eye sockets and open mouths. And they were faces Baz *knew*: Travers, Lia, Jordyn, Lizaveta, Keiran . . .

Romie.

His sister's body was as withered as Travers's had been, as pale as the Ilsker girl who'd tried to break through the wards and the Vanished Four that had just been found. As if void of blood, magic, life.

Someone moving closer to the shadows snapped Baz out of his stupor. Thames, trying to help Kai and Luce. But there were too many umbrae, and the nightmarish flowers seemed to grow and grow, as if trying to swallow everything in rotting darkness.

Clover came to stand beside Baz, face drawn with horror. He looked like he wanted to help, to draw on his own mighty power to stop all of this, but with the students at their backs watching the scene with dreaded curiosity, he couldn't.

But Baz could.

He stopped time. The umbrae stilled, the flowers became immobile, the students gathered outside the door and in the library beyond froze. The only ones he left untouched were the people in this room. Kai met his gaze with a mixture of relief and–*fear?*– before turning on the umbrae and becoming the Nightmare Weaver, the lord of nightmares, his voice quiet and commanding as he willed them to sleep. The umbrae fell away to nothing, dissolving into dust around them like any other nightmare thing that Kai took with him into waking. Then the flowers, too, and finally the cadavers, until the room was just a room again, if a bit ruined.

They all stared at each other in the resounding quiet. Baz didn't let go of the threads keeping the other students immobile, too scared to let time resume just yet.

Luce was panting as she looked between Baz and Kai and the frozen students with suspicion. "That kind of power . . . how are you two not Collapsing?"

Clover's eyes glimmered with intensity, seeming to share none of Luce's trepidation. "I believe, dear Luce, it's because they already have."

✳

"It's not what you think," Baz said quickly at Luce's and Thames's fearful expressions. Clover alone seemed unperturbed as Baz explained the truth about Collapsing, that it was not a curse at all but an expansion of their limits.

Luce was hugging herself, glancing nervously around the room as if she expected the nightmarish scene to return any moment. "Does Emory know about Collapsing? When she said she was Shadow-cursed . . ."

Baz whipped toward Kai. "What about Emory?" Understanding bloomed in his mind as he realized whose nightmares they'd just seen, the mind from which Kai had pulled such horrors. "You found her, didn't you?"

"Yes." Kai avoided his eye. "I've spoken to her twice now."

Twice. And this was how Baz found out. He glanced at the spot where his sister's corpse had been and felt his knees buckling. "Romie . . ."

"She's fine, Brysden. It was just a nightmare. Emory's worst fears drawn up."

"I can't believe you didn't tell me."

"We've got company," Thames muttered, jerking his chin at the door. Outside the secret room, the students had started moving again, Baz's grasp on his time magic having slipped without his notice. They blinked, peering into the room with puzzled expressions as they no doubt wondered if the darkness they'd glimpsed had been a hallucination.

"All right, everyone, let's clear out," Luce said, affecting the authority of the librarian she was posing as. She shooed everyone out, throwing a look back at Baz and Kai as if to say, *We'll discuss this later.* Clover and Thames followed after her and shut the door behind them, as if knowing Baz and Kai needed a moment.

"Tell me what happened," Baz said once they were alone.

Kai told him everything—how he'd seen both Emory and Romie that first time, and now Emory alone in this one. Anger and hurt simmered inside Baz. He'd thought he could count on Kai for the truth, always. But apparently not for this.

"Why didn't you tell me sooner?"

Kai let out a sigh. "Because Emory asked me not to, and I agreed to keep it quiet so that you wouldn't be thrown off your game during the Bicentennial."

That protective side again. Baz didn't find it quite as endearing now. "Are you sure that's the only reason?"

"What's that supposed to mean?"

"You get all worked up whenever Emory's name is even brought up. It's like you're jealous of her."

Something like hurt flashed in Kai's eyes at the insinuation, but he masked it with sarcasm. "Sure. I'm jealous of the girl who *used* you to get what she wanted, who you're still pining over like some pathetic, lovesick puppy."

"I am *not*. I don't—I don't think of her that way. Not anymore."

Baz realized it was the truth as he spoke it. What he'd felt for Emory . . . there would always be something there, but it was friendship more than anything. He could genuinely count on one hand the times he'd thought of her *that way* since she left. Because his mind was otherwise occupied. His feelings turned to someone else.

But Kai didn't seem to believe him. He snickered at him, saying, "You're telling me Emory is *not* who you've been drawing over and over again in that sketchbook of yours?"

Baz huffed a disbelieving laugh. "So you *are* jealous."

"I'm *concerned*. Because you don't want to hear that your precious Emory might bring about the end of the fucking worlds, but you have to face the facts, Brysden. She was never good to you, so why are you so quick to defend her?"

"Look, yes, she did use me, and I did have feelings for her, and it did push me to do things I might not . . ." He trailed off, shaking his head. "But you have no idea what that time was like for me, Kai. I was alone. Romie was gone. You'd gotten yourself into the Institute. Emory was the only one there for me. She understood me and made me grow, and I refuse to give up on her now. If defending her makes me weak in your eyes, then so be it. I won't apologize for it."

"I'm not asking you to. And I've *always* known what it's like for you, Brysden. I've seen your deepest fears, remember? Witnessed all the horrors inside that head of yours. I know the demons you fight against, and I know what you could do if you just let yourself accept that you're more powerful than anyone I've ever met. I know every part of you, and I'm here waiting for you to understand that. But you can't see it, can you?"

"See what?"

"If you don't know by now, then you never will." Kai scoffed, blinking rapidly as he looked anywhere but at Baz. "I don't know why I expected any different from you."

As Kai turned to leave, desperation smacked into Baz. He reached out a hand, gripping Kai's shoulder to keep him at his side, because he knew that if Kai walked away now, things between them would break irrevocably.

But Kai shoved him away with a snarled "Don't," taking Baz aback.

Their gazes met. There was nothing guarded about Kai's expression now, only a stark vulnerability that took Baz's breath away and made his heart ache in a way he couldn't explain. He'd been starting to see the cracks in Kai's armor, but nothing quite like this. This was Kai at his core, without any of the barriers he usually hid behind. Not the Nightmare Weaver, not the fearless fighter he'd made himself out to be, but simply a boy. A version of himself he showed to no one.

Except for Baz.

And Baz had been such a fool.

He took a step toward Kai and reached tentatively for his hand. Kai stood very still, breathing fast, that heartbreaking vulnerability still darkening his eyes. Baz wove his fingers through Kai's, palms flush against each other. He grabbed Kai's other hand, so that their hands were clasped on either side of them.

Baz didn't know what he was doing. His mind was blissfully blank and his movements so strangely assured, as if his body had taken the reins and were acting on pure instinct. He drew closer to Kai until he was in his space, breathing his air, discovering all the shades of his dark eyes, the hints of navy and brown and gray that could only be seen from up close.

They did not touch save for their entwined hands; there was a hairsbreadth between them, crackling with possibility.

"What are you doing?" Kai whispered, voice strained. His chest heaved with each quick breath, brushing slightly against Baz as it did.

"I don't know," Baz murmured in answer. He bowed his head toward Kai, eyes fluttering shut as he breathed him in. He pressed his mouth against the crook of Kai's neck. A plea, a sign, the only way he knew of to say *I think I finally understand*. Maybe he'd always known, but it was only now that he saw it plainly. That he felt it so completely.

"Baz . . ."

Kai's voice was hot against his ear, and there was a note to it that Baz had never heard. Hope and anguish and fear all tangled up together. Baz pressed another tentative kiss against Kai's neck, feeling Kai's throat bob against his mouth as he swallowed and said, "You don't have to do this."

I want to, Baz thought, and was surprised at how true the words rang in his mind. He untangled his hands from Kai's and reached for his collar, eyes searching Kai's desperately, thinking those words again. *I want to.* And because they were the truth, plain and simple and beautiful, they gave him the confidence to tug Kai closer, bringing his mouth down to his.

There was no hesitation in Kai. He grabbed Baz's face in his hands and deepened the kiss as if he'd been drowning until now, a man deprived of breath finally breaking though the surface and eager to fill his lungs.

A small sound rumbled at the back of Baz's throat. There was a want inside him that he'd never felt before, a desire that was clearly echoed in Kai. It left no room for questions. No burdening thoughts of, *Did I misread the signs?* or *Have I made a horrible mistake?* Nothing but a sense of rightness that blossomed and bloomed and expanded in Baz's chest. It was as if he and Kai had been heading here since the moment they met, two opposites beached on the same island, tortured souls learning to fill that space together and make it their own. Their home.

And now they were each other's only tether to that home, that sense of belonging. It was familiar and safe just as much as it was invigorating. Baz wanted to cling to this feeling and never let go.

Kai pulled away suddenly. Baz chased after his lips, wanting to keep melting into his kiss, but Kai leaned back farther, stopping Baz with a hand to his chest.

All the doubts and questions surfaced then, piercing through the blissful haze in his mind. Baz saw them reflected in the midnight depths of Kai's eyes. The Nightmare Weaver *never* doubted himself. He didn't show fear or hesitation or regret. But this was not the Nightmare Weaver. This was Kai, staring at Baz without all those layers of bravado. Only a boy, vulnerable and unsure of himself. A mirror reflecting back all that Baz felt.

Just as Kai was about to say something, a stern-faced librarian came bursting into the secret room, staring open-mouthed at the damage. Baz and Kai let go of each other, but not before she saw them entwined. She pursed her lips with displeasure, just as Luce appeared behind her with an apologetic wince.

"Out," the older librarian barked. "The library is no place for . . . *this.*"

As Baz and Kai rushed out the door, they heard her grumbling to Luce. "Secret library rooms for secret rendezvous. Humph! Not on my watch."

53

KAI

HUDDLED AROUND A TABLE IN A QUIET CORNER OF THE library, Clover and Thames spent what felt like hours asking hushed questions about what Collapsing was like—hanging on to every detail about silver blood, how it ran red again unless stoppered by the Unhallowed Seal, how the Selenic Order in their time had used that silver blood to create synthetic magics—and through it all, Kai could only think about Baz kissing him.

He found himself sneaking glances at Baz whenever he wasn't looking, committing to memory the shape of his mouth, the way it had pressed against his neck, how it had felt against his own. How those lips had chased his after Kai pulled away.

Doubt and fear were things Kai rarely let himself feel, but he'd felt it all in that one great, terrifying moment. He wasn't sure if Baz truly wanted this. If he might have felt pressured into the kiss by Kai's harsh words leading up to it. Baz definitely noticed him staring at him now, his cheeks going pink as he spoke with the others. And Kai was certain he felt Baz's eyes on *him* whenever *he* wasn't looking. But maybe that was regret coloring Baz's cheeks, shame making him sneak glances. Maybe Baz was prolonging this endless conversation so that he wouldn't have to find himself alone with Kai again, forced to deal with the consequences of that kiss.

Maybes. Something else Kai didn't like.

He'd been so sure with Farran back then. Convinced he'd found someone who truly accepted him, someone who would never abandon him. He couldn't have been more wrong. And though Baz was the furthest thing from Farran, Kai was hesitant to let himself trust this conviction in his heart.

People had a tendency to disappoint. He'd rather disappoint *them* before they had the chance to hurt him. It was like a chess match, and he was thinking five moves ahead, sacrificing parts of his game to protect his heart, the most vulnerable piece on the board.

Layer by layer, Kai built that armor back up around him, so that by the time they returned to the Eclipse commons later that evening, he had all but shut the metaphorical door on what had transpired. With Thames gone to bed and Polina nowhere to be found, it was finally just the two of them.

"It's been a long day," Kai said before silence could settle between them.

"Yeah." Baz sat down in his favorite armchair. He palmed the back of his neck in that nervous way of his. "Do you . . . I mean . . . That was . . ."

Kai figured he'd save him the trouble. "We don't have to talk about it."

Baz frowned. "What if I want to talk about it?"

There was something Kai didn't recognize in his voice, his expression, a confidence he was unused to seeing behind those glasses of his. "Look, if you regret it . . ."

"What? No, of course not."

"You can take it back if you do. It's been an emotional day, and I know there's Emory–"

"For Tides' sake, Kai." Baz fished a sketchbook out of his satchel and all but threw it at him. "Look."

Kai braced for the inevitable as he flipped it open. But unlike the sketchbook he'd seen back at the lighthouse, the one Baz had filled with drawings of Emory, this one was full of Kai's own face. Quick studies that only gave the impression of him, and more detailed pieces that had his throat closing with emotion: a replication of the tattoos on his collarbone; a sketch of his profile wearing a rare, unguarded smile; a beautifully rendered scene of the two of them dancing together, the world around them fading to a blur.

"I don't regret that kiss," Baz insisted. Horror seemed to dawn on him then. "Oh Tides, do *you*? You do, don't you?" He snatched his sketchbook back, looking embarrassed. "Let's just forget it."

Kai closed the distance between them, grabbing hold of Baz's face as he bent down to kiss his mouth. A surprised sound rumbled in Baz's throat, giving way to a soft sigh as he tugged Kai closer by the lapels of his shirt. Kai braced his hands on either side of the armchair so he wouldn't fall on top of him. Every nerve in his body was aflame as Baz's mouth opened to his and their tongues glided against each other.

Kai grazed his teeth over Baz's lower lip as he pulled back, delighting in how breathless Baz was, in the flush that crept up his neck. "Does that answer your question?"

"What was the question again?" Baz managed.

"If I regret this." Kai's mouth brushed his ever so slightly. "I don't," he rasped, "just so we're clear."

There was a yearning in Baz's eyes. "Thanks for clearing that up."

"Anytime." With another teasing brush of the lips, Kai drew himself up and plopped down on the sofa.

Baz cleared his throat, visibly flustered as he righted his glasses and pulled at his sleeves. Still, he couldn't hide the small smile playing on his lips, and Kai couldn't help but like him even more than he already did.

When Baz finally met Kai's gaze, it was with some of that earlier confidence. "So where does this leave us?" he asked.

Kai wanted to tell him he was all in, that he would follow Baz's lead and be whatever he needed him to be because this was *everything* to him. Instead, he asked, "Where do you want this to leave us?"

"I don't know. I'm not exactly good at this, in case you hadn't noticed."

"Brysden, I've been noticing every little thing about you since the first moment I saw you." Kai gave him a crooked smile. "In case *you* hadn't noticed."

Heat rose to Baz's cheeks, but he held Kai's gaze. "I noticed. It just . . . took me a while to make sense of it."

"Don't beat yourself up over it. I'm a tough one to crack."

Baz studied him in earnest, the firelight dancing in his glasses. "You don't have to hide behind that armor of yours," he said. "Not from me."

The words broke through whatever flimsy layer of armor still remained around his heart. "I won't," Kai whispered. He realized he never really had—not like he hid from other people. He'd never wanted to.

Kai must have fallen asleep on the sofa as he kept Baz company while he studied—because yes, even after the moment they'd shared, Basil fucking Brysden would obviously take the time to study.

Kai found himself seeking out the others in his sleep. Funny how the sleepscape used to be such a solitary place, and now he was flitting from mind to mind, following the tug on his soul wherever it took him. Clover. Luce. Baz, always. Emory, though he couldn't feel her in the sleepscape at present. Thames was nowhere to be found tonight either. Maybe unable to sleep.

But Kai slept. *Truly* slept, drifting from the sleepscape and falling into a magicless slumber, for once unencumbered by nightmares.

54

BAZ

"MORNING." KAI GREETED HIM WITH A CUP OF COFFEE. Their fingers brushed as Baz reached for it, his heart fluttering in his chest like a caged bird. His cheeks warmed as Kai's gaze lingered on his mouth. He didn't know what to say, his mind too full of the memory of Kai's lips on his. Tides, was this how he'd be now—acting like a lovesick fool anytime Kai so much as looked at him? Baz drowned himself in his cup, hoping the words would come—only to choke on the strongest coffee he'd ever tasted.

"Tides, what did you *do*?"

Kai snatched the cup back, taking a careful sip. He grimaced. "Oh."

"*Oh* is right. Out of the way, I'm in charge of the coffee from now on."

Kai did not get out of the way. In fact, he remained firmly in Baz's way so that they were in each other's space, making the bird in Baz's chest go wild again.

"Have either of you seen Thames?"

Baz jumped away from Kai at Polina's voice. She was coming down the stairs, her pale face drawn with worry, not seeming to have noticed the intimacy she'd interrupted.

"Haven't seen him, no," Baz sputtered.

Polina worried her lip. "I heard him leaving in the middle of the night, and he never came back. That's not like him." To Kai, she asked, "Did you encounter him in the sleepscape?"

"No. But I'm sure he's fine."

Polina didn't look so certain as she wrung her hands. "You don't think . . . I mean, he wasn't participating in the games. Surely he can't have turned up like those other students, right?"

"I'm sure he's fine," Baz repeated, though he suddenly didn't feel certain in the slightest.

They promised Polina to keep an eye out for him before she left for class. When Baz got to the Decrescens library for his usual meeting with Clover, he couldn't help but stop by the marble busts guarding the archway to the Vault. No sign of blood. No dead body.

His gaze caught on the silver engraving on each of the marble statues. He'd seen them before, but only now did they give him pause. He moved closer to read them.

The engraving on the left statue read *Blood spilt for the safeguard of knowledge.*

The one on the right: *Power eternal for the curious of mind.*

The blood of the four founders, spilled under mysterious circumstances.

The knowledge of the Vault, accessible only to the college's elite.

Like the very group who'd founded it.

A chill ran down Baz's spine as he hurried to Clover's table and plopped down in the seat across from him. "When exactly were the libraries completed?"

Clover combed through their research. "No specific date. But they were all completed on time for the college's grand opening."

"So, roughly around the same time the founders died?"

Clover blanched, looking up at Baz.

"We agree their deaths sound too ritualistic to be coincidence, right?" Baz said, heart pounding. "Four founding members from four different lunar houses, all of them dead within the same month, on their respective lunar phases, around the same time construction of their libraries ended . . . What if they were *sacrificed*? Their blood—their magical life force—spilled by the Selenic Order to erect the wards around the Vault. Wards that conceal the seat of the Order's power. Wards that their own leader—the person they'd appointed as the dean—could have designed."

Clover swore. "You think the Selenic Order would have murdered their own?"

"If it meant safeguarding the kind of knowledge they alone wanted access to? I wouldn't put it past them."

"The Selenic Order of old *were* known to conduct lethal rituals," Clover conceded.

"My guess is, the library founders knew they'd have to die. Why else would they not have grown suspicious of their peers getting killed one by one, each of them on their ruling moon phase?"

Clover rubbed his chin in thought. "The question remains: How do we unpick the wards?"

Baz's mind raced. The Ilsker student had nearly bled out before he saved her. Wulfrid and his friends had been drained of blood. *Blood spilt for the safeguard of knowledge. Power eternal for the curious of mind.*

All these stories of mysterious student deaths and haunting presences . . .

Suddenly it clicked.

"Porpentious Stockenbach," Baz murmured.

Clover raised a bemused brow. "The writer of ghost stories we were led to during the scavenger hunt?"

Baz rifled through their research. "Hilda Dunhall was a Shadowguide. Lutwin de Vruyes, a Purifier. Didn't he write that other book we found in the scavenger hunt? *Purifying Practices Against Evil*. A book on *exorcisms*." Baz's heart thudded against his chest. "It can't have been a coincidence what happened when the Ilsker student tried going past the wards. The library turning cold, that spectral wind howling between the shelves, the lanterns being nearly blown out . . ."

"Like a haunting," Clover concluded.

Baz nodded. "What if the wards are directly tied to the founders' deaths—more specifically, their *ghosts*?"

"How would that work?"

Blood spilt for the safeguard of knowledge. If all four founders had bled their magic—their lives—into the wards . . .

"Maybe Wulfrid and his friends had the right idea to form a group of four," Baz said slowly, mind racing. "Just like the initial challenge they had you all doing. There were four founders to match the four libraries that sit atop a fifth—the Vault. If each founder's ghost or soul is tied to the wards . . . maybe we need four people with the same magic. A Shadowguide, a Wordsmith, a Purifier, and an Unraveler."

Clover caught his eye. Understanding rippled between them. If Baz was right, they didn't need four people at all; Clover alone embodied all lunar houses, all tidal alignments.

He already had what they needed to break through the wards.

They went over their research again and again, coming up with ways to solve the ward equation. When at last they thought they had it, Clover's excitement dimmed as a grim realization set in. "If we do this, I'll be outing myself as a Tidecaller. My pull within the Order won't matter then. I'll be all but burned at the stake."

"If we do this," Baz countered, "we'll be able to go through the door. None of it will matter once we bring back the Tides and the Shadow."

Movement caught their eye as a group of students from different colleges–Karunang, Awansi, Ilsker, and Fröns–grew excited at a nearby table, appearing to have found something in the large tome the four of them bent over. The Karunang student noticed Baz and Clover staring and pointedly shushed her teammates.

The games weren't done. If Baz and Clover could figure out the solution, so might anyone else.

Clover seemed to realize the same thing. "Then let's be quick about it before someone else beats us to it."

"I knew I'd find you here."

Cordie stood with her hands on her hips, staring daggers at her brother.

"Delia." Clover raised a brow. "Why do I have a feeling I'm about to be scolded?"

"Are you really going to pretend like you don't know?" At Clover's impatient gesture, Cordie spat, "Louka is gone."

Students cast furious glances their way at Cordie's raised voice. She caught herself, wiping furiously at her cheeks before continuing in a lower voice. "I went to his apartment, his shop. All his things are gone. Everyone I spoke to told me he left for Trevel." She glared at Clover. "What did you say to him?"

"*Nothing–*"

"You never liked him. And Louka would never have left me. Not at a time like this."

"A time like what?"

Cordie ignored her brother's question, her gaze going unfocused as some sort of realization dawned on her. Her eyes welled with tears.

"Delia, I assure you, I said nothing to him." Clover gently grabbed hold of her, forcing her to look at him. "Whatever's happened, I'm sure it can be fixed. We'll find him, all right?"

Cordie nodded, lip trembling slightly. She composed herself, blinking at their research. "Does this mean you've figured out the wards?"

Baz realized with a sudden pang that Cordie didn't know the truth of what they were planning–that if they succeeded in getting past the wards, succeeded at going through the door . . .

She might never see her brother again.

The thought was unbearable as his mind filled with Romie, with how things might have been if they'd had the chance to say good-bye. Which is why, when he caught up with Cordie outside the library, he found himself saying, "I need to tell you something."

55

ROMIE

ROMIE COULDN'T HELP BUT MARVEL AT THE WASTES they traveled through.

"Wastes." Ivayne scoffed at the name. She'd been listening intently as Romie and Nisha spoke of this world's fictional depiction in *Song of the Drowned Gods*, drawing similarities to this real version they found themselves in. "These lands may be harsh and barren and strange," the draconic continued, "but they are not *wastes*."

Virgil snorted at that. "What else do you call a never-ending desert? We've been traveling for days now, and it's all the Tides-damned same. Nothing upon nothing. It's unsettling."

Ivayne looked like she might shove her sword through him for insulting her homeland. Thankfully, Tol jumped in with a more tactful approach.

"It's not unsettling if you care to see past the apparent nothingness," he said. "Look at how vibrantly the colors shine beneath the sun, even dim as it is. Look how the dew on these cacti catches in the morning sun, like glittering gems that dissolve before our eyes and return to us in the night. This is no wasteland. It's delicate and ethereal in its beauty."

Virgil huffed. "Well, when you put it like that . . ."

Romie caught the wistful look in Aspen's eye as the witch hung on Tol's every word. She'd been like this ever since they'd freed Tol, always listening to him wax poetic about the land and the beasts they encountered, hovering in his orbit, stealing glances his way when he wasn't looking, but never actually *speaking* to him. The one time Romie asked her about it, Aspen had looked miserable. "It's complicated. This connection I had to him, all these intimate details I know about him . . . How does one bring that up? He might hate me for it."

Romie doubted that. The witch might not have noticed the way Tol's gaze lingered on *her*, but Romie sure had. So had Nisha. It had become a bit of a running joke between the two of them, to count all the times Aspen and Tol secretly made eyes at each other.

Nisha caught her gaze now, a knowing smile playing on her lips. If Romie were the blushing type, she would have combusted right then and there at the thought of the heated kisses they'd shared that morning while everyone else still slept.

"What should we call your world, then?" Vera asked.

"I'm not sure it has a name," Tol said with a frown.

It does, Gwenhael's voice chimed in their minds. *We dragons call it the Heartland.*

"The Heartland, how fitting," Virgil singsonged. "Would this be a good time to address the fact that we're heading to a door that requires a heart for a sacrifice? Oh, that's right, it doesn't really matter anyway, because *someone* let the one person who can open the door leave in the middle of the night, and *another someone* is too stubborn to contact her in dreams to make sure she's safe."

Vera rolled her eyes. "This again?"

Romie crossed her arms. "Emory chose to leave. She can contact *me* if she needs to talk."

Her anger at her friend simmered close to the surface. It wasn't just that Emory had left without saying anything to anyone–except Vera, apparently–when they needed her most. It was the fact that she'd gone to *him*.

Romie wanted to trust that Emory knew what she was doing. Both Virgil and Vera seemed to believe she went to the Shadow to get a better understanding of her magic. And while Romie appreciated Emory's initiative to get this power that was hurting her and the other keys under control, she couldn't help but fear her friend would be seduced by this god that wore her ex-lover's face. That instead of controlling her Tidecaller magic, she would slip further into its dark depths.

Emory was right about her. Maybe she'd always been distrustful of Eclipse magic–and with good reason after what had happened with her father. And then to find out that *Baz* was the one who'd Collapsed, who'd killed those people . . . Tides, she'd always thought Baz was in utter control of his abilities. That he'd never let himself cross that line like their father had because he was always so careful. Too careful.

But this new version of Emory was nothing like Baz.

"Virgil's right, though," Nisha said, concern etched into the lines of her face. "If a heart is the sacrifice the door needs to open, how in the Tides' name is Tol going to survive it?"

Romie hadn't wanted to consider it until now, too focused on getting to the door first. "Any chance that gold heart of yours can be taken out and put back in again without killing you?"

Tol winced. "I'd rather not find out."

Romie's mind raced. There had to be a way to open the door without Tol having to *die*.

"I might have an idea," Aspen said, a small crease forming between her brows as she looked between Romie and Tol. "When we were on the ley line and Emory drew on our power . . . I felt your pain as my own. It's almost like I was scrying without trying to, like a conduit had been opened between the three of us so that I was in my own breaking body but also in yours. And the song was clearer than it's ever been, before it started to fade too. If we were to stand on a ley line again, without Emory there to hinder our connection . . ."

Romie caught on to what she was saying. "You think joining our power on the ley line would be like bringing the pieces of her back together?"

Aspen nodded. "That's what she seems to want, isn't it? Why we all feel this pull to one another." At this, her eyes flitted to Tol, who met her gaze with something charged.

"It's worth the try," Tol said. "Maybe the Forger—well, whoever she is—will make herself known to us then."

"Let's go," Romie said excitedly with a clap of her hands. As they moved in the direction of the ley line, she leaned into Aspen and said, "Will you tell him the truth already? He's clearly as infatuated with you as you are with him."

Aspen shushed her, affecting the stern look of her mother. "Don't you dare breathe a word of it to him. I'll tell him eventually."

Romie's gaze drifted to Nisha. "Take it from me: there are some things you don't want to put off saying, in case *eventually* never comes."

Standing on the ley line together did absolutely nothing—until they used their magic.

They started with Tol, who could see bright threads binding the three of them together, tethering Romie's veins to Aspen's rib cage to Tol's heart. Threads that sought a fourth part far down the ley line, on the other side of a distant door. These threads were visible only to Tol's eyes, but Romie felt them all the same, in the faint hum of the song that passed between them like a current.

Then Aspen scried into Romie's mind. Romie felt nothing at first save for a tingling sensation up her spine. She realized she'd felt this before at Amberyl House: an odd feeling that something was *there*, an instinct that had her glancing at her Selenic Mark thinking someone was calling her through it. Then she felt it: this presence inside her that was at once foreign and familiar, a song that hummed louder in her ears, as if the Tides—the Sculptress—found strength in the union of two of her pieces.

As Aspen blinked out of the scrying, Romie was left with a hollow feeling, like she was missing a piece of herself. Aspen looked at Tol with hesitancy. "Do you mind if I try it on you?" she asked. He gave a nod of approval, something like anticipation in his eyes, but still Aspen hesitated. Romie understood why: if *she* had felt Aspen scrying in her mind, then surely Tol would, too, and realize that it was her he'd been feeling all along, not the Forger. Aspen met Romie's gaze, a call for help. She wasn't ready.

"Why don't we switch it up," Romie suggested. "We've already determined we can hear the song in each of us, and it's definitely stronger on the ley line. But I want to try it where that song is strongest. In the sleepscape—the astral plane. Like that time I saw you there while you were scrying."

Aspen frowned. "But Tol can't access the astral plane."

"No." Romie gave them a crooked smile. "But I can bring you both there with me."

Romie had attempted a buddy-sleep only *once* before, but she wasn't called the brightest Dreamer of her generation for no reason. Guiding Aspen's and Tol's sleeping consciousnesses into the strangeness of the sleepscape was easier than anticipated, probably since their sleeping bodies were on the ley line. As the three of them stood together on the path of stars, Romie couldn't help but smile at seeing the awe with which Aspen and Tol looked at their surroundings.

"It's like the space between worlds that we traveled through," Aspen murmured.

"Do you hear that?" Tol said, frowning down the path. "The song is so clear here . . ."

Indeed, the song was a voice, layered and feminine. A star appeared before them—a dream burning brighter than all the rest. Romie touched it without question, taking the other two with her.

It was a strange dream, like they were at the center of a kaleidoscope, in a world flooded with dancing lights. There was a woman, ethereal in beauty, with long iridescent tresses and eyes of ever-shifting colors—silvers and blues and greens and reds and violets, like a diamond in the light. She smiled upon seeing them, opened her arms wide—

And suddenly it was like they were in her mind, listening to her story, this goddess of whom they each carried a piece.

She had always admired the mortals' ability to dream.

She felt a kinship with them over this singular quality, for she, too, was a dreamer of sorts, in tune with the endless possibilities that came of this ability to dream, to manifest, to imagine. The mortals loved her for it, and she loved them back. They were her whole world, and she would do anything to protect them.

It had been an easy decision to splinter herself into pieces for their sake. A necessary sacrifice. So long as a piece of her lived on in each world, the gods could not wipe clean the board. Evil would be kept at bay.

But oh, how she burned to be restored. She felt them, all her splintered parts. The blood she'd poured into the seas of a world flooded with moonlight. The bones she'd buried in the rich soil of the witches' woods. The heart that burned ever on in the fires of a sun-soaked land. The soul that kept singing in the storms between the peaks at the farthest reach of the universe.

If they would only answer her call, pour themselves into the mold from which she could reenter these worlds she had helped build.

But there was the small matter of his creature, a thorn in her side from the start. The dark deity that drove her to this splintered state, and the faithful servant of his that sought to diminish her power now.

Such thieves could not be trusted.

The woman's multicolored eyes met Romie's with a warning. Light flooded through the dream, the song growing fainter as it chased them back to waking.

56

EMORY

A T DAWN, WHILE THE DRACONIC KNIGHTS SLEPT, EMORY
slipped into their encampment, using the sunlight to render
herself invisible.

Using her magic was a relief, the pressure in her veins instantly
easing. She didn't feel guilty calling on her power here, far from
both the ley line and the keys. She only hoped the darkness would
stay away long enough for her to free the Shadow—and that his
presence would chase it away completely.

She found him in one of the tents, his eyes closed as if in sleep,
his hands bound together, and one of those magic-dampening
bands around his neck—which had to explain why she hadn't been
able to reach him in that liminal space these past few days. His
shirt was dark with dried blood where the sword had pierced
him at the Chasm, but the skin beneath was smooth, unblemished.
Emory's healing had worked.

Without those ecliptic eyes staring at her, it was hard to separate
the god from the boy she'd fallen for. The boy whose Lightkeeper

magic she wielded now. Emory took a careful step toward him—and jumped back when his eyes snapped open, locking on her face as if he could see through the invisibility. Her magic sputtered in shock.

Fury swept over his features, chasing away any lingering trace of Keiran as the god's murderous gaze met hers. "Behind you," he warned.

Emory spun around, but it was too late. The draconic knight barreled into her with a grunt, knocking her to the ground. The knight lifted his sword above her. Before he could bring it down to her chest, a chain wrapped around his neck. His eyes went wide as the Shadow stood behind him, tightening the chain until the knight's sword clattered uselessly to the ground and his eyes went empty.

The Shadow tossed the body aside. And then he was pulling Emory up roughly and wrapping a hand around her neck.

"I should kill you for leaving me in their clutches," he hissed.

His face was haggard, pale, as if he'd endured the worst sort of torture, or perhaps Keiran's reanimated corpse was finally running its course. Even his grip around her neck felt weaker than it ought to be. His eyes, though, burned with enough hatred to end them both.

"So do it," Emory said.

She thought he just might as his fingers dug in. And maybe this would be best, for someone to stop her before she hurt anyone else. But the Shadow released her with a frustrated growl, and relief surged into Emory despite herself. She didn't want to die.

"Why did you come here?" the Shadow asked.

Rubbing at her neck, Emory motioned to his chains, the collar around his neck. "You said we need each other. I'm here to propose a bargain."

"Like the one where I tell you who I am in exchange for you healing me? That didn't exactly end well for me, in case you haven't noticed."

"I kept my word. I healed you."

"And left me weak enough for the draconics to capture me and hurt me some more."

Emory crossed her arms. She wouldn't let herself feel guilty over that. "Do you want my help or not?"

There might have been a spark of a smile in his eyes as he asked, "What do you propose?"

"I need you to show me how to control my magic. And you clearly need me to get you out of these chains and heal you again along with whatever other reason there is that you've kept me alive so far. The deal is you don't go anywhere near my friends, and I hear you out."

The Shadow's eyes bore into her. Then he stuck out his hand, chains clinking together with the restricted movement. Emory hesitated for a breath before she shook it. She stifled a gasp as the Shadow gripped her tighter and pulled her close to him. They stood a hairsbreadth apart. She couldn't move, pinned as she was by his stare. For the first time she realized she wasn't looking at a demon, or even Keiran. This was *the Shadow*, the first Eclipse-born, the one she owed all her power to. A god in his own right, and one who was believed across realms to be the bringer of evil.

"If you betray me," he said, breath teasing her face, "I will not hesitate to kill your friends."

Emory found it difficult to swallow, her mouth going dry at the solemnity of his threat. She was certain she would never have the upper hand here, but still she said, "And if you betray me, I'll make sure you die in this corpse of a vessel."

Slowly, the corner of the Shadow's mouth lifted. "You make a fine adversary, Emory Ainsleif." His thumb stroked the spiral on her wrist. "You'll make an even finer ally, I'm sure."

Emory pulled away from him, disgust roiling in her stomach. "We're not allies."

"What, then?"

She had no answer. Instead, she simply used Virgil's trick with the Reaper magic and rusted off his chains and the metal band around his neck. "Let's go."

They made it out of the encampment without being seen thanks to Emory's Lightkeeper magic. It felt bizarre to her, to use it on the very body that had come up with the invisibility trick to begin with. When they were far enough, Emory let go of the magic and waited for ghosts to appear and visions of flowers choking her to swarm her mind. But the darkness was kept at bay, as she suspected it would be in the Shadow's presence.

"What are you doing?" he asked her as she suddenly stopped and sat down on a ridge.

"You're going to start by telling me what you really want with me and the keys. No more veiled stories. The truth."

"Fair enough." He sat down across from her. "Where do you wish me to start?"

"How about why you were imprisoned in the sleepscape and the Tides were splintered into pieces."

"The Tides," he said, forcing the word out between his teeth, "is not her real name. That is only what your world knew her as: the four-faced deity consisting of Bruma, Anima, Aestas, Quies. Her *real* name is Atheia."

Atheia. The name seemed to echo on the wind, as if a part of her lingered in this world.

"And yours?" Emory asked.

He thought it over for a second, as if pulling the name from the deepest recesses of his memory—as if the time he'd spent imprisoned in the dark between stars had made him forget it.

"Your people did not always know me as the Shadow. They called me Phoebus, once. The bright one. Associated with the sun because I appeared to them on an eclipse. Both were apt names, if not entirely accurate. My real name means he who dwells among the stars." When he finally spoke his name, it poured out of him like a prayer. "Sidraeus."

Emory tried to ignore how right the name sounded, how everything in her grew calm upon hearing it. "And what happened to them, Sidraeus and Atheia?"

"To understand that, I have to start at the beginning."

57

BAZ

"I CAN'T BELIEVE YOU GOT MY SISTER INVOLVED," CLOVER muttered.

"I can't believe *you* were planning to leave me here alone while you go traipsing off into the Deep without so much as a goodbye," Cordie snapped back.

Baz, Kai, and Luce exchanged a pointed look at the tension simmering between the two siblings. It was the middle of the night. They'd snuck into the Decrescens library, ready to face the perils of the wards. Clover, understandably, wasn't happy about his sister joining them–about Baz telling her in the first place.

Baz didn't regret it. And Cordie's mind seemed made up. Fueled by her sorrow over Louka and her anger at her brother, there was no convincing her to stay out of it now.

Thames was glaringly absent. They'd looked all over for him, knowing he'd want to be here. Polina's earlier worry troubled Baz. They'd talked about delaying things until they found him, but with the games drawing to their end and other students getting closer to figuring out the wards, they had to act now.

"Are we sure about this?"

Baz's question broke the resounding quiet. The five of them stood before the archway to the Vault, staring at the silver door. If they'd gotten it wrong, Clover would be exsanguinated by the wards–unless Baz stopped it in time, as he'd done for the Trevelyan student. The Tidecaller seemed unfazed as he said, "As sure as we'll ever be."

They all stepped back to give Clover space to perform what would be a complex sequence of magic that had to be done in the exact order of the founders' deaths. And so it started with Hilda Dunhall, founder of the Noviluna library.

Clover closed his eyes to call upon Hilda's Shadowguide magic. "Spirits of the four founders," he said, "with the dark of a new moon at my fingertips and the power of Shadowguides in my blood, I call on you from beyond the veil."

His voice had the cadence of an entrancing performer, brimming with gravitas. He looked like a supplicant at the altar of a great god. Yet nothing happened.

After a heart-stopping moment where Baz thought they might have gotten it all wrong, an unnatural chill ran through the quiet library. The air in front of the archway seemed to shift and part like a gauzy curtain caught in a breeze, and before their eyes appeared four translucent, shapeless forms. They were no more than tricks of the light, an out-of-focus impression that was there and gone as Baz blinked.

Clover didn't look surprised it had worked, only grew more confident in his stance. He breathed in deeply as if bracing for the next step: drawing upon the magic of Florien Delaune, the founder of the Crescens library.

"With the voice of a Wordsmith," Clover said, "I beseech you, spirits of the four founders, to make yourselves visible to us, just like a waxing moon growing into its light."

Kai swore. Baz gripped his arm, eyes wide as he stared at the *literal ghosts* that slowly appeared before them. With a Wordsmith's ability to manifest things into being, Clover had effectively *solidified* the founders' spirits, making them visible, tangible things.

Hilda, Florien, Lutwin, Suera–the four library founders of two hundred years past, dressed in robes and garments that screamed of another time. They were still somewhat translucent, but now they had faces and bodies and eyes that peered at them with a keen awareness that set Baz on edge.

And then the ghosts *pounced.*

Their eyes bulged in an unnatural way, their mouths opening on screeching, bloodcurdling screams to reveal pointed teeth. Their flesh had a green tinge, putrid and decaying, and their hands were clawed as they reached for those who dared to disturb their peace.

Baz and Clover had anticipated this–that surely the founders' spirits would have been enchanted to bar the way into the Vault by whatever means. Still, nothing could have prepared Baz for the pain.

His blood was boiling, bubbling in his veins, sprouting from his mouth. He clawed at his stomach and saw the others suffering in a similar way. They were being exsanguinated.

"Spirits of the four founders," Clover intoned over the chaos, blond hair fluttering wildly around him like on some invisible wind, turquoise eyes gleaming in the dark, "with the virtuous light of the full moon and the cleansing tide of Purifiers, I command you to be at peace and let us be."

The pain stopped. Baz's blood stilled.

With a Purifier's ability to balance energies–the magic of Lutwin de Vruyes, the founder of the Pleniluna library–the founders' spirits were appeased, settling back into their human forms.

Clover was panting now, but he seemed indomitable, eager to keep going so close to the end. "With the intuitive intellect of Unravelers and all the secrecy of a dark waning moon night," he said, "I urge you, spirits of the four founders, to unveil what you have so long kept concealed."

The magic of Suera Belesa, founder of the Decrescens library they stood in, was perhaps the most evident last step in picking through the Vault's wards, but Baz nevertheless held his breath, praying it would work. And it did. Like a key fitting into a lock, the ghosts suddenly went still at Clover's magic–and like a cloud of smoke vanishing on a sudden wind, they dispersed.

A shudder went through the library. Something prickled against Baz's magic, familiar and inexplicable. He watched as Clover stepped up to the door beneath the arch and froze with his hand hovering over the knob. He turned to Baz.

"The honor should be yours," he said with a smile.

"But you're the one who broke through the wards."

"And you're the one who figured the whole thing out." Before Baz could argue that this wasn't true, Clover added, "Besides, I'm afraid we won't know if the wards are truly gone if I'm the one to open the door, since I am technically already allowed entry into the Vault. You, on the other hand . . ."

Baz wasn't in the Selenic Order, and so the wards, if they were still intact, would not allow him through.

Gulping down his fear, Baz reached for the door–only for Kai to step in and pull it open in his place.

"What are you–" Panic sliced through Baz. He desperately tried to pull Kai back, but the Nightmare Weaver had already stepped over the threshold. He held the door open for them with an almost bored expression.

Nothing happened. No blood loss, no sentient wards attacking him in any way.

Baz shoved at Kai's chest. "Why in the Tides' name would you do that? The wards—"

"You would have saved me." Kai's eyes shone with fierce emotion. "None of us could have turned back time if *you'd* been attacked by the wards."

Baz couldn't exactly fault that logic. And as Clover and Cordie and Luce stepped through the door, all he could think of was that they'd really done it. They'd broken through the wards.

Together, they descended into the Vault of Knowledge.

The Vault was not *quite* as Baz remembered. For one thing, the silver door behind the permissions desk that he remembered was not there; the grotto-like space at the bottom of the stairs merely led to the Vault proper, where the aisles were laid out in the same clocklike fashion Baz remembered, with the Fountain of Fate spilling into the heart of the Vault, acting like the center of said clock. But the shelves were older, more sacred, in a way. The tomes they held looked like they were about to disintegrate. There were shelves covered entirely in scrolls of parchment that Baz did not recall seeing in his time, making him think they must have been moved in the next two hundred years, or perhaps had been lost to time.

Clover brought them to the *S* aisle, at the entrance of which stood a replica of the Fountain of Fate's statues of the Tides: Bruma, Anima, Aestas, Quies, all standing back-to-back.

"I thought there was supposed to be a spiral staircase here," Baz whispered to Kai, remembering how Virgil and Nisha had described the entrance to the Treasury.

"Maybe it was built later?" Kai suggested.

They watched as Clover stopped in front of the statue of Anima, the Waxing Moon Tide. A spiral was carved in the palm of her outstretched hand. At Clover's touch, the statue began to slowly spin on itself, stone grumbling beneath it as it unveiled an opening at its base. And there beneath their feet was a spiral staircase that wound on and on in the dark. A faint turquoise light was the only indication of there being something at the bottom.

Clover met their gaze. "Let's hope this worked."

They descended the steps and came into a large circular chamber carved from stone. *This* was exactly as Virgil and Nisha had described: sixteen throne-like chairs carved into the stone walls, one for each tidal alignment. In the middle of the grotto was a basin into which the water from the fountain high above them spilled, the sides of the pool adorned with carvings of the moon's phases. The turquoise light they'd seen came from the bottom of the pool, refracting prettily on the walls around them.

There was no door that Baz could see, nothing that resembled the Hourglass or a way to get to it. But he *felt* it–the magic of Dovermere close at hand, pulsing rhythmically like the beating of a heart. It was faint, as if it had just awoken from a long slumber, hidden as it had been behind the wards. The thrum of magic seemed to come from the glowing pool.

Baz froze when he spotted the body. It floated in the pool, face down and eerily still.

He knew who it was even without seeing his face, recognition shocking through him as he took in the curly hair, the half-moon glasses left at the side of the pool.

They'd found Thames after all.

58

KAI

CLOVER RAN INTO THE POOL TO PULL THAMES OUT. Instinctively, Kai went to help him, an unpleasant feeling in his gut. Thames was a dead weight when they hauled him out of the pool and onto the floor. His chest motionless. Eyes closed. Kai listened for breathing–there was none–and proceeded to administer compressions on Thames's chest while Clover stared at his friend, frozen with fear.

"Can't you heal him?" Cordie asked her brother in a panicked, broken voice.

This seemed to snap Clover out of it. He drew on his magic as Kai kept pressing on Thames's chest. Suddenly Thames spewed out water, choking on air as he came to.

Kai fell back with a heavy breath.

"Thank the Tides," Baz said, hands on his knees. He looked like he was going to be sick.

"You fool," Clover murmured as he gently wiped at Thames's face. "What did you do?"

"I did it," Thames rasped. "I survived."

"How did you even get down here past the wards?" Luce asked.

Her question remained unanswered as Thames went into a coughing fit, but Kai knew the answer. Baz had told him what Clover shared with him: that Thames was practically an Order member, benefiting in secret from all the advantages that came with membership. Like accessing the Vault.

"You were right." Thames beamed at Clover. "The silver blood, mixing it like that . . . I used the synth on myself, and I–it worked."

"What synth?" Baz asked in a strangled voice.

A horrible suspicion slithered along Kai's spine in the silence. His gaze trailed to the edge of the pool, where an empty glass vial lay forgotten.

Empty–save for a thin film of silvery blood.

Bleak realization hit him. He was on Clover in an instant, grabbing him by the collar of his shirt. "What is he talking about?"

Clover met Kai's menacing glare with unruffled calm. "Let go of me."

Kai felt Baz pulling on his arm to try to get him off Clover, but he ignored him, grabbing the vial and shoving it in Clover's face. "This is *silver* blood. You took this from someone who Collapsed and made a synth with it just like we told you about."

"I assure you I had no–"

Kai cut Clover off as he pressed harder on his neck, fury pounding in his ears. "Do you have any idea what it's like to have your magic put to sleep, only for others to take it and use it for their own gain? Because I swear to the Tides–"

"It's *my* blood!" Thames cried. "I gave it up willingly–just as I willingly Collapsed for the sake of this experiment."

The words cut through Kai's fury, replacing it with confusion.

Clover took advantage of Kai's lapse to break free of his grasp. He stared at Thames with horror. "Thames . . . what have you done?"

Thames blinked at Clover. "You said yourself that this was the answer. That for Eclipse-born to unlock our true potential and be as limitless as we once were, we need to become Tidecallers."

Kai looked between the two of them, suddenly understanding what the vial he still held contained. "You made a Tidecaller synth?"

Clover put his hands up in defense. "I assure you this is not what it sounds like."

"Then explain why Thames felt the need to *Collapse* and inject himself with a synth I'm assuming contains *your* blood."

Clover tipped his head toward Thames. "Ask him. I had no hand in this."

Thames seemed upset at their lack of understanding. His breathing was erratic, his eyes wild and frenzied. "You told us that Collapsing expanded your limits," he said to Kai and Baz. "But I've seen the way you both struggle. How you, Kai, bring nightmares to life against your will. And you, Baz . . . how frightened you are to use your power. You both claim Collapsing makes you limitless, but the Shadow's curse still has a hold on you. On all Eclipse-born."

"You're not making any sense," Baz said.

Thames looked desperately at Clover. "Tell them what you told me."

"Cornelius?" Cordie pressed at her brother's silence, a hint of suspicion in her voice.

Clover's throat bobbed. "When Baz and Kai mentioned how synthetic magics were made in their time, I thought it might be the key to unlocking Tidecaller magic in others–something I'd been puzzling over for some time." His gaze hardened on Thames. "I *never* meant for you to experiment on yourself like this. You should have told me what you were planning–what if your Collapsing had gone horribly wrong? What if you'd drowned in the pool before any of us got here?"

"Why were you in the pool in the first place?" Luce asked, brow furrowed.

"Because I had to die, of course," Thames said matter-of-factly. "Isn't that how a Tidecaller is made? A brush with death to unlock their latent Tidecaller powers."

"That's not exactly how it works," Baz argued. "I mean, yes, a near-death experience is needed, but not *anyone* can become a Tidecaller."

"But see, that's what Cornelius was trying to disprove. *Tell them.*"

Clover looked ashamed. "You must understand . . . what I did, I did for the sake of all Eclipse-born. I wanted to find a way to share the kind of limitless power that I have as a Tidecaller with others–with *you* specifically, Delia."

"Me?" Cordie gasped with a nervous laugh. "Cornelius, what is this? You're scaring me."

"You can't survive in this life without power, dear sister. Remember where we came from? Without power, we would have never gotten ourselves out of that place. We would have suffered more abuse at the hands of those who were meant to care for us if it weren't for my power finally getting us out of there. It was my magic that kept us safe, that lifted us from the hole of poverty and into the comforts of wealth. My power that gave the name Clover all the prestige it now carries."

"And I thank you for that, brother. But whatever you've done, whatever you're trying to achieve . . . isn't it enough to just be safe and comfortable?"

"No. Don't you see? My being a Tidecaller, your lack of magic . . . in our society, these are the kinds of secrets that have the power to destroy us. I wanted us to be *untouchable* so that no one could hurt us if our secrets came out. And I wanted *you* to have the same amount of power that I do, if only to protect yourself should something ever happen to me."

"I've never wanted such power," Cordie said.

"I know. It's why I kept this from you. I knew you wouldn't understand."

"Understand *what*? Please, brother, just tell us before I lose my mind."

Clover motioned to the pool, the Treasury at large. "It started with the Selenic Order. Everyone I experimented on was a willing participant, I assure you. I thought the key to unlocking Tidecaller magic was simply to have a brush with death, nothing more, just like what happened to me when I was a boy. I convinced my fellow Order members to make a ritual out of it, told them this would bring us closer to divinity—that it was a necessary step in bringing back the Tides. They thought I was a Healer with a morbid fascination with death and divinity, and they were more than eager to help. And so, for years, we would come down here, slice our palms open with a ceremonial knife, and bleed into the pool, which is said to be blessed by the Tides. Thus combining the magic of all four lunar houses. Well, all *five*, if you count my own."

Clover glanced at the glowing pool as if he could see the scene playing out. "And then we would drown one of our own in the water."

Cordie's hand flew to her mouth. Luce looked at Clover like she'd had him figured out all wrong—a sentiment that Kai shared.

"No one *died*," Clover added as he caught their horrified looks. "I never let it get that far, healing them when I felt they were close enough to death. Eventually, though, I realized my method wasn't working, and I thought maybe it was my own healing magic that was interfering. No one had saved *me* as a child. I had to claw my way back from the brink of death on my own. I suspected it would have to be the same for everyone else. To become a Tidecaller, they would have to fight for their life. If they did not survive death, then it must mean they were never fit for Tidecaller magic."

"Cornelius . . ."

"I stopped it then, the whole thing. It didn't go any further." Clover's gaze drifted to the glowing pool again. "The only thing that might give *everyone* that kind of limitless power now is going to the gods themselves. To the Deep, where the Tides and the Shadow reside. That is where true power lies. The source of magic itself, of godhood, kept locked behind a mighty gate, while most people here are left with only faint trickles of magic or none at all. I want to make magic whole again. To bring both the Tides and the Shadow back, and with them, the power that made us limitless. I will plead with the gods myself if I must–anything to elevate us all to what we were always meant to be."

"But don't you see? I did it," Thames said triumphantly. "Your original idea was right: we *can* make Tidecallers out of anyone. It's why I came down here to Collapse and try it for myself. I extracted my own silver blood, mixed it with your Tidecaller blood, injected the mixture into my veins–"

"I never asked you to, Thames. What you did was reckless–"

"I just wanted you to love me!" Thames yelled, eyes full of tears. "I wanted you to value me, to appreciate how far I was willing to go for your vision–*our* vision. Can't you see?"

Heartbreaking tenderness shone in Clover's face. "I've always loved you, Thames. You never had to prove anything to me."

Thames shook his head. "I did though. I still do."

He flexed his hands, eyes flitting around the Treasury as if in search of something. They settled on the glowing pool. He extended a hand, a look of deep concentration on his face.

Clover's face fell as he realized what Thames was doing. "Don't–"

Faint light drifted from the pool to Thames's outstretched fingers.

He was wielding Lightkeeper magic.

"See?" Thames smiled, a tear running down his cheek. "It works."

All at once, the light extinguished. Thames started coughing violently. Silver blood marred his hand as he took it away from his mouth, frowning at it.

"Thames?" Clover said. "Are you all right?"

"I . . ."

Silver veins rippled along Thames's skin, as if he were Collapsing all over again.

"What's happening to me?" he asked, eyes wild and full of fear. "It burns, it *burns*–"

Thames tipped his head to the ceiling and let out an earsplitting scream. The silver beneath his skin burned brighter than Kai thought possible. And though he didn't understand why Thames was Collapsing *again* if he'd already done so, Kai knew what came next.

He caught Baz's eye a second before the world erupted in silver, knocking them apart.

59

EMORY

"AS WITH MOST STORIES, THIS ONE BEGINS WITH THE gods."

The Shadow—Sidraeus—sat up straight as he settled into his story.

"The place you refer to as the Deep is the realm of gods, paradise locked behind a divine gate. It's where the moon, the earth, the sun, and the air convene as gods. And while this godsworld is the seat of their power, the center of the universe from which all magic flows, each god watches over a world of their own. A world they created in their image.

"There is a fifth god who reigns supreme over the others. The god of balance. His domain is the space between worlds—the sleepscape, as you call it. He was made to keep the balance between all things, and that meant keeping each world separate, never allowed to blend into one another despite the shared magic that coursed through them. The gods could rarely be bothered to leave their godsworld, and so they created messengers to do their bidding. Divine beings to help them keep this great balance between worlds.

"The first messenger was Atheia. She answered to the four gods who watched over the lunar, earth, solar, and air worlds–the realms of the living. Atheia's task was that of creation. She was a visionary, an artist who molded magic in ways not even the gods themselves had imagined possible.

"The second messenger was Sidraeus, who served the fifth god, and so his domain was the sleepscape. The realm of dreams, death, and everything in between. He was tasked with ferrying the souls of the dead across the sleepscape and into the godsworld. He was not allowed into the godsworld proper, nor was Atheia, and so he did not know what awaited these souls. His job was to alleviate their fears as he brought them to this final resting place.

"Atheia and Sidraeus could only exist in the realms they were created for. This meant that Atheia could not come into the sleeping realm–at least not physically, though her magic did allow her to access it in dreams, visions, and the like–while Sidraeus could not go into the four living worlds. There was one exception to this: the only way Atheia could jump from one world to the next was with Sidraeus's assistance crossing the space between said worlds. This was possible only when all four worlds were in perfect alignment. When the same eclipse happened at the same time in each world, which, back then, happened once every year.

"Time does not flow for gods the same way it does for mortals. Atheia and Sidraeus lived like this for centuries, millennia, but for them it felt like a few years only. They were young, and with youth came rebellion. Seeing each other once a year was at once a curse and a blessing as they tried to make sense of their respective existences.

"Atheia grew tired of being *lesser* than the gods, forced to follow all these rigid rules the gods themselves didn't abide by. She saw herself as worthy of their godlike status. After all, she was the hand of these four gods she served, a conduit for their power. Magic existed in each world because of her; she was the one to shape it in her gods' images, to share it with the people of each world. They worshipped her. She was the saint that would answer their prayers, the divine breath that allowed them to use magic. They called her many things: The Tides. The Sculptress. The Forger. The Celestials. Whatever shape she took, Atheia was seen as a creator, a dreamer. A giver of life and possibility.

"Sidraeus, on the other hand, was never allowed to dream or create. He ruled over endings and fear and death, the antithesis to dreaming and possibility, which is the very fabric of magic, of life itself. Sidraeus watched Atheia create and interact with these humans in the prime of their lives, and felt so alone in the sleep-scape, so burdened by the rigid constraints he was made to live within by his own god and by this heavy task he had of ferrying the dead to their final resting place. He wanted to know what it was like to be out there, in the world of the living, and be part of something more than sleep and death. He wanted to create his own kind of magic, to carve a new path for himself, to be something more than what he'd been made for.

"This, Atheia and Sidraeus realized, was something they had in common: a desire to go beyond their station—and to discover each other's worlds. To exist together in them. What started out as curiosity for each other became something more, a visceral need to know each other for more than the fleeting moments they were allowed to spend together. They fell in love."

There was no warmth to his voice, only a chilling sort of distance. As if he were recounting someone else's life instead of his own. Sidraeus blinked as if realizing this. He stared off into the middle distance, a small line creasing his brow.

"One day, Atheia found a way for me to come into the realm of the living, on the eclipse that saw our realms aligned. I could only come into this world as a nightmare version of myself, a creature of the sleeping realm given temporary form, which Atheia pulled from her dreaming."

A smile played on his lips. He was no longer just telling the story, Emory thought; he was reliving it. And in that smile, she saw the boy he might have been once, the inquisitive young messenger to what sounded like loveless gods.

"I was enamored with this world," Sidraeus said with affection. "And though I couldn't visit it as my full self, only as a being of shadow, I was corporeal enough that my presence created magic of my own. A new strain of magic inspired by Atheia's, something to act as a balance to what she'd created. It was the missing piece this world needed to form a true masterpiece. The kind of power that went beyond what Atheia had created in any of her worlds, because it combined both her power and mine into something entirely new."

"The Tidecallers," Emory murmured. The very first Eclipse-born.

Sidraeus inclined his head. "We wanted to share this new strand of magic across realms, not just this one. We were still so limited, confined to our respective borders. Yes, I could come into the realms of the living, but not freely, not as myself, and only on eclipses. And now that I'd tasted a sliver of what the realms of the living could be like, I wanted to know them in full. I wanted to create more than the Tidecallers. I wanted to see other worlds and create something there too."

Emory lifted a brow. "That's a lot of wanting for someone who called it a pathetic, mortal emotion."

Wry amusement danced in Sidraeus's eyes. "I never said I was impervious to it. My younger, more impressionable self certainly wasn't."

"How old are you now?" Emory asked tentatively, almost afraid to know the answer.

"In human years, I'm nearly as old as the worlds themselves." He tilted his head, considering. "Though in terms of the divine, I suppose I wouldn't be much older than you."

The thought made Emory flustered. She was suddenly very aware of his gaze on her. Clearing her throat, she said, "So you and Atheia wanted to expand your freedom."

"Yes. We knew the Tidecallers were the key to that dream, because they alone had the power to cross freely between worlds. Unlike Atheia and me, the Tidecallers did not have to wait for eclipses to move between the realms of the living and the dead. They were the eclipse itself. Through them, Atheia and I began to travel more often, a secret we kept from our gods. We gathered the best and brightest to us, an order of humans with whom we shared our knowledge and power and desire to break through boundaries.

"But this ability to cross worlds was still limited to Tidecallers. We wanted *everyone* to be able to travel between realms; ourselves, yes, but mortals, too. An impossible goal that would threaten the gods' divine balance. This angered Atheia and me. If *we* were gods, we would share our power and make all mortals as limitless as the Tidecallers."

He seemed lost in his memories for a moment. "I don't know what changed. One day, Atheia suggested we stop, telling me I should return to the sleeping realm and take my Tidecallers with me. She feared the gods were onto us. But I refused to abandon our goal. I refused to return to the grim existence I'd been confined to, void of dreams and creation. I wanted to fight back, take a stand, make the gods see that what we were striving for was just and right. And if they wouldn't listen, I was ready to wrest their very power from their hands."

His gaze grew dark, murderous. "Atheia betrayed me to the gods before I had the chance. She played the remorseful sinner and painted me as the vengeful rogue that needed to be stopped. The god of balance imprisoned me in the sleeping realm and stripped me of my true form, locking it away so that even in this realm that was mine, I was formless. Just another umbra like those who have always dwelled there.

"When the gods learned of the Tidecallers' existence, they saw their power as something that was never meant to exist, power that skewed the balance of the universe and threatened their own godhood. The gods saw only one solution: to restore balance, they would have to seal the doors between worlds and wipe clean the magic that had created this imbalance in the first place. And so, the gods killed all Tidecallers, sealing the doors with their spilled blood."

Emory felt the world tip beneath her, her own blood rushing to her head. Sidraeus didn't give her the time to consider what it all meant.

"As for Atheia," he said, grinding out each syllable of her name as if they cut his tongue, "she was meant to be punished by the gods too, for she was the one to bring me into the realms of the living to begin with. The gods planned to confine her to their godsworld, never allowing her to set foot in the worlds she cared so deeply for. But Atheia foiled the gods at the last. She escaped their punishment by splintering herself into pieces to keep her magic–her very life force–alive in each of her worlds."

Blood, bones, heart, soul.

"So it's revenge you're after," Emory said. "You don't want Atheia to be put back together again."

The golds and silvers in his eyes flared bright in answer. "I have had a long time to contemplate what was done to me and my Tidecallers," he said. "The retribution I seek is for them. Atheia might as well have led them to the slaughter. She chose her worlds over me and found a way to keep her magic alive while mine was sacrificed in the name of balance."

Emory thought she understood the pain he carried, the choices he'd made. He'd been betrayed by the one he loved, forced by cruel gods to see his creations die, and imprisoned in the sleepscape for ages as punishment.

His story didn't exactly paint him as a saint either. But if she were him, she'd want retribution too.

"When the god of balance confined me to the sleepscape," Sidraeus continued, "he kept me in stasis so that time lost all meaning, and I became nothing. I could feel the nightmares of mortals, but my consciousness could no longer slip into them as it once could. And I could still feel the souls of the dead pass through, but I was no longer able to ferry them to their resting place."

"How did they find their way to the godsworld, then?"

"Most souls manage well enough on their own, following the source of magic that calls to us all, that created life itself. It's the stray souls that I dealt with. The ones unwilling to go." He frowned, as if only now considering the question. "I don't know if another was appointed to take my place as ferrier of lost souls. All I knew was darkness. And then . . . you."

Her face heated at the quiet intensity in his words. "Me?"

"When you came into the sleeping realm and healed the umbrae, it broke through this stasis I was in. Suddenly I could move freely within the sleeping realm, could feel the souls of the dead again and slip into nightmares as I once did. I didn't know what you were then. I didn't even know Tidecaller magic had lived on before I saw you using the very powers I'd created. This dream I thought had been extinguished."

"What does that have to do with your desire for revenge?"

"*Everything*. I told you all magic comes from the godsworld. From the fountain of the gods, the source of all their power, of all magic, of the universe itself. It spills into all worlds, drawing paths through them. Lines of pure energy."

"The ley lines," Emory breathed.

"You feel them, as the Tidecallers that came before you did, because your magic is liminal, transcendent. Just as you can cross through worlds, this thing that the gods themselves never thought possible, you can also harness the power of the ley lines in a way no other being can. Not even Atheia and me. But what you feel in them now pales in comparison to the power the ley lines once held. Because when the gods sealed the way between realms, these doors became dams, allowing only a small trickle of the fountain's magic into each world. A meager resource that grows thinner and thinner until it is bound to die out entirely." He motioned to the dim sun. "It's already begun."

Understanding dawned on Emory. "That's why the worlds are rotting? Because magic is dying?"

"Ironic, isn't it? That the gods' solution for restoring their precious balance ended up causing an imbalance so great it will inevitably destroy us all. Unless we break the dams open."

"But I thought opening the doors between worlds is what caused this rot to spread in the first place."

"Only because opening them takes magic away from the ley lines. Every time a door opens, this finite resource grows ever thinner, taking longer and longer to get replenished by the minuscule trickle allowed to come through from the fountain. It's not supposed to be this way. When all the doors were open, the ley lines could never be depleted, because magic flowed straight through them from the fountain, and the fountain is infinite. But now the gods sit in their precious godsworld, a place so perfect that none of this sickness can ever get to it, because the fountain spills freely there, a source of eternal life and power. Magic powerful enough to heal all worlds if it were to flow freely through them once again."

He leaned toward her. "*You* have the power to make that happen. If you learn to tap into the ley lines, you can blow the dam wide open and heal these crumbling worlds in the process."

"But that's not all you're after, is it? You want to wrest the power from the gods—and you need me for it."

The corner of his mouth lifted. "If you can tap into the ley lines, you can tap into the fountain. And you can siphon that power off to me."

Emory crossed her arms. "And what about my friends? The pieces of Atheia you want so badly to destroy?"

"I do admit I sought to destroy them at first. But they are needed for us to reach the godsworld." He didn't seem pleased about it.

"And yet you still tried to kill them multiple times."

"It's difficult for me to sense these pieces of Atheia nearby and *not* want to kill them. I have spent a millennia in the sleeping realm stewing in my rage and revenge. Those feelings don't go away so easily. You learn to live in the dark when you have no choice. Can you blame me for making the darkness mine?"

His words resonated within her. Emory had been in the dark herself for so long, she was adapting to it against her will. Becoming someone who hurt her friends because she couldn't help herself wanting more power. Becoming someone who would do anything to protect them—even let herself become a killer.

If it weren't for the unnatural color of his eyes or the otherworldly power that thrummed from him, Emory might believe she had gone back in time, to a bonfire on the beach with that same boy staring at her. But this was not Keiran. He might look like him and sound like him and have his memories, but it was not *him*.

And yet she hated him all the same.

So why then did her blood sing at his proximity? Why did she relate to Sidraeus's story in such a way that she *believed* him, despite all the warning bells in her mind?

Emory didn't want to trust him, didn't want to feel even the tiniest fleck of kinship toward him. She tried to find the faults in his story, to see where he might be twisting the truth to dupe her. And yet she couldn't deny the power she'd felt from the ley lines. Couldn't deny the trepidation she felt at the idea of Atheia being brought back and what that might mean for her friends.

Sidraeus was offering a solution to the dying worlds–and to her own twisted magic. He was offering answers, and a way to master herself. She couldn't pass up such an opportunity.

When the time came, she could choose whether or not to do what he wanted of her.

He might be a deity, but he needed her, perhaps more than she needed him. He couldn't cross through worlds without her or the keys. He couldn't even use all his powers while in Keiran's body. And though she couldn't truly trust him, wouldn't let herself, she *could* use him as long as it suited her, just as he would use her as it suited him.

At least this time, they both knew where they stood.

60

BAZ

BAZ CALLED ON THE THREADS OF TIME TO CONTAIN THE blast of Thames's Collapse. He managed to keep it from reaching him and the others as they stumbled as far back as they could. But Baz couldn't stop Thames entirely, the power emanating from him too strong, burning too bright, that his magic simply eroded against it.

Baz didn't understand. If Thames had already Collapsed, how was he doing so again now? It was as if the Tidecaller synth he'd injected himself with were blazing through his body, liquid silver burning him from the inside out. The blast flared bright, then subsided for a fraction of a second, before flaring brighter than before, and again subsiding. Over and over and over again in quick, successive spurts, as if he were experiencing multiple Collapsings one after the other, each more terrible than the last.

Thames's screams ripped through the Treasury as silver light shot out in every which way. Clover was screaming too as he fought against the hold Kai had on him, trying desperately to get to Thames despite the danger of the blasts. Behind Baz, Cordie and Luce huddled close together, in the small bubble of protection that Baz was keeping out of time's reach. Around them, the silver light shot through the Treasury, splitting the grotto's walls in numerous places. This whole place was going to fall apart if this lasted much longer.

But then, at last, the light died out completely. Thames fell limply to the scorched cave floor beneath him, his body unrecognizable.

His veins had turned black, his skin shriveled in a way that echoed Quince Travers, eyes wide and unseeing, mouth open on a silent scream like Lia Azula.

It was as if his magic had consumed him from the inside. Rotted him to the core, depleting him of every last drop of power and life until he was nothing but a husk.

Clover was instantly at Thames's side, falling to his knees with a broken cry. He gathered Thames's body in his arms. Tears fell in earnest down his face. His head whipped to Baz, a bright fervor in his eyes as he said, "Undo this. Bring him back."

When Baz did not move, Clover's face turned feral. *"Bring him back!"*

Kai stepped in front of Baz, as if ready to take the brunt of any attack Clover might launch his way. Baz gripped his wrist to say it was all right.

"I can't," Baz said to Clover. "There are limits to my power. To *all* our power."

What happened to Thames was proof enough.

But Clover seemed undeterred. "You may be limited," he said, "but I am not."

He turned his attention back to Thames and closed his eyes in concentration, taking a deep breath in.

"What are you doing?" Cordie asked. "Cornelius—stop!"

Something prickled against Baz's magic, a sort of recognition he couldn't make sense of. Before his eyes, Thames's deteriorated body started to change, blackened veins slowly fading back to silver. Abruptly, they turned black again, and Clover swore in frustration as Thames's corpse remained that: a corpse.

It dawned on Baz what Clover was doing: he was trying to call on *his* Timespinner magic. To use the kind of power Baz would not allow himself to use.

Baz remembered the time Emory had tried calling on Eclipse magics, finding it more difficult to do than lunar magics. A warning was on his lips–because if a Tidecaller had limits, surely this was it–but just then the Treasury trembled with enough strength to send Baz lurching into Kai.

Debris started to fall around them as the cracks from Thames's Collapsing lengthened and expanded. Baz heard Cordie crying out as rubble fell around her. He used his magic to stop the rocks from harming any of them.

"We need to leave!" Luce yelled as she helped Cordie to her feet.

Baz gazed at the stairs up to the Vault, then at the glowing pool he suspected led to the door, that echo of Dovermere's power pulsing ever so much stronger from it. If they wanted to get to the Hourglass, this might very well be their only chance.

Clover locked eyes with him, as if the same thought had occurred to him. His gaze shifted to Cordie, something pained in his expression. "Delia," Clover said. "You need to return to the Vault."

"Me? What about all of you?"

"We're going to find this door."

"Then I'm coming with you."

"No, you're not. You're in no condition to take such risks. I need you to be safe, Delia."

Something private passed between them that Baz didn't understand.

"You know?" Cordie said in a small voice.

Clover gave her a watery smile. "I suspected." He gave Cordie a kiss on the cheek and whispered something in her ear that had her lip wobbling and tears forming in her eyes. "Go back up to safety. And please, get someone to come down here for Thames's body. He should not have to stay down here."

Cordie grabbed his wrist. Her eyes were wide and pleading. "Be careful."

Cordie gave each of them a quick hug, tears running down her cheeks. Baz couldn't bear to say goodbye. She'd become his friend. And if he never saw her again . . . He bit back all his emotions and focused on keeping a hold on his magic as Cordie went back up the stairs.

Only once she disappeared from view did they all turn to the pool. Clover was the first to step into it. He edged toward the cascade in its middle.

"There's something here, at the bottom," he said with a frown. "Something that wasn't there before when the wards were still intact."

Before they could ask what it was, Clover dove below the water and did not reemerge.

With a sad look back to Thames's body and whispered words that sounded like *Sleep well, my friend*, Luce dove in after Clover. Then it was just Baz and Kai, staring wide-eyed at each other.

"We can still back out," Kai said haltingly.

"Do you want to back out?"

"No. You?"

Baz shook his head. They'd gotten this far—if anything, he had to see for himself where this led.

Kai grabbed his hand, and together they dove in after the others.

Whatever made the pool glow turquoise seemed to emanate from the bottom, where a hazy light shone. But as Baz and Kai kicked toward it, there seemed to be no bottom at all. Suddenly, light particles danced around them, forming into a great spiral that spun quicker and quicker as it pulled them farther down.

Just when Baz was certain he'd run out of breath, an odd sensation overtook him, and the light drowned the world in white.

Solid ground rushed up to meet him, too quick–

Pain lanced through his wrist, then his head, as he collided.

"Baz. *BAZ!*"

He opened his eyes to a blurry Kai hovering over him. "Thank the fucking Tides."

Baz blinked. His vision remained blurry. Or maybe that was his glasses, all wet and askew. He lifted his hand to right them and winced. His wrist was leaden with pain, and his head–

"Easy," Kai said as Baz tried to push himself up. "You landed pretty hard."

"Where are we?" Baz managed. He was sopping wet and on solid ground, that much he could tell.

"Take a wild guess."

Baz ventured a look as his vision slowly focused. They were in yet *another* cave, this one utterly familiar. "The Belly of the Beast," he breathed.

Clover and Luce stood at the base of the Hourglass, staring at it with parted lips. Luce seemed to be limping, and Clover's cheek was scraped, but otherwise, they seemed fine. So did Kai, with only a scratch on his chin, from what Baz could tell.

And the Hourglass stood in the middle of the cave as it always had, pulsing with power.

Before Baz could make sense of how they'd gotten here, the cave shook as chunks of rock fell from above. He glanced up. There on the cave ceiling was a mirage-like reflection of water, as though they were looking up from the bottom of the Treasury's pool. There was no way to reach it from this distance. No wonder the fall had been so brutal.

It was only then that Baz noticed the cracks that ran like veins along the ceiling, emanating from the magicked pool bottom, and growing rapidly. They spanned all the way to the far end of the cave, where it should have opened onto the rest of Dovermere's tunnels. There was only a wall of solid rock there, the same wall Baz and Kai had come up against when they'd tried getting back to the door after first arriving in this time.

The fissures in the wall *groaned.*

And burst.

The tide rushed in, the cave wall shattering beneath the full, raging force of the Aldersea. Baz flung his magic toward the tide, freezing the waves before they could reach them. But he wasn't quick enough to stop the growing cracks or the rocks that fell onto the Hourglass.

Baz had an unsettling sense of déjà vu as the Hourglass *split*, the stalactite that formed the upper part of it crumbling at the foot of the dais. The stalagmite still stood, though the spiral etched on its surface was cracked.

The door was broken. Their only way out of here, and it was gone.

Baz grasped at the threads of time around the door, thread by flimsy thread. They were all over the place, scattered and cut to pieces and lying in shambles, as if the door's brokenness had disrupted the very fabric of time itself. Baz couldn't fix it–did not know how, not with all his focus and power fighting to hold back the sea. The magic of Dovermere did not speak to him as it once did because it was not *there*; it was broken just like the door itself.

"You can do this, Brysden," Kai said at his side, a tethering presence, steady as he'd always been.

Baz tried to breathe. He forgot how it was supposed to go.

In. Hold. Out.

Like the rhythm of the sea, the slow breathing of the tide. Ebb and flow. A cycle so continuous it could never be broken.

Something sparked in his mind. Grabbing hold of a single thread–the biggest he could find, the one fragment of time and magic that was still somewhat intact–Baz took a deep inhale. As he breathed in, he called the other threads of time toward him. And they answered. When he exhaled, they wove themselves back together.

Again and again he breathed threads in and breathed time out, until he held in his hand the very life force of what used to be or would become again the door, this thing that was made up of time itself. His skin tingled with warmth. Power that felt at once vast and familiar coursed through his veins. He was the Timespinner, and here he was spinning time, unspooling and weaving until he had remade the very fabric of time around him.

Perhaps it would have been a more fitting metaphor to call him the lungs . . .

The Hourglass righted itself, its scattered pieces mending back together. Baz kept breathing, pushing back on the tide and pulling on time. Push pull. In out. It seemed to be working, but his power was not limitless, despite him being Collapsed. He felt it leaving him in a way that made him certain he was giving up a part of himself he would never see again. The magic left his veins to seep into the stalactite and stalagmite, the veins of power in the rock, the silver in the Hourglass.

This exchange of power only seemed to amplify the pain in his wrist, on his head. He fell to his knees, grinding his teeth against the agony of his body.

He was vaguely aware of Kai's bracing hand around his elbow, of him calling out his name, of the edge of concern in that midnight voice of his. *I'm all right,* Baz tried to say, and perhaps he did say it. But it was a lie he was telling himself, because he knew there was no avoiding this.

With his magic, the Hourglass was reborn. It felt, strangely, like this was what Baz had been destined for.

And here stood the Hourglass once more, the same as it had always been.

And here were the whispers of Dovermere's magic, chittering in Baz's ears, thanking him for bringing it back, for healing it.

Your magic is ours and our magic is yours and we are the same because time runs through our veins.

They were the same, he and Dovermere. He and time. He and the Hourglass. It was all the same, connected in a way Baz still did not entirely understand, but it was there, a faint glimmering thread that bound them together, that breathed in sync, as if his lungs were what powered the threads of time that lived here, or they were what gave breath to his lungs.

Baz had thought, for a second, that his magic would leave him entirely to do this one great feat. But it was still there, as much a part of him as time was a part of life. It could not be severed from him.

But he was weakened, and the rushing tide still battered against the magic he was using to keep it from engulfing the Belly of the Beast. It wouldn't hold forever.

Clover wasted no time as he slashed a blade across his palm and pressed it against the Hourglass. The door didn't open for him until Luce did the same. Silver particles danced around them, seared a spiral onto their wrists, and then the door opened wide onto a dark expanse of stars. Both Tidecaller and Dreamer were full of wonder as they gaped at the dark, starlit expanse that appeared before them.

"That song," Luce breathed. "Can you all hear it?"

Baz looked at Kai, whose arms kept him steady. He knew the

song must be calling Kai's name. But Kai only watched *him* with a quiet sort of wonder, as if Baz were the only song he would ever follow.

Clover turned his back to the door to peer at the three of them. The light from the stars formed a sort of halo around his pale blond head, and his eyes shone like the turquoise pool they'd emerged from.

"We can do this," he said. "We've come this far, and I am certain now that together we can bring back the Tides and the Shadow. We can save the world."

A Tidecaller, a Dreamer, a Nightmare Weaver, standing before a door to other worlds, steps from sailing toward the sea of ash and their possible salvation. Perhaps this was the way it had always been intended.

Clover went through without a single look back, the darkness swallowing him up like it had always been waiting for him. Luce followed as if in a trance, the stars reflected in her eyes. Kai tugged at Baz's elbow, but Baz stopped him.

"Go," he said, straining against the force of the tide. "I'll hold it, just go."

The wonder in Kai's eyes gave way to a sadness so profound it sliced through Baz's heart. Then anger. "Don't be ridiculous, Brysden. We can make it through the door together."

But the door seemed so far away, the effort of walking too daunting. His grasp on his magic would fail him before he got there.

And maybe a part of Baz didn't think he deserved to go through the door. To become one of the heroes of this story, to step into a role beyond the guardian of the door he'd made himself out to be. He wasn't brave like the rest of them were.

Luce was willing to travel through time and worlds and all the unknowns in between to save her daughter. Emory and Romie were doing just that somewhere in the future to save the fate of the universe. Clover was willing to sacrifice himself in Emory's place to save all of them. And Kai . . . Kai was a fighter through and through, willing to face the dark, ugly truths of the world so others need not have to.

Baz wanted to be as brave as them. But maybe this was enough.

"Go," he said again, heart breaking at the tears that glistened like stars in Kai's eyes. He willed himself not to shatter at the thought that, for the second time in his life, Baz would watch a person he loved disappear through the door to a place where he could not follow.

Before he knew what was happening, Kai reached for him, hands snaking behind his head to pull him in for a kiss. There was nothing sweet about it. Kai's lips crushed Baz's, full of desperation. He pulled away too quickly.

"I'm not letting you be a self-sacrificing prick," Kai said angrily. He laced his fingers through Baz's and tugged him toward the door. "We go together or not at all."

They ran into the awaiting darkness of the sleepscape, the tide nipping at their heels as Baz's grasp on time slipped and the sea rushed in unencumbered. Kai turned to him with a wicked smile, because they had made it, and here they were with their literary idol, about to go with him through the very worlds they had read of, together and unafraid.

Baz's hand slipped from Kai's grasp as something *shoved* him back, as if the darkness itself were a solid thing barring him access.

Your work is not yet done, Timespinner, the magic of Dovermere whispered in his head.

The last thing Baz saw was Kai's wide eyes as he tried to reach for him, Baz's name tearing from his throat.

The door shut between them.

And then Baz was drowning in the Belly of the Beast.

PART IV

THE SCHOLAR

CORNELIUS HAD ALWAYS FANCIED HIMSELF A SAINT. It was something his sister said to him once, about how she and the other children at the orphanage looked to him as their champion. He was their patron of protection and healing, their bringer of luck and laughter. As long as they were with him, they felt safe. Invincible against the evil that lived in that vile place.

No child was sacred in the eyes of the gods who ran the orphanage. And they were particularly rotten gods, the husband and wife who called themselves their caretakers. *Caretakers* was a laughable term; *care* was not something they ever took of their charges, nor even their decrepit house.

They saw the children as spoiled goods, undeserving of any love or kindness. Most children came to believe this, seeing the gods' mistreatment of them as proof they were unwanted. But Cornelius had too stubborn a mind and too big an imagination to accept that this was the life any of them deserved.

He found early on that he could heal those that would come out of the husband's office bruised and battered. He hated to see anyone hurt, but he reveled in this small sainthood of his. Maybe it was selfish of him, but he liked feeling useful and valued. He knew he would forever chase that feeling.

For someone who fancied himself a saint, he never expected death to find him so quickly.

Gods never expect to die, seeing immortality as their divine right. But Cornelius was not a god, and so death came for him, abrupt and premature. It was, in truth, a heroic death. A martyr's passing. The uncaring caretakers had been fighting, as they often did. The man drank too much, as he always did, and slipped into a fury he only ever took out on the children. He was the most terrifying of the gods because death sang in his blood, and the children lived in constant fear that his Reaper magic might slip during one of his rages.

Cornelius's sister was his intended victim that night. But Cornelius wouldn't have it. He stepped in and took the beating for her. The god did not like that. Cornelius was never certain whether it was the god's fists or his magic that did it, but here he met his end.

Or should have.

Cornelius clung so desperately to life that he managed to claw his way back to it. He found himself forever changed after that, with power that surpassed that of healing. Magic that felt godlike in its own way. Now the gods of the orphanage feared *him*, but they only became viler for it. This, Cornelius thought, could not stand.

With his newfound power, he took the orphanage down. He gave death to its cruel gods, and freedom to the children who had been forced to bow to them. He made the whole thing look like an accident—wielding the man's own Reaper magic against him and his wife, so that it would look like a marital dispute gone horribly wrong. Cornelius liked the poetic justice of it. He also liked that no one would ever suspect he'd had a hand in it, because the world knew him as a Healer, not a Reaper, and certainly not a Tidecaller. He would do everything he could to keep it that way.

All gods needed secrets.

The children scattered after that, making lives for themselves on the streets or finding places at other orphanages with kinder gods, caretakers who actually cared.

Cornelius and his sister carved their own path. Power belonged to Cornelius now, and he swore he would never again be made to feel helpless or bow to others. He had the ability to speak his way out of trouble, to swindle money and steal food from unsuspecting victims, to make his own fortune with the power of all four Tides at his fingertips.

We make our own luck, dear sister, he told her the day he purchased an estate in their new name. *Clover.* The four-leafed symbol for good luck and fortune.

It wasn't the money or the fame or the access to all the prestigious circles that Cornelius was after, but this feeling of making a difference in the world. This feeling of sainthood, of godhood, which only grew and grew the more powerful he became, the more his ideas and his magic expanded, the more he knew he was meant to help those like him who had once felt powerless.

Like many saints, Cornelius was blessed with prophecy. He saw visions of other worlds, of futures that could be his, of people he might help. Always they painted him in a bright light that further proved he was blessed. So when *this* vision first came to him, he couldn't make sense of its darkness.

His hunger for holiness only deepened as he traveled through worlds, eager to prove this contradictory vision wrong. Cornelius drew followers to him as he always had, disciples who believed he was ushering in their salvation. He believed it too, for a time. Until their salvation started to matter less and less in the face of his own ambition. He gave them hollow promises of power that fell on their ears like burnished prayers. The more adoration he garnered, the more greed chipped away at him, until nothing was ever enough to sate him.

Only godhood would.

Cornelius had defeated gods before–small, cruel, human gods, but gods nonetheless in the eyes of a child. He knew strength and cunning were needed to triumph over them. So he did the unthinkable. He gobbled up the power of those who trusted him most, draining them dry of it, until he carried their life force within him. And he set off to wrest the gods' power from their greedy hands and take it into his righteous ones.

The thing about godhood was this: one always fancied themselves a god when basking in their own self-importance, until they met a real one and realized they were nothing in comparison. A mere speck of dust next to a great sea of ash.

But ash had a tendency to shift. Power could be taken. Godhood could be created out of that tiny speck, if one only wanted it badly enough.

And Cornelius wanted nothing more.

He was a saint who'd made himself into a god. He was a power-hungry demon who'd let himself become a god-killer. He was a boy grown into a man turned into a monster, all sense of right and wrong long forgotten.

Saint. God. Demon. God-killer.

Tidecaller.

Tidethief.

It mattered not to him what they called him anymore, so long as power remained his.

61

EMORY

SIDRAEUS MADE HER STAND ON THE LEY LINE FOR hours on end, simply listening to the static hum of its power. It was an exercise in trust as she closed her eyes and tuned everything out, knowing this vengeful god was mere feet away from her.

"What am I even listening for?" she asked, her distrust making her annoyed and on edge.

"How the magic flows, the motion of its currents. Familiarize yourself with it like you would your own breathing."

She was even more annoyed that it worked. She could indeed feel the ley line in ways she hadn't before if she just concentrated enough. The spiraling paths it carved through the world. How it began at one door and ended at another.

It was pure possibility. Or *should* have been. Emory felt the wrongness within it, like moldering ash corrupting this divine power that should have been incorruptible. She wondered if she might heal it the same way she'd healed the umbrae. Tentatively, she called on different magics–Healer, Amplifier, Purifier, Unraveler–blending them to cleanse the rot.

All it did was call on the darkness that followed her magic, like a corruption of its own.

"Easy," Sidraeus warned.

Emory couldn't let go as the ley line coursed through her, beckoning her to use more. But there wasn't enough power in the ley lines themselves. She felt her magic running along them in search of something else to tap into, something that sang to her in a different way.

"No," she murmured as she felt herself drawing closer to the blood and bones and heart that would fuel her, as silver began to ripple along her veins and her ghosts flocked around her.

Solid hands grabbed her firmly by the arms. She was forced to look into Sidraeus's eyes, a tether to reality. "Resist her call," he said.

Her call. Atheia's. Because that's what called to her, what she kept taking from the keys: the parts of Atheia that lived in them, the power of creation that Sidraeus never had . . . until he created Tidecallers like her.

Tidethieves.

She began to panic, unable to breathe as that pull drew her closer, closer–

Sidraeus dug his fingers into her skin and, with unnatural strength, shoved off the ley line with her in his grasp. They fell to the ground, Emory landing on top of him. For a second, she saw only Keiran in his face and was reminded of moments spent similarly entangled. Disgusted, she pushed off him and stood.

Only then did she notice the darkness around her had receded as it seeped into him, just like it had at the Chasm. She realized what it reminded her of: a Nightmare Weaver drawing the darkness from a nightmare.

"Do you do that on purpose?" she asked.

"What, save you from yourself?" he said dryly. He got up and dusted himself off. "A thank-you would be appreciated."

Emory hugged herself, watching the still-crackling ley line with wariness. "Did the first Tidecallers experience any of this? The pull to Atheia, the darkness that follows."

"There's a reason they're referred to as Tide*callers*. Their magic was reliant on that of the Tides. Like you, they could mimic the lunar magics that Atheia created by calling on her power of creation. Some found they could even twist that magic in different ways, creating various new strains—magics that exist now in those who are born under regular eclipses in your world. But always they needed to borrow from Atheia's power of creation to use this magic, otherwise they would burn out. They could not exist without her. A cruel joke of the universe, to finally allow me this gift of creation, but to have what I create be so dependent on another."

So it was true. Tidecallers had always been Tidethieves, in a sense. And from the sounds of it, they ran the risk of Collapsing just like any Eclipse-born today. Except, hadn't Virgil said Collapsing wasn't the curse it was believed to be, but a broadening of their limits? It was as if, once Sidraeus and Atheia had left, once the doors between worlds were shut, magic dwindled for everyone *but* Eclipse-born.

Maybe Sidraeus *had* created something entirely his after all.

Emory thought it best not to mention this. She wondered again why *she* apparently couldn't Collapse—always coming close to it, but never quite. And suddenly it clicked. The ley line. All those times she'd almost Collapsed, she'd been on the ley line, unwittingly tapping into its power. It was as if her magic sought to replenish itself by tapping into another source—whether that be the keys or the ley line or both—so that she never did burn out.

"There has to be a way for me to power myself up without

hurting my friends." To use magic without taking something away from anyone else. It made her feel dirty, made her think of Keiran and what he'd been doing with silver Eclipse blood.

Sidraeus studied her. "You fear it, this power in your veins. You hate it like those of your world taught you to."

In her mind, she saw Romie's fear, and she understood it. She felt that same fear at the thought of hurting her friends. But could she say she hated her magic? This thing that had saved her, that had pulled her out of mediocrity and given her a reason to see herself as something more than the girl who lived in her best friend's shadow? Her magic had made her see her own worth–a worth tied not only to what power she had but to everything that made her *her*.

"I might have, once," Emory said. "Not so much anymore."

This magic might be a burden, but she loved it all the same. There was beauty in it, even if it was hard to see.

You learn to live in the dark when you have no choice. Can you blame me for making the darkness mine?

Emory would make this magic hers. She would fight for it because she wanted it all–her power, her life, her friends. Not one over the other, but all of it at once.

Something proud and eager flashed in Sidraeus's eyes, as if he could see the determination in her. She imagined it was an echo of his own, this desire he'd had to break through the limits imposed on him. He'd wanted what Atheia had, and once he got it, he didn't want to give it up. He wanted to fight for it, for himself and his Tidecallers and all mortals alike.

Emory saw in his eyes the deity he must have been once, the enthusiasm with which he'd wanted to share his power with mortals. She found herself imagining what he might have looked like, a near god that was only a boy, starved for purpose and connection beyond the souls of the dead and the creatures of nightmare he was bound to.

"Is there any way you can regain your true form?" she asked.

"I suspect the gods are keeping it safely tucked away in the godsworld, where they believed I could never reach it."

"What happens to *him* if you regain your own body?" She motioned to Keiran. His revived corpse.

Sidraeus considered her. "What do you want to happen to him?"

Emory didn't know how to answer that. Part of her wanted Keiran to have some awareness of what was going on, if only so that he could see how strong she'd gotten. No longer the vulnerable girl he'd taken advantage of, but someone who was taking her fate into her own hands—even if that fate was closely linked to a god who might be using her too.

If anything, she wanted Keiran to know that the Shadow of Ruin himself was using him as a vessel the same way Keiran had wanted *her* to become a vessel for the Tides. She wanted him to suffer for what he'd done and everything he'd wanted to do to Eclipse-born. He deserved it.

And yet.

Perhaps death had been punishment enough.

It was a death she might have prevented. Perhaps the first real death she had on her hands; where Travers's and Lia's and Jordyn's deaths had been accidents, Keiran's could have been avoided. His final plea as the umbrae ravaged him still rang in her ears. The look in his eyes as she'd ignored him, letting him be dragged to his death.

"I can't tell you he forgave you in the end," Sidraeus said, as if he knew exactly what she was thinking. "He was too selfish for that, I think, and valued his life too greatly. But this guilt you carry over his death . . . the longer you let it weigh on you, the harder it will be to set it down."

"Are you speaking from experience?"

"Am I that obvious?"

"Would that be such a bad thing? Not everything has to be veiled behind double meaning, you know. Honesty is a nice change."

Sidraeus considered this. "Honesty, then. I had centuries to think of what I might have done differently to avoid what happened to the Tidecallers. They would never have been killed by the gods if I had listened to Atheia and chosen to give up on our dream before it got that far. They would never even have been created had I not set foot in your world to begin with."

There was such devastation on his face, it gave her pause. She didn't want to sympathize with him, but she knew this guilt, this blame. The thirst for power that remained all the same.

"You're not the one who killed them," Emory said, forcing forgiveness into her tone. Not for him, but for herself.

"Neither are you." He watched her intently, as if trying to make sense of something. "Perhaps you and I are more alike than we think."

Well, I do have your magic, she thought to herself bitterly, ignoring the way her blood sang at his words.

Emory woke with his hand covering her mouth.

A scream of protest died in her throat as Sidraeus pressed a finger to his own lips, the solemnity of his expression urging her to be quiet. It was a wonder she saw him at all in the dark: their fire, she noticed, had been doused.

Slowly, he let go of her mouth. "We need to move." He was close enough that when he whispered, she felt his breath on her face. "The knights are nearby."

She heard it then, the subtle clink of armor, the faint shuffle of footsteps. They looked over the edge of the canyon they had set up camp atop for the night. In the canyon pass below were at least two dozen draconics marching toward the east, carrying a few torches between them. There were armored knights and robed sages alike, as well as a young page Emory recognized as Caius. Tears glistened on his cheeks. He made to wipe them away, and the sage beside him–Master Bayns–seemed to admonish him for it.

Sidraeus tugged urgently at Emory's sleeve, dragging her under a copse of spindly trees just as the sound of flapping wings assaulted them. Above them, a handful of draconic knights passed, surveying the canyon from the air. Two of them set themselves down a few feet away from where Emory and Sidraeus hid. A screeching growl rent the night skies from somewhere in the distance, drawing the two knights' gaze.

"Is it wise to leave the beast there?" one of them asked.

In the other, Emory recognized the voice of the Knight Commander: "If the Night Bringer comes across it, it'll send him a message."

"Remind me why we're not prioritizing going after him instead?"

"Because Anatolius is with the Golden Helm. They hold all the secrets of the dragons. More importantly: they know where the Sun Forger slumbers. If we follow them, we can find an unlimited resource of dragon flame to make more of our kind with. The Night Bringer will be no match for us then."

"What about Anatolius?"

A pause. "I won't let him escape death a second time."

Emory's heart raced. If the knights caught up to her friends before they made it to the Sunforge . . .

She had to stop them. But before she could think of drawing on her magic, the knights were off in a great flap of their wings. And Sidraeus was no longer at her side.

"What– *Where are you going?*"

He was bounding off in the direction the growl had come from, his silhouette barely visible against the dark. Emory tore after him. She nearly knocked into him at the base of the canyon. His face was twisted with horror and anger as he stared at an eldritch beast that had Emory backing up a step. It had the body of a wild-cat, fur black as the night, and the torso and head of an owl, with feathers the silvery gray of the moon. Vibrant blue eyes stared back at them as the creature uttered a broken cry.

Its wings were pinned to the canyon wall, pierced through with golden swords.

Sidraeus seemed heartbroken and outraged all at once. He walked up to the creature and stroked it gently on its neck, speaking to it in a language Emory didn't know. The eldritch made another plaintive cry, closing its eyes as it leaned into Sidraeus's touch. Distracting it with his soothing words, Sidraeus took out the swords with quick, efficient movements. Dark blood pooled from the wounds as the creature stumbled forward.

"Can you heal it?" Sidraeus asked. His mouth was set in a grim line as he met Emory's gaze, but there was something desperate and broken hiding behind his eyes.

She looked at the beast, at the way Sidraeus knelt beside it, and understood. The eldritch were his, creatures that carried a trace of his power after he entered this world alongside Atheia. Creatures who lived in the balance between life and death, creation and destruction. They weren't the bloodthirsty, wicked underworld beings that the Fellowship wanted the world to believe. They were just misunderstood.

And maybe it was because she, too, was a creature born of Sidraeus's power that she drew on her healing magic and sent it toward the beast. Its wings mended themselves in no time. The eldritch shook them off and tucked them close to its sides with a pleased coo. Its blue eyes met hers, and then a voice was in her mind, just like when the dragon spoke.

Thank you, Tidecaller.

"You know what I am?"

I know many things. Such is my gift.

"Is it talking to you?" Sidraeus asked with a frown. "What's it saying?"

"You don't hear it?"

I choose who to speak with, the creature said, its tail flickering idly as it sat on its hind legs. *You healed me, and so my gift is yours if you want it.*

Emory felt a chill at its words despite herself. "What is it?"

Put your hand on my heart and find out for yourself.

Emory's eyes flicked to Sidraeus, who watched the silent exchange with a raised brow. Curiosity had her moving closer to the beast. She rested a tentative hand on the soft down on its breast. Mesmerized by its blue eyes, she gasped as images swam in her mind. *Knowledge. Truth.* Such was the creature's gift, and it washed through her like the tide.

Emory snatched her hand back, heart pounding. The eldritch inclined its head to her.

Farewell.

And just like that, it leapt toward freedom—but not before exchanging a weighted glance with Sidraeus. His expression changed; Emory could practically see the wheels spinning in his mind, leaving her to wonder if the beast had spoken to him, too. She was still trying to make sense of what *she'd* seen when Sidraeus met her eye. He quickly composed his features, trying for a bemused slant of his mouth that couldn't quite hide his suspicion.

"Care to share what it said?"

Emory had trouble breathing as the truth the eldritch had showed her nestled in her heart. She steeled herself against it. "It just wanted to thank me for healing it. Did it speak to you?"

"It did not. I guess my freeing it deserved no thanks," he said dryly. He searched her gaze. "Is there nothing else?"

"No." Her mouth went thick with the lie. Her cheeks warmed under his scrutiny. She jerked her chin to the canyon pass where the knights had gone. "Other than a shared thirst for vengeance. They should pay for the way they treat the eldritch."

"I couldn't agree more."

"So let's."

He raised a bemused brow. "While I appreciate the bloodthirsty enthusiasm, I don't think you and I can take all of them on. I may be a deity, but this body is frail. And you–"

"Not just the two of us. I have an idea."

The appreciative look in his eye as she told him her plan made her think he was seeing her for the first time. Fitting, she thought, that she had seen the truth of him, too.

62

BAZ

BAZ WOKE IN THE INFIRMARY, BRUISED AND BATTERED but with all his limbs intact. At least he thought so. Bleary-eyed, he surveyed his surroundings. All the beds around him were occupied with bandaged-up students. Cordie, he noticed, stood near the windows, red-eyed and with her arm in a sling, but *alive*. She spoke with a white-faced Polina. Outside, the sun was setting, casting them both in a golden glow.

Cordie noticed he was up and was instantly at his side. "How are you feeling?" she rasped.

Baz winced as he sat up. "Like I should be dead."

His mind raced back to what had happened. The magic of the door barring him entry into the sleepscape, whispering about his work not being done. "How did I get here?"

His right wrist was bandaged. He lifted his good hand to his head–still fuzzy from when he'd landed in the Belly of the Beast–but found he was bound to the bed, a damper cuff around his wrist. "What–"

"A precaution," Cordie said. "You were found on Dovermere Cove, half-drowned and barely breathing." Tears glistened in her eyes. "Cornelius is gone, isn't he?"

Baz nodded. Clover was gone. Kai and Luce too. And Baz was left here stranded in the past, with not the faintest clue if he would ever see Kai again.

Polina shuffled uncomfortably by the bed, hunched as if she were trying to make herself smaller or disappear entirely. She too wore a damper cuff, though hers wasn't keeping her tied to a bed. Baz noticed the stares from injured students around them. They were glaring at them–at *him* specifically.

"What happened?"

"There was a blast," Polina explained. "It ripped through the Vault and the Decrescens library and the whole quad, and, well . . ." She gave a furtive glance at the glaring students, lowering her voice. "They assume the blast was from Thames's Collapsing. That he cheated his way past the wards. And that you must have helped him, even though you were found on the cove, not in the Vault. They thought you'd Collapsed too, but don't worry, they tested your blood. Red, not silver."

Equal parts anger and sadness rushed through Baz. All the progress he'd made with these students, all the animosity that had started to fade around him . . . it had all been for nothing. He was Eclipse-born, and so they would find a reason to blame him for this.

"What happened to Thames's body?" Baz asked.

Cordie suddenly plopped down at the foot of Baz's bed, her shoulders racked with sobs. "I'm sorry. I just–I can't believe he's gone. I don't understand how he ended up down there. After I thought he'd left for Trevel? Why was he there at all?"

Polina threw her arm over Cordie's shoulders as she broke down, whispering to her in soothing tones. She met Baz's confused gaze. "They found another body down in the Treasury. It was Louka."

Baz's stomach fell. *Louka?* It made no sense. How in the Tides' name would he have found a way past the wards? And how had they not seen the body? "Cordie, I'm so sorry."

His heart broke for her as she cried in Polina's arms. A Healer brought Cordie to an empty bed to calm her down.

"None of this makes sense," Baz muttered.

Polina looked at him, worrying her lip. "I may have done something." She fished out two silver lockets from her pocket, laying them on the bed. "I took both Thames's and Louka's memories and imbued them in these. The pertinent ones, at least. I haven't shown Cordie yet, but . . . I needed someone else to know."

Baz's heart raced as he reached for the lockets. He'd nearly forgotten about Polina's Enshriner magic–the ability to extract memories from the dead. He hesitated before touching the lockets. "What did you see?"

Polina shook her head. "I can't say. You have to see for yourself."

Baz wasn't sure he *wanted* to, given the sickly tint to Polina's face. But he had to. "How does it work?"

"Put the necklace on and open the locket. It'll pull you into the memories it contains. You won't be . . . *yourself* when you're there. You'll experience the memories through the bearer's eyes, with their thoughts, their feelings." She handed him the bigger of the two lockets. "Start with this one."

Haltingly, Baz slipped the chain over his head. With fingers that were surprisingly steady, he opened the locket–and gasped as the infirmary and everyone in it disappeared. As Baz himself disappeared, his mind replaced with another's.

"This isn't working."

Cornelius's frustration was evident as he shoved his journal aside, nearly knocking over an ink pot. Thames looked up from where he sat reading on Cornelius's bed. The sheets were undone from their earlier tumble, and Thames luxuriated in the silky feel of them on his skin.

Cornelius ran a hand through his hair, mouth set in a petulant line as he leaned back in his desk chair. It always fascinated Thames, how close to the surface Cornelius's emotions were when he wasn't out in public–when he wasn't being the unflappable scholar everyone saw him as, but the passionate idealist Thames knew.

"What are you thinking?" Thames pried.

Cornelius rubbed pensively at his lip. "For the experiment to truly be successful, I would have to not interfere. Let them fight for their lives on their own, without my healing magic to fall back on."

"And if they don't survive?" Thames asked. "Surely people will notice if Aldryn's best and brightest start dropping like flies."

Cornelius gave an exasperated sigh. "You're right."

Pride soared in Thames's chest at this small recognition of his worth. "You could keep it outside of the Selenic Order," he suggested. "The Bicentennial would provide the perfect cover-up."

"Students dealing with notoriously deadly wards?" Cornelius's eyes glimmered with excitement. "No one would bat an eye should something happen."

"Precisely. You'd have to be careful who you target, but . . ."

"I think I have an idea." Cornelius's mouth curled up in a smile. He joined Thames on the bed, tenderly grabbing his face between his hands. "Whatever would I do without this brilliant mind of yours?"

The scene dissolved just as Clover's mouth descended on Thames's. The memory bled into another before Baz had time to consider what any of it meant.

Cornelius was being strangled by Wulfrid and still had the audacity to smile–to laugh–in the face of death.

"Do your worst," he croaked.

Veins bulged on Wulfrid's neck as he squeezed tighter. Cornelius's eyes rolled to the back of his head, legs flailing and kicking as his body spasmed beneath Wulfrid's. Thames had seen enough. He pounced, tearing Wulfrid off Cornelius and driving his fist into him again and again, something wild coming loose inside him.

"Enough, Thames."

Cornelius pulled him up, looking completely unruffled. He righted Thames's glasses for him, fixed the lapels of his suit, a crimson mirror to the white one Cornelius had donned for the party. He grabbed his trembling hand between his and pressed a gentle kiss to his bloodied knuckles. "There," Cornelius murmured, and Thames felt the brush of healing magic against his skin, erasing the evidence of what he'd done.

Thames glanced at Wulfrid. "Is he . . ."

"Not yet. Though he'll make for the perfect target, don't you think? It was so easy to bait him."

"What have you done?"

Thames and Cornelius whipped to the voice behind them. Three students looked at them with wide eyes—Wulfrid's teammates. The burly Fröns student opened his mouth to alert the librarian on duty, unaware that Cornelius had already paid off Luce to be absent from her post tonight, given the party.

"Keep your mouths shut and do as I say," Cornelius said, voice laced with the compulsion of Glamour magic. The three students went quiet. "Now grab your friend here and follow me."

Thames was in the secret library room, assaulted by loud music and laughter. He flexed his hand, a phantom soreness after pummeling Wulfrid. His gaze caught on Baz, who watched Cornelius and Kai on the dance floor with an expression Thames knew well. "Cornelius is like that with everyone," he said.

"Like what?" Baz asked.

"A shameless flirt. It used to bother me, too, at first."

Lie. It still bothered him. He wanted Cornelius to have eyes only for him, but he was always chasing after those with the most interesting stories and magics. Everyone could be replaced at a moment's notice in Cornelius's eyes, his sister being the one exception, of course. But no one knew him like Thames did. Not even Cordelia.

If they knew the real Cornelius, they might see a monster. Thames only saw a scholar willing to go to lengths no other had the courage to.

"You've got something there," Baz said to him.

Thames looked at the stain on his shirt.

Blood.

It must have gotten on him earlier. Thank the Tides his jacket was already red, making the stain look like nothing more than spilled wine. Still, he couldn't risk raising suspicions.

He left the party to wash up, checking in on the four students as he did. Cornelius had Glamoured them to remain unconscious, hiding them away in a dark corner of the library. "Don't worry, I put up a ward to shield them from unwanted eyes," he'd said.

The plan was to deal with them after the party. But as Thames vigorously tried to scrub away the blood on him, doubt crept in. If Cornelius's theory proved wrong, if none of these students turned into a Tidecaller, they would have four deaths on their hands.

They would be killers.

The party was over, the secret library room empty except for Thames and Cornelius and the three bodies splayed out at their feet. Dead, all of them.

The first to go had been the Fröns student. Drowned in a shallow bloodletting bowl that Cornelius had filled with the closest available liquid: moonbrew. Fitting.

He'd slashed a ceremonial knife across his palm, then the student's, to combine their blood in the bowl, creating swirling trails of red amid the cloudy drink. Just like during the Selenic Order rituals.

Then he'd grabbed hold of the student almost lovingly, whispering in his ear, "Now fight for your life."

Thames had watched, heart pounding with a hint of remorse and a grim sort of hope, as the student flailed against Cornelius's hold, head thrashing in the shallow bowl. Eventually he'd stilled. Air bubbles had risen to the surface. And Cornelius had waited, waited, waited, desperate for his theory to be proven right.

The student didn't rise.

Next had been the two Aldryn boys, Wulfrid's acolytes. A different method for each. One strangled. The other stabbed. "Since drowning doesn't seem to work," Cornelius explained.

Neither of them survived.

Only Wulfrid now remained. His eyes were wild with fury and fear as Cornelius approached him. This one was personal, Thames could tell. "You remind me of my first kill," Cornelius said to Wulfrid. "He was a bully too. Maybe if I give you the same death he tried to give me . . ."

Thames didn't see the Reaper magic. He only saw the light leave Wulfrid's eyes. Dead like the others, never to rise.

"What do we do with the bodies?" Thames asked.

"The Treasury," Cornelius said. "I have an idea."

Thames panted with the effort of hauling the body up the stairs. Every breath he took made him want to gag; they had left the bodies down in the Treasury for too long, and now the stench of wet, decaying flesh spoiled the air.

"Almost there," Cornelius said ahead of him, grunting with the effort of dragging Wulfrid's body.

The first two bodies they'd hauled up were waiting for them at the top of the stairs. "Wait here," Cornelius said, hand braced against the wall. "I'll ensure the coast is clear."

Thames watched him disappear behind the silver door. His heart nearly stopped when he heard Cornelius say, "This isn't what it looks like."

A familiar voice exclaimed: "Really? So you haven't found a way around the very wards we're trying to break through?"

Thames's mind raced. That was Baz–and there, that was Kai's voice that followed soon after. They'd been caught, and now everything would come to light. Remorse churned in his stomach, making bile rise in his throat. Or perhaps that was the stench of the corpses. He suddenly wanted no part in this. But then he heard Cornelius's smooth voice, and Luce's, and after a moment the voices disappeared altogether.

Thames's shoulders relaxed ever so slightly. They'd been given an out. And now it was up to him to see the rest through.

He got to work hauling the bodies through the door. The library, thankfully, was empty. Thames laid the bodies out at the foot of the arch, following Cornelius's instructions down to the letter. We'll make it look like the wards did this. They had already drained them of their blood, just like the wards had nearly drained that Ilsker student of hers. The apparent signs of drowning were an added flair of mystery, easily blamed on the deadly wards.

When Thames was done, he fled the scene, welcoming the cold bite of night air in the quad. He spilled his guts on the lawn and proceeded to break down into tears.

Thames watched Cornelius's nightmare unfold as they always did. But something felt different this night, as if Cornelius's guard were down where it usually stayed up even as he slept. Cornelius's veins rippled silver, then black, before he transformed into a veritable monster. A dark, deadly power blasted from him. It turned everything and everyone around him to ash.

The world was dark and bleak. Lifeless. And it was Cornelius's doing.

In the great expanse of ash, a light appeared. At first Thames thought it was Luce, bursting into the nightmare like a dream, a shining star. But this girl was not Luce. Light emanated from her as she stood against Cornelius, and when Thames looked at her, he felt a great sense of hope wash over him.

Cornelius turned to him then, noticing his presence in this bleak dream that was not quite a dream but a memory, a vision. Something not easily forgotten. His mouth formed a grim line. "Now you know, dear Thames," he said in a small voice. "This is the fate that awaits me."

Thames shook his head, refusing to believe it. He grabbed Cornelius's face between his hands, willing the darkness of Cornelius's nightmare to seep into him. "We have time yet to change it," he said fiercely.

A promise. A vow. Whatever it took to keep Cornelius from this fate.

Cornelius kissed him softly, then said, "Perhaps, if we can create a Tidecaller synth like the kind that Baz and Kai described . . ." He cut himself off. "But no. That would require silver blood."

They kissed among the darkness of the nightmare, Cornelius's words making an idea bloom in Thames's mind.

Another nightmare. The worst one Thames had been able to find. Umbrae flocked toward him, called by the heaviness of this person's dreaming. Thames didn't know them, and he never wished to, given the twisted nature of their mind.

Thames wasn't adept at pulling things out of nightmares the way Kai was. He knew how, but even the smallest things brought him too close to Collapsing. But now he needed to Collapse. So he let the umbrae overtake him, and willed himself to wake–

He was in the Treasury, having gone to sleep here knowing he would Collapse. Knowing the blast would be contained behind the Vault's wards. The umbrae screamed in the shadows around him, as if to contest their strange entry into reality. Thames glanced down at his hands. Silver rippled in his veins. And then he was Collapsing, the force of it burning through him so brightly he screamed in agony. He had to do this. He could weather the pain. He must–

Thames came to in a daze of confusion. His Collapsing had stopped, yet silver still swirled in his veins. Rising to his feet, he quickly got to work extracting his blood and mixing it with one of the vials of Cornelius's Tidecaller blood that they kept down here for experiments. He infused the mixture into his veins, then waded into the glowing pool, heart pounding an angry rhythm in his ears.

He would not be another failed experiment. He would survive this and be reborn a Tidecaller.

Thames plunged into the water and let himself sink to the bottom as the air left his lungs.

Thames took a deep breath in. He was in Cornelius's arms. He had done it! He had survived what the others had not!

But then Cornelius was whispering in his ear, telling him–no, commanding him–to take the blame, to hide the full truth of what they had done. Confusion wormed its way into Thames's mind. Why was Cornelius using Glamour magic on him? Why was he pretending he hadn't killed those students?

Thames wanted to rage, to claw his way out from under Cornelius's influence, even as his betrayal shattered his heart into a million pieces.

After everything Thames had done for him . . .

He had to at least prove to Cornelius–to himself–that this had not *been for nothing. Thames pulled on whatever magic he could think of, and suddenly he was wielding Lightkeeper magic, and surely the look of wonder and affection in Cornelius's eyes was real, and–*

Thames was Collapsing all over again. Power burned through him, rotting his flesh from within, turning his blood to ash, draining every drop of magic and life from him as it razed through him.

Someone help, *he thought.*

His last, before the end.

Baz gasped as he was again in his own mind, in his own body, in the infirmary he had never actually left. He tore the locket off his neck, tossing it at the foot of the bed. Polina watched him with sad eyes, handing him the second locket before he had a chance to say anything.

"I'm afraid it gets worse," she said quietly.

Baz hesitated. He felt like throwing up. But he had to know the whole truth, and so he picked the locket up and braced himself for the onslaught of memories to come.

"I'm pregnant."

Cordelia's words made the floor pitch under Louka's feet. A joy so poignant he thought he'd burst soared through him, the feeling so clearly mirrored on her face. He laughed. Kissed her mouth. In hushed whispers, they began to make plans. Marriage. Trevel. A life full of beauty and art, far from Aldryn College, from the constraints of magic.

Leave her, an intrusive voice said in his mind. Do it gently, so that *she doesn't suspect.*

"I . . . I must go," Louka found himself saying against his will.

Confusion banked in Cordelia's eyes. "Go?"

"There's much to be done."

"But you're happy about this, right? This is a good thing."

"This is a good thing," he repeated, monotone voice so unlike his own. Of course I'm happy, he wanted to shout. But that other voice in his mind was telling him to leave. So he turned on his heel and left Cordelia standing dumbstruck before the door of her art studio.

Outside, Louka ran into Cornelius. He was still too confused by what just happened to realize how odd it was that Cordelia's brother should be here. He never went anywhere near her studio, as if art was too far beneath him to bother with.

"Let's you and I go have ourselves a little chat," Cornelius said, his demeanor oozing deceitful ease.

Louka's back went rigid. His feet began walking of their own volition. Was that magic that had been used on him? And that voice, so like the one that had been in Louka's mind . . .

Before he could ponder it further, he found himself sitting in a private taproom with Cornelius.

"I would like for you to tell me the whole truth, tailor. All of it."

The words came tumbling out of Louka's mouth without his meaning, as monotone as before: "Cordelia is with child. We wish to marry. I have a business opportunity lined up in Trevel, where your sister wishes to study art. We will leave when the spring comes, after the school year is done. She knows how you value her education."

"Does she now," Cornelius said tightly, a storm brewing behind his polished exterior. "And what is the plan if I decide not to give my blessing?"

"Respectfully . . . I think your sister knows you won't approve of this union, or the child we are to raise, or the kind of life we wish to live. She intends to leave with me for Trevel regardless of your blessing."

Why was he saying all of this? It was meant to be their secret . . .

Cornelius pondered his words in an agonizing stretch of silence. Then he said: "Here's what I want you to do, tailor." He pushed a piece of writing paper and a pen toward him. "You will write a letter to my sister breaking things off with her. You will say that you have reconsidered the relationship, that you are not ready to become a father, and so you have left for Trevel without her. You will end this letter by saying you never wish to speak to her or see her ever again."

Tears formed in Louka's eyes. His heart broke, but for the life of him, he found he could not refuse. His hand moved of its own volition, writing the very words he was told to write. He watched, powerless, as Cornelius sealed the letter. "That's a good lad," he said.

"Please," Louka managed. "I beg you."

"Begging will not help you, I'm afraid." Cornelius tilted his head. "Though there may be something you can help me with . . ."

Louka was in a strange, damp grotto with a glowing pool in its center surrounded by stony thrones. Death clung to the air. He knew he would die here.

Cornelius instructed him to step into the pool. "I've yet to test the experiment on a blank canvas," he said, talking to Louka in a conversational manner, "someone without magic. If you can survive it and emerge a Tidecaller, perhaps Delia might too."

Louka tasted salt on his tongue from the tears falling in earnest down his face, the only thing he still had control of after being told not to speak or move without Cornelius saying so. When his head was shoved underwater, he did not kick, he did not scream, he did not fight back.

He only thought of his darling Cordelia, and hoped she would sail far from this place and the monster she called brother.

63

EMORY

THE LANDSCAPE AROUND THEM CHANGED AS SUDDENLY as the weather.

Gone was the beauty of the desert they'd traveled through, the red sandstone arches and spindly trees and ridges that overlooked miles and miles of curiously striated rock. Here was a scorched land, charcoal rocks where nothing grew, sharp as a beast's gnashing teeth. A large volcano emerged from the soot-stained land, and Emory knew it had to be the Sunforge. She only hoped it wouldn't decide to unleash the sea of fire within its belly while they were here.

The sky had lost its dim sun and washed-out blues. A storm brewed, electricity forming in the depths of angry dark clouds.

"Are you certain you're ready for this?" Sidraeus asked.

They stood shoulder to shoulder on a ridge, their backs to the Sunforge. Emory twisted her neck to look up at him. There was that appreciative glimmer in his ecliptic eyes again, twisting her stomach into knots. She swallowed thickly, returning her gaze to the horizon. "I am."

The ley line crackled with anticipation under her feet, begging her to unleash her magic. But she managed to hold off, imagining the ley line powering her up the longer she waited.

At last they appeared on the horizon, specks of gold armor and gold swords and gold wings. The Knight Commander and her company.

Emory and Sidraeus had raced to get ahead of them so they could stop them before they reached the Sunforge. They'd gotten here not a moment too soon. At last Emory called on the Darkbearer magic she'd been waiting to use, opening herself up to the ley line's power to make a grand spectacle out of it. Darkness fell all around her, pitch as night, spreading across the barren plain between the Sunforge at her back and the knights moving toward her.

She wondered what they must look like: she and the Night Bringer, standing on a ridge together as darkness bloomed around them. Judging from the glint of swords being drawn as the approaching draconics got into formation, they must look terrifying enough.

Emory faltered slightly as power rushed from the ley line through her. Sidraeus's hand on her elbow steadied her. She realized no ghosts had been called by her magic, thanks to him. She shook away the thoughts drawn up by his touch and focused on the task at hand.

The Knight Commander came to stand before them, hand on her sword. Hovering close behind her were three knights, as well as the sage Master Bayns, and his page Caius. Caius's eyes were wide with fear as he looked at Emory.

"Night Bringer," the Knight Commander said. "Did you receive my message?"

"I did," Sidraeus said evenly. "You'll be displeased to know the eldritch lived."

"You won't be so lucky." The Knight Commander motioned to her knights. "Seize them."

Emory studied Caius. He looked haunted–ashamed even–at the mention of the eldritch. She wondered if his love of all beasts had opened his eyes to the cruelty of his masters, after what they did to the eldritch in the canyon pass. Pointedly, she looked up at the darkened skies above them, where something moved in the clouds. Caius frowned as he caught the motion.

Emory could only hope the young boy understood as Sidraeus said to the Knight Commander, "It's you and your knights who are out of luck, I'm afraid."

Gwenhael emerged from the dark clouds above on silent wings, jaws open wide to reveal gold-white flames at the back of its throat. The Knight Commander barely had time to jump out of the way before dragon flame shot down toward her, lethal and precise in its trajectory.

The company of knights descended into chaos as they ran for cover they wouldn't find. Gwenhael's flames razed the barren rock, and Emory desperately tried to spot Caius, hoping he'd made it out safely. The sky above Gwenhael split open as a dozen armed draconics appeared bearing the crest of the Golden Helm.

Ivayne led these draconics with a fierce smile as they descended upon the Fellowship of the Light. With the dragon on their side, the Knight Commander's company would be no match.

Emory turned to Sidraeus. He surveyed the chaos with grim satisfaction, and she knew what he must be thinking. That they'd gotten retribution for the eldritch. That the knights deserved to burn.

"You were right about the eldritch I healed," she said in a conversational tone, drawing his attention away from the battle. She moved closer to him, pulling him into her orbit. "It did tell me something else. A truth it shared with me as a thank-you."

She might have imagined the way his gaze flicked to her mouth. "And what truth was that?"

"Something I'd suspected but hoped would turn out to be false."

His brow knit in confusion. Before he could realize what she meant, a magic-dampening collar like the one she'd freed him from only days ago was snapped shut around his neck. He whirled on the draconic who'd chained him, but Vivyan pointed her sword at his heart.

Emory stepped away from him. Vivyan gave her a curt nod. "You all right, girl?"

"Fine. The others are at the Sunforge?"

"Waiting for us as planned."

Confusion slowly gave way to anger as Sidraeus looked between them. "What is this?"

Emory forced steel into her words. "The truth the eldritch showed me," she said, "was about you. You omitted something from your story. You'd already tried wresting the gods' power from them before they imprisoned you. You got Tidecallers to stand before the fountain and siphon its power off to you. Except it didn't work. The Tidecallers burned out completely, too much power ripping through them, and they died. And despite this, you were willing to risk it again on me. The last Tidecaller who might do alone what four of them died trying."

"Emory . . ."

"But that's not even the worst part, is it?" she added with a bitter laugh. "The worst part is that *you* were the one to sacrifice the Tidecallers in the end. *You* were the one to give them up to the gods so they could be bled dry."

His gaze turned stony. "I did what I had to."

No denial. No remorse. Emory shouldn't have expected any different. "You're just like him," she muttered, studying Keiran's face. Someone else who'd meant to use her. Suddenly they seemed like a single person.

Sidraeus's eyes flared, a reminder of the deity beneath. "I am *nothing* like him." He pulled on his chains to no avail, reduced to human frailty under the magic damper. "If I didn't give up the Tide-callers," he seethed, "the gods were going to destroy *everything*. Wipe clean the realms of the living and the dead, burn everyone and everything in them—myself and Atheia included—just so they could build something better out of the ashes."

"And why would they do that?"

"Self-preservation, fear, spite—does it matter? They saw Tide-callers as something that was never meant to exist. The one threat to their godhood. That's the kind of power the gods have, to end us all in the blink of an eye if they choose. I couldn't let that happen."

"So you offered your Tidecallers as sacrifice." Their blood on his hands. "And now me."

His jaw tightened. "Believe me, if I had known—"

"I'm done believing you." The sounds of battle raged on around them. Emory motioned to Vivyan. "Take him."

The draconic tugged on his chain, but Sidraeus dug his heels into the ground, trying to fight back. Vivyan yanked him to her with ease, Keiran's body too frail with the deity's power dampened.

Sidraeus stilled, seeming to accept his fate despite the feral edge of his scowl. To Emory, he asked: "What will you do to me?"

"I'm not sure yet. Maybe we'll leave you in the sleepscape where you belong. But I'm done being used and lied to."

Anger brewed in Sidraeus's gaze, a storm on the brink of vio-lence. But there was something else there too. Something like hurt, and betrayal. Maybe even . . . pride?

"You see?" he murmured, a note of appreciation in his voice. "We're the same, you and I."

"We're nothing alike."

"We could have set these worlds right together. Now I'm afraid we're doomed to remain rivals."

She walked up to him, anger roiling in her stomach. "Let me

make something very clear. There is no world that exists in which we could be *anything* but rivals. I despise this body you wear, and I hate the monstrous soul that fills it. *Rivals* doesn't even *begin* to cover it."

Something heated flashed in his gaze.

Emory stormed off ahead of him and Vivyan, barely sparing a glance to the battle still raging. Most of the Fellowship of the Light had been rounded up by the Golden Helm, kept alive for now. Gwenhael had landed amid the golden flames and bloodshed, munching on something Emory didn't want to consider.

Suddenly Ivayne was catching up to them, blood splattered on her face, her smile a flash of brilliant white. She clasped Emory on the shoulder. "You did good."

Emory tried to smile back, tried to be proud she'd successfully duped Sidraeus, but all she felt was hollow. After the eldritch had shown her the truth of him, she'd found Romie in dreams and told her everything. They'd devised this plan for Emory to make Sidraeus believe she was still on his side. He knew of Vivyan and Ivayne calling on the help of their fellow knights-errant to ambush the Fellowship, but he hadn't known it was meant as a distraction to capture *him*.

She would not die for him, would not play into his quest for revenge.

She'd gotten what she needed from him, and now she had a door to get through.

When they caught up to the group, Virgil was the first one to greet her, arms crossed and lips pursed in a way that was almost comical. "You have some explaining to do, young lady." He threw Sidraeus a narrow-eyed look as Vivyan drew her captive past him. To Emory he said: "You know I would have come with you if you'd asked me, right?"

Emory's heart went out to him. "I know," she said, squeezing his arm in a gesture she hoped conveyed how sorry she was to have left without saying anything, and how much she valued his friendship–especially as she spotted Romie looking at her with a guarded expression. Giving Virgil one last squeeze, Emory went over to her.

"Glad to see you went through with it," Romie said. "I wasn't sure you'd actually turn on him."

The iciness in her tone sliced as much as the words themselves. Even after all this, Romie's wariness about her remained. Emory felt unmoored, wondering if there was anything left to save or if she'd destroyed their friendship beyond repair. Maybe it had always been doomed to come to this, the nature of their magics pitting them against each other in some predestined way. A key, a Tidecaller. Atheia, Sidraeus.

"I'm on your side, Ro. That's never going to change, even if *I've* changed. Even if *we've* changed. I know I've hurt you, but I'm try-ing here, I really am."

Romie softened at that, some of the tension leaving her shoul-ders. She gave Emory a wobbly smile. "Things were so much eas-ier before, weren't they? I wish we could go back."

It was so very Romie to want to hold on tight to who they'd been, the version of themselves that existed in a perfect bubble, think-ing it would make it easier to face the hard things. But the bubble had burst a long time ago. They were no longer those people, and Emory didn't want to be.

She thought of what Sidraeus had told her. That when forced to live in the dark, he'd had no choice but to become the darkness itself. Maybe that's what Emory had done. She'd been molded by darkness, and some of it had taken root inside her. Maybe it had always been there, waiting to be let out. Whatever the case, that darkness–her selfishness, her hunger for power–didn't mean she was beyond forgiveness.

All she could do was be her best self, darkness and all, and hope that was enough for the people who loved her. True friendship would survive such darkness.

She just wasn't sure Romie saw it that way.

64

ROMIE

THE SUNFORGE WAS BUILT AT THE VERY BASE OF THE looming volcano. Ivayne and Vivyan told them it was known to erupt sporadically over the years, and Romie only hoped it wouldn't do so while they found their way inside.

A large arched doorway was built into the jagged rocks, its carved columns intricately wrought, with threads of gold running through them and etchings of eldritch beasts and dragons in flight. The archway was big enough to accommodate a dragon, but Gwenhael did not follow them into the Sunforge. It chose instead to remain with the Golden Helm draconics, who, after taking care of the Fellowship, would lead Gwenhael back to freedom—and to other dragons.

Romie expected scorching heat as they trod carefully inside the mountain. They found themselves in a gigantic cave, with columns like the ones outside lining a path that cut deeper into the darkness. Rivers of steaming water ran through the ground they walked on. In some places, geysers shot water and steam up into the air, as if warning them of what lay beyond.

"There is death here," Vivyan said eerily. "I can feel it."

The words made Romie's spine tingle. But all *she* could feel was that song tugging inside her, beckoning her on. *So close*, it seemed to say, brimming with excitement that warred with the dread that permeated this place.

But the draconic was right: death did await them, in the form of a mound of bones.

A carcass. That of a colossal dragon that must have been twice the size of Gwenhael.

Ivayne and Vivyan fell to their knees, looking utterly heartbroken. "We thought, at the very least, that the Sunforge would be a haven for dragons," Vivyan said. "Instead it is a graveyard."

"What do you think happened to it?" Tol asked, eyes bright with unshed tears.

"Maybe it died guarding *this*."

Ivayne motioned to the wall of smooth, black rock behind the carcass. It formed a natural arch and was flanked by two steaming, roiling geysers. The rock was shot through with veins of fire, as if on the other side of it were the fiery belly of the volcano itself.

Romie spotted the golden spiral etched in the middle of the arch.

The door to the fourth world.

Tol stepped up to it as if in a trance, called no doubt by the same song in Romie's blood. Aspen grabbed his arm, pulling him back. Something loaded passed between them.

"The sacrifice," Emory said, face blanching. "How are we going to get the door open without Tol giving up his heart?"

As if she'd *just* now emerged from whatever dark hole she let herself sink into to ask herself this. Romie shouldn't have been surprised.

Tol squared his shoulders as he faced the door, fingers searching along the groove at the center of the spiral. It was shaped like a heart, the same way the Wychwood's door had had a place in which to fit Aspen's bone.

"If I have to risk my life to bring back the many-faced goddess and stop the worlds from dying, then I will gladly give up my heart."

"You can't be serious," Virgil said. "*Nothing* is worth dying for."

"I won't have to stay dead." Tol's eyes flashed to Emory. "Right?"

Emory shook her head. "This isn't something I can heal you from like I did Aspen. You can't survive this."

Romie looked at Keiran. The Shadow. This dark god wearing the body of a corpse.

A corpse that had been revived.

"What if someone had the power to bring him back?" Romie said.

Emory caught on to her meaning. "I'm not using *Reanimator* magic on him. I can barely use other Eclipse magics as it is, and this one . . . we don't know how much of Keiran actually came back as *him*, before Sidraeus took over."

Sidraeus. Atheia. That was what Emory had called the Tides and the Shadow when she visited Romie in dreams the other day.

Romie couldn't help but see the clear divide between them now. Emory, a product of Sidraeus. Herself, a creation of Atheia.

I'm on your side, Ro. That's never going to change.

Except they weren't on the same side, were they? They were friends, allies, but opposites by fate's design. She wanted to believe they could defy these roles destiny had laid out for them, that their friendship could survive it. But it was hard to do with Atheia's warning still in her mind.

Such thieves could not be trusted.

"So, what, we just give up?" Romie snapped, angry at this wavering conviction inside her. "We didn't make it this far to turn back now, not with us so close to reaching Atheia." She looked between Aspen and Tol. "Right?"

Aspen swallowed, looking uncertain. "There has to be another way," she whispered. "One that doesn't require Tol's sacrifice."

"There *is* another way," Emory said, her eyes locked on Sidraeus. "Blasting the door wide open."

65

EMORY

EMORY COULDN'T TELL BY THE LOOK IN SIDRAEUS'S eyes if he was pleased or not that she was willing to do what they'd set out to do in the first place.

She didn't care. She wasn't doing this for him.

They couldn't open this world's door if it meant Tol had to give up his heart. This wouldn't be like Aspen's rib bone–the second they took his heart out, he would die. Emory couldn't heal what was already dead. And she wasn't playing around with reanimation magic.

What she could do was break down the door so that Tol's sacrifice wouldn't be needed. If she was the only one able to fit keys into locks, she would instead kick this door right off its hinges.

And then she would march up to the sea of ash and confront the gods herself if she had to.

There had to be another way to heal this corruption seeping through the worlds. Emory thought of what Sidraeus had said about the gods having the power to destroy the universe and start over again. That kind of power . . . she was beginning to see why Sidraeus and Atheia had wanted things to change. Why they'd felt compelled to wrest the gods' power away from them and share it with the mortals instead.

If the gods had such control over their fates, surely they could save the worlds without them having to sacrifice any of the keys. The gods had wanted Atheia imprisoned, hadn't they? As punishment for her part in the skewed balance between worlds. And she had evaded such punishment by splintering herself into parts.

Well, maybe they could plead with the gods to heal the worlds if they could guarantee the pieces of Atheia were never put back together–and maybe they'd hand Sidraeus over too. No more messengers. Balance restored.

"And how exactly are you going to blast the door open?" Romie asked.

Emory could see the wheels turning in her mind, the careful hope in her eyes, the wariness that remained all the same. Romie had to know this was their best shot, but she also knew that kind of magic would require power–power Emory would undoubtedly take from the keys.

"We have to try," Emory said. "I understand the ley line better now. I can–I'll try to avoid your power as best I can."

Romie's mouth thinned as she considered.

Aspen pleaded with her. "Dying isn't a guarantee for any of us if Emory does this. It is for Tol if he gives up his heart."

At last Romie relented, but her reluctance was clear.

Emory waited for Sidraeus to argue. He didn't. Only watched her with a begrudging anticipation.

She stepped up to the door that was not yet a door, and let herself plunge into the power of the ley line. It built and built inside her until she was certain she had enough that she could throw it back into the door and will it to open.

But she felt that corruption again, tainting the ley line, pulling on her focus, dimming the very power she sought to fuel herself with. Again she attempted to cleanse it, calling on different magics in her arsenal. But the sickness did not recede, and her own darkness only grew, looking to consume her, a corruption of its own. Both that darkness and the ley line's power rushed into her, and suddenly she was burning brighter than she ever had, silver veins rippling wildly on her skin.

Emory yelled against the pain of it. It was again like she was Collapsing, but instead of a blast that *ended*, there seemed to be no end in sight. With difficulty, she rested her hand on the golden spiral in the middle of the rock wall, willing the power into it. Slowly, the fiery red lines that ran through the rock turned silver instead, and Emory knew it was working, the power of the ley lines and her Tidecaller magic seeping into the rock, looking to blow open the door.

But she felt herself slipping. Burning out. The ley line was too powerful, searing through her like she was a conduit, and she knew she would die like Sidraeus's Tidecallers had.

But then she felt the traces of other magics tied to her own. The keys. The parts of a deity her magic couldn't help but call on. Emory had sworn to herself she wouldn't hurt her friends again. She resisted the urge to dip into their reservoir of power, even as she realized she was going to burn out without it.

The darkness around her pressed closer, closer. It didn't have anywhere to escape to–couldn't seep into Sidraeus, because he had that magic damper around his neck and would likely not help her now anyway. She was either going to drown in darkness or extinguish the bright lights that were her friends to keep herself afloat.

But she *was* darkness, wasn't she? Like Sidraeus, she'd been forced to become it. So maybe she could make it hers.

Emory pulled the darkness into herself, the same way Sidraeus had siphoned it from her. It was a power source of its own, a magic that was part of her in some twisted way, but one she hadn't wanted, one she'd been fighting all this time instead of truly accepting it. It rushed into her, a missing piece she made space for.

But the force of the ley line was still burning through her, and the dam would still not burst. Suddenly Romie was at her side, resting a hand on her arm. "You can do this, Em. Take what you need."

"If I start, I won't be able to stop," Emory gritted out.

Aspen and Tol were right there with her too, offering her their power.

With great effort, Emory found Virgil's gaze. "Promise you'll stop me. Promise you won't let me hurt them."

Grim understanding settled in Virgil's eyes. He nodded.

Emory opened herself up to Romie's and Aspen's and Tol's magics, their lifelines.

This wasn't like the other times. Their magics soared inside her, but it didn't feel like she was *taking* anything from them. She wasn't a Tidethief; she was a Tidecaller invoking their help, a creation of Sidraeus calling to the creations of Atheia, so that together they could create something more, something *better*.

The keys weren't being depleted of their energy because they were sharing it with her willingly.

The power that poured out of Emory burned bright and true, until the wall before her cracked open in a burst of silver.

There was a great *whoosh* like that of an explosion, and all of them fell back, shielding their eyes from the light.

For a disorienting moment, Emory thought she was dead—that she had doomed them all.

She made out faint silhouettes in the lingering brightness of the blast, like ghosts rising from their deaths. The ringing in her ears made it impossible to hear anything else. In the silent, hushed chaos, someone grabbed hold of her face. Emory blinked rapidly until Keiran's face materialized before her. His lips were moving, but she couldn't hear what he was saying. Had she died and joined him in the afterlife?

No. Keiran wasn't *in* the afterlife. Which meant neither was she. And this wasn't Keiran at all.

Emory shoved out of Sidraeus's grasp. The light had faded some, and she could see that the ghostly silhouettes were her friends, looking just as dazed and disoriented as she felt. She grabbed hold of Romie. Unhurt. Alive.

Everyone was alive, if a little shaken.

"Look," Romie said, her voice sounding muffled to Emory's ears, but at least she was starting to hear again.

Emory looked. Where there had been a wall before was now a gaping hole in the rock, on the other side of which was the darkness of the sleepscape.

"You did it," Romie said, her voice clearer now. She was smiling at Emory, her fear at last giving way to awe.

"We did it," Emory said.

They helped each other to their feet, staring at the open door, the stars beyond.

Something was making its way toward them on the starlit path.

Emory's first thought was that it was an umbra. It didn't seem to have a material body, though it was still humanoid in shape. She and Romie stumbled back as it stepped out of the darkness. It *wasn't* an umbra, but it wasn't entirely human, either. It was made up of swirling clouds of shimmering dust, interspersed with the rotten roots of a tree and rivulets of water and dying embers and the faint crackling of energy, like an electric storm brewing in a darkened sky.

The creature stepped into the cave and seemed to tip its head to the side to study them. Then it shook itself a bit, and the strange magical clouds around it began to dissipate, revealing a young man in a suit of emerald velvet. His face was still handsome despite the black veins that appeared stark against his neck and at his temples. The veins flashed silver and gold every now and then, as if the blood running through them held some odd power, like that of a Collapsing Eclipse-born, but twisted, corrupt. The young man's blond hair was perfectly coiffed, and though his eyes appeared sunken on his pale, sallow face, they glimmered with life, a shade of turquoise so bright that Emory couldn't decide if they were beautiful or haunting.

Romie swore under her breath, staring at the man with wide-eyed recognition. "That's Cornus Clover," she said.

66

BAZ

THE VAULT WAS INDEFINITELY SHUT DOWN UNTIL IT could be rebuilt. The wards, it seemed, were forever broken. This came as no surprise for Baz, given the intensity of Thames's Collapsing and the fact that, two hundred years from now, those wards did not exist. The Vault he knew didn't have such deadly defenses.

Maybe this would serve to open Aldryn College's eyes to the dangers of keeping such knowledge locked away, accessible only to those who they deemed the best and brightest. Power had the ability to corrupt anyone and everyone, Baz thought bitterly.

Clover was proof enough of that.

It was a few days since the incident now. Foreign students were starting to leave the college, and by tomorrow Baz would be expected to leave too, having been cleared of any involvement in the Vault's blast. Except he had nowhere to go.

The Hourglass had rejected him. He'd even gone back and tried to open it again, but it was as if the threads of time around the

Hourglass were eluding him on purpose. Somewhere beyond it, Kai was in the company of a killer, and Baz could not give him so much as a warning.

With nowhere else to go, he'd asked Cordie to arrange travel to Harebell Cove for him, where he might be able to get the time rift Luce had come through to open. He could find his way back to his time. Professor Selandyn, Jae, his father, the Eclipse-born—they still needed him, after all.

Yet he couldn't bring himself to leave on the off chance Kai returned.

Baz went to knock on the door to Cordie's art studio and found it was already open. He pushed his way inside. "Hello?"

"Good, you're here," Cordie said with a smile that didn't reach her eyes. All her artwork had been packed up.

Baz scrunched up his brow. "Are you leaving?"

She hugged herself. "I have to get away from this place. Start fresh. Away from . . ."

Away from the stain her brother had left behind.

The school had asked questions about Clover's sudden disappearance, which Cordie had explained as an unexpected trip to some distant relative having taken ill. Baz supposed it made sense for her to leave before anyone unraveled that lie.

"My brother was my whole world," she said now. "I would have nothing without him, and he would be no one without me. He wouldn't–he wouldn't have done the things he did if it weren't for me." She scowled. "Do you know how toxic that is? He *murdered* people and told himself it was to save me. But I don't need saving. I never have. I just want to lead the life I want, free of the burden of his suffocating love."

"Will you be all right on your own?"

"I have my art and my wits and the Clover fortune to tide me over in Trevel. But I think it's time I shed that name, leave it to die here in the rubble of Cornelius's mess. I'll take Louka's name." She stroked her stomach absentmindedly, her face lighting up at the thought. "Cordie Kazan has a nice ring to it, no?"

Kazan.

Of course. The name was a puzzle piece that finally painted a full picture. The Kazans–Adriana, Alya, Vera, even Emory–they didn't get their Clover blood from Cornus at all. Their line originated with *Cordie.*

"There's something I wanted to pick your brain about," Cordie said, fishing something out of a box full of sketchbooks and paintbrushes. It was Clover's journal. "I found it in Cornelius's room. It used to be warded to reveal its contents to his eyes only–he was so paranoid about everything–but look, see?"

She flipped through it to reveal pages full of words and sketches, and for a moment Baz thought it might be the future version of Clover's journal that *he* had. But a quick pat on his person revealed that journal to be in his pocket.

He frowned. "Would the wards have lifted when Clover left?"

"I imagine so. But here, this is what I wanted to show you."

She flipped to a page that Baz remembered poring over, early passages of *Song of the Drowned Gods* that painted character portraits of the witch, the warrior, the guardian, and their respective worlds.

Cordie looked at Baz oddly. "I told you how my magic works. How it lets me see glimpses of people's past, things that have emotional resonance and significance. They're most often the faintest impressions, but these drawings . . . I've seen them so clearly before. In your mind." She unveiled drawings she'd made of the characters, and Baz realized they were the original illustrations that were included in the first edition of Clover's work.

"These are the worlds he's going through, yes?" Cordie asked. "So why am I seeing them in your past?"

Baz explained everything to her—that Clover was supposed to pen a famous book, that these were the images Baz had grown up poring over. Cordie handed him the drawings once he was done. "I don't think my brother's coming back," she said. "And even if he does, I don't think that story actually belongs to him at all." The words were slow to sink into Baz's mind. But she was right. Clover was the very evil he had foreseen in the sea of ash. *He* was the Tidecaller who would bring about the end of the worlds, not Emory. That was what Thames had seen in Clover's nightmare, the truth behind this vision of his. Clover, the force of evil. Emory, the light that would go up against him.

And if Clover was still in the sea of ash two hundred years from now, then surely he must never have made it back here. Must never have gotten the chance to write *Song of the Drowned Gods*.

Which meant Kai would never come back here either.

Without *Song of the Drowned Gods*, history itself would be altered. Baz would not be here if it weren't for Clover's story. Romie and Kai would never have chased after the epilogue. Emory would not have become a Tidecaller. They might all still be together at Aldryn, safe and ignorant to doors to other worlds.

Luce had the epilogue when she went through the door with Clover—at least, the future version of the epilogue that Baz had brought back here with him and that Kai had given to Luce. But if Clover never wrote it, would it simply come to disintegrate in her hands? Would Luce and Kai disappear from Clover's side, going back to their own world, their own time, because the epilogue would have never brought them here to the past? Would Baz vanish from this time, too, and reappear back in his own, having forgotten all of this?

And then what? The worlds might still be crumbling, still be in need of saving. And none of them would know.

No. Baz couldn't take that risk.

He was done being scared. Done coasting along while others did the brunt of the work and put themselves in harm's way while he did *nothing*. He'd always seen everyone around him as heroes in a story, while he was nothing more than a side character. But heroes were heroes because they did what others couldn't or didn't want to do. They embraced what made them special and faced their problems head-on. It was time for him to step up.

Power had the ability to corrupt everyone, sure enough. But in the same way, everyone had the capacity for bravery.

Baz knew what he had to do.

67

EMORY

CORNUS CLOVER GAVE A POLITE SMILE, SEEMING pleased with himself that someone recognized him. "Excellent, we can skip the introductions, then."

"How is this possible?" Vera asked with wide eyes as she took in her supposed ancestor.

Clover looked no older than his midtwenties. But he'd existed *two hundred years* ago. He should have been dead, not looking like that, alive in the here and now.

"Good genes," Clover said with a shrug and a slanted smile, "and a bit of luck. Time in the godsworld doesn't flow quite the same."

"The godsworld?" Romie repeated. "All this time, you were in the sea of ash?"

Clover's eyes fell on Romie, then Aspen, then Tol. "You must be the heroes of the story I've been waiting for. Scholar. Witch. Warrior . . . and the Tidecaller who tore down the door that kept us apart."

He spoke that last title like a prayer as he looked at Emory. She remembered that Clover himself was believed to have been a Tidecaller–that he was, in fact, her own flesh and blood.

Someone like her.

Someone who understood her power.

The same thoughts seemed to be echoed in Clover's gaze. "You look so very much like someone I knew," he said, an emotion she couldn't place in his voice. But he seemed to remember himself and squared his shoulders, smoothing his suit. "Shall we get on with it?" At their blank stares, he motioned to the door. "Saving the worlds. Restoring the balance of things. Is that not what you came here for? What you were called here to help fix?"

"Wait, back up," Romie said with a confused expression. "How are you even here?"

"You already know the story. The scholar on the shores who travels through worlds and gets himself stuck in the sea of ash at the last, doomed alongside his otherworldly comrades to oversee the damned in the Deep." Clover motioned to himself with a sad flourish, his mouth twisting in a frown. "I am that scholar. But my comrades from other worlds . . . they didn't make it. I've been trapped alone in the godsworld for so long, waiting for the next set of keys to be called. And here you are. Together, we can replenish the fountain of the gods and stop this blight on the worlds."

"He's lying."

Sidraeus's ecliptic eyes, intent on Clover, flared dangerously. Clover turned to him like he hadn't noticed him before. His expression darkened, the power in his veins rippling black and silver and gold as if in answer to Sidraeus's own godly power.

"I sense magic in you." Clover squinted as if he were trying to see who hid beneath Keiran's mortal face. "Who are you?"

"I am the Shadow you once worshipped. The deity your Tidecaller magic comes from."

"So we're all here, then." Clover sounded delighted. "The

splintered parts of Atheia and the runaway soul of Sidraeus. I wondered why I couldn't sense you in the sleeping realm."

"What do you want?" Sidraeus seethed.

Clover raised a brow. "The same thing you do: to bring Atheia back. Is that not how you'll be able to regain your true form? The gods and their sense of humor, ensuring balance would always be kept."

Emory frowned, trying to make sense of Clover's words. "What is he talking about?"

Sidraeus avoided her eye.

Clover looked between the two of them. "He didn't tell you? The only way Sidraeus can regain his true form is if the pieces of Atheia are brought back together again. Of course, the gods failed to imagine the doors would ever be reopened, so they never thought you would get this close to being truly freed from your prison in the sleeping realm."

"How do you know all this?" Sidraeus asked.

"I've been in a cage of my own for these past centuries. But the godsworld proved fruitful at least. An opportunity to gain both knowledge and power through the fountain of divine magic that flows there. Well, *flowed*."

Replenish the fountain, he'd said. Meaning it had dried up. All its magic depleted.

Emory's thoughts raced as she watched the power rippling from Clover in odd bursts and clouds. Power, she realized, that echoed each of the living realms.

Power he might have drawn from the keys and kept for himself.

Emory took a step backward. "You're the one at the root of all this sickness spreading through worlds, aren't you? The reason the ley lines are corrupted. Because you took all the magic from the fountain and corrupted it for the rest of us."

Clover squared his shoulders. "I did what Sidraeus and Atheia failed to do. I took power from the gods and made myself into divinity."

It hadn't made sense to her, why the rot would have set in so quickly when she opened the doors, if these same doors had been previously opened by Clover in the past. The doors being sealed by the gods might have limited magic, made it slowly die, but that didn't explain why the ley lines felt corrupt. Though if Clover had tainted it somehow . . . if whatever meager power trickled from the fountain was not divine but monstrous . . .

"That power was never yours to take," Sidraeus growled.

"You're right. I suppose it was yours first, wasn't it? And you would have oh so generously shared this power with mortals, or so you claim."

"I wouldn't have stolen it all for myself like you did."

Clover dipped his chin in what looked like remorse. "I can admit I made a mistake there. That's why the power of the gods is festering in my body. Why I need to replenish the fountain. I was foolish when I first traveled through worlds and didn't know how to control myself on the ley line. I took and took every last drop of power from the keys, unable to stop. Constantly craving more." He eyed Emory. "You're a Tidecaller. You've felt it, haven't you, this unquenchable thirst inside you, the constant pull of Atheia's power?"

Emory stared at him, horrified. Was this what would have become of her if she'd kept hurting her friends by gorging herself on their magic?

"With the power of Atheia that I imbibed and the magic of Sidraeus coursing through my blood," Clover continued, "I tapped into the fountain itself, using up all of the power of the gods until there was nothing left."

That must be why he'd been able to tap into the fountain without burning out completely like Sidraeus's Tidecallers had: if he'd leeched the magic from the original keys he'd traveled with, then he'd had both the power of life and death inside him. Just like Emory did earlier when she blew the door open. Power to rival gods.

"But *why*?" Romie asked. "What do you want with that kind of power?"

Clover seemed to think about it. "You know, it started off as wanting to help my fellow Eclipse-born. To create more Tidecallers, so that everyone could know the kind of limitless power that we have access to. I believed the only way to do that was to bring back the Tides and the Shadow. To combine the magic of death and night-mares with that of creation and dreams. But as I crossed through worlds, I discovered they were both to blame for the closure of doors. That they'd been willing to sacrifice the Tidecallers to the gods. Why would I bring back deities who could just as well decide I was not worth it? Instead, I decided to take power for myself. To take away the gods' power for what they did to the Tidecallers. I thought I could do a better job at ruling the worlds and keeping our kind safe than the gods ever did.

"But that kind of power . . . I've realized I am not limitless, as much as I would like to be. Neither are the gods, clearly, if their fountain can be so easily diminished. But Sidraeus and Atheia? Why do you think the gods kept them apart, confining one to the realm of the dead and the other to the realms of the living? They knew that together they had power to rival their own." Clover's gaze darkened. "And with it, I can finally make myself into a true god and ensure that this sickness that runs through the worlds is cured and never happens again."

"If you think I'm going to let you use me to make yourself into a god," Sidraeus said, "you've got me all wrong."

Clover smiled indulgently at him, motioning to his neck. "I don't believe you're in a position to stop me."

The magic damper around his neck.

Sidraeus met Emory's gaze just as the idea formed in her mind. She drew on her Reaper magic and rusted the metal right off as she'd done before.

Sidraeus wasted no time. He lunged at Clover, more beast than man, and so lethally quick that Clover didn't stand a chance against such a force.

But then, Clover was not exactly a man himself.

Before Sidraeus could reach him, Clover disappeared behind his strangely swirling clouds again. He clasped his hands together, and a great blast of power–lightning and water and fire and roots combined–hit Sidraeus with such a force, it sounded like an ear-splitting, earth-shattering thunderclap.

Sidraeus shot backward, hitting the rocky cave wall. For a second, or perhaps not even that, Sidraeus seemed to split into two: there was Keiran's body splayed out on the ground, and a phantom shadow–an umbra crowned in obsidian–hovering over it. As if Sidraeus's spirit had been ejected from its vessel.

Emory thought she glimpsed fear and confusion and relief in those hazel eyes–*Keiran's* eyes, burning with a humanity that was entirely his–before the phantom returned to the body, and all that was left in that gaze as it settled on Clover was a murderous hatred that was all Sidraeus's.

Before Sidraeus or any of them had time to react, Clover had them all immobilized with some remnant of Glamour magic, Emory was sure. He stepped on the ley line and breathed in deeply, hands tilted up. His black veins were burning silver as he drew energy from the ley line. With it, he made creatures appear as if from thin air, drawn from the dust of the blasted cave wall and the broken bits of bones from the dragon carcass. The dust and bones swirled and drew together until they formed what looked like a dozen umbrae, made not of shadow and nightmare but ash and death.

The creatures flocked to each of the keys—Romie, Aspen, Tol—and set their pale, bony hands on their shoulders, like grim reapers ready to take them to meet their end.

"I apologize for this," Clover said to the keys. "It's a shame, really, that you have to die for Atheia to be rebuilt."

"What?" Romie said in a small voice, face blanching.

"You hadn't figured it out? You have to give the pieces of her back to her, which means that you can't exist if she does. For Atheia to come back, you have to die. But I promise yours will be a worthy sacrifice."

Emory knew the horror on Romie's face was mirrored on her own. Their panic-stricken gazes met. Before either of them could move, before Emory could beg the ley line to lend her its power and break free of the Glamour, before Romie and Aspen and Tol could rage against this impossible fate that awaited them and fight back against the creatures holding them, it was over.

Clover's creatures tightened their grip on the keys and vanished with them in clouds of billowing dust.

They were gone.

A scream tore through Emory's throat. Desperation and anger had her breaking through the Glamour like it was nothing. Clover set his sights on Sidraeus. Emory refused to let him take the only leverage she might still have. She barreled into Clover, taking him by surprise. They stumbled past the door's threshold and fell onto the starlit path.

"Bring them back!" Emory raged at him.

Clover easily drew himself up, wiping away a trickle of blackened blood at the corner of his mouth. "This is for our own good, Emory. Imagine what the worlds could be with someone like us at their helm."

"I'm not letting you kill my friends to make yourself into a god."

"We all have to make sacrifices."

"You're a monster," she spat at him. Her Tides-damned ancestor. Another Tidecaller like her who'd gone corrupt with power, wanting more than what he already had, the same way she'd wanted more power and significance for herself. Seeing what he'd become, she knew that wasn't a path she wanted to ever go down.

"God, monster." Clover waved her off with a shrug. "It's all the same in the end. There are simply those who have power and those who do not."

"Maybe you're right," Emory said, advancing a step toward him. "But the thing about power is that it can be taken."

She called on *his* power, trying to tap into his limitless Tidecaller reservoir and all the power of the fountain that he had gorged himself on.

"What are you–" Clover laughed. "Stop this. You cannot possibly win against me."

Clover looked annoyed now as she tried harder, but he was right; it was like trying to move the stars in the sky itself. Still, she did not relent. Clover came at her with murder in his eyes. His intent was clear: he meant to finish her off, kill her for trying to bleed him of his own stolen power. He fashioned a blade from the twisted magic that clung to him–rotten roots and white-hot silver and sizzling electricity–and aimed it at Emory's heart.

Only it never found its mark because someone stepped in front of her.

"No!" Emory yelled, lurching toward Sidraeus.

Clover seemed to realize his mistake at the same time she did. He had driven the blade right through Sidraeus's heart–or at least, the heart of his vessel. Of Keiran.

And as he fell to his knees, Emory knew it was Keiran–not Sidraeus–that looked down in confusion at the blade sticking out of his chest. Because Sidraeus stood right behind him, nothing but shadows swirling with faint stars. An umbra with a crown of obsidian. The ruler of the sleepscape, returned to his realm.

Clover called on a maelstrom of power he aimed at Sidraeus, but the deity dissolved into shadows before it could reach him, blowing away on a nonexistent breeze. Clover raged against the darkness. His plan worked only if he had Sidraeus. Fury marred his features. He turned to Emory instead, looking to take his anger out on her.

But then a veritable army of umbrae descended upon them. They swarmed Clover, forcing him away from Emory. As if they were *protecting* her.

Clover didn't fight back against the umbrae–he didn't need to, with the power of gods in him. With a narrow-eyed look at Emory, he simply vanished like his creatures had with the keys, in that strange cloud of billowing dust.

With him gone, Emory turned her attention to Keiran. Because it really *was* Keiran, just him now that Sidraeus's spirit had left his body. His hazel eyes found hers, glassy and hurt, but so clearly his. Blood dripped down the side of his mouth. He toppled over, the blade still lodged in his chest.

The world narrowed to just the two of them as Emory knelt at his side. "Keiran . . ."

He coughed up blood, looking at his wound, then at her. Emory couldn't stop the tears that fell down her face. Instinctively, she reached for her Healing magic, resting her hands on Keiran's chest to take the blade out and heal him. To save him.

"Don't." Keiran stopped her with a light touch to her wrist, too weak to muster anything more. But there was a desperation in that touch, a pleading look in his eyes. "Let me die so that I can be freed of the stain he left on me."

"You felt it? The whole time Sidraeus was in there?"

A plaintive sound escaped his lips in answer.

Emory imagined what it must have been like for him. Being

reanimated and then possessed by the Shadow himself, the thing he hated most. When he'd died, had Keiran glimpsed the afterlife, seen his parents and Farran and Lizaveta again for a blissful second, before being dragged back to this half-life? Would he find them again, if she gave him the death he asked of her now?

Keiran lifted a hand to her. For a second, she thought he would brush a strand of hair from her face like he used to do, and she found herself leaning into his touch, despite everything he'd done. But his fingers closed around her neck instead, not strong enough to bruise, but enough to make her mouth go dry with fear.

The look in his eyes was clear: he would have a hold on her always. If he couldn't kill her here, then he would haunt her still.

And as the light left him, as his fingers slid from her neck and death took him once more, Emory knew that wherever his soul went, if he had one at all, it would be waiting for her.

PART V

THE SLEEPERS

KAI SALONGA WAS NOT SUPPOSED TO BE AFRAID. HE was the Nightmare Weaver, made to be fearless in the dark. But fear was all he knew as the door shut between the sleepscape and Dovermere. Between him and Baz.

The door wouldn't open again no matter how hard Kai slammed his fists against it. He screamed Baz's name until his throat sliced itself on the edges of it, until he tasted blood and all the defenses around his heart shattered at his feet like glass. He fell, defeated, to his knees.

The stars looked on, mocking him.

A hand squeezed his shoulder. "There's nothing for it, Kai," Luce said in a quiet, forlorn voice. "The door won't reopen. We owe it to those we left behind to keep going."

The boy he'd left in the past. The daughter she'd abandoned in the future. How would they ever make their way back to them now?

"Come along, you two," Clover called out in a voice that was far too chipper. He was already moving down the path of stars, his gait light, his grin full of bright confidence. "We've got a universe to save."

Luce helped Kai to his feet. They stared at each other, him the boy of nightmares, she the girl of dreams. And as they started walking through the dark, following the only hope they had left, Luce said, "Don't be afraid."

But Kai was. It was impossible not to be. Baz was gone, and without him, the dark Kai had known became an unfathomable abyss.

There was no pretending here. No armor to hide behind. Only visceral fear and the certainty that he had seen the boy he loved for the very last time.

68

EMORY

EMORY STARED AT THE DARKNESS OF THE SLEEPSCAPE and forced herself to her feet. She had to get to Romie and Aspen and Tol before Clover could reunite them with the fourth piece needed to bring Atheia back. Behind her, Virgil, Nisha, Vera, and the two Golden Helm draconics appeared on the star-lined path, panting as they asked what happened.

Nisha fell to her knees. Romie's name escaped her in a sob. Virgil pulled her to him, his face grim. Vera held tightly to the compass Emory had returned to her, staring angrily down the path to where Clover had disappeared.

"What do we do?" Nisha asked, a note of desperation making her voice tremble.

Movement caught Emory's eye as the crowned umbra hovered nearby, quiet as a wraith. Sidraeus. He wasn't gone, had simply left his vessel behind now that he was back in the sleepscape.

Conflicting emotions warred inside Emory. She could have used his help now more than ever, but without a vessel, he would have to remain here, formless. And maybe that was a good thing. Because the alternative was him regaining his true form–which meant Atheia was back, and her friends were dead.

She would not let that happen.

The crowned umbra seemed to realize the same thing. Something passed between them, an understanding that this wouldn't be the last time they saw each other, for better or worse.

And then Sidraeus slunk back into the darkness he had come from.

"We go to the next world," Emory said to her friends with renewed conviction. "We find Romie and Aspen and Tol, no matter what. Then we storm the godsworld," she vowed, "and we make Cornus Clover pay."

69

BAZ

B AZ SAT IN HIS FAVORITE SPOT IN THE DECRESCENS
library, at the small table where he and Emory would speculate
two hundred years from now about her Tidecaller powers. Above
him, a shaft of rare wintry sunlight made the stained-glass window
come alive, softening the deep purple of the poppies it portrayed.
The lunar flower he associated most with his sister.

He stared at the stack of blank pages before him, the dip pens
and steel nibs and ink pots he'd taken from Clover's room sitting
idly by. The library was quiet, familiar. If he closed his eyes, he
could imagine he was back in his own time, poring over Clover's
journal or his famed book. Instead, here he was, trying to convince
himself that what he was about to do was not complete heresy.

If Clover was not here to write his story, someone had to. And
who knew it better than Baz? It had shaped who he was, had
carried him through every chapter of his life. He knew most of it
by heart. And he had Clover's journal to help him fill in the blanks
where his memory might fail him.

Still, Baz could not bring himself to pick up the pen. All he saw in his mind was the power-hungry look in Clover's eyes, the corpses of the students he'd experimented on, Thames's emaciated body. *That* was Clover's true legacy, and Baz felt crushed and helpless and foolish for ever having believed Clover had good intentions. His literary idol–someone he had looked up to all his life, had made into this hero in his head–turned out to be the villain of the story.

In truth, Baz realized he'd been idolizing someone who wasn't real. The artist rather than the man behind the art. They were two separate beings, but how could he see them as anything but one? The story that had gotten him through childhood felt tainted now. Darkened by ill intent, crooked desires. He felt like he would never be able to read its words the same way again.

Maybe it was time he let it go. He had the power to ensure *Song of the Drowned Gods* never saw the light of day. Clover's name could fall into oblivion right here, right now, if Baz did not pick up that pen.

But so much of his own story revolved around this book. How much of history would be rewritten if *Song of the Drowned Gods* didn't exist? How much of *him* would be rewritten? It was not something Baz wanted to mess with. Time, he had learned, had a way of making things happen as they should.

With a sigh, Baz picked up a pen. On the middle of the top page, he inscribed the title. *Song of the Drowned Gods* by Cornus Clover. Before he could talk himself out of it, he started writing.

There is a scholar on these shores who breathes stories.

With those first words, purpose thrummed through him, a feeling of *rightness* singing at his fingertips. Baz wrote the rest of it in a frenzy. His hand cramped, but he paid it no mind, so focused was he on the task. He stayed true to the story he knew, telling it in the same way, with the same words that were imprinted on his soul.

Two lines stuck with him as he wrote them from memory: *The first to find her is the scholar from our shores, with the stories he inhales and the words he exhales, as much sustenance to him as air. (Perhaps it would have been a more fitting metaphor to call him the lungs, but in truth he is much more like a bloodstream, for magic runs in his veins as he runs through worlds like rivers to the sea and blood through arteries.)*

The scholar was always believed to have been Clover, and in a way it was. But here Baz was writing the story in Clover's place, a scholar exhaling the same words he'd inhaled as a kid. Something shifted in his heart as he wrote. Clover's words–the words Baz had grown up loving, the words he feared would be forever changed now that he knew the vile truth of Clover–were not Clover's words at all, but his. *Baz* was the one to have written *Song of the Drowned Gods*, not Clover.

It felt to him like he was reclaiming the story of his childhood in a way he'd never imagined he might. And maybe that was all he could hope for.

Breathing time and stories–that was Baz's role. He was the lungs of the story, the sixth part of the equation, the unnamed puzzle piece of it all. The unsuspected breath of creation that blew through all of it, with no one ever the wiser.

When he got to the end, Baz stopped, paused, read over his work. He would leave the manuscript with Cordie so that she could get it published on her brother's behalf, and hopefully benefit from what money it would bring in. Money that might help her raise this child of hers and keep the Clover estate afloat now that her brother wasn't here to use whatever Tidecaller magic he'd relied on to make his fortune in the first place.

But as he read over the end, he paused again, uncertain as he considered what to do for the epilogue. Did he have to write it at all, if it had always been lost? It already existed–had been in Luce's possession when she left. Baz suspected she might leave it in the sleepscape now, where Romie would find it two hundred years later. But what if she didn't?

In the end, Baz wrote the epilogue anyway. When he was finished, he ripped the page out from the rest of the bound manuscript and stared at it, thinking of Kai and Luce and Romie. *The Sleepers Among the Stars.* He could only hope they, like the epilogue's characters, would be the unsuspecting heroes of the story.

Before Baz could fold up the epilogue and put it in his pocket, the page shone with a light so bright Baz had to avert his gaze. He squinted down at it through splayed fingers, heart pounding in his chest. The light had dampened somewhat, flecks of it hovering over the page like tiny specks of dust.

Or *ash.*

This couldn't be real. He had to be imagining this, his mind so full of the story he'd been writing that it had conjured this strange dream or hallucination or whatever this was. All he heard in the back of his mind were the words he himself had written, pounding to the rhythm of his heart.

It is a song that carries on the wind like ash as it flutters across worlds, and perhaps a piece of it lingers here on this very page. Look closer. Strain your ear. The drowned gods are calling; will you answer?

Baz leaned down, bringing his face closer to the shimmering page. It smelled of possibility. Of sea salt and damp earth, sooty coals and storm clouds. The light particles emanating from it were cool on his skin, like the brightness of starlight and the velvety touch of the dark.

Baz took a breath and felt himself enveloped by the intensifying light.

Whatever magic this was pulled him into the epilogue.

Through a literal portal on a page.

When his feet struck ground, Baz half expected to find himself beneath a colorless sky, alone in the stillness of a great expanse of ash. The epilogue still hung from his hand, but it did not turn to dust like the manuscript had for the scholar in the story, and he was not pulled back to Aldryn like the scholar was, the memory of this place fading like a dream before he could make sense of it.

Baz was still here, with the page intact in his hand, with the strange desire to laugh at the inconceivability of the situation.

Here was not the sea of ash at all but what looked to be the sleepscape.

Baz was on the familiar star-lined path. This *had* to be a dream, yet it felt entirely real. Instinctively, he moved down the curving path, clinging desperately to the epilogue. There must be some kind of magic to it if it had brought him here.

He came upon the door to the Wychwood, unimpeded by umbrae or strange tapestries of threads pulling him back through time. His hand hovered over the vine-covered marble door as he marveled at it, every fiber of his being itching to see what lay on the other side. But *something* told him to keep going. Not a voice, not a song, but this feeling of inevitability that made him pull his hand back and, without another look, walk away from the door.

Deeper down the path he went. It curved inward and downward, in a pattern he knew now to be a spiral. He came across the golden door of the Wastes and thought of the warrior's strength. Again he pushed onward, until he reached the icy door of the fourth world. Here he hesitated.

If a single door into the sea of ash existed, then it was in this world, at the top of the mountain where the cunning guardian sat playing his lyre. All logic said Baz should push open this door and find his way to that very mountain.

So why then did the path keep curving onward?

Baz kept going. The spiral here was tighter, and it felt to him like he was coming down a narrow spiral staircase. Darkness pressed in closer around him, the stars making themselves scarce. Until at last, he found himself at the very center of the spiral–where a giant, ancient loom sat in the middle of what appeared to be a workshop.

Baz struggled to make sense of his surroundings. The loom, which was on a raised platform in the middle of the space, seemed to be weaving on its own, animated by a rhythmic, invisible force. Translucent threads that shimmered faintly stretched themselves taut on one end of the loom, coming out the other in a woven piece of cloth that looked just like the fabric that had pulled Baz and Kai back in time. The woven cloth spilled onto the workshop floor in a great heap, as if waiting for someone to come lay it out flat and marvel at its design.

While the loom was clearly the focal point, the rest of the workshop drew Baz's attention, for it was full of strange clockwork.

Everywhere he looked were complex series of interlocking gears, wheels and oscillators and pendulums made of silver and gold and brass and obsidian, their movements like that of a great orchestra. There were devices he recognized, sundials and hourglasses and grandfather clocks–clocks of all kinds, old and new and some the likes of which he'd never seen before–as well as instruments that were not clocks at all, like astrolabes and sextants and measuring wheels.

A bell chimed, loud and clear and crystalline.

"Ah, Mr. Brysden, right on time."

Baz whirled around to see a stocky man with a scruffy, graying beard appear between the clocks. Peculiar-looking goggles sat atop his thick dark hair, and his mismatched three-piece suit was adorned with not one but four pocket watches. He was glancing at one of them–silver, and adorned with grooves that mimicked waves–and shut it with a flourish before turning on his heel.

"Come along," the man called out–supposedly to Baz, as there appeared to be no one else here.

"Um . . . I'm sorry, what . . . Who are you?" Baz asked as he trailed uncertainly after him.

A strident whistle coming from a peculiar engine that hovered near the giant loom caught the man's attention. He veered toward it, looking flustered as he muttered something under his breath. His movements were frayed, erratic, like he was a ball of tightly wound nerves. Ignoring Baz's question, he climbed the steps of the loom's platform and proceeded to fix a snag in the threads.

"There," he said, sounding pleased with himself. He climbed down and looked at one of his pocket watches–gold, with what appeared to be flame-like details. He grumbled something else that Baz couldn't hear.

"Excuse me," Baz said, voice strained with annoyance now.

The man's gray eyes lifted to his. "Ah yes, Mr. Brysden, sorry. You were saying?"

Baz stared at him. "Who are you?" He gestured to the clock-work around them, the giant loom. "How did I get here?"

"I called you here, of course. Through a portal on a page." He grinned. "Clever, no?"

"I . . . yes, but where is *here*?"

The man lifted a bushy eyebrow. "Isn't it obvious? This is where the threads of time are spun, where the mechanisms of life itself operate, keeping the balance between this moment and the last and the next and every other in between."

Baz pinched the bridge of his nose. He was losing his mind. "Please," he said. "Just tell me what's happening."

"We have business, you and I. But–clocks, where are my manners, you still don't know who I am." The man adjusted his jacket, puffing out his chest. "I am the god of balance. And I have been expecting you, Timespinner."

EPILOGUE:

THE
DAMNED

ROMIE CAME TO IN A WORLD OF ASH.

Ropes bound her hands and feet. Ash dusted her clothes, filled her mouth. Before her was a great fountain that called to mind the one at Aldryn, though nothing flowed from it. It was dried up, like everything else in this godsforsaken world. Used up by Clover to quench his thirst for power.

Next to her, Aspen and Tol were similarly bound. Offerings awaiting sacrifice.

It should have been a grim affair, but all Romie felt was the hopeful note of that song in her veins, which soared louder than it ever had as she laid eyes on the fourth person who was with them. She would have known the boy was the guardian even without the spiral mark on his forehead.

The four pieces of Atheia, reunited in the sea of ash.

They all looked between each other as the song became complete, conviction and hope mirrored on each of their faces. And beneath it all, the dark thrum of damnation they knew they couldn't possibly escape.

Tol couldn't give up his heart and survive. The guardian couldn't part with his soul. Aspen had nearly died getting her rib bone ripped out of her before, and Romie . . . how much of her blood would be spilled to bring Atheia back? A single drop? Or would she be drained dry and die too?

Patience, Atheia's song whispered in her ear. *Take heart.*

And Romie did. If death was her destiny, then she would meet it willingly, like she'd always meant to.

ACKNOWLEDGMENTS

T HIS BOOK WAS NOT EASY TO WRITE. IN FACT, I'M PRETTY sure it tried to kill me a few times, but I survived thanks in large part to the Forest app, Scrivener backups, and all the people in my life who stuck by me during what was a very difficult year.

To Adrian Graves and Kapri Psych: thanks for being the glue that holds my often-frazzled writer brain together. This book would have never seen the light of day without our many writing sprints and brainstorming sessions and laughter-filled conversations. You two keep me going, even when the going gets rough.

To my agent, Victoria Marini: thanks for continuously being the fiercest champion for me and my books. You're an absolute dream to work with, and the same goes for the entire High Line team (shoutout to Sheyla Knigge).

To my editor, Sarah McCabe, and assistant editor, Anum Shafqat: thank you for always asking the most thoughtful questions and pushing me to dive deeper into these characters and worlds. I couldn't ask for a better editorial team.

Thank you to all the people at Simon & Schuster/McElderry

Books who had a hand in the making of this book: Justin Chanda, Karen Wojtyla, Anne Zafian, Bridget Madsen, Jennifer Strada, Elizabeth Blake-Linn, Greg Stadnyk (you've truly outdone yourself with this cover!), Lisa Vega, Chrissy Noh, Caitlin Sweeny, Alissa Nigro, Samantha McVeigh, Thad Whittier, Bezi Yohannes, Perla Gil, Remi Moon, Amelia Johnson, Ashley Mitchell, Yasleen Trinidad, Saleena Nival, Amy Lavigne, Lisa Moraleda, Nicole Russo, Christina Pecorale and her sales team, Michelle Leo and her education/ library team, Ali Dougal and Rachel Denwood (and the whole UK team), Cayley Pimentel and Miranda Rasch (and everyone at Simon & Schuster Canada). Thank you also to Lara Ameen for the thoughtful sensitivity read.

I can't forget to thank the many writers who've loudly cheered me on from the start and helped celebrate the launch of my debut; the authors who generously blurbed *Curious Tides*, participated in events and giveaways with me, and imparted nuggets of wisdom and encouragement along the way, whether they're aware of it or not; the people who read early versions of *Stranger Skies* and reassured me when I was having doubts; my fellow 2023 debuts; and the friends, colleagues, and mentors that make this publishing journey feel not quite as intimidating or isolating as I feared it might be. To name but a few of you, in alphabetical order: Chelsea Abdullah, Isabel Agajanian, Jen Carnelian, Emily Charlotte, Emma Clancey, Lyndall Clipstone, Kamilah Cole, Erin Cotter, Tracy Deonn, SJ Donders, Kat Dunn, Emma Finnerty, Chloe Gong, Joan He, Suzey Ingold, Bailey Knaub, Hannah Laycraft, Claire Legrand, Ania Poranek, Aamna Qureshi, Allison Saft, Birdie Schae, Laura Steven, Emma Theriault, Sarah Underwood. And to anyone I might have forgotten to name, please forgive my tired brain and know I appreciate you dearly.

To Mom, Dad, Éric, Crys, Gab, Marv, Mylou, Val: thanks for keeping me grounded and reminding me to emerge from my make-believe worlds every now and then. Same goes to you, Roscoe.

Thank you to all the talented artists I've commissioned *Stranger Skies* artwork from, for bringing these scenes and characters to life in the most beautiful ways.

And a massive thank-you to the booksellers, librarians, and bloggers who have shown so much love for this series since *Curious Tides* hit the shelves. The incredible work you do is greatly appreciated.

Finally, to my readers–I hope you've enjoyed returning to this universe and all the worlds it contains. Thanks for being here.

PASCALE LACELLE is a French-Canadian author from Ottawa, Ontario. A longtime devourer of books, she started writing her own at age thirteen and quickly became enthralled by the magic of words. When not lost in stories, she's most likely daydreaming about food and travel, playing with her dog, Roscoe, or trying to curate the perfect playlist for every mood. *Stranger Skies* is the sequel to *New York Times* bestseller *Curious Tides*. You can find her on Instagram and X/Twitter @PascaleLacelle.